The Blonde Venus
Becomes A Gypsy Vixen

"You look like a she-devil!" Sara exclaimed.

"And I shall be a she-devil until I have my revenge!" Catherine vowed.

"Have you thought of all the men you are going to attract, who will stop at nothing now that you have no name and rank to protect you? Now you are nothing but a common gypsy girl, a creature to rape or hang as one sees fit."

"Do you think I like it? But I know that until I do what I have set out to do I shall have no rest, either in this life or the next. I must avenge Arnaud, avenge the destruction of Montsalvy, avenge my impoverished son!"

~

CATHERINE AND ARNAUD is one of a series of historical romances written with all the dramatic brilliance of a colorful era. Watch for CATHERINE'S TIME FOR LOVE, the next novel in the series.

Other Avon Books by:
Juliette Benzoni

BELLE CATHERINE	36525	$1.95
CATHERINE, ROYAL MISTRESS	37069	1.95
CATHERINE'S QUEST	37895	1.95

JULIETTE BENZONI
CATHERINE AND ARNAUD

Translated by
JOCASTA GOODWIN

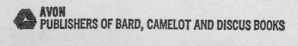

AVON
PUBLISHERS OF BARD, CAMELOT AND DISCUS BOOKS

Originally published in Paris by Editions de Trevise
as *Catherine ma Mie*.

AVON BOOKS
A division of
The Hearst Corporation
959 Eighth Avenue
New York, New York 10019

© Opera Mundi, Paris 1967
Published in Great Britain by William Heinemann Ltd.,
as *Catherine and Arnaud*
Translation © Opera Mundi, Paris 1967
ISBN: 0-380-40493-1

All rights reserved, which includes the right
to reproduce this book or portions thereof in
any form whatsoever. For information address
Avon Books.

First Avon Printing, January, 1969
Fifth Printing

AVON TRADEMARK REG. U.S. PAT. OFF. AND
FOREIGN COUNTRIES, REGISTERED TRADEMARK—
MARCA REGISTRADA, HECHO EN CHICAGO, U.S.A.

Printed in the U.S.A.

Contents

Part I

GAUTHIER

◆◆◆◆◆◆◆◆◆◆◆◆◆◆◆◆◆◆◆◆◆

CHAPTER ONE

The Accursed Diamond

The black diamond lay sparkling with all its sinister brilliance in the hollow of Catherine's palm, lightening the gloom of the great hall of Carlat, the fortress where Catherine and her people had taken refuge after the destruction of Montsalvy. She held it suspended before a candle-flame for a moment so that every glittering facet took fire and it seemed as though a stream of fiery red stars were cascading from her hand. Before her in glittering heaps on a velvet-covered table lay all the other jewels she had been wont to wear as Queen of Bruges and Dijon, all-powerful and beloved mistress of Philippe of Burgundy. She had scarcely looked at them. They included the fabulous necklace of amethysts from the Oural Mountains which Garin de Brazey, her first husband, had given her on the occasion of their betrothal. There were rubies, too, and sapphires, diamonds and aquamarines, Hungarian opals and lapis lazuli from Badakshan, and finally the magnificent collar of Indian diamonds and immense emeralds from Djebel Sikait which, among others, the Duke Philippe had given her. But it was the black diamond which caught her eye, when Brother Etienne Charlot reached into his shabby monk's robe and flung the fabulous treasure down before her.

Garin de Brazey had bought it long ago from a Venetian sea-captain. And he in his turn had stolen it from an Indian idol and had been only too glad to get rid of it: the diamond brought bad luck. It would seem that it had continued to do so. Garin, condemned to death, had poisoned himself in his dungeon to avoid the shame of being dragged through the town before execution, and had not Catherine, who had inherited it, been dogged by the same ill-fortune? Sorrow and bad luck had pursued her ever since, herself and those she loved. There was Arnaud de Montsalvy, her husband, decreed a traitor and felon for having attempted to free Joan "the witch," and flung into a dungeon by Georges de la Trémoille, all-powerful favorite of Charles VII. It had almost killed him; and on being rescued from there he had returned to his estates only to find that the Castle of Montsalvy had been burned and razed to the ground by order of the King. And then the horror had come, the dreadful horror which had befallen them some eight months earlier and which still made Catherine shudder with anguish when she thought of it: the leprosy which Arnaud had contracted in La Trémoille's filthy dungeon. For the last eight months Arnaud had been leading a form of life-in-death, cut off from his own people and from the world for ever more, in the leprarium of Calves. Life for him now meant only suffering.

Catherine's fingers closed about the diamond. It had grown warm in her clasp so that now it seemed almost a living thing. What was the evil power enclosed in this inky brilliance? Hidden in her hand it seemed no more than a hard pebble, and yet it held so much more tragedy in store. More men would fight for it; blood would be spilled in order to gain possession of it; and for how many centuries would this go on? For a moment she was tempted to throw it into the fire and destroy it; but who there, the faithful monk or that old lady, her mother-in-law, sitting speechless with awe in her high-backed chair, would understand the motive for this act? The black diamond represented an immense fortune . . . and Montsalvy, in ashes and ruins, stood waiting to be rebuilt! Catherine opened her hand and let the diamond roll on to the table.

"What splendor!" sighed Isabelle de Montsalvy. "I have never seen anything like it in my life! It shall be the treasure of our family."

"No, mother," Catherine interrupted gently. "I shall not keep the black diamond. It is an accursed jewel. It has brought nothing but misfortune. And besides, it represents so much gold! That black pebble there means a new castle, men-at-arms, and all that is needed to rebuild Montsalvy and restore it to what it was, and to give my son the rank which only power and money can bring. . . . The black diamond means all that!"

"What a pity!" said Madame de Montsalvy. "It is so beautiful!"

8

"More dreadful than beautiful," said Brother Etienne. "Did you know, Dame Catherine, that Nicole Son, who kept the draper's shop in Rouen and gave you shelter there, is dead too?"

"Dead? But how?"

"Murdered! She went to take a superb, gold lace head-dress to Madame the Duchess of Bedford, and she was found in the Seine with her throat cut. . . ."

Catherine did not speak but the horrified glance she cast at the black diamond was explicit enough. So, even when it was entrusted to someone else's care, the black diamond still killed! She must get rid of it, and the sooner the better.

"All the same," said the monk with a kindly smile, "don't let us exaggerate or be superstitious. All this may be no more than a chain of coincidences. You must admit that I have transported it across the greater part of the kingdom, through starving countryside swarming with brigands and . . . no evil has befallen me!"

And it was indeed something of a miracle. In deep winter —for it was now the beginning of the year 1433—the Corde-lier of Mont Beuvray had succeeded in crossing the unhappy land of France, ravaged by poverty, bled white by bands of outlaws and the English garrisons still scattered here and there, without anyone suspecting that he carried an emperor's ransom in a linen bag hidden within his coarse-spun habit. The night that Catherine and Arnaud de Montsalvy had escaped from Rouen, the very night of the Maid's death, the jewels had been placed in the care of their friend Jean Son, master-mason, until the time when Brother Etienne Charlot, trusty secret agent of Yolande, Duchess of Anjou, Countess of Provence and Queen of the Four Kingdoms of Aragon, Sicily, Naples and Jerusalem, should find the time and occasion to return them to their rightful owner.

For many years past Etienne Charlot's big feet, bare in their Franciscan sandals, had trudged the highways of the kingdom, taking messages and instructions from Queen Yolande, mother-in-law of Charles VII, even to the least and humblest of her subjects. No one suspected the plump little monk with his ready, beaming smile, or dreamed that his candid good humor masked an acute intelligence.

He had reached Carlat some hours after noon, toward sunset. His rotund silhouette had apparently materialized out of the snow at the very moment when the Scots governor of the castle, Hugh Kennedy, was supervising the changing of the guard, and he had been immediately escorted to Catherine's quarters. To be reunited with her friend after more than eighteen months' absence had been both a joy and heart-break for the young countess. For Brother Etienne had always been the instrument chosen by fate to bring Arnaud and herself together. His presence brought back memories of golden hours which could not but torment her now. This time, for all his goodwill, Brother Etienne could do nothing for them. The leper and the lady who mourned him in this world were separated as surely as by the gates of the tomb. . . .

Catherine got up from the table and walked over to the window. It was quite dark now beyond the great white circular expanse of courtyard where the kitchen lights cast a ruddy glow. But it was a long while since the young woman's eyes had need of daylight to gaze in the exact direction of the lazar-house of Calves. Through space and darkness the tie which bound her to her beloved husband, Arnaud de Montsalvy, was as strong and painful as ever. . . . Sometimes she stood there for hours on end, staring out as in a dream, with tears rolling unchecked, silently, down her lovely face.

Brother Etienne coughed, then chided her gently: "Madame . . . you are destroying yourself! Is there nothing, truly, which can soften your grief?"

"Nothing, father! My husband was all my life. The day that . . . that day I ceased to exist!"

She closed her eyes. . . . Against the dark curtain of her lids her pitiless memory traced the outline of a vigorous man, dressed in black from head to foot, walking off in the sun-light with his hands buried in the living gold of a woman's tresses, her own hair, which she had cut off in a transport of grief, to fling them like a fabulous carpet beneath the feet of the man whose brother men had cast him out. Since then her hair had grown again. It clustered about her cheeks like showers of gold, but she dragged it back sternly from her face and hid it beneath the black veils of widowhood or the white, starched caps which hid everything but the pure oval of her face. If she could, she would have been glad to dull the beauty of that face too, especially when she intercepted an admiring look from Hugh Kennedy or felt the gaze of passionate devotion which her squire Gauthier bestowed upon her. . . . She had never left off her black widow's weeds. Brother Etienne ran his eye meditatively over the slender form whose austere black garments could not cloak its grace. Then he looked at the soft face with its delicate lips which grief had only rendered more ethereal and touching, and the long violet eyes which smoldered with pain as once they had smoldered with passion. And the good monk found

10

himself wondering. Could God really have formed such beauty in order to leave it languishing, smothered by widow's weeds, in the depths of an old castle in the mountains of Auvergne? Had it not been for her little son of ten months old Catherine de Montsalvy would, as she freely admitted, have followed her beloved husband among the lepers and thus inflicted upon herself the worst of slow and lingering deaths. Now Brother Etienne searched for words to pierce the armor of grief which enveloped the young woman. What could he say? It was useless to speak of God. What could God do for this woman, passionately in love with one man; a woman who had raised up her love, like an idol, on a secret altar? For the sake of Arnaud, for the sake of this husband to whom she would never cease to belong, body and soul, Catherine would gladly, joyously, have consigned herself to hell itself. . . . Therefore he was surprised to hear himself saying:

"Dame Catherine, one should never despair of Providence. Often she strikes down those whom she loves only to reward them the more generously. . . ."

The sad, beautiful mouth curled scornfully. Catherine shrugged her shoulders wearily.

"What do I care about rewards? What do I care for the Heaven about which you are doubtless going to speak, Brother Etienne? If by some miracle God himself were to appear before me I should say to him: 'Lord, you are God omnipotent. Give me back my husband . . . and take the rest, even my share of life hereafter, but give him back to me!' "

Inwardly the monk cursed himself for a fool, but nevertheless he allowed his face to cloud over.

"Madame, that is blasphemy! And among the rest you speak of do you include your son?"

The narrow face framed in white linen turned toward him in a sort of horror.

"Why do you say that? Don't you think I've been through enough? Of course not, of course I didn't mean my son—I was speaking of all those vain things like power, or beauty . . . or this!"

With one finger she indicated the sparkling heap on the table. She walked across rapidly and plunged her hands among the jewels so that she could hold them up to the light.

"There is money enough to buy lands here! Ah, how glad I should have been of it a year ago when I could have given it all to him . . . to my husband! In his hands they would have meant a lifetime's happiness, for us and all our people. Now . . ." Slowly she let the jewels cascade in a sparkling

11

colored stream between her fingers, "Now they're nothing but jewels, dead stones."

"But they can restore life and power to your family name. Now, Dame Catherine, enough of this bleak philosophizing! I did not come here solely to restore your treasure to you. In fact I was sent to you: Queen Yolande wishes to see you."

"Me? I am surprised her Majesty remembers my existence at all."

"She never forgets anyone, madame, anyone at all . . . and least of all those who have served her faithfully. One thing is certain: she wishes to see you. Don't ask me why, the Queen did not tell me . . . although I think I can guess."

Catherine's somber eyes studied the monk. It seemed as though his wandering existence was a source of perpetual youth, for he had not changed. His face was as round, as fresh, and as candid. But Catherine had suffered so much that she had grown suspicious of everyone and everything. The most angelic figure seemed to her to hold a concealed threat, even when it was an old friend like Brother Etienne.

"What did the Queen say to you when she sent you to me here? Can you remember her exact words?"

He nodded, but his eyes never left hers for a moment.

"Of course. 'There are some griefs which time can never heal,' the Queen said to me, 'but in certain cases of extreme suffering vengeance can bring relief. Go and find Dame Catherine de Montsalvy and remind her that she is still one of my ladies-in-waiting. Her mourning shall not relieve her of her duties.' "

"I am grateful to her for remembering me, but has she forgotten that all the Montsalvy family are in banishment, that they have been decreed traitors and felons and that they are wanted by the Royal Provost? That one would have to be either dead . . . or a leper to escape the men-at-arms? The Queen mentioned my mourning, you said. Does she know the truth then?"

"She knows everything. Messire Kennedy told her about it."

"Which means, I suppose, that at Court they talk of nothing else!" said Catherine bitterly. "What a triumph for La Trémoille to know that the most valiant of the King's captains is buried away in the depths of a lazar-house!"

"Only the Queen knows this. And the Queen knows how to hold her tongue, madame," said the monk reproachfully. "Messire Kennedy informed her of this under the seal of secrecy . . . just as he has promised everyone here, country people and soldiers alike, to personally cut the throat of anyone who reveals what has happened to Messire Arnaud. As far as the outside world is concerned, Madame, the King himself included, your husband is dead. You seem to know very little of what goes on under your own roof."

Catherine flushed. It was true. Since that evil day when the monk took Arnaud away to the leprarium she had never once left the castle, even refusing to go as far as the village where the sight of the people and the familiar places sickened her. She stayed shut up in her quarters, only leaving them for a short while after dark to take a walk round the battlements. She would stand there for a long time, motionless between two merlons, forever gazing at the same place. Her squire Gauthier, the Norman whom she had saved from the gallows, accompanied her but always stayed ten paces or so behind, unwilling to disturb her thoughts. Hugh Kennedy was the only person who dared to approach her when she came down again. The men-at-arms regarded her with pity tinged with awe, this black-veiled woman who stood so erect and proud but hid her face as soon as she passed outside her quarters in the castle. In the evening, round their fire, the soldiers talked about her, describing the resplendent beauty which none of them had seen during the past eight months. The strangest tales circulated. One of them said that the beautiful countess, after shaving her head, had disfigured herself deliberately, so that no one should ever fall in love with her again. The villagers crossed themselves whenever they perceived her dark veils fluttering high up against the sunset sky. Little by little the beautiful Countess of Montsalvy was becoming a legend. . . .

"You are right," said Catherine, sighing. "I no longer know anything because nothing interests me any more, except perhaps that word you uttered just now: vengeance . . . strange though it may sound on the lips of a holy man. Nevertheless I am astonished that the Queen should wish to assist in revenging a banished woman like myself."

"From the moment you are recalled by the Queen, madame, you are no longer in banishment. With her you will be safe. As for your desire for vengeance, it so happens that it coincides with the wishes of Queen Yolande herself. You do not realize, madame, that the insolence of La Trémoille knows no bounds, and that the troops of the Spaniard, Villa-Andrade, who is in his pay, last year pillaged, burned and sacked Maine and Anjou, both lands belonging to the Queen. The time has come to dispose of the favorite, madame. Will you come? I might add that Messire Hugh Kennedy, who has

13

also been recalled by the Queen, will serve as your escort together with your humble servant."

For the first time Brother Etienne saw Catherine's eyes brighten and a little color came up into her pale cheeks.

"Who would protect Carlat? And my son and my mother?"

The monk turned toward Isabelle de Montsalvy, still sitting motionless in her chair.

"Madame de Montsalvy and the child must go to the Abbey of Montsalvy. The new abbot, who is young and courageous, awaits their arrival. They will be safe there till the time when you can persuade the King to restore your husband's rights and properties to him. A new governor is to take over Carlat, one of the Count d'Armagnac's men. Besides, Messire Kennedy was only here temporarily. Now will you come?"

Catherine turned toward her mother-in-law. In a gesture which had become familiar to her she went and knelt before her, clasping the beautiful wrinkled hands between her own. Arnaud's departure had brought the two women closer together than Catherine could ever have believed possible. The great lady's frigid reception of her daughter-in-law was now but a distant memory, and a feeling of deep tenderness, which did not need to be expressed in words, united the two women.

"What should I do, mother?"

"Obey, daughter! One does not refuse the Queen, and our House can only derive profit from your sojourn there."

"I know. But it is so painful for me to leave you . . . and Michel . . . and go away from . . ."

Once again she turned toward the window but, gently, Isabelle turned the fair countenance back toward her own.

"You love him too much for distance to mean anything! Go and do not fear. I shall watch over Michel with redoubled care."

Catherine kissed the old lady's hand rapidly and then got to her feet.

"Very well. I shall go." Her eye fell upon the heap of jewels on the table. "I shall take some of these," she said, "because I shall need money. You must keep the rest, mother, and use it as you think fit. You will find no difficulty in exchanging these stones for gold."

She picked up the black diamond again and squeezed it tight in her hand as if she wanted to crush it.

"Where am I to rejoin the Queen?"

"At Angers, madame. . . . Relations between the King

and his mother-in-law are still somewhat strained. Queen Yolande is only safe on her lands at Bourges and Chinon."

"To Angers then. But if it is not inconvenient I would like to pass through Bourges on the way. I want to ask Maître Jacques Côeur to find me a buyer for this unlucky jewel."

The news that they were soon to depart left three people overjoyed: Hugh Kennedy first of all. The Scotsman felt ill at ease among these Auvergne mountains which reminded him of his own country without being at all familiar. Besides the atmosphere of the castle, heavy with Catherine's grief, was becoming stifling. He could stand it no longer. He was torn between the violent attraction he felt for the young woman and his deep desire to help her forget her sorrows, and his longing to return to the good old life he loved, a life of battle and feats of arms, the rough camp life and the virile companionship of his brother officers. It would be good to return to the smiling cities of the Loire valley, and to do so with Catherine beside him would be a double delight! He lost not a moment in preparing for his departure.

Their departure was good news to Gauthier Strongitharm too, but for another reason. The giant Norman, a former woodcutter, worshipped his young mistress with a blind, fanatical but silent passion. He passed his life as if his spirit were prostrate before her, like a believer before an idol. This man, who did not believe in God, but drew his faith from ancient Nordic superstitions, the legends of the swan-ships, had elevated his pagan love into a sort of religion. Ever since Arnaud de Montsalvy had retired into the leper-house and Catherine had plunged into mourning for him, Gauthier himself seemed to have lost all appetite for life too. He no longer even found pleasure in hunting and never left the fortress. He could not bear to leave Catherine, even for a moment, and he had the strange idea that she would cease to exist if he ever took his eyes off her. But how the time dragged! Days piled on days, all alike, with no indication that a time would ever come when Catherine might shake off her grief. And now, miraculously, the moment had arrived! They were going to leave this accursed castle and set out once more, do something at last! And Gauthier, in his simple soul, was not far from considering the little monk of Mont Beuvray as a worker of miracles.

The third person was Sara, the faithful gypsy-woman who had brought Catherine up and stayed by her throughout all the trials of her turbulent life. Now more than forty-five years old, Black Sara was as youthful and vigorous as ever. There was scarcely a gray hair to be seen in her black locks.

There was not a wrinkle on her brown, smooth and well-filled skin. She had merely acquired a comfortable corpulence which did not augur well for long hours in the saddle. Yet her hereditary love of the open road prevailed over creature comforts and, like Gauthier, she could not bear to see Catherine buried alive in the Auvergne, ony living for the frail thread which attached her to the recluse of Calves. The arrival of Brother Etienne was a blessed event. The Queen's summons would force the young woman to shake off her grief and willy-nilly pay some attention to this world which she had so resolutely been avoiding. In the depths of her loving heart Sara wished to see Catherine learn to love life again. She did not go so far perhaps as to wish another lover on her: Catherine was a single-hearted woman; but then life sometimes made all things possible! Often, in the silent watches of the night, Sara the Gypsy had tried to pierce the veil of the future by fire and by water. But the fire went out, the water remained clear and untroubled and not one of the visions which sometimes came to her had manifested itself. The Book of Fate stayed firmly shut after the departure of Arnaud.

One thing alone tormented her: having to leave little Michel for whom she felt a passion amounting to adoration. But Sara would not have dreamed of letting Catherine go off alone. The Court was a dangerous place, and the gypsy had every intention of looking after Catherine herself. Stricken in spirit as she was, Catherine would need to be looked after. Michel, as Sara well knew, would want for nothing in the care of a grandmother who idolized him, finding in him a living image of the son she had lost long ago.

In a few weeks' time the child would be a year old. He was tall and strong for his age and in Sara's eyes the most superb child ever seen. His small round rosy face was illuminated by large pale blue eyes and tight golden curls blossomed all over his round head. The gaze he turned on everything around him was infinitely solemn, but when he laughed he laughed till he cried. He showed proof already of great courage, and only the red patches in his cheeks showed that he was teething, for he never cried. When the pain was intense large silent tears rolled down his cheeks, but his little mouth never uttered a sound. The garrison, like the peasantry, adored him wholeheartedly and Michel, already conscious of his power, ruled over his little world like a young tyrant, his favorite slaves remaining his mother, his grandmother, Sara, and old Donatienne, the peasant woman from Montsalvy who was

Dame Isabelle's personal maid. The little boy was more cautious with Gauthier. The blond Norman impressed him because of his prodigious physical strength and the child coped with him in his fashion; which is to say that he never inflicted on him any of the whims reserved for the four women. With Gauthier he entered a man's world and Michel always had a big smile for his gigantic friend.

It was a hard sacrifice for Catherine to leave her child. She surrounded him with all the love she could no longer give his father, and she watched over him with anxious tenderness. Catherine's behavior with Michel was a bit like a miser's with his gold. He was the single, marvelous memento of her absent love, this child who would never have either brothers or sisters. He was the last of the Montsalvys. Whatever the cost it was up to her to build a future for him which would be worthy of his ancestors, above all worthy of his father. And so, bravely holding back her tears, she devoted herself to preparing for the little boy's departure with his grandmother. But it was so difficult not to weep as she carefully folded up tiny garments and placed them in a chest, garments most of them the work of her own hands.

"My tears are selfish, don't you see," she said to Sara who was helping her, her face stern with repressed emotion. "I know mother will look after him as well as I could. I know nothing bad can possibly happen to him at the Abbey and that he will be safe from all harm and unhappiness there. And our absence, I sincerely hope, will not be too long! But even so it grieves me sorely to leave him!"

Noticing perhaps that Catherine's voice was faltering, Sara hurriedly fought back her own distress and came to her aid.

"Do you think I'm not miserable about leaving him too? But it's for his sake we've got to go! And I don't mind doing anything which could help him!"

As if to demonstrate the strength of this conviction Sara began to pack the child's little shirts into the chest hand over fist.

Catherine could not suppress a faint smile. Nothing ever changed her Sara! Even if she were half demented with misery she would rather cut her tongue out than say so. In her case sorrow changed to anger and the easiest way to work this off was to turn it against innocent, inanimate objects. Since she had learned that she was to be separated for some time from her young charge, Sara had managed to break two bowls, a plate, a pitcher, a stool and a wooden statue of St. Geraud, after which last exploit she had precipitated herself into the chapel to implore God's pardon for the involuntary sacrilege.

In between ferocious bursts of packing Sara murmured:

"I suppose it's better really that Fortunat should have refused to come with us. That way Michel will have at least one trustworthy defender and then . . ."

She stopped, almost biting her tongue, as happened every time she found her thoughts running in the direction of Arnaud. The young Gascon squire had in fact been almost as grief-stricken as Catherine herself. He worshipped his master with the ardent, unswerving devotion which some men alone can inspire. He admired him for his valor, and inflexible honor, for his warlike talents and also for what Charles VII's captains called "Montsalvy's appalling character," a highly personal blend of violence, humanity, inflexibility and unswerving loyalty. That his god should have been attacked by the abominable disease of leprosy had first horrified Fortunat, then angered him, then plunged him into a despair from which he had not yet recovered. The day Arnaud took leave of his family, Fortunat shut himself up in a tower and refused to be present. Hugh Kennedy found him huddled on the ground with both hands pressed to his ears to shut out the funereally tolling church bell, sobbing like a child. Since then Fortunat had dragged himself about the fortress like a soul in torment, coming to life only once a week, on Friday, when he took a basket of food to the lodge of the leper-house at Calves. He refused all offers of company on these weekly pilgrimages to a closed door. He wanted to go alone. Even Gauthier, whom he liked, was not allowed to accompany him. And the squire refused to make the journey on horseback. He covered the three half-leagues between Carlat and the leper-house on foot, like a pilgrim, laden with his heavy basket on the way there, bowed by grief on his return. Catherine had been so moved by the sight that she tried to make him take a horse. But Fortunat refused.

"No, Dame Catherine, not even a donkey. Now that 'he' can no longer ride as he loved doing I, his squire, will go to meet him on foot!"

The generous spirit and deep affection which the boy's words revealed had touched Catherine deeply. She did not try to persuade him further. Instead, her eyes shining with tears, she took the little squire by the shoulders and drew him to her and kissed him fraternally on both cheeks.

"You are braver than I am," she said. "I haven't the courage to go there myself. I feel I should die if I saw that door in front of me—that door which never opens! I try to content

18

myself with watching the chimney smoking, a long way off. . . . I am but a woman," she added, very humbly.

That last evening, however, when she summoned Fortunat to her to give him his last instructions before the journey to Montsalvy, she brought the subject up once more.

"It is more than five leagues from Montsalvy to Calves!" she said. "I think you should resign yourself to making the journey on horseback, or by mule. You can always leave your mount some distance from . . . from the . . ."

She could never bring herself to utter the painful name of the place. But Fortunat shook his head.

"I shall simply have to take two days over the journey, Dame Catherine, that is all!"

Once again Catherine did not reply. She instinctively understood the little Gascon's desire to suffer in his own way when he visited the man whose whole life was pain. But she murmured to herself, between clenched teeth, wringing her hands together: "One day . . . I shall go there too! And I shall never come back. . . ."

The following morning Catherine, attended by Sara and Gauthier, stood on the ramparts to watch the departure of her son and mother-in-law. From behind her black veil she watched the ancient litter, a clumsy conveyance closed in by leather curtains which had been exhumed from the castle stables especially for this journey, pass through the outer gateway. An icy wind swept the snow-covered valley but Michel would be warm enough in the litter between his grandmother and Donatienne. It had been furnished with as many footwarmers full of hot charcoal, and as many fur rugs as they could find. In the midst of his armed escort the little boy was journeying towards peace and safety, but all the same Catherine could not keep back the tears. Since no one could observe her behind her fluttering veil she allowed them to flow unchecked. She could still feel the child's velvety cheek against her lips where she had kissed him, repeatedly, ardently, almost wildly before returning him to his grandmother's arms. Inwardly she was torn to pieces by this enforced separation. Then the two women had embraced without a word. Just before climbing into the litter, however, Isabelle de Montsalvy had traced a rapid sign of the cross on the young woman's brow with her thumb. Then she had taken Michel in her arms and the heavy leather curtains had closed over them.

By now the procession was winding its way down the steep ramp towards the village. From her look-out post Catherine could just make out the red or blue caps of a crowd of peasants assembled near the church. Women ran out of their houses, some of them carrying their spindles covered with a hood of plaited willow to protect the wool. As the litter passed, bonnets were doffed all round. The countryside was enveloped in total silence. Here and there pale curls of smoke wreathed up from cottage chimneys. Beyond the mountains, whose chestnut forests were stripped of their summer verdure, a weak sun struggled through the clouds, its long arrowy beams gleaming sinisterly on the lances of the armed escort, yellowing the heron plumes on their bonnets. Ian MacLaren, Hugh Kennedy's lieutenant, was in command of the Scots detachment entrusted with the task of escorting the little lord and his grandmother to Montsalvy. They were to return the next day. And the day after that the expedition to the north would be leaving the castle.

When the last straggler in the party had vanished behind a tongue of woodland which stretched down into the valley Catherine turned round. Sara stood with hands clasped over her bosom and eyes brimming with tears, still gazing at the spot where the troop had vanished. Catherine noticed that her lips were quivering. Then she turned to look at Gauthier, but his attention was elsewhere. He stood facing westwards as if listening for something. The expression on his broad face was so strained that Catherine, who knew that he was as quick at picking up a scent as a hunting dog, was instantly alarmed.

"What's wrong? Can you hear something?"

He nodded without replying and ran towards the stairway. Catherine followed him but the Norman's long legs soon outdistanced her. She saw him race across the courtyard into the smithy and come out a moment later with Kennedy. And at that moment came the watchman's cry from the gate-tower:

"Armed troop in sight!"

At once she turned and raced back up the stairway and then, with Sara at her heels, started to run the length of the battlements towards the Black Tower. The news of an armed troop approaching filled her with terror for Michel's safety, despite the fact that the soldiers seemed to be traveling in the opposite direction from that which her son's party had taken. She reached the tower just as Gauthier and the governor, both flushed and breathless from their headlong rush up the steps, emerged from the stairway. With one accord they all rushed towards the battlements. Sure enough, on the road towards Aurillac, an armed band had just come into sight. Against the snow it looked like a long gray streak of wet,

20

glistening mud, and it was coming towards them, slowly, surely. . . . Few banners were to be seen—not that the colors were visible at this distance—but something long and red flapped at the head of the troop. Catherine narrowed her eyes in an effort to make out the coats of arms embroidered on it, but failed. Gauthier's eyes, however, keen as a hawk's, had already spotted them.

"Those look like the Castilian colors," he said.

Catherine allowed herself a thin smile.

"How learned you are becoming," she said. "You will soon be the equal of the kings-at-arms themselves!"

But Kennedy's face was unsmiling. There was a scowl on his sharp, ruddy features which boded ill. He turned and shouted some commands in his strange dialect, then he added:

"Lower the portcullis! Raise the drawbridge! Archers to the walls!"

Instantly the fortress seethed with activity. Men raced up to the walls dragging their bows and halberds, while others saw to the portcullis and drawbridge. Guttural cries, calls, clatter of arms, the sound of feet running in all directions. The castle, which had seemed to slumber beneath its coverlet of snow a moment earlier, had sprung to life. They were already piling up faggots and dragging cauldrons to the battlements for the boiling oil. Catherine went up to Kennedy.

"You have placed the castle on the defensive. Why is that? Who is coming towards us?" she asked.

"Villa-Andrade, the Castilian dog!" he said briefly. And to better illustrate the esteem in which he held the newcomer Kennedy spat contemptuously, then added: "Last night the watchmen caught sight of fires a long way off, near Aurillac. I didn't pay much attention at the time but now it seems I was wrong. It must have been him!"

Catherine turned away and leaned against one of the huge merlons. She adjusted her black veil the better to hide the sudden color which had risen to her face, then she wrung her chilly hands in the cover of her fur-lined sleeves. The Spaniard's name brought back so many memories!

Not only Gauthier, but she too had seen that red and gold banner before, a year ago on the ramparts of Ventadour, whence Villa-Andrade had driven its rightful owners, the Viscounts. And Arnaud had fought the Castilian's men. She shut her eyes hurriedly to keep back the scalding tears. She could see the cave at the bottom of one of the narrow chasms which acted as moat to Ventadour. It was a refuge for shepherds and the place where she had given birth to her son. She saw the firelight's red glow and the tall black silhouette of Arnaud standing protector between her weakness and the ferocity of the brigands without. And she saw, too, the Spaniard's bony face as he knelt before her with a gleam of desire deep within his eyes. He had recited a poem to her, but she had forgotten the words, and also, a courteous enemy, he had sent victuals to help build up the strength of mother and child. She would indeed have felt almost grateful to him had it not been for the appalling shock which met their eyes at the end of their journey—Montsalvy razed and burnt to its foundation stones by Valette, the lieutenant of Villa-Andrade, acting on his master's orders. Bernard d'Armagnac had hanged Valette but did this in any way lessen his master's crime? And now here he was marching towards Carlat, living image of the curse which pursued the Montsalvys.

When she reopened her eyes she saw that Brother Etienne was standing beside her. Arms folded in his long sleeves, the little monk stood gazing thoughtfully at the advancing column of men. He did not appear unduly anxious. Catherine even had the impression that a smile hovered round his lips.

"Do you find those men there amusing?" she asked somewhat dryly.

"I wouldn't go so far as to call them amusing. They interest me . . . and surprise me. A strange man, this Castilian! Heaven seems to have granted him a special gift of ubiquity. I could have sworn that he was now at Albi, whose inhabitants had no reason to rejoice at his presence. And then someone at Angers swore that this same stinking jackal . . ."

"Is that expression quite suited to your thoughts, Brother Etienne?" Catherine asked, lingering a little on the word Brother. The little monk blushed like a girl but smiled candidly at her.

"You are quite right. I meant to say that Messire de Villa-Andrade was spending the winter in Castile, at the Court of King John. Clearly his reception at Angers was not too welcoming . . . I wish you could hear Queen Yolande when she talks about him. Still, there he is! Why has he come?"

"I think we shall soon know."

Even as she spoke the armed band reached the gate-tower and the standard-bearer came forward, guiding his horse with one hand up the rocky ground below the castle walls. Another man followed behind, dressed in the gaudy costume of a herald, but one whose crimson and gold plumes showed the effects of traveling in winter along bad roads. The rest of the band had halted.

When the two men reached the palisade which encircled the gigantic rock they stopped and looked up.

"Who commands this castle?" the herald demanded.

Kennedy stepped forward, placed a stoutly shod foot on the battlement and thundered at them:

"I am Hugh Alan Kennedy of Gleneagle, Captain of King Charles VII. And I hold this castle for Monseigneur the Comte d'Armagnac. Have you any objection?"

The herald mumbled something, somewhat disconcerted, then he coughed to clear his throat, flung back his head and bellowed:

"I, Fermoso, herald-pursuivant to Messire Rodrigo de Villa-Andrade, Count of Ribadeo, Lord of Pusignan, Talmont and . . ."

"Come, come," the Scotsman interrupted impatiently, "what does Messire Villa-Andrade want with us?"

The man in question, no doubt deciding that the negotiation had gone on long enough, spurred his horse forward till he was standing between his standard-bearer and the herald. Under the raised visor of his helmet, which was decorated with two gold wings, a coronet and fluttering red pennants, Catherine could see the flash of sharp, white teeth amid the short, well-trimmed black beard.

"Merely to pay you a visit," he said pleasantly, "have a little conversation. . . ."

"With me?" Kennedy inquired doubtfully.

"S'truth, no! Please don't think that I despise your company, Messire Kennedy, but my business is not with you. I wish to speak to the Comtesse de Montsalvy. I know she is here!"

"What do you want with her?" the Scotsman asked belligerently. "Dame Catherine receives no visitors!"

"What I have to say to her concerns herself alone, if it please you. And I dare to hope that she will look kindly on a visitor who has traveled far to see her. I might add that I do not intend to leave without speaking to her!"

Without stepping out of her hiding-place behind the merlon Catherine whispered:

"We may as well find out what he wants! Tell him I will see him . . . alone! He must come unescorted. . . . That should give my son time to reach his destination, I hope."

Kennedy made a quick gesture of comprehension then he continued his parley with the Spaniard while Catherine, escorted by Sara and Brother Etienne, left the battlements. She had made her decision unhesitatingly because she knew that Villa-Andrade was La Trémoille's man, and she believed in

23

looking dangers in the face. If the Castilian's arrival spelled danger, and she was certain it did, it would be as well to know straight away.

A moment later Rodrigo de Villa-Andrade, followed by a single page carrying his helmet, entered the great hall where Catherine awaited him. She was sitting in a tall high-backed chair placed on a raised dais, with Sara and Brother Etienne on either side of her. She sat very straight, with her slender hands clasped around her knees, facing the visitor. Her demeanor was so impressive that at first sight of this black-veiled statue the Spaniard hesitated in astonishment on the threshold. Then, with faltering step, he came forward into the room, and the triumphant smile vanished from his face like a snuffed-out candle-flame.

When he reached Catherine he bowed deeply but could not resist stealing a quick look at her.

"Madame," he said in measured tones, "I am grateful to you for granting me these few moments. But I would fain speak to you alone."

"Messire, you will readily understand that I cannot welcome you to my presence before I know what errand it is that brings you here. I might add that I have no secrets from Dame Sara, who brought me up, or Brother Etienne Charlot, my confessor."

The monk repressed a smile at this flagrant untruth but he noticed that the Castilian was gazing at him with deep mistrust.

"I know Brother Etienne," he muttered. "Monseigneur de La Trémoille would pay dearly to get hold of that wrinkled hide and those gray whiskers!"

Catherine jumped up as if a bee had stung her. A flush of anger swept her cheeks and she retorted furiously:

"I do not know what your reason for coming here may be, Seigneur Villa-Andrade, but you do not begin your visit very auspiciously by insulting those I revere and love. Without more ado let us have the reason for your visit, sir!"

Rodrigo now stood erect. Despite the two steps which raised her chair above the floor his face was almost on a level with Catherine's. An angry light kindled in his black eyes and he narrowed them insolently, trying to see through her veil. But he forced himself to smile.

"I regret the clumsiness of my behavior and even more that it should have offended you. Especially since I have come here with the very best intentions, as you may judge for yourself."

Catherine slowly sat down again but she neglected to offer a seat to this visitor of hers, whose motives still filled her with misgivings. He spoke of good intentions. It was just possible perhaps, if one remembered that basket of victuals sent to the cave; on the other hand the smoking ruins of Montsalvy were sufficient to inspire mistrust. And that sharp grin of it—it was uncomfortably wolfish looking.

"Speak!" was all she said.

"Fair countess," he began, bending one knee on the first step of the dais, "news of your misfortunes has come to me. It touched my heart. Young . . . beautiful, and encumbered with the responsibility of a young child . . . surely you have need of protectors. You need a strong arm, a stout heart. . . ."

"There is no lack of strong arms . . . nor of stout hearts to watch over my son and me in this very castle," Catherine cut in dryly. "I don't understand you, messire, please express yourself more clearly."

The Castilian's olive features darkened slightly. He bit his lips but once more succeeded in mastering his anger.

"So be it! I will speak as frankly as you could wish. Dame Catherine, I have come to tell you this: by the grace of King Charles VII of France, whom I loyally serve . . ."

"Hm!" Brother Etienne coughed with unmistakable meaning.

"*Loyally* serve!" the Spaniard repeated angrily. "Also by the grace of King John II of Castille, I am Lord of Talmont, Count of Ribadeo in Castille . . ."

"Bah!" the monk interrupted pleasantly. "All King John has done is return to you what was rightfully yours. Your grandfather, who married the sister of Begues de Villaines, was already Count of Ribadeo, it seems to me. As for the lordship of Talmont, I congratulate you! The Lord Chamberlain is generous to those who serve him . . . especially with property which does not belong to him!"

At the cost of an immense effort Villa-Andrade ignored the interruption, but Catherine saw the veins of his temple swelling and thought for a moment that he was about to explode. However, he merely breathed hard two or three times.

"Be that as it may," he said between gritted teeth, "I have come to lay these estates and goods at your feet, Dame Catherine. The veils of widowhood ill become such beauty. You are a widow, I am free, rich, powerful . . . and I love you. Agree to marry me!"

Although she had felt herself proof against all surprise, Catherine could not help starting with astonishment. Her

25

gaze wandered and she twisted her hands together nervously.

"You asked me . . ."

"To be my wife! I would be a husband and willing slave to you, and a strong arm to defend your cause. And your son would have a father. . . ."

The mention of little Michel aroused Catherine's indignation. That this man should dare to think he could replace Arnaud, the very man who . . . No! This was intolerable! Trembling with rage she threw back the heavy veil and presented her pale slender face to Villa-Andrade's gaze. Her huge violet eyes gleamed like amethysts in the sun. Instinctively she gripped the arms of her chair, as if seeking some support.

"Messire, you are pleased to call me a widow. It is true that I wear a widow's weeds, but I would have you know that I shall never think of myself as one. My beloved husband is still alive to me, and will remain so as long as I live. But even if it were not so you are the last, the very last person I should consider as his successor!"

"Why is that pray?"

"Go and consult the ruins of Montsalvy, messire. For my part I have said all I intend to say. I wish you good day."

She was getting up to put an end to the interview, but now the Castilian's red lips curled in an ambiguous smile.

"It appears, madame, that you have not understood me. I asked for your hand . . . but it was purely from courtesy. The fact is that you *must* marry me. That is an order. . . ."

"An order? That is a curious word! And from whom, if you please?"

"From whom do you suppose? King Charles, madame! His Majesty, at the intercession of the Lord Chamberlain, La Trémoille, is prepared to overlook your crimes and those of your late husband, on condition that you become my wife, thereby returning to the ranks of obedient wives . . . and a decent life!"

The pallor of Catherine's face changed to pink, then red, then scarlet under the pressure of such a fury that Sara laid a restraining hand on her arm. But Catherine was wild with rage and beyond restraint. Was it written into her Fate then, in the Book of Destiny, that a prince should always dispose of her in marriage? First the Duke of Burgundy, and now the King of France! Clenching her fists and making superhuman efforts to keep her voice level, she cried:

"I've rarely listened to a more impudent cockscomb than you, messire! When I think that I actually entertained some grateful feelings towards you because of the food you sent me once—well, you have made me thoroughly repent of them now! So, not content with having reduced my husband . . . to his present state, La Trémoille now thinks he can dispose of me too? I would like to know how you propose to force me, seigneur? For, doubtless, you have thought of such a contingency?"

"The army I have brought with me," said the Spaniard with silky insolence, "is ample proof of the importance which I attach to obtaining your hand. I have a thousand men below Carlat, madame . . . and if you refuse, I shall lay siege to this mole-hill till you come to me begging for mercy."

"That might take a long time . . ."

"I have all the time I need . . . and I would be surprised if you had enough food for many months. You will soon surrender, madame, if only so as not to see your son starve."

Catherine repressed a sigh of relief. He knew nothing of Michel's departure then, and it was better he should not learn of it yet. She hid her feelings with a shrug.

"The castle is strong and its defenders are brave. You will be wasting your time, messire!"

"And you would merely be foolishly causing the death of many people. You would do better to accept now, madame, since you will have to sooner or later. Consider that I have turned down a very flattering alliance: the hand of Madame Marguerite, daughter of Monseigneur the Duke of Bourbon. . . ."

"Born . . . the other side of the blanket?" Brother Etienne insinuated gently.

"Her blood is princely! Besides your governor here is a Scot, Dame Catherine. The Scots are poor, needy and grasping . . . and they love gold more than anything else . . ."

He was not allowed to finish. Neither Catherine nor the Spaniard had seen Kennedy, followed by Gauthier, enter the hall. The Spaniard did not notice him till the moment the great Scot flung himself bodily upon him. With a great roar Kennedy seized Villa-Andrade by his collar and the hem of his doublet and half dragging, half carrying him, bore him to the door.

"There is one thing the Scots love more than gold, and that is their honor, master brigand! Go and tell that to your master!" he bellowed furiously.

Seeing this, Gauthier, rather annoyed at being left such a pitiful prey, snatched up the little page under one arm, and raced after the irate governor. When they had both gone

Brother Etienne turned towards Catherine who was still trembling and said, with a sweet smile:

"There, madame, now you have no need to reply. What do you think of that?"

She did not answer but merely looked at him, ashamed to find herself close to laughter for the first time in months. The sight of Villa-Andrade struggling like a red spider in the Scottish captain's grip was not the sort of thing one could forget in a hurry.

CHAPTER TWO

Footsteps in the Snow

By the time evening came this brief moment of gaiety had been forgotten. Catherine, Sara, Gauthier, Brother Etienne, Hugh Kennedy and the Steward of Carlat, a Gascon called Cabriac who had held this position for the past ten months, were gathered together in the high-ceilinged chamber in the keep, where Kennedy had established his own quarters since the death of old Jean de Cabanes, three months earlier. Cabriac was a plump, simple, good-natured fellow who loved peace and quiet above all. He was quite without ambition and had never wished to be appointed governor of the fortress. He preferred to see the responsibility for its defense rest on more martial shoulders than his own. But he knew the massive building and the surrounding countryside like no one else.

A little earlier, at the moment when the brief winter's day was extinguished as abruptly as a snuffed candle-flame, the party had climbed up to the watch tower to examine the enemy positions. They were already preparing to lay siege. Their rude canvas tents were clustered about the castle walls like a rash of poisonous mushrooms which had pushed up through the snow. Some soldiers had quartered themselves in the village. The terrified peasants had fled, seeking refuge within the massive walls of the fortress. They were dispersed all over the place, some in the empty barns and stables, others in the old armory. The scene within the castle was something like the bustle of a market day, because they had all brought their livestock with them. Now that darkness had fallen the assailants' camp, drawn up round the base of the castle mound, looked like a crown, with fires replacing scintillating jewels. Red plumes of smoke soared through the inky darkness lighting up faces here and there, faces so blue and tormented with the intense cold that they looked scarcely human. As she leaned over the walls of the keep Catherine felt as if she were staring down into an inferno peopled with demons. But the sight had considerably lessened Kennedy's optimism. He stood watching the menacing red tentacles closing round Carlat.

"What are we going to do, messire?" Catherine asked.

He turned his arrogant bulldog face towards her, and shrugged.

"For the time being I am less anxious for us than for MacLaren, madame. We are almost completely surrounded. How is he to reenter the fortress tomorrow on his return from Montsalvy? He will stumble upon these people and be taken prisoner . . . or worse! Villa-Andrade is ready for anything to force your consent. They will question him thoroughly, with all the unpleasant little refinements that such a procedure is likely to suggest to the Castilian. Our enemy will doubtless want to know where they have been."

Catherine went white. If MacLaren were tortured until he talked, the Spaniard would learn where Michel was. And what better hostage than a little child to make his mother surrender? Catherine knew that she would endure anything to keep her baby out of Villa-Andrade's clutches.

"Well, then," she said faintly, "I ask you again, Messire Kennedy, what are we to do?"

"Damned if I know!"

"A man must leave Carlat secretly during the night," Brother Etienne said calmly, "and set out for Montsalvy so that he can intercept them and warn them. The important thing is to get the man out. It does not look as though the walls are completely surrounded yet. I see a large area to the north where no fires are burning."

Kennedy shrugged his massive leather-covered shoulders impatiently.

"Have you ever looked at the rock on that side of the castle? It is smooth, black cliff falling sheer to the valley below and the wall above it makes the descent almost twice as high. It would take a damn great rope and enormous courage to undertake such a descent without breaking one's neck."

"Let me try," Gauthier interrupted, stepping forward into the circle of light cast by the leaping flames in the hearth. Catherine was about to protest when the Gascon, Cabriac, spoke.

"No need of a rope for the wall . . . or the rock. . . . There is a secret stairway!"

Instantly all eyes were upon him. Kennedy laid a hand on his shoulder and drew him closer.

"A stairway? You must be dreaming?"

"Oh no, messire. A real stairway, very narrow of course, cut through the rock itself. It starts from inside one of the towers. Only myself and the old Sire de Cabanes knew of its existence. It was via the same stairway, Dame Catherine, that Escorneboeuf made his escape the day. . . ."

Catherine shuddered at the recollection of the day that the treacherous Gascon had tried to throw her into an *oubliette* in this very keep. Sometimes in her nightmares she was visited by the sergeant's red, sweating face, convulsed by a hideous lust for blood.

"How did he discover the secret?" she asked.

The little steward hung his head and twisted his cap nervously in both hands.

"We . . . we are from the same part of Gascony," he stammered. "I did not want him to die . . . for that."

Catherine did not reply. It was not the moment, when he had just given them information of inestimable value, to start upbraiding him for protecting a murderer. Kennedy, who seemed lost in thought, would certainly not have allowed it in any case. He stood with arms folded and head on one side staring at the fire without a trace of expression on his face. Almost mechanically he asked whether women could use the stairway, and when told they could he said:

"Then I have a better plan. We must take advantage of the fact that Villa-Andrade has not had time to encircle the castle completely. He presumably imagines that the north wall is not so urgent, in view of the height of the rock; but he might well think differently by tomorrow. So tonight is our one chance. Dame Catherine, you must go and get ready to leave."

Catherine's cheeks colored faintly and she clasped her hands together.

"Must I leave alone?" she asked.

"No. Sara, Brother Etienne and Gauthier will naturally go with you. Once you have left Carlat safely behind Gauthier will go on to warn MacLaren while you proceed to Aurillac and wait. He will take orders to MacLaren to join you with all his men and serve as your escort for the rest of your journey."

"But meanwhile what will happen to you?"

The Scot gave a hearty laugh which, miraculously, dispelled the tense atmosphere of the high, vaulted chamber. It was a laugh which chased off all the demons of fear and doubt.

"Me? I shall remain quietly here for a few days, to keep Villa-Andrade happy. I must remain here in any case till the arrival of the new governor, and he is not likely to approach while the castle is under siege. After giving you a good start in case of eventual pursuit, I shall summon Villa-Andrade here and pretty soon convince him that you have all flown the nest. Then, with nothing left to wait for, he will surely leave. And all that will remain for me to do is hand over the keys to my successor and pack my bags."

Brother Etienne went up to Catherine and took her two cold hands in his own.

"What do you think, my child? It seems to me that the captain speaks with the voice of wisdom."

This time Catherine smiled, a lovely warm generous smile which embraced the little monk and the tall Scot, who grew suddenly scarlet with emotion.

"I think it's an excellent plan," she said softly. "I shall go and get ready. Come, Sara! Messire Kennedy, I should be very grateful if you would procure some men's clothing for myself and for Sara."

She heaved a great sigh. She loathed men's clothes which were uncomfortably restricting on her abundant curves. But, apparently, her life of adventure was not yet at an end and there was nothing for it but to resign herself to the inevitable, with good grace.

A moment later, in her room, Catherine stood gazing in astonishment at the clothes which Kennedy had sent to her. The Scottish captain had borrowed them from his page, and they consisted of the traditional costume worn by his countrymen with one or two slight variations. The hardy Highland Scots were used to a harsh climate and they had skin as tanned and tough as leather. Their usual costume consisted of a large piece of checked wool in their clan colors which they draped around themselves, a flannel jacket and a mail shirt. A brooch of wrought metal held the folds of material pinned to one shoulder. On their heads they either wore a pointed helmet or a flat beret adorned with a heron's feather, and they went bare of leg and frequently of foot too. In the service of King Charles VII, whose celebrated Scots Guard they had been since they were first formed by Constable John Stuart of Buchan, they wore silver breastplates and magnificent white heron plumes, but in the country they reverted to the traditional dress which they found more comfortable.

Kennedy had sent Catherine a tartan in the clan Kennedy colors: green, blue, red and yellow, a red jacket and blue beret, short stout leather boots and a goatskin bag. The only concessions to the rigors of the winter weather were a pair of blue woolen stockings matching the beret and a large black ponyskin coat.

32

"When MacLaren rejoins you you can pass for his page," the captain told her, "and like that you will not attract attention among the troop."

He had sent another costume in the same style, though considerably larger, and somewhat less elegant, to Sara. The gypsy categorically refused to wear it, at least to begin with.

"One can be a fugitive without making a fool of oneself!" she declared. "What am I going to look like in this preposterous getup?"

"What about me?" Catherine asked. She had undressed and scrambled into her strange costume the moment Kennedy left the room. Then she ran her fingers through her blonde curls, clapped the beret on top of her head and placed herself in front of a long mirror of polished tin where she stood looking critically at herself, hand on hip. It was lucky she was so slender because these bright colors were fattening; and she would a hundred times rather have worn black, if only to remain faithful to the vow she had made, never again to wear anything but black or white. But tonight was an exception, a case of necessity since it had not been possible to find any men's clothes in her size. All the same she felt a thrill of pleasure. The quaint costume gave her the piquant charm of a young page with an overly pretty face. She twisted a lock of hair round her fingers. It seemed to be growing back a shade deeper in color. The bright gold had taken on a bronze tinge which made it a warmer color and contrasted flatteringly with her delicate complexion and large dark violet eyes. Sara, who was watching her silently, grumbled:

"It's not fair for anyone to be so beautiful! I fear the mirror won't hold such a pleasant surprise for me!"

Sara had pushed her thick black locks under her bonnet, but there was an irresistibly comic air about her in the costume.

"You must drape the plaid over your chest a bit more," Catherine advised. "You look too much like a woman."

She had done the same herself, as well as taking the precaution of binding her breasts with a bandage to flatten them before putting on her jacket. Then she flung on her leather coat and went to the door, where someone was knocking.

"Are you ready?" came Kennedy's voice.

"I suppose so," Sara shrugged.

"Come in," Catherine called. She was busy putting the black diamond and a whole mass of other jewels into her goatskin bag. Sara would be taking some more. The Scotsman's tall figure loomed on the threshold. He smiled.

33

"What a handsome page you make," he remarked, in a voice charged with emotion. But Catherine did not smile.

"I don't find this masquerade at all amusing. I've bundled up some of my clothes and I shall put them on again the moment I can. Now then, let's be off. . . ."

Catherine took a last look round the chamber which had been the scene of her last hours of happiness, and then of so many long days of sorrow and suffering. Those bleak walls seemed to her to harbor the reflection of Arnaud's smile, the echo of her baby's laughter. She realized that they had grown dear and familiar to her and she felt a lump in her throat. But she would not let emotion get the better of her. She needed all her courage and presence of mind. She turned her back resolutely on the familiar scene and laid one hand on the hilt of the dagger which she had slipped through her belt. This was the sparrow-hawk dagger, the one which Arnaud had used to slay Marie de Comborn, and Catherine valued it more highly than anything she possessed. Besides these few inches of blue steel which had so often been warmed by her husband's hand, the black diamond itself seemed no more than a pebble and she would unhesitatingly have changed the one for the other.

She found Kennedy waiting for her in the courtyard, a lantern swinging in one hand. Gauthier and Brother Etienne were with him. Without a word the Norman took Sara's bundle of clothing from her, and the little party set out on the first stage of their journey. Walking one behind the other they made their way toward the outer wall. It had grown colder since nightfall and the frost nipped cruelly. From time to time a gust of wind caught them, raising white clouds of snow so that they could only make their way across the vast courtyard bent almost double. But as they drew nearer the walls the currents of air in the center subsided. From time to time the lowing of a cow or a baby's cry broke the silence; or it might be a loud snore from one of the refugees from the village, rolled in blankets next to a dying fire.

In spite of her thick leather coat, Catherine's teeth were chattering by the time they reached the tower Cabriac had mentioned. The latter was waiting for them inside, stamping and slapping his thighs to keep himself warm. Under the low, dripping vaulted roof the cold struck like a mantle of ice.

"We must make haste," said Cabriac. "The moon will soon be rising and you will show up as clearly against this snow as if it were broad daylight. The Castilian must have watchmen out everywhere."

"But how will we get through the barrier around the rock?" Catherine objected.

"I'll take care of that," Gauthier said. "Come, Dame Catherine. Messire Cabriac is right; we have already wasted far too much time."

He took her arm to lead her towards the black hole of the secret stairway, revealed when Cabriac had lifted up a layer of rotting straw from the floor. But Catherine paused and held out her hand to Kennedy:

"Many thanks for everything, Messire Hugh. Thank you for your friendship and the protection you have given me. I shall never forget these days I have spent here. Thanks to you . . . they won't seem quite black. And I hope we shall meet again soon, at Queen Yolande's Court."

In the flickering candlelight she saw the Scot's broad face brighten and his white teeth flash.

"If it only depended on me, Dame Catherine, we would meet again in a few days. But now one never knows what the morrow will bring. And since I may never see you again in this world . . ."

He did not finish the sentence but seized her by the shoulders, drew her towards him and kissed her soundly before she could find breath to protest. Then he let go of her as abruptly, and burst out laughing with the spontaneous gaiety of a child who has pulled off a good joke. And he finished his sentence:

". . . at least I can die without regrets! Forgive me, Catherine, that will not happen again . . . but I just had to kiss you once!"

His candor was so disarming that Catherine merely smiled. She was touched, more deeply perhaps than she would have cared to admit, by the warmth of this brusque caress. But Gauthier had gone pale. Once more he took her by the arm.

"Come, Dame Catherine," he said roughly.

He picked up the lantern and began to descend the narrow stairway. Catherine followed with Sara behind her and Brother Etienne bringing up the rear. As she plunged down into the heart of the rock Catherine could hear him making his farewells to Kennedy, urging him not to tarry too long in Auvergne.

"The wars will be beginning again soon, and the Connétable will have need of you," he added.

"Don't worry. I shan't keep him waiting!"

Catherine heard no more. The steep, uneven steps of rough-hewn rock plunged almost vertically between two great walls of rock, which time had furrowed and cracked. Catherine had to keep all her wits about her merely to keep from falling. The exercise was not made any easier by the fact that the steps were iced over in many places and dangerously slippery. When at last they reached the exit of the secret stairway, well hidden among a thicket of low shrubs, Catherine breathed a sigh of relief. Thanks to Gauthier, who held back the brambles for her to pass, she got through this obstacle without too much trouble, but then she noticed that the high barrier of pointed stakes which composed the palisade stood almost flush with the rock. They were trapped in a deep, narrow hole.

With one eye Catherine calculated the height of the formidable wooden wall:

"How are we going to get through that? We might just as well give up straight away. The stakes are too sharp to let us use a rope-ladder."

"Well, naturally," Gauthier said calmly. "That's what they are for."

Starting from the bushes where they were he began counting the planks going towards the right. When he reached the seventh one he stopped. Catherine watched in astonishment as he seized the massive tree-trunk and started to haul it little by little out of the stockade. Then she saw that the stake had been cunningly sawn through half-way up, in such a way that it still looked exactly like the others. Through the narrow gap which now appeared they could see the steep slope which led down to the river, as well as the few houses of the hamlet of Cabanes on the opposite slope. Just then the moon appeared between two dark clouds and its pallid light streamed down, illuminating the whole pale expanse of snow. Tree-trunks, and even bushes showed up as clearly as in broad daylight. The fugitives, huddled behind the palisade, gazed despairingly at the immaculate white slope below them.

"We shall be as visible as black ink blots on a white page," Brother Etienne murmured. "One of the sentinels need only glance this way once to catch sight of us and give the alarm."

No one answered. The monk had expressed only too clearly the thoughts in everyone's mind. Catherine was growing agitated.

"What can we do? Our only hope is to escape tonight, before the fort is completely surrounded. But if we are seen we are lost."

As if to lend force to her words, just then the sound of voices reached them, from close enough to make their danger seem all the more imminent. Gauthier cautiously passed his head through the gap and then hastily drew back again.

"The nearest guard post is but a stone's throw from here. A dozen men or so . . . but it would not help us much to put them out of action," he said, with a shadow of regret. "The best thing to do is to wait."

"What?" Catherine said nervously. "Till day-break?"

"Till the moon is covered again. Thank heaven dawn comes later in winter."

There was no help for it but to stay as they were out in the snow and the cold. All four of them held their breath as they craned their necks hopefully upward at the moon's pallid face. It seemed almost deliberate the way the black clouds scurried from one horizon to the other without ever completely hiding the treacherous orb. Catherine's feet and hands were frozen. The sequestered life she had been leading for the past few months had left her more vulnerable, and she suffered more than the others from their enforced immobility in this icy corridor. Once in a while Sara would rub her back vigorously but the relief this gave was fleeting, especially as she was beginning to lose her nerve.

"I can't go on like this," she whispered to Gauthier. "We must do something. We'll have to take a chance, it's our only hope! Listen, everything's quiet now. Perhaps the guards are asleep."

Gauthier peered out again. Just then a violet gust of wind swept up a powdery snowdrift into a white whirlwind. And simultaneously the moon vanished behind a black engulfing cloud. The light dimmed considerably. Gauthier glanced at Catherine.

"Can you run?"

"I think so."

"Then start . . . now!"

He passed through the gap and then helped the other three out. While they began racing down the snow-covered hillside he hurriedly replaced the sawn stake. Catherine ran as fast as she could but her frozen legs were clumsy and sore. The steep slope seemed to fall away beneath her feet and her heart pounded with terror. Gauthier caught up with her just as she was about to crash into a tree and snatched her up in his arms.

"We must run faster," he said gruffly, somehow managing to hurry his own pace in spite of his extra burden. Over his shoulder Catherine suddenly caught sight of their footprints clearly marked in the snow.

"Our footprints . . . they'll see them! We must rub them out!"

"We haven't time. Hey there, you two, walk in the stream for a bit and come up over there in that clump of trees."

He sprang down into the shallow brook. The thin sheet of ice cracked under his weight and the icy water splashed over Catherine. Gauthier kept an eye on the moon as they hurried along. It was still covered but it would soon reappear. The light was growing brighter already. They climbed up the bank at the spot he had chosen. By some good chance there was a pine wood close at hand. The Norman set Catherine down and started to cut off a branch.

"Make for the wood," he told the other three, "I'm going to get rid of our footmarks."

Catherine, Sara and Brother Etienne raced into the wood, while Gauthier used the fir branch to sweep their footprints away. The fugitives reached the shelter of the wood just as the moon swam up out of the clouds. They sank down on a fallen log to get back their breath after their headlong flight down the hill. Now they could see Carlat in its entirety: the rock like a ship's prow crowned by its immense fortress, the powerful bastions, steeples and towers, and at its feet, the menacing circle formed by the besiegers. Catherine thought gratefully of Hugh Kennedy. Thanks to him she had escaped the trap; she was going to be able to get to Angers . . . Gauthier's voice broke into her thoughts:

"This is not the moment to take a rest! We've some way to go before day-break. And that won't be long in coming now."

They set off again through the forest. It was the first time for many months that Catherine had come into contact with nature, with the countryside and the forest she loved. She was surprised to find all her old feeling of kinship with the giant trees returning, almost intact. It was not the first time she had sought shelter among them, and they had never yet failed her. The forest floor, mantled in snow, had a dreamlike quality. The cold was less bitter here, and the fir trees with their long skirts trailing in the snow had an air of majestic calm. Patches of moonlight in the clearings shattered into a million tiny scintillating crystals, and the silence was the simple, gentle silence of the sleeping countryside. War and wickedness, like the troubles of the heart, melted away in such surroundings as at the door of a sanctuary. Catherine suddenly found herself thinking of the hermits who were to be found sometimes living in the depths of the forests. She suddenly felt that she understood them. Such beauty would take the sting from any suffering, however cruel. She was not even conscious of her weariness or the cold. Gauthier's tall shape moved forward with a rhythmic, plodding step and she tried to keep pace with him and walk in his deep footprints. The others did the same. The giant too belonged to the forest where he had seen the light just like any one of these trees. He was at home here and the confidence which Catherine felt in him was strengthened still further. Then suddenly he stopped and hearkened and motioned to the others to stop. In the distance they could hear strident trumpet blasts.

"Reveille already?" Catherine asked. "Is day breaking?"

"Not yet. And it isn't reveille. Wait here a moment."

In the twinkling of an eye Gauthier caught hold of a fir trunk and scrambled up it, as agile as a monkey. The trumpet could still be heard, muffled and far away, proof of the distance they had already covered. . . .

"Is it the camp . . . or is it the castle?" Brother Etienne whispered.

"The castle would only sound their trumpets if there were an attack . . ." Catherine began. But just then Gauthier plummeted down between them.

"It's the camp! There's a group of men heading for the north wall of the castle. This damned moon must have shown up our footprints. I saw some men on horseback."

"What can we do?" Sara moaned. "We can't possibly hope to outdistance the horses if they find our footprints by the stream."

"True," said Gauthier. "The only thing for us to do is to separate at once."

Catherine was about to protest, but he bade her keep silence so firmly she did not dare to argue. Wasn't it to be expected that he should be the leader in an adventure like this? He went on: "We should have had to break up in any case at dawn. You must head for Aurillac, if you remember, Dame Catherine. I have to rejoin MacLaren. I shall leave alone . . . and they will follow me."

"Unless they prefer to follow us," Sara pointed out.

"No. The three of you will climb into this tree and hide there . . . until our pursuers have disappeared. Don't worry. I shall lead them such a dance you will be able to continue your journey without fear of being surprised."

All the fairylike beauty of the woodland scene seemed to Catherine to have vanished. Having to part from her friend was bad enough, but in addition there would now be the knowledge that he was in danger, the fear of what could happen to him. Shared dangers are so much less intimidating.

"But what if they catch up with you," she said miserably; "what if they . . ."

She could not bring herself to utter the word. Great tears

sprang from her eyes and rolled down her cheeks. They glittered in the moonlight. At the sight of them the giant's broad face shone with delight.

"Kill me?" he said gently. "I am proof against them, Dame Catherine. Now that you have wept for me, nothing can befall me. Now do what I tell you. Climb!"

He took her by the waist and swung her up effortlessly on to a branch. Then he helped Sara up, and finally the monk. Sitting like that, in a row, they looked like three sparrows in a storm. Gauthier burst out laughing.

"A funny little nestful you look, sitting there like that! It's an easy tree to climb. Climb as high as you can, and try not to make any noise. If I reckon right you should see the soldiers here within an hour. Don't get down again till you are certain they have passed by. Courage, my friends!"

They watched, motionless on their perch, while Gauthier trampled the snow industriously in a different direction so that the soldiers would not be led to the oak tree, then started a brief false trail in another direction and finally, with a great wave of the hand, set off at a run in the direction of Montsalvy. Only then did the three turn and look at each other.

"Ah well," Brother Etienne said good-humoredly, "I am afraid we shall have to carry out his instructions. Forgive me, Dame Catherine, but I am afraid I shall have to shorten this habit of mine—it is not very practical for tree-climbing."

Suiting the deed to the word, the little monk hauled up his frock and secured it firmly about his middle with his rope girdle, revealing slender, wiry legs which made his feet in their sandals look quite huge by comparison. He gallantly helped Sara clamber up the tree. Catherine, her old agility suddenly restored, climbed up unaided. It was not long before they reached the first fork in the tree-trunk. The branches were so many, and so tightly latticed together that they almost hid the ground below them. The three fugitives must have been all but invisible from below.

"We must just be patient," said Brother Etienne calmly, leaning back against the gnarled trunk. "I intend to make use of the time to say a decade or two of the rosary for that brave lad. I have an idea he may need our prayers, even if he doesn't think so himself."

Catherine tried to follow suit but her heart was too heavy, and her thoughts were far away, racing through the forest with Gauthier. She did not dare let herself think what she would feel if any harm were to befall him. He was very dear to her now; his devotion and loyalty had conquered a whole corner of her heart. Like Sara he was one of the bonds which attached her to the past. His calm strength and clear and lucid spirit were both reassuring bulwarks against life and its sorrows. From the moment his tall figure vanished among the trees she felt strangely vulnerable and fragile.

"Please God, don't let anything happen to him," she prayed silently, gazing up at the sky through the branches. "If you take my last friend from me what shall I have left?"

A noise of horses, clattering arms, men's voices and dogs barking was drawing closer to them every minute. Apparently Villa-Andrade's men had discovered their traces. Brother Etienne and Sara crossed themselves fervently.

"Here they come," the little monk whispered. "They will soon be here. . . ."

Catherine looked up again. There was no doubt about it; the sky was growing paler. Dawn was breaking. The forest was full of tiny rustling noises which meant that it was coming to life around them.

"If only . . ." she began

Then she stopped and gripped Brother Etienne's arm. She had just caught sight of a steel helmet gleaming between the trees. The deep snow muffled their footsteps, but the sound of crashing branches revealed their presence. They were busily hacking a way through the forest with their swords. The three fugitives hidden in their oak tree held their breath. . . .

The soldiers went by with agonizing slowness, peering at the ground; they numbered twenty or so archers, with their bows slung from their shoulders, followed by ten horsemen. They were all Castilians, and Catherine could not understand what they were saying. But it was growing lighter every minute and she could make out their olive-hued faces and black mustaches quite clearly now. She saw to her horror that one of the men had a string of human ears hanging from his saddle-bow, and almost cried out with dismay. The man stopped just beneath their oak, as if he had guessed that she were there, and shouted something in a hoarse voice. A soldier came running up and Catherine's heart missed a beat. But the man with the hideous trophy only wanted to have his girth tightened, and once this was done, he set off again. A few moments later there was no one left beneath the tree. All three fugitives heaved a simultaneous sigh of relief. In spite of the cold Brother Etienne's brow was streaming. He flung back his hood.

"Lord, I was frightened!" he whispered. "Don't move yet!"

They waited a few minutes longer in accordance with Gauthier's instructions. When the only sound to be heard in the wood was the distant crowing of a tardy cock, the monk stretched his cramped limbs, yawned till his face seemed in danger of splitting and then flashed an encouraging smile at his companions.

"I think we might risk getting down now. These good people have trampled the ground so thoroughly there's not much likelihood of their picking up our traces now."

"I agree," said Catherine, starting to slither down the tree. "But how are we going to know if we are going in the right direction?"

"Don't worry. It so happens that I know this countryside well. When I was a boy I spent several months at the Abbey of St. Geraud d'Aurillac. Follow me. If we keep going due west we should reach the priory of Vezac where we can rest for a while. Night falls quickly at this time of year. As soon as it is dark we can set out again. . . ."

The first pale rays of winter sunshine cheered the two women up. The sun was not hot but it was confortingly bright. When they were all standing at the foot of the great oak where they had been hiding Catherine burst out laughing at the bizarre appearance they presented in their outlandish clothes.

"You know what we look like?" she said to Sara. "We look like Gedeon, the parakeet which Duke Philippe gave me at Dijon."

"Very likely," said Sara, wrapping herself up as warmly as possible in her colorful plaid. "But I'd far rather be Gedeon himself at the moment, sitting snugly in a corner of your uncle's hearth!"

They set out once more and Brother Etienne's prediction was presently confirmed. The squat bell-tower of the Priory of Vezec appeared as soon as they reached the fringe of the forest; veiled in mist, it was a peaceful and reassuring sight.

At dawn the next day Catherine, Brother Etienne and Sara reached the gates of Aurillac just as they were about to open. A horn sounded on the battlements and the clear sharp air was full of hammering from the smithies. From time to time a nauseating odor reached them from the direction of the tanneries. In spite of the intense cold there were men to be seen on the banks of the river Jordanne, holding strange sloping trays under the icy water.

"This river is reputed to wash down particles of gold," Brother Etienne commented. "Those men are filtering it through coarse sieves to catch the particles. Look how closely they are watched!"

And indeed there were armed guards standing over them,

following their every move. They stood, motionless, leaning on their pikes, just a few paces from the workers. The workmen themselves were skinny and raggedly dressed, and the skin which showed through the holes in their clothes was quite blue with cold. Their appearance was in painful contrast to the sturdy, well-equipped guards. There was one man in particular who seemed hardly able to stand in the rushing river water. He was old and bent, and his arthritic hands clutched painfully at the sieve. He was trembling with cold and exhaustion, and this sight seemed to be exquisitely diverting to one of the soldiers. When the old man tried to climb up the bank he knocked him off balance with a blow from his lance. With a cry the old man tumbled into the icy water and disappeared. One of his companions, a sturdy-looking young man, plunged after him, but the river was swift at this point and he too lost his footing amid the laughter of the guards.

Catherine's heart swelled with indignation. She was not the sort of person who could stand by and watch such a scene without doing something about it. Almost without thinking her hand flew to Arnaud's dagger at her waist. Before Brother Etienne could restrain her she snatched it out of its sheath and leaped towards the guard with her dagger held high. She had not stopped to think of her own weakness pitted against these armed men. She had merely obeyed an impulse which was stronger than she was . . . perhaps because she had seen too much of the poor and weak being oppressed and maltreated.

To begin with she had the advantage of surprise on her side. The dagger plunged into the man's shoulder and he stumbled and fell to the ground with a howl of pain. Catherine clung to him like a wild cat and fell with him:

"Brute! Swine! You won't live long enough to kill any more old men. . . ."

Like a wasp's sting the dagger struck again and again, quite at random, while the man reared like a stuck pig without succeeding in defending himself effectively. Fury lent Catherine astonishing physical strength. But the other men had come to their senses by now and were attacking her viciously.

"The Scotsman!" one of them shouted. "Kill him, kill him!"

"Onward, by St. Andrew!"

The sievers just had time to scramble out of the way, as a troop of horsemen clattered down into the foaming river-bed and then pressed forward to attack the guards, swords flashing. Catherine, whom a dozen pairs of hands had seized, now found herself abruptly released. She stood up. Her hands were wet with blood and the man she had attacked was no longer breathing. He lay motionless at her feet, eyes wide open; and the snow around him was splashed with blood and mud. Catherine realized that she had killed him, but the strange thing was that she felt neither remorse nor revulsion. She was still seething with indignation. Quite coolly she went down and washed her dagger in the river and then stuck it back in her belt. Then she looked round and found that the battle between the guards of Aurillac and her unexpected rescuers was drawing to a close. She recognized Gauthier in the thick of the fray, fighting next to a tall blond Scot. All around them ten or so Highlanders were battling bravely: MacLaren and his men. The young woman's heart swelled with joy.

"Heaven be praised! He found them again!"

She ran along the river-bank, where the sievers stood watching the skirmish with frightened, bewildered faces, till she came up to where Brother Etienne and Sara had taken shelter, huddled under a ruined wall. Sara sprang out upon her like a tigress rediscovering her young, and first embraced her in floods of tears and then slapped her soundly on the face.

"Crazy idiot! Do you want to break my heart?"

Catherine reeled from the blow and her hand flew to her burning cheek. But by now Sara had collapsed in a sobbing heap at her feet, imploring her forgiveness. Catherine raised her up and hugged her and stroked her hair. But she met Brother Etienne's look proudly.

"I killed a man, father . . . and I do not regret it!"

"Who would?" sighed the monk. "I shall say my next mass for the villain's soul, if a mass can do anything for so black a soul! As for you—I absolve you herewith."

The fight was ending. The riverside guards had all been beaten down and lay dead or wounded in the snow. MacLaren was collecting up his men. Gauthier leaped from his horse and came towards them, his eyes shining with happiness.

"Are you all right, Dame Catherine? By Odin, I thought I must be dreaming when I saw a little blond Scotsman spring at that great brute's throat. But you're quite safe and sound, I see."

In his joy he had seized her by the shoulders and now he shook her, none too gently, fighting against an almost irresistible desire to crush her against him and kiss her. But suddenly Catherine went limp in his grasp. Her body seemed quite devoid of feeling but for this burning sensation in one shoulder. Her head began to turn, and the day went dark. Through the humming sound in her ears she could just make out a voice protesting angrily:

"Stupid fool! Look at the blood on your hand! Can't you see that she's hurt?"

Catherine felt herself abruptly released and then everything went black. In the excitement of the fight she had not even noticed the dagger sinking into her shoulder! And she had the good fortune to faint before the pain could grow too intense. While Gauthier picked her up gently and laid her across his saddle-bow, MacLaren raised himself in his stirrups.

"It would be unwise to linger here," he said. "I see a band of armed men leaving the abbey and in a moment we shall have the abbot's soldiery to contend with! Let us be off!"

"But she needs care," Sara cried.

"She will get it later. But first we must make our escape. Get up in front of two of my men. You there. Forward!"

Two sturdy Scots took charge of Sara and Brother Etienne, and the troop broke into a gallop, followed by the curses of the men-at-arms who came running up dragging bows and crossbows. A few arrows and lead shots fell about them but no one was hit. MacLaren's laughter fell on their ears like a thunder-clap.

"A monk's soldiers are no better than nuns in armor! They know more of telling beads and tumbling wenches than drawing a bow!"

Catherine's wound was not serious. A narrow blade had struck her shoulder causing a wound about an inch deep. Her shoulder and arm were swollen and painful but she had rapidly regained consciousness during their headlong flight. As soon as MacLaren judged that they were out of danger he called a halt. While his men snatched a bite of food and drink, Sara took Catherine on one side to dress her wound. Her skillful hands had speedily concocted a dressing from strips of linen torn from a chemise and smeared with a little mutton fat and herb balm which one of the Scots provided. Then they too ate a little bread and cheese and drank a few mouthfuls of wine before MacLaren once more gave the signal to depart. Catherine was weary. The strain of her night's march between Vezac and Aurillac plus the excitement of the fight had exhausted her. She felt an overpowering drowsiness stealing over her, and it was only with the greatest difficulty that she managed to keep her eyes open.

This time she rode behind MacLaren. The lieutenant had

resolved to take charge of her personally despite Gauthier's furious protests.

"Your horse already has quite enough weight to carry," he said sharply. "It doesn't need an extra burden."

"She won't be safe riding behind you," Gauthier retorted. "Can't you see she's dropping with sleep?"

"I shall tie her on. Anyway I am in command here!"

Gauthier had been obliged to give way, but Catherine had intercepted the look of fury he darted at the young Scot, who seemed quite oblivious of it. MacLaren was a striking example of that type of man who never hesitates over the right course of action and having once taken it never goes back, whatever the consequences. He made sure Catherine was firmly lashed to him and then rode up to the head of the column. Before long the party had entered the wild plateau at the heart of the formidable Cantal range.

Catherine jogged along behind MacLaren, leaning against his back. Soon the heavy silence of the region, with its deserted mountains, wooded volcanic ranges and deep, tree-lined gullies, encompassed them, intensified eerily by the snow. The occasional hamlet and dwelling they passed on their way seemed sealed hermetically round the warmth of man and beast within. The only sign of life was a thin, frail plume of smoke twisting up amid the snowy wastes. Inside their huts of black volcanic rock the peasants huddled beside their little cows with their curly reddish pelts. Catherine thought that the harsh outlines of this part of the country had a strange beauty, which the snow rendered more striking.

A strange feeling of well-being stole over her, in spite of the dull throbbing in her shoulder and the slight fever she felt circulating through her veins. She felt the warmth of the man in front of her. His sturdy body was a solid barrier against the cutting wind. She leaned her head against it and closed her eyes. She had the strange sensation, all of a sudden, that there was another tighter bond between herself and Mac-Laren. Yet she had never properly looked at him before. Enclosed within her proud grief, hidden by her heavy widow's veils as by a convent wall, the men who guarded Carlat had merged in her eyes into a faceless blur, and she had seen nothing but the invisible face of her lost love. Paradoxically it seemed that she had to don these boy's clothes to rediscover her woman's nature. Despite the despairing and hopeless love which consumed her, she had not been able to help noticing MacLaren's strange good looks.

He was tall and thin, but with the supple strength and grace of a steel blade. In profile his narrow face looked like

46

some bird of prey, arrogant and tight-lipped with square jaws suggestive of mulish obstinacy. His icy blue eyes were mocking, devoid of tenderness, and deep-set beneath fair brows. His longish hair was so fair as to be almost silvery. When he smiled only one corner of his mouth curved upwards, and that brief mocking smile, which did not reach his eyes, gave him a curiously lopsided look.

A little while earlier, as he lifted Catherine up on to his horse, he had looked at her hard and long: a look which pierced like a dagger. Then he smiled without saying a word. Confronted by this vaguely teasing stranger, Catherine felt strangely helpless. The look he had given her earlier seemed to say that the Dame de Montsalvy without her widow's weeds was only a woman like the rest, an accessible woman into the bargain. And Catherine found it hard to decide whether this impression was agreeable or not.

When they halted for the night in a barn belonging to a frightened peasant, who did not dare refuse them black bread and goat's cheese, Catherine had this feeling again. Sara had made her up a bed as far as possible from the men, but since their fire was small it was not possible to keep at a very great distance without freezing. Catherine was wet through, dead tired, and her wound throbbed painfully. The blood pounded heavily in her injured arm but all the same she was trying to get off to sleep when MacLaren approached.

"You are not well," he said, letting his clear, disquieting gaze rest on her. "That wound of yours needs different treatment. Let me see it."

"I've done everything necessary," Sara interposed. "There's nothing to do but wait for it to heal."

"I can see that you have never had to tend a wound made by a bear's claws," said the Scot with his rapid, tight-lipped smile. "Show it to me, I said."

"Leave her alone," came Gauthier's voice threateningly. "You will not lay a finger on Dame Catherine without her permission."

The Norman's tall shadow interposed between the fire and MacLaren, and Catherine thought that he resembled nothing so much as one of those bears MacLaren had just mentioned. His face was ominous and his large hand lingered menacingly on the battleaxe at his waist. Catherine felt a thrill of fear as she realized that the two men were on the point of falling to blows. Ian MacLaren replied, disdainfully:

"You are beginning to get on my nerves, friend! Are you Dame Catherine's squire or her nurse? Stay where you are

. . . I only want to help cure her, or would you prefer her shoulder to rot quietly away?"

"It hurts badly, Gauthier," Catherine said gently. "If he can help at all I should be grateful. Help me, Sara. . . ."

Gauthier did not answer. He turned on his heel and went and sat down in the furthest corner of the barn. His face was like stone. Meanwhile, helped by Sara, Catherine stood up and unrolled the long piece of woolen cloth in which she was dressed.

"Turn your backs, you lot!" Sara commanded the few soldiers who were not yet asleep.

She unfastened Catherine's jacket and mail shirt, and then when she was dressed in nothing but the clinging tights and coarse yellow shirt, she made her sit down and undid the shirt herself to reveal the injured shoulder.

MacLaren waited, with one knee on the ground, but his eyes never left Catherine for a moment and she felt herself blushing. Those strange eyes insolently followed the line of her long legs, the curve of her hips and climbed up to her bosom whose roundness was revealed even beneath the bandage of coarse linen she had put on. But she said nothing and allowed him to remove the dressing while Sara stood by holding a lighted brand. MacLaren gave a little whistle and frowned. The wound was a nasty sight, the cut was swollen and it had turned an ominous color.

"It is beginning to suppurate," he muttered, "but I can take care of that. I warn you, it will hurt for a moment, but you are brave, I know."

He went off and returned with a goatskin flask and a little leather bag. Kneeling once more he took his dagger and, quick as a flash, reopened the wound before Catherine even had time to cry out. A thin trickle of blood appeared. Then the Scot damped a piece of rag with the liquid from the flask. And then he began to clean the wound with it, far from gently.

"I warned you," he said, "this burns."

It burned like the fires of hell, as it turned out. In spite of his warnings Catherine had to grit her teeth with all her might to keep back the cry of pain rising to her lips. Tears sprang to her eyes but she said nothing. One of them fell on MacLaren's hand. He looked up at her with unaccustomed gentleness and smiled:

"You are brave. I guessed you would be. That's over now."

"What did you put on her?" Sara asked.

"A liquid the Moors call spirits of wine, which they use to

revive the sick. It was noticed that wounds washed with it did not become infected."

As he spoke he smeared a little ointment over the wound and placed a clean dressing over it. His hands were astonishingly gentle now and Catherine, all of a sudden, held her breath. One of his hands slid from her shoulder to the small of her back and lingered there so caressingly that she gave an involuntary shudder. A flush of shame and anger mingled rose to her cheeks. The strange, troubled feeling which swept through her at the touch of this man's hand horrified her all the more because it made her so sharply aware again of her smothered youth. She had believed that her body was reduced to silence now that her heart was dead to hope, and yet, in this fleeting moment, it had brusquely proved her wrong. She turned away her head to avoid the eyes which probed her own, and drew up her shirt abruptly.

"Thank you, messire. It scarcely hurts at all now. I shall try to get some sleep."

Ian MacLaren's hands fell to his sides, and he bowed silently and went off. Meanwhile Catherine, scarlet to the roots of her hair, put on her clothes again hastily under Sara's suspicious eyes and slid beneath the straw. She was about to close her eyes when Sara bent over her and her white teeth flashed in the dying fire's glow. Her eyes gleamed maliciously:

"My dear," whispered the gypsy, "merely wishing yourself dead is not enough. You are going to have a few surprises yet. . . ."

Catherine preferred not to answer. She closed her eyes tight, hoping to fall asleep straight away, so that she would not have to think. All around her rose the deep snores of the Scotsmen and the lighter, almost melodious snores of Brother Etienne. In a moment Sara's vigorous breathing joined in. For some time this strange concert prevented Catherine from finding any relief from her tiresome thoughts in sleep. The dying fire flickered briefly, then went out, leaving the young woman lying wide-eyed staring up into the darkness.

At the far end of the barn Gauthier was sleepless too. Outside the deep cold of a winter's night reigned, but the untutored instinct of this man of the woods told him that spring was not far away.

CHAPTER THREE

A Blow from an Axe

By the time they set off again on their journey the next morning Catherine was feeling better. Her fever seemed to have gone. Encouraged by this she asked MacLaren whether it would not be possible to find her a mount. She was apprehensive of having to spend a long journey in such close proximity to the young Scot. He met her request with stony displeasure.

"Where do you expect me to find a horse for you? I gave your Norman the horse your squire Fortunat used to go to Montsalvy. Sara and the monk are riding pillion on two of our horses. I can't very well force one of my men to dismount so that you can gambol about at your ease. Do you find it so unpleasant then to travel with me?"

"No," she answered, a little too quickly. "No, of course not . . . but I thought . . ."

He leaned forward so that his words were audible only to her:

"But you are afraid because you know that to me you aren't just a black-draped statue to be admired from a distance but a flesh-and-blood woman whom one can desire and not be afraid to say so!"

Catherine's beautiful mouth curved in a disdainful smile but her cheeks were noticeably flushed.

"Don't flatter yourself, messire, that I am at your mercy simply because I am weak and injured and without protectors. If you are suggesting that any contact with you might unsettle me, I can easily give the lie to that. I should like to mount, if you don't mind!"

With a shrug of the shoulders and a mocking grin he leaped into the saddle and gave her his hand to help her up. When she was safely ensconced behind him he held out the cord to lash her to him but she refused it.

"I am much stronger today! I shall be all right. It's not the first time I have been on horseback, Messire Ian!"

He did not insist and instantly gave the signal for departure. The journey throughout that day was without incident.

Everywhere the countryside was bleak, windswept, ravaged. The few peasants they met fled at the sight of an armed troop. The ravages of war had taken such a toll of these poor folk, endlessly pillaged and looted and maltreated, that they no longer even cared which side any new arrivals might belong to. Friends or enemies—all were equally cruel and destructive. The sight of a lance glittering in the sun was enough to set them bolting all the doors and barricading the windows. One sensed them holding their breath behind their walls, hearts pounding, brows sweating anxiously, and Catherine could not help feeling almost physically ill in sympathy.

The horse on which she and MacLaren rode was a sturdy but inelegant roan, a real warhorse, bred for charging and violence and not for speed, for gallops across country or through the forest in the teeth of a gale or a snowstorm. It was no Morgane!

At the thought of the little mare Catherine felt a lump rise in her throat. She rubbed a tear from her eyes angrily. She was an idiot to grow so attached to an animal! Morgane had left the stables of Gilles de Rais with her, and now she would doubtless leave for other stables just as cheerfully . . . but somehow the idea pained Catherine. When she left she had begged Kennedy to keep an eye on Morgane but the Scottish captain would be too busy to devote much thought to a horse, even a thoroughbred one. From Morgane Catherine's thoughts flew to Michel, and then to Arnaud and she was filled with bitterness. She would have liked to remain at Carlat for the rest of her days, leading a monotonous but peaceful existence there till she died, but fate, apparently, had decided differently. For her son's sake she would have to take up the struggle again, and plunge back into the hurly-burly of a life which no longer interested her. . . .

While Catherine's thoughts followed this path the road they were traveling on unrolled beneath their horses' hooves. All day she and MacLaren spoke not a word. That evening they halted at Mauriac. It consisted of low black granite houses clustered round the square towers of a roman basilica, a poor guest-house for pilgrims on their way to the shrine of St James of Compostela in Galicia. For Catherine it was more than enough. It was a relief to be spared the company of the soldiers that night, particularly that of their enigmatic leader. One thing was certain: MacLaren was not easily discouraged. When he helped her down from her horse he had surely squeezed her waist tighter than was necessary, and yet no sooner had she set foot to ground than he released her and went off without a word to see to his men's lodgings for the night. Sara came up to Catherine:

"What do you think of him?" she asked point-blank.

"What do you?"

"I don't know. He's extraordinarily vital, full of sap . . . and yet I could swear that death rides at his saddle-bow."

Catherine shivered.

"Have you forgotten that I share the horse with him?"

"No," Sara said slowly. "I haven't forgotten. But it occurs to me that you might represent this man's death."

To hide her agitation Catherine entered the low gateway to the hospice. A monk came towards them over the cobbled yard carrying a lighted torch.

"What are you looking for?" he asked, misled by the two women's costumes. "The Scots soldiers' lodgings are at the other end of the yard and . . ."

"We are both women," said Catherine briefly. "And we travel thus so as not to attract attention."

The monk's scanty brows knitted together, and his yellowish face, the color of old parchment, was furrowed by deep lines.

"Such an immodest dress is unsuitable for the Lord's house. The Church does not tolerate such garments on those of your sex. If you wish to enter here you must don women's clothes again. Otherwise you must spend the night with your companions."

Catherine scarcely hesitated. Besides she felt ill at ease in this foreign costume. It did not protect her efficiently—perhaps because she was not skilled at wearing it—against either bad weather or designing men. She tore off her bonnet and shook her golden curls.

"Let us enter. As soon as we are in a private place we will change back into more fitting clothes. I am the Comtesse de Montsalvy and I would have shelter for the night."

The frown disappeared from the monk's face and he even bowed with a certain deference.

"I shall take you to one. You are very welcome!"

He escorted her to one of the rooms reserved for more important guests. It consisted of nothing more elaborate than four stone walls, a large bed with a scanty coverlet, a stool, an oil lamp and a large stone crucifix, carved with a naïve skill, on one wall. In the fireplace a pile of logs waited for tinder to set them alight. But at least here the two women would be alone.

The moment they were in the room Sara started to light

the fire while Catherine scrambled, with suspect haste, out of
the clothes Kennedy had lent them.

"You seem to be in a great hurry?" Sara remarked. "You
might have waited till the room warmed up!"

"I couldn't. I'm in a hurry to get back into my own
clothes. At least I shall be treated respectfully then. And anyway I don't like these eccentric garments."

"Hum!" said Sara, unmoved. "I can't help feeling you are
trying to reassure yourself more than impress others! But
please observe that I am heartily in agreement with you. You
may not like this costume but I loathe it! In my old dress at
least I don't feel grotesque." And suiting action to words Sara
too began to undress. At day-break Catherine together with
Sara heard mass in the icy basilica, kneeling before the oldest
of the monks to receive a blessing. Then she returned to her
companions. When MacLaren saw the black lady of Carlat
appear on the doorstep, in the red glow of the sunrise, he
started back. Then he frowned in annoyance, while a somber
glow of pleasure shone in Gauthier's eyes. For the last two
days the Norman had not uttered a word. He rode a little
apart, behind the troop, obstinately resisting all Catherine's
attempts to get him to talk to her. She had finally given up
the attempt. The hatred which had grown up between the
man of the woods and the Highlander was almost palpable.

But before the lieutenant could say a word Gauthier had
run to meet her.

"I am pleased to see you once more, Dame Catherine," he
cried as though they had been parted far longer than one
night. Then, with the arrogance of a king, he offered her his
huge fist for her to place her hand upon. Side by side they
returned to the rest of the troop. MacLaren watched them,
hands on hips, with a malicious curl of the lip. When she
came up he looked Catherine over from head to foot.

"You aren't thinking of riding in that rig-out?"

"Why not? Isn't that how women usually travel? I asked
for men's clothes because I thought it would be more practical, but I found I was wrong."

"What's wrong is that black veil! It's a crime to hide such
a pretty face!"

And he was just about to push the fragile chiffon veil aside
with a nonchalant finger when Gauthier's hand fell on his
wrist and imprisoned it.

"Enough, messire," the Norman said quietly, "unless you
want me to break your arm."

MacLaren began to laugh, with deliberate insolence. "You

53

are beginning to get in my way, clodhopper! Hey there, you men . . ."

But before the rest of the Scots could fall upon Gauthier, Brother Etienne, who had just come out of the hospice, ran between the two men. He put one hand on Gauthier's wrist and the other on MacLaren's:

"Stop this, both of you! In the name of our Lord . . . and the name of the King!"

The monk's quiet voice was suddenly so authoritative that the two men obeyed mechanically, without thinking.

"Thank you, Brother Etienne," said Catherine, with a sigh of relief. "Now let us depart. We have wasted too much time. As for you, Sire MacLaren, I hope that in future you will conduct yourself as a knight towards a lady."

By way of reply the Scot bowed his tall body and offered the young woman his clasped hands to mount her horse with. It was both a tacit avowal of defeat and a chivalrous gesture of submission. Catherine smiled triumphantly, and then with a movement of unconscious coquetry she flung back her veil. Her eyes plunged into the young man's pale blue ones. What she read there brought a slight crimson to her cheeks, but then, with a light pressure of her feet on his clasped hands she sprang on to the horse. Peace was restored. Everyone else followed suit and the party galloped out of Mauriac without anyone noticing the shadow which had reappeared on Gauthier's face.

This incident as it turned out was the prelude to something far more serious. Towards midday the riders drew near to Jalleyrac. The dense woodlands gave way here to a large stretch of well-cultivated country, with fields of barley and oats; and in the midst of them stood a great abbey and small village. The whole place gave an impression of profound tranquillity. Perhaps this was due to the pale sunlight gilding the snow, or the pealing of a church bell, but there seemed to be something else, something unusual about this modest village and rustic convent. The strangest thing of all was that the villagers did not run for shelter at their arrival as they had everywhere else along their route. There was a large crowd of people in the one street which led up to the church. When they came in sight of the village MacLaren reined in his horse till Brother Etienne's could catch up. The little monk had been riding pillion behind a skinny Scotsman during the entire journey, which he had given every appearance of intensely enjoying.

"What are all those folk doing?" MacLaren asked him curtly.

"Going to church," said Brother Etienne. "At Jalleyrac they worship the remains of St. Meen, a monk who came originally from Wales across the sea and settled in Brittany where his abbey was burned and sacked by the Normans. The monks fled before them. The reason there is such a crowd is that St. Meen is thought to occupy himself particularly with lepers."

The word pierced Catherine to the heart. She went white to the lips and had to take a stern hold of herself.

"Lepers!" she echoed faintly.

She said no more, the words dying in her throat. And now the crowd was at its thickest, pressing and pushing up the narrow street. They were a horrifying sight. Beings one could no longer identify as men or women dragged their way through the snow, supporting themselves on T-shaped sticks or canes, displaying limbs which had either gone black or rotted to mere stumps, strange ulcers on their faces, swellings, tumors and boils; a terrifying rabble which might have been spewed up from hell itself. Groaning, chanting, crying out, they inched their way towards the sanctuary, one holding out a hand, another a greedily outstretched neck. Gray-robed monks, with a blue enamel insignia pinned to one shoulder, inclined their shaven heads toward them and assisted them along the road.

"Beggars!" MacLaren exclaimed disgustedly.

"No," Brother Etienne amended, "they aren't beggars. Some of them have the itching sickness, some erysipelas, some have the burning illness from eating rotten tubers and mildewed flour in times of famine, and so their skin burns and blackens all over their bodies. Here come the lepers now!"

And just then from a collection of huts standing quite apart from the rest of the village another procession came wending slowly towards them. They were men dressed all alike in gray tunics bearing a scarlet cross, with red hoods shading their faces beneath their broad-brimmed hats. They all rang bells as they went along and the sound echoed mournfully through the clear mountain air. At the sight of these men the hideous crowd in the street fell back in horror. Those rags and tatters of humanity ran as fast as they could towards the monastery, or else pressed back against the walls in an effort to save themselves from contact with the unclean, unclean though they might be themselves. Catherine watched speechlessly, eyes dimmed with tears. This ugly, wretched, suffering world was the whole life of the man she could never cease to love, the man she would adore as long as any breath remained in her body.

Uneasily Sara saw the signs of mounting grief in her mistress's pale face. Now the tears were coming thick and fast, running unchecked down her cheeks. She saw that Catherine's large dark eyes had fastened upon one man in particular, a tall monk, in a brown habit. And quite suddenly the gypsy realized why. This was the guardian monk of the lazar-house at Calves. He must have brought some sufferers hither to see whether St. Meen could cure them.

But the train of Sara's thoughts was brutally interrupted by the sound which, all unconsciously, she had been dreading: a desperate, heartbroken cry from Catherine herself.

"Arnaud!"

The lepers had by now gone past the little knoll where the riders were standing and were already moving off. But there could be no doubt about the tall figure walking beside the brown-frocked monk—that tall slender figure whose broad shoulders carried the livery of suffering with so much instinctive elegance could only be Arnaud de Montsalvy!

It was Catherine's love which had recognized him rather than her eyes. Before MacLaren could stop her she had slipped to the ground and begun running through the snow, holding up her long skirts with both hands. At once Sara, Gauthier, and Brother Etienne, prompted by their common affection for her, followed suit. The Norman's long legs rapidly outstripped the other two, but Catherine ran so fast under the spur of her passion that he could not catch up with her. Neither snow nor uneven ground could hold her back. She seemed almost to be flying, her long veil flapping behind her like a pennant. She was possessed by a single, wild, intoxicating thought: she was about to see *him,* speak to *him.* A flood of happiness swept her heart like a torrent bursting its banks. Her eyes, sparkling now, were fixed on that tall form walking before her.

The wild delight which Gauthier sensed in Catherine filled him with dread. How could it last? What would she see when the man turned to face her? Surely Arnaud de Montsalvy must have changed in those months he had spent in the leper-house? What if the face she saw had rotted already, and been eaten away? He forced himself to run faster and cried out.

"Dame Catherine . . . for mercy's sake, wait! Wait for me!"

His strong voice carried so far that it reached the lepers

56

themselves. The monk turned, and his companion with him. It was indeed Arnaud! Joy breathed new hope into Catherine's breast. What if a miracle were to take place! What if they were at last to be reunited? Had God taken pity on her at last? Had he listened to the prayers of those long sleepless nights? Now she could clearly see his beloved face, tightly framed in the red hood but as proud and handsome as ever. The terrible disease had not yet attacked it. One more burst of speed, one moment more, and she would reach him. She held out her arms imploringly and ran still faster, deaf to Gauthier's cries.

But Arnaud had seen her too by now. Catherine saw him grow pale, heard him cry out:

"No! No!" and start to repel her in advance by a gesture of both gloved hands. He murmured something to the monk who immediately stepped forward, barring the way with outstretched arms. Catherine flung herself against him blindly and was brought up sharply by his solid torso in its rough serge habit. Then she snatched at his arms as at a barrier.

"Let me pass!" she cried, through clenched teeth. "Let me pass! He is my husband! I must see him!"

"No, my child. You have not the right to go nearer . . . and besides he does not want you to."

"You are lying," Catherine shrieked, beside herself. "Arnaud! Arnaud! Tell him to let me pass!"

Arnaud stood a few paces further off, as if rooted to the spot. His face was ravaged by grief, a veritable mask of suffering. But when he spoke his voice was firm and clear.

"No, Catherine, no, my love! Go away! You must not come any closer. Think of our son!"

"I love you!" Catherine moaned. "I shall always love you. Let me come nearer."

"No! . . . God is my witness that I love you too and that I would tear this love from my breast if I could, because it is killing me. But you must go!"

"St. Meen could work a miracle!"

"I doubt it."

"My son," said the monk reproachfully, still holding on to Catherine, "that is blasphemy!"

"No, it isn't. The reason I came here was to help my companions rather than myself. Who remembers the last miraculous cure here? It is hopeless."

He turned, and with suddenly leaden steps rejoined his companions in misery who were moving off now, chanting a psalm, quite unaware of the drama being played out in their midst. Catherine burst into tears.

57

"Arnaud," she sobbed, "Arnaud . . . I beg of you . . . wait for me. . . . Listen to me!"

But he refused to listen. He went off without turning back, leaning on his long stick. But Gauthier came up now and gently took her from the monk and cradled her against his broad chest, sobbing desperately.

"Go, go now, brother, quickly! . . . and tell Messire Arnaud not to grieve himself. . . ."

The monk left them while Sara and Brother Etienne came running up, out of breath and puffing heavily. The Scotsmen brought up the rear at a trot. Catherine made one last attempt to free herself and follow Arnaud but she was so blinded by tears that she could see nothing but a wavering gray and red blur against the snow and Gauthier was able to recapture her without much difficulty.

MacLaren's cold voice fell on their ears and they found the Scotsman behind them, astride his horse.

"Hand her over to me and let us be off! This affair has wasted too much time already."

But Gauthier ignored him and lifted Catherine up on to his own animal which one of the soldiers was holding nearby.

"Whether you like it or not, Dame Catherine travels with me today, even if it breaks this horse in two. You seem to me to have very little understanding of a tragedy like hers. She might as well be in exile as be with you."

MacLaren's hand flew to the hilt of his sword and he half drew it and growled:

"By God, varlet, I'm sorely tempted to thrust your insolent tongue down your throat!"

"I should think twice if I were you," the Norman answered with a baleful smile. And he allowed his own hand to drop almost accidentally on his battle-axe. MacLaren did not press the point and, spurring his horse viciously, swung round and cantered out of the village.

Catherine did not even notice the inn where they spent that night, a small building nestled in a curve of the Dordogne river. She had wept so much that she was almost numb. Her eyes were red and so swollen that she could scarcely open them, and when she did everything appeared so misty and blurred it seemed scarcely to repay the effort. Anyway there was nothing to interest her now. She suffered as she had never suffered before, not even on that atrocious day when Arnaud had been banished from among the living. In that burst of optimism which had come to her it had seemed that this chance encounter with Arnaud must be a sign from Fate,

God's answer to her incessant prayers. And now all those months of suffering had gone for nothing and the wound of her love, which had perhaps been healing a little, had reopened and bled more than before.

All that day she had huddled against Gauthier's chest like a sick child, bumping up and down as the horse trotted along, without even opening her eyes. Then someone had helped her up a rickety staircase to this inn chamber. Chamber? Hardly! More like a rude hovel with a charcoal burner for warmth and a narrow wooden bed taking up almost all the space. But what did it matter to Catherine? Sara put her to bed as she might have put little Michel, and she curled herself into a ball under the coverlets which were so thin and worn they were almost transparent. She wanted to make herself as small as possible, melt into this cruel hostile world, take up as little room as she could. . . .

The burst of vitality and energy which she had felt on leaving Carlat had evaporated. She was tired of struggling, of living . . . even Michel did not really need her so much. He had his grandmother with him, and Brother Etienne would know how to plead the cause of the Montsalvys with the King, helped by Queen Yolande. What Catherine longed desperately to do was to rejoin Arnaud. She could not bear this dreadful emptiness he had left in her heart, this wound which only seemed to get bigger as time went on. . . .

She opened her eyes painfully. The room was all but dark and silent as a tomb. Catherine had begged Sara to leave her alone. She felt as if she had been skinned alive so sensitive was she to the slightest alien presence. In the red glow of the dying fire she could just make out a heap of clothes. Arnaud's dagger lay on top of them. Catherine struggled to raise herself to take hold of it. One blow and it would all be over: pain, despair, her undying grief. One blow, one simple movement . . .

But her torrents of weeping and the cruel shock to her nervous system had worn her out. She fell back on her pillow, shuddering. . . . The sounds from below were growing louder. The soldiers must be sitting down to eat. But these sounds of life were as remote and foreign to Catherine as if she had been sealed up in the heart of a mountain. She closed her eyes and sighed. . . .

The sounds of heavy footsteps and upraised voices from below prevented her hearing the soft creak as her door was gently pushed open. She did not see a tall shape steal toward the bed, but she shivered with alarm when a hand descended on her shoulder and the bed creaked as a knee was placed heavily on it. She half-opened her eyes. A man stood leaning toward her, and the man was none other than Ian MacLaren. The sight did not astonish her unduly. Sunk in the depths of despair, she felt that nothing could surprise her now, nothing could touch her.

"You aren't asleep, are you?" the Scotsman asked. "You are eating your heart out, torturing yourself unnecessarily."

The young man's voice betrayed a rising anger. Catherine was aware of his exasperation but did not even trouble to explain it to herself.

"What difference can it make to you?" she asked.

"What difference? Just that I have been watching you destroy yourself for months and months now! Oh, from afar of course! Have you even noticed our presence at all—only Kennedy's perhaps, and that only when you needed him! We all know that you have suffered, but in our northern country people do not consume themselves with vain regrets. Life is too harsh in my country to be frittered away in tears and sighs."

"What has that to do with me? Just say what you have to say, and speak plainly. I am so weary . . ."

"Weary? Who is not weary in this time we live in? Why should you be more so than the next woman? Do you think you are the only sufferer on this earth, or is that all you are capable of—huddling in a corner like a frightened beast and crying till you are half insensible . . . ?"

The man's harsh, contemptuous and yet passionate voice pierced the protective stupor which enveloped Catherine. She could not altogether ignore what he was saying because in her heart of hearts she knew that he was right.

"In my country too there are men dying, swiftly or slowly, and women stricken in heart and body but there is not enough time to dwell on one's misfortunes. The country is too harsh, and life itself too much of a battle to afford the luxury of tears and sighs."

A feeling of revolt galvanized Catherine. She sat up, clutching her coverlets to her bosom.

"And so? What is the point of this harangue? Why have you come here to torment me? Can't you leave me in peace?"

MacLaren's face broke into its brief, teasing grin. "Some reaction at last! That was what I wanted . . . and something else besides!"

"Something else?"

"This . . ."

Before she realized what he was about, he had taken her into his arms. She found herself completely immobilized,

60

helpless, as his hand slipped among her curls and dragged her head backward. When Ian began to kiss her she instinctively pushed him away. But she might as well not have bothered: he had fast hold of her. After a while an insidious enjoyment stole over her, as it had when he had tended her wound. His lips were soft and warm and his arms were solid and reassuring about her. Suddenly Catherine stopped thinking and abandoned herself to the feminine instinct which is as old as life itself and which whispered to her that she should enjoy the young man's caresses. Some people find oblivion in drink, but the love and caresses of a man can prove no less powerful an intoxicant, and it was this that Catherine was discovering now. . . .

When he lowered her down on the shabby cushions he threw back his head a moment and gave her a look of burning passion and pride.

"Let me make love to you and I'll make you forget your tears. I'll love you so much that . . ."

But he wasn't allowed to finish. This time it was Catherine who glued her lips to his in the grip of a sudden frenzy of passion, and drew him down to her. All at once he had become the one reality in her tottering world, a warm, breathing reality which she longed to cling to with all her strength. The two of them rolled, embracing tightly, into the hollow of the old mattress, oblivious of the wretched surroundings, of everything but the approach of pleasure. Catherine's shattered nerves made her long for total oblivion and submission to a stronger will. She closed her eyes with a little moan.

What happened next thrust her right back into the nightmarish, demoniac world from which MacLaren had briefly rescued her.

First there came a dreadful cry, which seemed to Catherine to explode inside her own skull, then the body she clasped in her arms shuddered convulsively, MacLaren's eyes seemed to burst from their sockets and a jet of blood spurted from his mouth. With a cry of horror Catherine wrenched herself aside, pulling the covers with her. Almost without thinking she wrapped herself in them. Only then did she see Gauthier standing by the bed staring at her with a madman's eyes. His hands hung motionless by his side. His axe was buried deep between MacLaren's shoulder-blades.

For a moment Catherine and the Norman gazed at each other in silence, as if seeing each other for the first time. Catherine was paralyzed by fear. She had never seen Gauthier's face twisted into this mask of implacable hatred and cruelty. He was quite out of his mind, and when he slowly

lifted up his enormous hands she thought that he was going
to kill her, but she did not stir because, although her mind
worked, her body seemed bereft of power and strength. For
the first time in her life Catherine literally experienced that
nightmare sensation when one struggles vainly to flee from a
pursuer, but one's feet refuse to leave the ground and the
scream dies in one's throat. . . .

However, Gauthier's hands fell back nervelessly to his
sides and the spell which seemed to have bewitched Catherine
was broken. She looked away and glanced at MacLaren's
body with a mixture of alarm and astonishment. How easy
and how rapid death was! In the space of a scream, life and
passion could be extinguished and nothing be left but dead
matter. This man in whose arms she had been swooning only
a moment before, had disappeared! "I'll make you forget," he
had promised her, but he had not had time to bend her to his
will! She swallowed painfully, then asked in a faint voice:

"Why did you do this thing?"

"You dare to ask?" he answered brutally. "Has all your
love for Messire Arnaud come to this? Do you have to find
yourself a lover the very day you see him again? I set you up
so high . . . higher than any woman deserves! And just a
moment ago I heard you purring like a cat in heat!"

A sudden gust of anger swept away Catherine's fear. This
man had committed murder, and now he thought he could
stand there in judgment upon her!

"What right have you got to interfere with my private life?
Have I ever given you the right to meddle in my affairs?"

He took a step towards her, his fists clenched, with a
wicked gleam in his eyes.

"You entrusted yourself to me and, by Odin, I would have
shed my last drop of blood in your service! I silenced my
love for you, and the wild desire I felt for you because it
seemed to me that the love between you and your husband
was too fine and beautiful a thing: others had no right to
touch it or interfere in any way. Everything else had to be
sacrificed to a love like that!"

"And what's left to me of it?" Catherine cried, beside herself suddenly. "I am all alone, always alone—I have no more
love, no husband. . . . Only a short while ago he sent me
away, he rejected me!"

"And all the while he yearned to hold his arms out to you!
Only he loves you too much to want to see you rot alive as
he is doing! Your poor little woman's mind saw no further
than the act—he rejected you! So what did you do then? You
threw yourself into the arms of the first man who came

along, and for just one reason—spring is coming and that's the time when animals go in heat, and you are just an animal like the rest. But if it was a man you wanted, just a man, why did you have to choose this cold-eyed foreigner? Why not me?"

The Norman's magnificent chest reverberated like a drum as he struck it, and his angry voice growled like thunder. Catherine had returned to her senses, and with the return of her self-control she was forced to admit that she could not imagine what had thrown her into the Scotsman's arms only a little while earlier. In her innermost self she knew that Gauthier was right. She was ashamed as she had never been ashamed before, but she understood only too clearly the meaning of the cloudy gleam in the Norman's gray eyes. In just a moment he would fling himself upon her, without a thought for the man he had just slain. After what he had seen there would be no restraining him. In that "Why not me?" of his there had been a world of anger, bitterness, frustrated love and contempt. Catherine was no longer sacred to him. She was just a woman he had desired for too long.

She tried to check the convulsive trembling which had taken hold of her and looked squarely into his eyes.

"Go away," she said icily. "I dismiss you from my service!"

Gauthier gave a ferocious roar of laughter, and his strong white teeth flashed.

"You dismiss me? Well, that is your right after all! But first of all . . ."

Catherine shrank back against the wall the better to resist the sudden onslaught, but at that precise moment the door opened and Sara entered the room. In one rapid glance she took in the whole scene—Catherine flattened against the wall, Gauthier about to spring, and between them both MacLaren's pitiful corpse, outstretched upon the bed like a human cross.

"Gramercy!" she cried. "What has happened here?"

Catherine's agonized breathing relaxed in a long sigh. The gypsy's solid presence seemed to have dispelled the evil atmosphere from the room. The devils were fleeing and cold reality taking their place. Calmly and without trying to gloss over the less admirable aspects of her own behavior Catherine described how Gauthier had come to kill the Scotsman. Meanwhile the Norman slumped down at the foot of the bed without looking at his victim, his fury suddenly drained away. He sat with his head in his hands apparently quite indifferent to anything which could befall him now. With tacit accord he and Catherine left the decisions to Sara.

"What a mess!" the gypsy murmured when she had finished recounting her story. "I'd like to know how you think we're going to get out of it? What are the Scots going to do when they find their leader has been killed?"

As if to underline her words a cry arose from the room below.

"Ian! Hey, Ian MacLaren! Come and drink with us! For once the wine is not too bad! Come on down!"

"They will come up here in a minute," Sara whispered. "We must hide the body. If they learn the truth there will be more bloodshed. . . ."

Gauthier still did not move, but Catherine fully understood what Sara was saying. The Scots would demand Gauthier's head. They knew one law only—an eye for an eye! Their leader was dead, and his killer must pay with his life. And Catherine realized that that was a thing she could not endure. After all, what was MacLaren to her? She did not love him. She had not even been seized by one of those infatuations which might have excused her behavior. It had just been a passing madness! But the idea that Gauthier should be offered up as a sacrifice to their swords, no, that was unthinkable! On a sudden impulse she threw herself down on her knees before him and tried to prise his hands away from his face.

"You must flee!" she said. "I beg you! Escape from here before they find the body!"

He let drop his hands revealing a ravaged face and tragic eyes.

"What difference does it make whether they find out that I killed him? They can only kill me. And what then?"

"I don't want you to die," Catherine spoke hotly.

"You dismissed me just now . . . death would be a far surer way of getting rid of me!"

"I didn't know what I was saying. I was mad. You insulted me and hurt me . . . but you were right. You see now it is I who ask your forgiveness."

"What a to-do!" Sara scolded from her corner. "You would do better to listen to the din they are making down below."

The Scotsmen were calling for their chief now at the tops of their voices, banging their mugs and plates on the table. They heard the crash of a bench being overturned, then suddenly there was the sound of feet on the stairs and voices coming nearer. Catherine gripped Gauthier's hand in terror.

"Have pity on me! If you have ever thought kindly of me do what I tell you now, and escape!"

"Where should I go? Somewhere where I can never see you again?"

"Go back to Montsalvy, to Michel, and wait there till I return. But hurry, hurry . . . I hear them coming!"

Sara had already opened the small window which fortunately led on to a sloping roof. The winter wind burst into the small room like an icy whirlwind and Catherine drew the covers more tightly round herself. The steps were coming nearer. The men were already drunk. . . .

"I'll talk to them and gain a little time," said Sara. "But he must be off at once. The horses are in the barn. If we can give him an hour or two's start he will be safe. Now make haste; I will get them to go downstairs again. . . ."

She slipped hurriedly through the half-open door. Not a moment too soon. The light of a candle flickered briefly and the sound of a man's voice reached them from apparently just outside the door.

"What's all this din?" Sara scolded. "Didn't you know that Dame Catherine was worn out? It has taken her all this time to get off to sleep and now here you are bellowing like pigs right outside her door! What do you want?"

"I beg your pardon," came the contrite voice of one of the soldiers, "but we were looking for our chief."

"And do you expect to find him in here? A curious notion."

"It's just that . . ." the man broke off abruptly, then gave a coarse laugh and went on: "He told us that he wanted to pay the gracious lady a little visit . . . see if she was all right!"

"Well, he isn't here! You had better look elsewhere. . . . As a matter of fact I saw him going out not so long ago. He went toward the stables at the back of the inn . . . and I think he was after some wench."

Catherine listened to this exchange avidly, heart pounding. Her hand tightened its clutch on Gauthier's. She felt him tremble; and yet she knew it was not from fear. They could hear the men roaring with laughter now beyond the door, but their voices were already receding, and Sara's with them. No doubt the gypsy woman was accompanying them to make certain that they were searching in the right direction and didn't catch sight of Gauthier escaping from the window.

"They have gone," Catherine whispered. "Now you must go. . . ."

He obeyed her this time and crossed over to the window and stuck one leg out. But before leaving he turned back.

"Do you swear that I shall see you again?"

"If we live long enough for that, I swear! Now quick!"

"And . . . you forgive me?"

"If you aren't out of here in one minute I shall never forgive you as long as I live!"

Gauthier's teeth flashed in a quick grin, then, with a feline suppleness astonishing in such a massive man, he slipped through the window. Catherine watched him slide down the roof and then jump down. Then he vanished from sight but a few moments later she caught a faint glimpse of a man on horseback galloping off into the night. Fortunately the thick snow muffled the sound of the hoof-beats. Catherine breathed more freely. Then she shut the window and put some more fuel on the fire to warm up the room. She was shivering. But the desperate weariness and lassitude she had felt earlier had quite gone. She took care not to look at the tall body stretched out on her bed, but its presence there no longer filled her with terror and dread. She found that her mind was working with crystal clarity, and she was quite calm as she planned what she would have to do next. The first thing was to get the corpse out of the room. It must not remain there. With Sara's assistance she would have to smuggle it out through the window and leave it somewhere near the inn, by the river for instance. That way the Scots would not find it till morning and Gauthier would be assured of a night's start. For she had no illusions as to what would happen when they found their captain dead—they would all fling themselves in pursuit of the man who had murdered him, and there could be no doubt as to the murderer's identity; the axe blow which had killed MacLaren could only point to Gauthier.

When Sara returned she found Catherine dressed and seated by the brazier. She looked up at her.

"Well?"

"They are all convinced that MacLaren is wooing one of the maidservants in the stable. They have all gone back to their meal. And now, what are we going to do?"

Catherine explained her plans to Sara, who gaped at her.

"You mean to say you are thinking of passing this great corpse through the window? We'll never do it . . . we'll break our necks!"

"Where there's a will, there's a way. Now go and fetch Brother Etienne. He must be told. We shall need him."

Sara did not argue. When Catherine spoke in that particular tone of voice it was a waste of time. She knew that of old. She went out and returned a few minutes later with the monk. She had already explained the situation to him, and Brother Etienne had seen too much in the course of an adventurous life to be surprised by anything. When occasion demanded, he could be remarkably efficient. He wholly approved of Catherine's plan and instantly placed his services at her disposal.

"Just give me time for a short prayer and I'll be with you," he said.

He knelt beside the lifeless body and murmured a rapid prayer, then he traced the sign of the cross over it and stood up, rolling back his sleeves.

"The best thing would be for me to get out on the roof," he said. "I can get him down from there."

"But he is tall and heavy in spite of being so thin," Catherine objected.

"I'm stronger than you imagine, my child. Now, come, let us to work."

He helped Catherine and Sara carry the body to the window and then stepped out. The cold was more intense but the night was still and peaceful. The Scotsmen must have fallen asleep down below after having eaten and drunk their fill, because there was not a sound to be heard.

The unfortunate MacLaren's body had already stiffened and was unwieldy to carry. Catherine and Sara needed every ounce of strength to lift him through the window. They were both dripping with sweat despite the cold, and they had to grit their teeth to keep back their panic. If anyone were to hear them now God alone knew what would happen to them! In their fury the Scotsmen would almost certainly string them up from the nearest tree, without further trial. But no one appeared, and there was not a sound to be heard. Brother Etienne took hold of the body and let it slide to the edge of the roof.

"One of you will have to come here and keep hold of it while I get down," he whispered.

Catherine got out of the window and crept cautiously down to join Brother Etienne. The tiled roof was slippery with ice but Catherine negotiated it without mishap, and she held on to the corpse to prevent it crashing down, while Brother Etienne leaped to the ground with astonishing agility.

"All right. Now let him slip down gently . . . gently now! There, I've got him! Now go back to your room. I'll take care of the rest."

"But how will you get in again?"

"Through the door! This habit I wear allows me to come and go without attracting attention. I've often noticed that. In fact there are times when I wonder if that was the real reason why I went into the monastery."

Catherine sensed that he was smiling, but she said nothing. Now that the corpse was out of sight she was suddenly experiencing a violent attack of nervous tension. She remained for a moment crouching on the edge of the roof, eyes closed in an attempt to ward off a fit of giddiness which threatened to make her lose her footing and overbalance. Heaven and earth seemed to be wheeling around her in a wild dance.

"What's the matter?" Sara whispered anxiously from the window. "Do you want me to come and fetch you?"

"No . . . no . . . there's no need. Anyway you wouldn't be able to get through the window!"

Catherine began to crawl back up the roof on hands and knees. Slowly her giddiness disappeared. Sara's hands seized her and drew her into the room which was now as cold as ice. Sara helped her to the bed where she sat down, wiping her damp forehead with one hand. Her teeth chattered.

"I'll go and find something to light the fire with," Sara said, "and I'll bring you back some soup."

She bustled about while she spoke lighting the candle and examining the bloodstained coverlets with an expression of disgust.

"We shall have to burn them. I'll find some way of discreetly compensating the innkeeper for them."

Catherine did not speak. Her thoughts were with Gauthier, galloping through the night toward Michel and Montsalvy, and a bitter despair filled her heart. Deprived of his solid presence and protection the days ahead seemed suddenly darker and more threatening. Was she to see all the people who loved her best taken from her one by one? Once again she and her old Sara were alone together, with a new life to build. But she refused to allow self-pity to swamp her in spite of her sad thoughts. What had happened was her fault, entirely her fault. If she had sent MacLaren away when he leaned over her bed, none of this would have happened. The young Scot would still be alive, and poor Gauthier would not have had to set out once more on the perilous road to adventure.

When Sara returned bringing a faggot of wood and a bowl of soup with her, her handsome brown face was full of satisfaction.

"They are all asleep down there. The Scotsmen are all snoring on the floor or on the benches. Gauthier will have the entire night to get away from them. All is well."

"You're easy to please! Let's say that everything is going as well as can be expected in the midst of an avalanche of disasters."

The events of the next day came about exactly as Sara and Catherine had predicted. At sunrise one of the Scotsmen discovered MacLaren's body lying in the snow by the river, close to the stable, and all at once Sara, Catherine and Brother Etienne found themselves in the center of a storm of revolt. The oldest of the men-at-arms, a soldier of fifty or so called Alan Scott, naturally assumed command of his companions and it was he who silenced the hubbub for a moment and informed the three travelers of their intentions.

"Sorry, lady," he told Catherine, "but we have to avenge our chief's death."

"On whom? How can you know who the murderer was?"

"It was your squire. The axe blow proves that beyond a doubt."

"The men around here also use axes," Catherine parried nervously. "Sara told you she saw MacLaren going toward the stables with one of the maids."

"First we should have to find the girl. No, lady, it is useless to argue. We are determined to go after the man. His tracks are easy to follow in the snow. Anyway if he wasn't guilty why did he run away?"

"Would you have given him a chance to defend himself?"

"No, by God! He did right to flee from us while he could. But now it is our duty to seek him and punish him. Continue your journey alone."

"And is that," Catherine asked haughtily, "your way of obeying Captain Kennedy's orders?"

"When he learns what happened, Kennedy will agree that we did the right thing. Besides it seems that you bring bad luck, noble lady . . . and my men do not want to serve you any longer."

Anger took hold of Catherine. It was pointless arguing with these narrow-minded peasants. But she was inwardly daunted by the thought of the journey she must make alone, or almost so. But she hid her feelings.

"Very well," she said curtly, "be gone with you. I shall not try to detain you."

"One moment!" Scott interrupted. "I shall need your monk. Half my men will be leaving at once, but the rest will stay here to cope with the funeral of Messire MacLaren. He has need of prayers and there is no priest here."

It was quite natural that he should want to give his chieftain a Christian burial and Catherine did not dream of objecting. It would be the work of a moment to dig a grave and say the Office for the Dead over it. That would hardly delay

69

them. There was a little chapel not far off as it happened, and a small cemetery round it.

"Your desire is perfectly natural," she said. "We will remain here then till you have buried him."

"It may take longer than you expect!"

It did in fact take infinitely longer, and Catherine had to live through an interminable day, sickened by disgust.

When she saw Scott going towards the few houses in the village, she supposed that he had gone to find a carpenter to made a coffin. But a few minutes later she saw him returning with his four men dragging an immense cauldron used for making cheese. They set up the cauldron, supported by some large stones, by the river-bank. Then they half-filled it with water and set about amassing a huge quantity of wood. Some of the peasants watched them, half-curious, half-alarmed. Catherine, standing between Sara and Brother Etienne under a chestnut tree, watched too, racking her brains to understand what it meant.

"Are they preparing a funeral feast perhaps?" she asked the monk. "It must be a gigantic feast then."

Brother Etienne shook his head. He too was observing the preparations but without apparent surprise.

"This means, my dear child, that this Scot has no intention of leaving his captain's bones in Auvergne."

"I still don't see."

"Oh, it's quite simple! That huge cauldron will receive the lieutenant's body. They will boil him there until his bones can be removed, so that our Scotsmen can transport them back to their own country in a casket. The rest will of course receive Christian burial on the spot."

Catherine and Sara had both gone green. Catherine placed a trembling hand on her throat which suddenly seemed too restricted to swallow.

"It's appalling! Don't these people know any less barbarous practices? Why don't they burn the body?"

"It is an honorable practice," Brother Etienne remarked tranquilly. "People use it when embalming is impossible or the corpse has to be transported for too great a distance. And I regret to have to tell you that this custom is not exclusively Scottish. The great Connétable du Guesclin underwent the same fate when he died before Châteauneuf de Randon. They embalmed him first, but when the funeral cortège reached Puy they discovered that the embalming had not been entirely successful. So they boiled him up, as Scott is going to do today. He is doing his chieftain great honor . . . but if I were you I wouldn't stay here."

By now the fire was crackling beneath the cauldron and two men went off to fetch the corpse, which they carried solemnly back on a litter made of latticed branches. Catherine was appalled by the thought of what was about to happen and she snatched at Sara's hand and ran towards the inn, while Brother Etienne slipped his hands in his sleeves and went calmly across to the cauldron. During the entire time that the horrifying operation lasted he would recite the prayers for the dead, kneeling by the river Dordogne.

The grisly cooking went on all that day and Catherine spent the whole time huddled under the chimney-breast in the main room of the inn. She stared absently at the fire, incapable of eating or drinking a morsel. The frightened peasants had barricaded themselves into their houses where they sat with teeth chattering, no doubt imploring heaven to spare them from the fury of these wild barbarians. The innkeeper's wife herself did not dare set foot outside her inn. Catherine had told her of Brother Etienne's explanation and she knew now that no infernal witchcraft was involved, but she was still too frightened to step outside. All that could be heard was a shouted order from Scott, or the hammer blows of the carpenter, who was busily making a little chest for the bones in the safety of his own home. Sara, who was as terrified as Catherine, sat mumbling prayers in an undertone. But Catherine was unable to pray. More than ever she felt she was living in a nightmare.

It was pitch dark by the time the operation was over. By lantern light they buried MacLaren's remains in the little churchyard. Catherine forced herself to attend and even the peasants stood and watched from some way off. There was so much fear in their eyes that it made Catherine shiver. Had it not been for the monk's presence they would certainly not have let Scott practice his strange rite, and the five Scotsmen would doubtless have found themselves threatened with sickles and axes.

The last spadeful of earth had dropped over what now had no name in any language, but which once had been a young and ardent man. Now the Scotsmen, their wooden faces frozen in expressionless impassivity, climbed on to their horses and set off into the mountains, without even saying farewell to Catherine and the others. A crude wooden box was strapped to Scott's saddle-bow.

The night was cold, and when the men had gone only Catherine, Sara and Brother Etienne were left standing in the darkness by the river-bank. They could not see the river but they could hear its thundering waters. A little way off the windows of the inn glowed like two yellow eyes in the darkness. Brother Etienne waved the torch which he had taken from one of the Scots so that sparks glowed.

"Let's go back now," he suggested.

"I want to leave at once," Catherine implored. "This place makes me feel ill. . . ."

"I can believe that, but all the same we must wait till dawn. We have to cross the river by the ford. The river is swollen and dangerous. Trying to find the way across in the dark would mean almost certain death . . . and I'm not sure that any of the people here would come and pull us out of the water."

"Well then, let's wait for morning in the inn, all together. I couldn't go back to that horrible room."

CHAPTER FOUR

The Traveler

The Saracen's Head at Aubusson had seen better days in the time when the region was rich and fertile, when the great fairs were held there, when starvation and the English were not yet ravaging the land. In those blessed times travelers thronged to Limoges where the wondrous skill of the enamel-workers attracted great crowds of merchants. Others came to buy the wool of upland sheep. In those days the fire roared all day and the spits never stopped turning. The laughter and cries of the drinkers mingled with the clacking sabots of the pretty maidservants who bustled about the place from dawn to nightfall.

But when Catherine, Sara and Brother Etienne reached the inn after an exhausting day journeying across the wild, deserted wastes of the plateau of Millevaches, the only sound to be heard was the melancholy creaking of the inn sign, which had once been brightly painted but had now grown faded and weatherbeaten. The night watchmen had just sounded the curfew and the little town seemed almost to be drawing its tiny streets closer down into the valley which enclosed it, as tightly as a miser hoards his treasure. Up on its rock stood the crumbling walls of the old seignorial château, looking like a fat melancholy cat curled into a ball for the night. Few people were about in the streets. The passers-by quickened their steps and darted nervous glances at the three travelers until they discovered that they were merely two women and a monk.

Nevertheless the sound of the horses' hooves brought a white-aproned figure out on to the threshold of the Saracen's Head, a man whose round belly contrasted pitifully with his yellow face and skinny legs. He had the pendulous cheeks of those who have lost weight too quickly, and the sigh which he sent up at the sight of the three travelers testified eloquently to the state of his larder. However, he doffed his cap and went forward to meet the three newcomers who were already dismounting.

73

"Noble ladies," he began politely, "and you, most reverend father, how can the Saracen's Head be of service to you?"

"By finding us board and lodging, my son," Brother Étienne answered good-humoredly. "We have had a hard day's ride. Our horses are weary . . . and so are we. Can you accommodate and feed us? We have money to pay you."

"Alas, reverend father, all the gold in Christendom would not buy you more than a little herb soup and some black bread. The Saracen's Head is only a shadow of what it was, alas, and your stay here will not give you a very favorable notion of it. . . ." A huge sigh interrupted this tale of woe, but just then the sound of hooves in the street outside gave rise to another.

"Lord!" said the innkeeper, "I hope that is not another customer!"

Unfortunately for Maître Amable it was indeed a traveler, as the great dusty cloak he wore testified, not to mention his horse's muddy hooves. Catherine, who had grown tired of the innkeeper's problems and chiefly wanted to get warm, was on the point of entering the inn when the sound of the newcomer's voice asking for lodging for himself and his horse, made her turn round. She tried to make out the traveler's features under his large gray hood, but then the innkeeper settled her doubts for her as he replied.

"Lord, Maître Cœur, you know very well that empty or full, rich or poor, my house is always at your disposal . . . Would to heaven that the Saracen's Head could receive you in a style worthy of its past."

"Amen," said Jacques Cœur good-humoredly. He dismounted, and his boot had no sooner touched the ground than Catherine flung herself into his arms, transported with joy.

"Jacques! Jacques! Can it be you? How wonderful!"

"Catherine! Well . . . Madame de Montsalvy! What are you doing here?"

"Call me Catherine, my friend! You always used to. Oh, if you knew how happy I am to see you again! How are Macée and the children?"

"Very well, but let us go in! We can talk more comfortably inside. If you have any firewood left, master innkeeper, we can all sup together. There are two hams in my saddle-bags . . . and lard, cheese and nuts. . . ."

While Maître Amable flung himself on the provisions, offering thanks to heaven, Jacques Cœur slipped his arm through Catherine's and led her into the inn, giving Sara a friendly greeting on the way. In the main room of the inn, where the huge blackened beams exhibited only a few melancholy strings of onions instead of the hams of happier times, they found Brother Etienne calmly warming himself in front of the fire. Catherine was about to introduce the two men when she perceived that they already knew each other of old.

"I didn't know you had returned from the East, Maître Cœur," said the monk. "The news had not yet reached me."

"The fact is that I have returned as it were on tiptoe. I had built great hopes on this journey, and while it has been full of places and people of interest it has also cost me every penny I had. . . ."

While Maître Amable and his one remaining maidservant bustled about preparing the meal and laying the table, the travelers installed themselves on the seats built round the huge open hearth. Catherine was so pleased to find such a loyal friend again she could not stop looking at him. And not infrequently her eyes met Jacques's. The brown eyes of the furrier of Bourges would sparkle then with a light which was not entirely due to the flames, and his thin lips parted in a happy smile.

He described how he had set sail the previous spring in the good ship *Notre-Dame and St. Paul* of Narbonne, belonging to the merchant Jean Vidal. He and various other merchants from Montpellier and Narbonne had made a tour of the eastern Mediterranean countries to sow the seeds of future commercial enterprises. He had visited Damascus, Beyrouth and Tripoli, Cyprus and the islands of the Archipelago, finishing up at Alexandria and Cairo; and he brought memories back with him whose enchantment could be read in his eyes as he talked.

"You ought to live in Damascus," he told Catherine. "The town was sacked and burned thirty years ago by the Mongols led by Tamberlaine, but you would scarcely guess it to look at the town now! Everything there is consecrated to making women more beautiful! There are glittering silks and transparent veils woven with gold and silver thread, incomparable perfumes, magnificent jewels and delectable sweetmeats for their consumption—best of all a delicious black nougat, and crystallized plums in syrup which are called myrobalans."

"I trust you have brought some of them back," Brother Etienne cut in. "The King adores that sort of thing, not to mention the Court ladies."

Maître Cœur heaved a sigh almost as heartfelt as the innkeeper's had been at the mention of these culinary dainties.

"Alas I have brought back nothing at all! I sold my cargo of furs, cloths from Berry and Marseilles and corals at a good price, and I managed to buy many beautiful and rare things. Unfortunately the *Notre-Dame and St. Paul* was on its last journey, which is to say that it was no longer very young. When our ship was in sight of Corsica a great storm blew up and drove the ship on to a rock, where it sank. We were all thrown clear of the ship. The coast was not far and despite the heavy seas we managed to reach the shore . . . and further disasters. The people of Corsica are all but savages and they stick at nothing. If the sea does not throw up the goods they want they light fires on the cliffs to lure ships on to the rocks. So that as you can imagine they had little respect for our cargo—whatever they managed to salvage they flatly refused to return to us. And it could have been dangerous to insist; they would have killed us without compunction. So we let them have their way and as a result they treated us in a friendly and hospitable fashion. They escorted us very courteously to the port of Ajaccio where a boat was found to take us to Marseilles on condition that we paid on arrival. So you see me returning to Bourges a ruined man, as poor as Job," Jacques Cœur finished up, with a hearty laugh.

"Quite ruined?" Catherine asked in astonishment. "But you seem to take it very calmly?"

"What point is there in lamentations? I've already been ruined once before over that disagreeable business of coining money, which I undertook on the King's behalf with Ravand the Dane. And I began again then just as I am starting again now. I am on my way back from Limoges where I have been buying up enamels and I have hopes that this town may yield up one or two of the carpets which the Saracens are said to have taught the townspeople how to make. I managed to persuade my father-in-law to lend me some money, only a little unfortunately, but I hope it will be enough to get together a little cargo for my next voyage."

"Are you planning to go on another one then?"

"Of course. You cannot imagine the future there is in trade with the Orient, Catherine. Take the Sultan of Cairo for instance. He has gold, fabulous quantities of gold, and no silver, or very little. I know of ancient mines myself which the Romans worked and then abandoned but which were never exhausted. If I could extract silver from them and transport it to Cairo I would be able to buy gold with it at an infinitely lower price than it fetches in Europe, and make a fantastic profit. If I had some capital now what could I not do with it!"

While Jacques Cœur talked, Catherine's imagination wa. voyaging. This man, whose shrewd intelligence, courage and daring were well known to her, was capable of moving heaven and earth to make a fortune. And he was brimful of ideas. She did not hesitate for a moment.

"I think I might be able to provide you with the money you need."

"You?"

The furrier's sincere astonishment was patently obvious. During her long stay at Carlat Catherine had written to Macée telling her of the disaster which had befallen Montsalvy and he knew, as well as anyone else in the royal entourage, that Arnaud and his family were banished and outlawed. And certainly Catherine's style of travel held out small hope of riches. She smiled sweetly and looked in her bag.

"I should imagine that this stone alone would buy you a whole ship's cargo."

Three cries of astonishment arose simultaneously. In her hand Garin's diamond blazed like a little black sun. Maître Amable was so moved by the sight that he dropped a dish while the maidservant clapped her hands together in amazement. Jacques's suddenly narrowed eyes went from the superb jewel to Catherine's impassive face.

"The famous diamond of the Lord Treasurer of Burgundy!" he said slowly. "What a splendid stone! I don't think I have ever seen anything comparable."

He stretched out his hand and took the stone delicately between two fingers so that the light could play on it. A shower of fiery sparks seemed to pour from his hand. Catherine's cheeks flushed a little.

"Take it, Jacques, and sell it, and make what you can from it."

"But don't you want to keep possession of such a spectacular jewel? Do you realize that this little stone is worth a king's ransom?"

"Yes, I know. But I also know that it is accursed. It brings misfortune wherever it goes, and those who possess it never find happiness. You must sell it, Jacques . . . perhaps misfortune will overlook me then," she said dully. The faint tremor in her voice did not escape the furrier, who laid his hand over hers.

"I don't believe these stories, Catherine. Beauty can never be evil and this diamond is beauty itself. If you entrust it to me I will make it yield prosperity for the entire kingdom. I shall send out fleets of caravels across the sea, I shall establish trading-posts and force the plundered soil to yield its deeply hidden treasures . . . I will make your fortune, my own and the King's to boot."

77

He offered the jewel to Catherine, but she gently but firmly refused to take it.

"No, Jacques, keep it. It is yours. I hope that you will really succeed in triumphing over its evil reputation and using it for the benefit of all. But if you do not succeed you need have no regrets. I give it to you."

"I will accept it purely as a loan, Catherine. And I will return it to you a hundredfold. You will rebuild Montsalvy and your son will be one of the great ones of this earth, with a fortune to match his illustrious name. But . . . this innkeeper is letting us starve to death! Hoy there, Maître Amable, what about our dinner?"

Startled out of his reverie the worthy innkeeper rushed off to the kitchen to fetch the herb soup mentioned earlier. Jacques Cœur got up and offered his hand to Catherine.

"Come to dinner now, my dear business partner, and the Lord be praised for bringing us together. We will go far, the two of us, or my name is not Jacques Cœur." He led her to the table and waited till Amable and his maid were out of earshot. Then he whispered:

"You shouldn't have brought that stone out in front of the innkeeper. Amable is a good fellow, but you may not have heard that La Trémoille is after that diamond. His cousin Gilles was foolish enough to mention it to him and now he can think of nothing else. You will have to take care when you reach Court, my dear."

"What a perfect solution! Sell him the diamond!"

Jacques Cœur laughed dryly and shrugged.

"You can't still be so innocent! If the Chamberlain knew I had the stone my skin would not be worth a farthing! Do you think he would pay when it is easier to take . . . and kill, if necessary?"

"I suppose that's why the Castilian Villa-Andrade had La Trémoille's blessing for his marriage with me. The Spaniard would acquire the Montsalvy lands and La Trémoille would get the black diamond for his part in the enterprise."

"You are being overmodest, my dear. The Castilian is really attached to you, I believe. He wants you first of all, but that doesn't mean that he would object to taking your property too. The King has confiscated them and would doubtless make them over to him in due course."

"In any case," Brother Etienne intervened, "I take it the diamond will be departing with you tomorrow?"

"I shall stay here long enough to do a little trading and then go on to Beaucaire. The Jewish community there is rich and powerful. I know a rabbi, Isaac Abrabanel. His brother

78

is one of the leaders of the Jewish community in Toledo and the family is extremely rich. I shall find all the gold I need there. . . ."

As a signal that the innkeeper was returning Brother Etienne coughed warningly. Then he folded his hands and bent his head over his bowl and began to say grace, to which they all listened piously. Then everyone fell to restoring the strength which had been depleted during a long and rigorous journey. Catherine felt her heart amazingly lightened since she had seen the diamond disappear into Jacques Cœur's pouch. She had made a wise decision there. Thanks to it Michel would one day be rich, and even if the royal pardon were never vouchsafed to his parents he would be able to live a free and comfortable life outside France. But Catherine wanted more than that, more and better. A fortune was but a part of her plan. What she really wanted was the death of the Lord Chamberlain and a royal amnesty for Arnaud and herself. The name of Montsalvy must get back all its former luster or her life would be without meaning.

Dinner, which the innkeeper served up with every mark of respect, passed in listening to Jacques Cœur making plans for the future. He had not asked Catherine any questions about her husband or the motives for this journey of hers, making it a point of discretion to avoid touching on what might have been a painful topic. Catherine had in fact told Macée that Arnaud was dead, part of her determination to keep his name free from any taint of horror or disgust. And the furrier was clearly anxious to avoid any tactless or clumsy remarks which could reopen an old wound. And Catherine was grateful to him for his delicacy. But several times, catching his eye in the course of conversation, she thought that she could detect a look both anxious and questioning. He must be trying to find the right words to question her about her plans for the future without appearing either tactless or wounding. At last he decided to approach the subject obliquely.

"I said that life in the Orient would suit you, Catherine. Why don't you come with me on this trip?"

She smiled back at him but shook her head a little wearily.

"Because that sort of adventure would not suit me at all, Jacques. I have other souls to account for now, and too many things left to do in this world. I would gladly exchange the trials ahead for all the storms in the Mediterranean, believe me, but I must see this undertaking through to the bitter end and . . ."

She was interrupted by a discreet but peremptory sign from Jacques bidding her be silent. She fell silent instantly and glanced inquiringly at the furrier. Jacques Cœur's eyes seemed to be probing the shadows in the part of the room where Maître Amable had vanished a moment earlier with a strange fixity and concentration. When he gave his attention to Catherine again it was only to chatter about unimportant topics, carefully avoiding any subject which might have a compromising ring to it. And as soon as the meal was over he rose and offered his hand to Catherine asking if he might have the honor of escorting her to the door of her room. As if by magic Maître Amable reappeared, holding a candle high above his head to light the way to the upper story. Sara and Brother Etienne brought up the rear of the procession and Sara seemed to have the greatest difficulty in keeping her eyes open. But Catherine's were wide open still, surprised to find something vaguely sinister about the long shadows which the candlelight cast on the yellow walls. Why had the feeling of relief and lightheartedness she had experienced a little while earlier disappeared already? Why had this nameless apprehension crept into her soul? The ill-omened diamond had changed hands and with this act she had made her own fortune, and she was as certain of this as she had been of anything. So why this anxiety?

They separated ceremoniously in front of the door to the room which Catherine and Sara were to share. The two women went in, while the furrier and the monk went up to their rooms on the floor above. Soon the Saracen's Head was shrouded in silence. Sara was so exhausted she threw herself down on the bed fully dressed and was soon asleep. Catherine made do with removing her dress and stockings and crept in beside her.

She was awakened from a deep sleep by the sound of gentle tapping at her door. Or rather, to be precise, a gentle scratching which at first she was inclined to attribute to a mouse. But no, there was definitely someone knocking at her door. . . .

The room was pitch dark and the candle had burned itself out. Catherine groped her way to the door where the scratching had started up again, trembling with fear lest she trip over something and wake up the whole house. Whoever it was at the door must be anxious to avoid exciting suspicion, to knock so discreetly? At last the door opened and Catherine saw that Jacques Cœur was standing on the threshold with a candle in one hand. He was fully dressed, with coat and hat on. He put his finger swiftly to his lips to enjoin silence and then gently pushed her back into her room, followed her and then shut the door carefully. His face was alarmingly grave.

"Forgive this intrusion, Catherine, but if you wish to avoid a closer acquaintance with the local prison at dawn I would advise you to get dressed and wake Sara and follow me. Brother Etienne must be at the stables by now."

"But . . . why so early? What time is it?"

"An hour after midnight, and I agree with you that it is a little early but we do not have much time."

"Why?"

"Because the sight of a certain diamond has clouded the judgment of a man who has hitherto always been honest. I mean to say that a little while ago Maître Amable closed up his inn and ran straight round to the provost's to denounce us as dangerous malefactors wanted by the Lord Chamberlain. Sara's exotic appearance and the fact that I mentioned the Jew Abrabanel have combined to give his denunciation a faint whiff of sorcery. In short Maître Amable is ready to send us all to the stake to get his hands on a little of the value of that fabulous diamond."

"How do you know all this?" Catherine asked, too thunderstruck to be really afraid.

"Firstly because I took the precaution of following our worthy host when he left the inn. I thought there was something suspicious about his behavior during our meal. He kept blushing and going pale in turn, his hands shook like leaves in the wind and he couldn't keep his eyes off my pouch. I have known him for many years 'tis true, but I have learned to trust no one where there is gold at stake. Luckily the room I share with Brother Etienne is just above the front door. I kept watch there for a while, prompted by this obscure presentiment I told you about, and sure enough I saw our innkeeper mysteriously creeping out when he must have supposed us all asleep. I was in too great a hurry to use the stairs, let me tell you—I slid down the roof, jumped down and hastened after Maître Amable. When I saw him heading towards the castle I realized that I had been right to keep an eye on him."

"And then?" said Catherine, shivering as she slipped into her dress. "What happened then? How can you be certain that he denounced us?"

"You wouldn't ask that if you had seen him coming out again rubbing his hands with glee. Besides I was able to make certain of all this. A troop of armed men sent by the provost is due to arrest us at daybreak before the town gates are opened."

"Who told you that?"

Jacques Cœur smiled and Catherine thought to herself that he seemed strangely relaxed and calm for a man in danger of his life.

"It so happens that I have two or three friends in this town, something which Maître Amable does not know. The oldest son of one of the two men who received the secret of the tapestries brought by Marie de Hainaut is a sergeant in the garrison. I went boldly up to the castle and presented myself to the watch, without disclosing my name naturally, and asked to speak to him."

"Without difficulty?"

"A gold piece is a wonderful thing, Catherine, and it appears that young Esperat has a good business head. Desirous of pleasing a good client of his father's he lost no time in acquainting me with the orders which he had been given for the following morning."

Catherine had finished lacing up her dress and now she shook Sara, who was loth to wake up.

"It's all very well to be so well informed," she said crossly. "But that's not going to help us escape. Other than by equipping ourselves with birds' wings, I don't see how we are to get out of a town which is surrounded by high walls, and massive gates which are kept carefully locked and guarded. We might as well be caught in a mousetrap. The town is far too small for us to be able to hide."

"No, we will have to get out of the town. And I hope we will be able to. Now hurry, Catherine. Brother Etienne must already be at the stables."

Catherine opened her eyes wide and stared at Jacques as if he had gone out of his senses.

"I suppose you are planning to leave on horseback? Well, I must say you are not lacking in confidence. A horse makes a lot of noise. As for four!"

The furrier's grave face softened in a brief smile. Then he gave Catherine's shoulder a quick squeeze.

"How about trusting me a little, my dear? I don't swear that I'll get you out of this scrape. But I will do my best. Anyway, that is enough of talk! Come!"

In the twinkling of an eye both women were ready. Sara, with her instinct for danger, had hurried without even asking the reason why. And now, cautiously following Jacques Cœur, they started down the old staircase, walking as near the wall as possible to prevent the treads from squeaking. The silence was so profound that the noise of their breathing seemed quite terrifying. They reached the foot of the stairs without mishap. Jacques Cœur took Catherine by the hand and hurried her across to the back door of the inn. Here the only things to watch out for were tables and benches because the stone floors were not likely to creak. But just as Jacques reached for the door handle a sharp cracking noise sent them all huddling against the walls with pounding hearts.

But it was only a hot coal which had escaped from the layer of ashes with which the maid had covered the fire to bank it up for the night. Jacques took a deep breath and Catherine let out a sigh. They exchanged looks, and somewhat tremulous smiles. Then inch by inch he opened the huge chestnut wood door. Jacques blew out his candle and set it down on the ground. Then he led Catherine and Sara out and shut the door. Across the yard a faint glimmer of light came from beneath the stable door. They went across.

"It is us, Brother Etienne," Jacques whispered.

Brother Etienne was hard at work in the stable. With the help of linen cloths which he must have stolen from the innkeeper's kitchen he was calmly and efficiently wrapping up the horses' hooves. Jacques and Sara went to his assistance. In a few seconds they were ready to leave. While Jacques ran out to open the gate used by carts entering the inn the others took the horses gently by their leading reins and led them as quietly as possible out to the street, one by one. This road overlooked the church of St. Croix. And from there a sort of fair ground led up towards the castle, whose squat silhouette stood out blackly against the sky. Catherine drew her coat closer round her neck. The wind which whistled down from the plateau was icy cold and penetrating. There was no light to be seen anywhere except just outside the drawbridge where a brazier glowed like a dull red star. The huddle of houses seemed almost to be spilling out of the rustic fortress, whose stone tower reared up above their close-heaped gabled roofs. A little lower down, towards the church, stood a sort of tower without windows.

"The prisons!" was Jacques's only comment. "Follow me. We have to go up towards the château."

"The château?" Catherine echoed faintly.

"Yes. Justin Esperat will be waiting for us near the outer wall. It seems that the town wall and the castle wall run into each other at some point up there, near the plateau."

"Well? I still don't understand."

"You'll soon see. Heaven apparently is with us this time. The frost was so severe this year, it seems that some of the stones have crumbled and there is a breach in the wall. Naturally the breach is guarded, and will continue to be until the weather is fine enough to repair it. But it so happens that Esperat is on guard from one o'clock onwards."

Catherine said nothing this time. There was nothing to object to anyway. Besides the climb was steep, and the higher they climbed the colder it grew and the harder it became to breathe freely. And they had to hold the horses' heads carefully to prevent them slipping. Soon the darkness grew inkier still and they realized that they must be skirting the castle walls. The great drawbridge was raised but not that of the postern gate. An armed guard stood watch there leaning heavily on his pike. It was there that the brazier stood. Jacques Cœur signed to them all to halt, then he went up to Catherine.

"We shall have to pass almost under the guard's nose. There is only one way to do that—and that's to keep him occupied!"

"But how?"

"I think Brother Etienne has an answer to that. It's quite amazing what one can do with a monk's habit!"

Catherine was about to ask for further explanations but just then Brother Etienne handed Jacques Cœur his horse's reins.

"Leave it to me. All you need do is watch for the best moment and make as little noise as possible."

Brother Etienne pulled up his hood, slipped his hands inside his sleeves and then stepped boldly towards the circle of light where the man stood dozing on his weapon like a melancholy heron. The others stood watching breathlessly from behind their outcrop of rock. The sound of the monk's footsteps had awakened the guard who stood to attention.

"Who goes there?" he asked in a voice grown hoarse with fatigue. "What do you want, father?"

"I am Brother Ambrose from St. John's Monastery," the monk lied with superb aplomb. "I have come to bring the succor of religion to the man who is dying in there."

"Someone dying?" the soldier echoed, astonished. "Who can that be?"

"How should I know? All I know is that someone came to the monastery asking for a priest who could hear confession. That was all they said."

The guard pushed back his helmet and scratched his head in evident bewilderment. He was clearly at a loss. Finally he shouldered his pike.

"I have not received any orders, father. Can't very well take it on myself to let you in, y'know! Wait here a moment."

He disappeared under the low archway of the postern gate. He must have decided to go to the guard room to get instructions.

"Now," said Jacques Cœur.

They left their hiding-place and hurried across the lighted area. The horses' muffled hooves were quite silent. Three frightened heartbeats later they were once more safely in shadow, but Catherine was breathing as hard as if she had run a mile. They hid in the angle of a turret. Just then the soldier returned.

"Sorry, father, you were misinformed. No one's about to croak here tonight!"

"But I am sure . . ."

The man shook his head with a look of genuine embarrassment.

"Afraid not. There must have been a mistake. Or perhaps a practical joker . . ."

"A practical joker? Playing tricks on a servant of God? Oh, my son!" the monk cried with convincing horror.

"By Our Lady, nothing would surprise me in these times of ours, father! If I were you I should get back into the warm as quickly as possible."

Brother Etienne shrugged and pulled his hood further down over his face.

"Since I am out already I think I'll go to the Clermont gate to see old Marie who is very sick. Nights drag on for ever when one is nigh to death and the small hours are the ones where courage is weakest! God be with you, my son!"

Brother Etienne made a sign of the cross and then walked out of the circle of light while the soldier once more propped himself on his weapon and continued his morose vigil.

A few seconds later he had joined the others. As the night wore on it grew colder, and they could hear the wind howling behind the rugged stone walls of the township, sweeping across the plateau. Without a word Jacques Cœur had gone on ahead of the little band. Now they were making their way along a narrow alley between the town wall and the wall of the castle. It was an alley which led nowhere and the appalling stench which arose from it was so pervasive that even the frost could not lessen it. Catherine struggled bravely against mounting nausea but she began to feel as if she were entering a squelching, sticky universe where the very air was a foul gas. The horses' hooves kept stumbling over the rubbish. The river was far away and the people of the neighborhood had found this spot a convenient place to throw their rubbish and slops. Suddenly a gap appeared in the wall through which they could see the sky once more, and a dark figure detached itself from the shadows.

"Is that you, Maître Cœur?"

"Yes, here we are, Justin! Are we late?"

"Very late. It is important that you should have gained a head start on your pursuers by dawn. You must make haste!"

Catherine's eyes were growing accustomed to the dark and she could make out the silhouette of a young archer, and the pale blur of his face under a steel helmet. A horn was slung from a belt round his hips. She was briefly aware of a pair of bright, lively eyes.

"Are you certain you won't get into trouble, Justin?"

"Do not fear. The provost will merely imagine that the innkeeper had too much to drink, and no one will think of looking here. Besides your horses' hooves will not leave any recognizable traces in all this muck."

"You are a good lad, Justin. I'll reward you for this one of these days."

The young man's lighthearted laughter rang out comfortingly in the night.

"Reward my father, Maître Jacques, by ordering some fine thing from him when you are rich and powerful. He dreams of weaving the most beautiful tapestry in the world and he never stops drawing lovely ladies and fantastic beasts."

"Your father is a great artist, Justin; I have always known that. There is no danger of my forgetting him. Till our next meeting then, my boy, and again thank you! For I know that you are taking a greater risk than you will admit!"

"Where would friendship be if it could not take risks, messire? May God go with you, and do not worry about me, but for pity's sake make haste!"

Without another word Jacques wrung the young man's hand, then he helped Catherine clamber through the gap in the wall. Outside the air was fresh and clean. They found themselves on a little plateau where the wind raged ceaselessly. Further off the ground rose up once more in a steep hill. The travelers walked on several minutes without speaking, still leading their horses by the bridle-reins. The night seemed to be growing lighter, or perhaps their eyes were growing accustomed to it. Catherine could make out the shape of trees tossed and tormented by the sudden blasts of wind.

Jacques halted at a cross-roads marked by a stone cross.

"This is where we must separate, Catherine. This road," he said, pointing to the right-hand one which led over the brow of the hill, "is mine, and it goes to Clermont and thence into

Provence. Yours is the left-hand one. A little further along it will reach the Priory of St. Alapinien where, if you wish, you can wait for dawn and take a little rest."

"Certainly not, Jacques! My one desire is to place as much distance as possible between ourselves and the prison of Aubusson. But it grieves me that we should have to part. . . ."

Instinctively, to gain a moment alone together, the furrier and Catherine strolled beyond the cross and left Sara and Brother Etienne unbinding the horses' hooves. Catherine felt a deep regret at seeing the last of Jacques. He represented the solid reassuring masculine presence which Gauthier's flight had deprived her of, and which she sorely missed. All the anguish of the early hours before dawn weighed down her spirits, and she found her heart failing at the thought of the unknown roads she must travel. Never perhaps had the nostalgia for a normal life and proper home struck her as forcibly as it did now, at the foot of this wayside cross. She sought Jacques's hand wordlessly and squeezed it, while tears came unbidden into her eyes.

"Jacques," she murmured, "am I condemned to eternal wanderings and endless solitude?"

A spasm of emotion crossed the furrier's face; Catherine stood looking up at him, and such was the magic of her beauty, even in the heart of a dark night, that his eyes grew troubled and a wild thought insinuated itself into his sensible soul. He could not know that Catherine's depression was a temporary one, born of the night, the cold and her own weariness rather than good sense. He gripped her small hands and laid them against his breast.

"Catherine," he cried, and his voice was dark with passion, "don't leave me! Come with me! We can travel into the East together, to Damascus where I will make you a queen and pour the treasures of the Orient at your feet! For you and with you I could achieve anything!"

Such an ardor had arisen in him that his hot breath burned against Catherine's brow. But her moment of weakness had passed. She had been happy to find Jacques again and sad to part from him so soon, but in what folly had this led him to believe? She gently withdrew her hands and smiled.

"We were tired and frightened and I think we just lost our heads a little, Jacques? What would you do with me during your adventurous voyages? And how about that grandiose scheme of yours which was to bring wealth and prosperity to the kingdom?"

"What does all that matter? You are worth a kingdom!

The first moment I saw you among all Queen Marie's ladies-in-waiting, I knew that I could renounce everything and everyone for you. . . ."

"Even Macée and the children?"

There was a moment's silence. Jacques had stiffened at the mention of his family. She heard his breathing come faster. Then his voice reached her as from a great way off, and it was somber but quite steady:

"Yes, even them, Catherine!"

She did not let him say more. It might have been dangerous. She had always known that Jacques had a soft spot for her but she had never imagined a love so passionate. He was not the sort of man to form impulsive attachments. What if she were to take him at his word and force him to abandon everything—fortune, family, his whole future—for her? She shook her head slowly.

"No, Jacques, we would always regret taking such a mad step. I spoke as I did because I was tired, and frightened too, perhaps. And you answered me too impulsively. Both you and I have a task to perform in this country of ours. Besides, you love Macée too much—even if it doesn't seem so at this moment—to hurt her so badly. And for my part . . . ah well, my heart died with my husband!"

"Come now! You are too young, too beautiful for that to be the case!"

"It is so nevertheless, my friend," Catherine said firmly, lingering intentionally over the word "friend." "I have lived, breathed and suffered only through and for Arnaud de Montsalvy. He and he alone was my life, my love and my whole reason for being. Now that he is gone I am like a body without a soul, and that may be as well since it will help me achieve the task I have set myself without weakening."

"What task is this?"

"What does it matter? But it could cost me my life. And in that case, Jacques Cœur, remember that you have the fortunes of Michel de Montsalvy, my son, in your hands, and pray for me. Good-bye, my dear friend."

Gathering up the folds of her coat she turned back to where Sara and Brother Etienne stood waiting. Jacques's sorrowful protest reached her like a sigh on the wind.

"Not good-bye, Catherine . . . but farewell!"

She hid a grimace of pain under the shadow of her hood. Those were almost the very words she had cried out despairingly in the solitary road at Carlat, half mad with grief but clinging obstinately to a hope which would not die. The same words, yes . . . but the feeling behind them could not be the

88

same. As soon as they were out of sight behind the bend in the road Jacques would once more be swept up by the excitement of his turbulent life. And that was as it should be!

She leaned towards Sara who was sitting huddled on a stone trying to keep out the cold and helped her up, smiling meanwhile at Brother Etienne.

"I'm sorry I kept you waiting! Maître Cœur asked me to say farewell to you both. Now let us be off."

Wordlessly they set off along the road. The route slanted off down to the left and for some of its way skirted along the margin of a lake. A thin sickle moon which had appeared in the sky glistened softly on its waters. Catherine turned in the saddle and looked back. The dim light allowed her to faintly make out the distant silhouette of Jacques Cœur, mantle flapping behind him as he rode into the wind. He was climbing the hill now and he did not look back.

She sighed and straightened up once more in the saddle. The moment of sentimental weakness had passed, and it would be the last she would allow herself till La Trémoille had been destroyed. In the hazardous Court life to which she was returning there was no room for that sort of thing.

Part II

VENGEANCE

◆◆◆◆◆◆◆◆◆◆◆◆◆◆◆◆◆◆◆◆◆◆◆◆

CHAPTER FIVE

Cavaliers of the Queen

Catherine stood in one of the deep window embrasures of the château at Angers, looking absent-mindedly at the scene outside. She was so weary after her long journey that she found it hard to take in her surroundings as yet. When she and Sara and Brother Etienne had reached the Loire a little while earlier she had been on the point of swooning with exhaustion and horror. For the past twelve days their journey had taken them through starving Limousin, Marches and Poitou, where the bloody stamp of English oppression could be seen on all sides, in hanging corpses, sacked villages, plague spots. They had to fight for their lives, against cold, against men, even against the wolves, who hurled themselves howling against the walls of the barns, where often they had been forced to take shelter at night. Finding food had become a problem, and each meal was a challenge which grew more and more pressing and difficult to meet. Had it not been for the abbeys, to which the friar's habit admitted them, and Catherine's safe-conduct from Queen Yolande, the three companions would doubtless have died of starvation long before reaching the royal river. Childishly, Catherine had imagined that once in the Duchy of Anjou, Yolande's favorite country, their troubles would be over. But things had grown worse still!

Under the torrential rain which greeted them when they crossed the frontiers of the Duchy, Catherine and her friends crossed countryside which had been systematically sacked the previous autumn by Villa-Andrade's men. They saw villages so brutally devastated that there was not a soul alive to bury the dead whose only grave-digger had been that winter's snows. They saw trampled vines, fields where no grass would grow that spring, gutted churches, burned abbeys and castles. They saw blackened deserts, spiked here and there by the charred stumps of trees where whole forests had once stood, and the skeletons of animals which the wolves had abandoned by the roadside.

They had seen men, women and children driven by misery and fear to find refuge in caves, like animals. And from those too it was necessary to flee. For to those poor wretches any traveler was fair prey. On one occasion, they were saved in the nick of time from being lynched at the hands of one of these bands by some of the Queen's sergeants, who had traveled into the stricken countryside with cartloads of food for the wretched inhabitants.

When at last the Ponts-de-Ce, their turrets as stoutly fortified and buttressed as little castles, came into sight, with their four bridges straddling three islands, Brother Etienne could not help murmuring to himself:

"At last! We've arrived!"

Their safe-conduct allowed them to pass without hindrance and soon, to their great relief, the massive walls of the city of Angers had closed about them. Although the ducal city had not been ravaged by the Spaniard's troops and the misery of the countryside had not made itself felt in so rich and well-manned a town, some reflection of it could still be seen in the closed, mistrustful faces of the inhabitants. Everywhere there were people in mourning, and the streets showed none of the commotion and activity which usually marks a large and prosperous city. People spoke to each other in undertones as if they were in church. Nevertheless there was an air of energy and orderliness about the place. There were no beggars or drunken soldiery, or loose women. This city which had been created as a setting for easy and graceful living, with its gardens and white walls and blue roofs, had been transformed into a fortress which was constantly on the alert. The refugees even, who had crowded into the city like chickens sheltering under the mother hen, had been organized so that they did not impede the orderly life of the city or its defenses. Everything here proclaimed that Yolande d'Anjou knew how to rule, to succor and to fight!

This impression was reinforced by the sight of the mighty castle itself: its black and gray rock and granite towers grouped round their immense central keep reflected in the waters of the river Maine. Its walls were crowned by a forest of blue, pepperpot roofs gleaming like steel, bristling bell-turrets and crenellated roundways. Men stood guard all the way along the battlements, armed with pikes, halberds and battle-axes, and from the highest tower an enormous banner flapped in the sea wind. It glowed blue, crimson, white and gold: cross of Jerusalem, lambel of Sicily, lilies of Anjou and pales of Aragon; the coat of arms of the Duchess-Queen which was also to be found carved above the city gates, surmounted by a gold crown and angel's hands.

Brother Etienne could move through the town and castle as he liked, and the guard did everything but salute him. But once they had crossed the huge moat, a mist of rain clouded Catherine's vision. And her eyes, under the rain-sodden hood, were beginning to dim with fatigue. All she could think of at the moment was a bed, a real bed with sheets and coverlets where she could stretch herself out after so many nights of lying on stone or bare earth. But first she would have to present herself to Queen Yolande. Brother Etienne left his two companions in a large room in the ducal lodgings whose tall windows overlooked the Maine, cordoned off at intervals by massive chains, and the rest of the town. Sara flung herself down at once on a little bench near the fire and was soon fast asleep. Catherine remained standing. Her muscles were so sore and aching that she couldn't help fearing that if she sat down she might not be able to get up again. . . .

She did not have long to wait. After a few minutes the monk reappeared.

"Come, my child! The Queen is waiting to see you."

Catherine glanced back at Sara who had not stirred, and followed Brother Etienne. He escorted her through a low archway where two guards stood watch, legs straddled, motionless as statues, leaning on their halberds. Beyond it was a large chamber all hung with tapestries depicting allegorical scenes. For light there were the leaping flames in the carved chimney-piece, where a whole tree-trunk was burning, and the soft glimmer of tall yellow tapers standing in a bronze tripod. An enormous bed, whose draperies of crimson velvet were embroidered with fleurs-de-lis, took up almost a quarter of the space of this chamber, large though it was. In the opposite corner a lady-in-waiting sat embroidering and she was so discreet she did not even lift her head when Catherine came in. Not that Catherine would have noticed if she had. She only had eyes for the Queen!

Yolande sat in a huge ebony chair piled with cushions, her narrow feet resting on a foot-warmer, and watched her advance across the room towards her. Catherine's heart was smitten to observe the ravages which the last three years had wrought in the Duchess-Queen's proud and delicate face. The raven hair which could be seen under her severe widow's coif was going white, deep lines had appeared on her face and her smooth skin was yellowing to the color of old parchment. All those months of incessant struggle against the evil genius of France, and against her English and Burgundian enemies, seemed to weigh heavily on Yolande's shoulders. The capture of her son, the Duke René de Bar, who had fallen into Philippe of Burgundy's hands after the battle of Bugneville, had been a cruel blow. At fifty-four the Queen of the Four Kingdoms was an old woman. Her huge black eyes alone, with their imperious gleam, kept something of the fire of youth. Her wasting body was almost lost in the flowing black draperies she wore and in the heaped cushions where she sat.

But as Catherine knelt at her feet Yolande smiled suddenly and all at once her face regained its old charm. She held out an exquisite white hand to her.

"At last you are here, my child!" she murmured. "I have waited to see you for so long!"

Catherine was moved by a surge of deep emotion. So often had she dreamed of the time she would kneel at the feet of the only woman at Court she could trust, hold out imploring hands to the Queen of Sicily in expectation of her help and succor, that she was at a loss for words. She covered her face in shaking hands and burst into tears.

For a moment Yolande contemplated the slender figure in its worn clothes prostrated before her. She too had noticed the weariness of that ravishing face, the sorrowful expression of the large violet eyes, the suffering revealed in every line of her face and body. Then, with an exclamation of compassion, she stood up and took her in her arms, and much as Sara might have done, drew her closer and cradled Catherine's weeping face against her shoulder.

"Weep, little one," she murmured. "Weep! Tears bring relief."

Without losing hold of Catherine she turned and raised her voice:

"Leave us for a moment, Madame de Chaumont! I would like you to return here presently, and meanwhile see that a room is prepared for Madame de Montsalvy."

The lady-in-waiting sank into a deep curtsy and left the room as silently as a shadow. Then the Queen led Catherine to a long seat heaped with velvet cushions and made her sit down beside her; she waited patiently till Catherine's sobs quietened a little. When she had calmed down a little she took a little flask of the Queen of Hungary's water from her reticule and sprinkled a few drops on to a handkerchief which she used to mop Catherine's face with. The soft but pungent scent revived her, and all at once she felt ashamed of her behavior and would have dropped on her knees again had the Queen not restrained her.

"Let us talk as one woman to another, if you please, Catherine! I did not send Brother Etienne to fetch you merely to treat you as another ordinary lady-in-waiting and join in your tears. The time is ripe for getting rid of the man responsible for all your misfortunes, of that sorry gentleman who is selling off his country piecemeal for no other purpose than to fill his own pockets and complete Queen Isabeau's melancholy work. You have suffered too much at his hands not to wish him destroyed."

"We have been pursued, and hunted, and banished like criminals, and had all our goods and possessions taken from us. We would have died not long ago if the Comte de Pardiac had not come to our assistance. My son has no name, no lands . . . and my husband is a leper!" Catherine said somberly. "What worse evil could befall us?"

"Something worse can always happen," the Queen amended gently, "but the important thing now is to give back to the Montsalvy name its former glory, and prepare a worthy future for your son. Look . . . I was much attached to your husband. Beneath that rough exterior he was a perfect gentleman and one of the most valiant knights this country has ever known. La Trémoille's victims are too distinguished for their ruin to go unavenged. Will you help us?"

"That was the reason I came!" Catherine cried fiercely. "But Your Majesty will have to guide me."

Yolande was about to reply when a clamorous trumpet-call sounded from without the castle, followed by an immediate bustle and confusion within the walls. The Duchess-Queen herself got up and hurried to the window overlooking the chapel and the huge courtyard, and Catherine followed her automatically. Outside soldiers came tumbling out of the guardroom and began racing towards the gates, arming themselves hurriedly as they went. A whole wave of pages, squires and lords came running out of the ducal lodgings. In this twilight hour, Catherine reflected, they looked as if they could have stepped straight out of the tapestries hanging round the walls. But Yolande of Aragon was stamping her feet with impatience.

"Why this din? What can it all mean? Who is it arriving?"

As if in answer to her question the door opened and Madame de Chaumont appeared smiling and greeted her:

"Madame! It is the Lord Constable just arrived from his estate at Parthenay. Your Majesty . . ."

She was interrupted by a delighted exclamation from the Queen.

"Richemont! Heaven must have sent him here! I shall go to meet him!"

She turned towards Catherine with a gesture as if to beckon her to follow, but then she checked herself, after a quick look at the young woman's exhausted face.

"Go and rest, my dear," she said kindly. "Madame de Chaumont will take you to your room. Tomorrow I shall send for you and we can make our plans."

Catherine bowed silently and followed the lady-in-waiting as Yolande left by another door. Her head felt dreadfully empty, and she felt as though she were walking through fog.

She let herself be led to a room on the floor above, whose two large windows overlooked the courtyard. She had no desire at all to chat, and Madame de Chaumont respected her silence. She was a pleasant, fair-haired young woman with a round face and lively brown eyes and she seemed to have the utmost difficulty in keeping her native high spirits under control. She was very young, only twenty, but she had already been married these five years to Pierre d'Amboise, Lord of Chaumont, and she had two children, though one would never have suspected it. She seemed to have to make a constant effort to curb her exuberant nature into the somewhat formal pattern of Court life. She was clearly bursting to talk and gossip, but equally clearly Catherine was in great need of rest and peace. So little Madame de Chaumont contented herself with flashing her a brilliant smile.

"Here you are, Madame de Montsalvy. I will send your maid to you now and two chambermaids who will help you unpack. Would you like a bath?"

Catherine's eyes shone at the mention of this almost forgotten luxury. A bath! It must be months since she had had one! It had been far too cold in the rather rudimentary bathhouse at Carlat since the autumn, and since leaving Auvergne, her voyage had been too rough to afford such comforts.

"I'd love one," she said, smiling at the young woman. "I feel as though all the dirt of the kingdom were stuck to me!"

"It won't take a minute!"

And Anne de Chaumont vanished in a whirl of red velvet and gray satin. Left to herself Catherine had to struggle with herself not to collapse straight on to the bed but the din from the courtyard drew her to the windows. There were so many torches and braziers down there that it was almost as light as day and the reflection of all those flames danced on Catherine's ceiling, brighter by far than the glow of the fire and the candle flames which were to keep her room warm and light.

Down below a veritable army of liveried servants, pages and knights, ladies and gentlemen crowded round a group of mailed knights who formed an intimidating gray steel wall in their midst. Their armor was enlivened by the white tabards and black ermine tails which formed the device of the Dukes of Brittany. They were clustered round a large white banner bearing a boar rampant before a little green oak, and the motto "He who dares" embroidered on a red scroll. Some paces ahead of the rest a man whose helmet bore the crest of a crowned lion in gold, was dismounting with the help of a squire. The visor was up and Catherine recognized the scarred visage of the Constable himself. Moreover, the great sword of France, encrusted with fleurs-de-lis, swung at the doughty Breton's left thigh.

Catherine saw Queen Yolande step swiftly down the steps and come forward with outstretched hands and a warm smile to greet the new arrival. She saw Richemont's stern face soften as he knelt to kiss the beautiful hand. From where she stood Catherine could not hear what they were saying, but it was obvious that the understanding between the Duchess-Queen and the military leader was perfect, absolute, and the thought was a comforting one. She remembered the liking Richemont had shown Arnaud and the dogged determination with which he pursued his chosen aims. Yolande and Richemont were the two solid pillars on which she hoped to build a future for little Michel.

Half an hour later she sat soaking in a great tub full of hot scented water, her weariness and travel soreness almost forgotten. She closed her eyes, leaned her head back against the cushioned edge of the tub and relaxed completely, letting all her nerves and muscles go. The hot water seemed to seep into every corner of her body so that she felt pleasantly drowsy. She felt obscurely as though she had sloughed off not only the dirt of the journey but her fear and misery and ten years of her age. Her mind was clearer and her blood circulated better. Once again she became aware that she was young and strong, and that her feminine charms were intact. She had seen confirmation of this in the admiring eyes of the servants as they helped her into the bath before opening up chests and taking out linen sheets and covers to prepare her bed. Yes, she was as beautiful as ever, and it was good to know it!

Sara slept in the alcove where she had been lifted rather than conducted. She had barely opened so much as an eyelid between the river and her bed, but for once Catherine did not need her.

Now her bed was ready, the bath-water scum witnessed to

the amount of dust and dirt which had accompanied Catherine from the Auvergne, and one of the chambermaids was already holding up a warmed towel to wrap her in. She stood up in the bath for a minute, running her hands down her body to get rid of some of the water. Just then they heard the clank of rapid, mailed footsteps outside in the narrow gallery; the door was pushed open impatiently and a man stepped into the room.

His exclamation of astonishment found an echo in Catherine's cry of horror. Such was her confusion that she noticed nothing about the newcomer except that he was gigantically tall, and blond. Instantly she snatched the towel from the chambermaid and covered herself up in it as best she could.

"How dare you? Get out! Get out at once!" she cried.

The spectacle which met his eyes, together with Catherine's angry speech, seemed to have plunged the man into a stupor. His eyes popped and he opened his mouth but not a sound came out of it. Catherine meanwhile was shrieking at him:

"Well, what are you waiting for? I've already told you, haven't I? Get out!"

He seemed to have turned to stone, and when at last he got back the use of speech he stammered helplessly:

"Who . . . who are you?"

"That's none of your business! But I'll tell you what you are, you're an impertinent oaf! Now get out!"

"But . . ." the poor man began.

"No buts . . . you mean you *still* haven't gone!"

Wild with rage Catherine snatched up a huge sponge which was lying in the tub and flung it, all swollen with water, right at the foe. Her aim was impressive. The sponge hit the intruder full in the face. In a second the blue silk tunic he wore over his chain mail was soaked. He started to beat a hasty retreat. Mumbling vague apologies he ran out of the room in a great clatter of steel. Then Catherine stepped out of her bath with the dignity of an offended queen. But the two petrified servants did not lift a finger to help her.

"Well?" she said curtly.

"Does the noble lady realize who it was she has just treated like that?" one of them uttered at last. "It was Monseigneur Pierre de Breze, who is a great favorite of the Queen and one of her closest advisers. And besides . . ."

"That's enough!" Catherine cut in. "I should have done the same if it had been the King himself. Now dry me! I'm cold!"

Catherine lost no time in putting the indiscreet visitor out of her thoughts, and she sincerely hoped that she would not have to meet him again because she couldn't help realizing what a ridiculous position he had put her in. However, he was the very first person she clapped eyes on the next morning when she reached the great hall of the château, in answer to a summons from the Queen. But the funny thing was she was less embarrassed by the encounter than she would have expected. A good night's sleep, a large breakfast, and a careful toilet had worked miracles. She felt like a new woman, and ready for anything.

Guessing at the threadbare state of her wardrobe Yolande had sent her several dresses to choose from. The one Catherine chose was of heavy black brocade under a surcoat of silver cloth trimmed with sable. The tall pointed head-dress she wore was of the same brocade, and the long veils which floated from it were of black mousseline shot with silver. The look was one of sumptuous mourning and it was well calculated to set off Catherine's beauty. If she had been in any doubt on that score, however, the appreciative murmur which greeted her appearance in the council chamber would have set them at rest. She approached the throne where Queen Yolande sat, however, in a silence so profound one could have heard a pin drop.

Other than the Queen and herself all the others—not that there were more than seven or eight people altogether—were men, the tallest of them being Pierre de Breze and the most impressive the Constable de Richemont, who stood on the steps to the throne. To one side of Yolande's throne, but a little below it, a high-backed chair held an ancient man in priestly vestments, still upright despite his eighty-six years but wearing spectacles over his weak eyes; this was Hardouin de Beuil, Bishop of Angers.

The hall was enormous and Catherine had to fight against a sudden attack of shyness as she made her way across it. Multi-colored pennants fluttered gently against the stone, fan-vaulted roof, and the walls were hidden by an immense and fanciful tapestry in blue and red predominantly, showing the Apocalypse of St. John. It was so silent that the swishing of her silk skirts sounded like a rushing wind in her ears. But when she was about half-way across the room she heard rapid steps and the Constable appeared before her.

As he drew near Arthur Richemont bowed and then offered her his closed fist to rest her hand on, and said:

"Welcome among us, Madame de Montsalvy! We are particularly glad to have you with us because you have suffered so much for a cause which is also ours. Your husband was still very young when he fought at my side at Agincourt but

98

his valor was already noteworthy, and I loved him dearly and my heart grieves at his death."

Now that it was not covered by a helmet, the Breton Prince's face showed up in all its battered pride, criss-crossed by old war wounds but lit up by a pair of clear blue eyes. Catherine rediscovered all the confidence in him which she had felt on the occasion of their first meeting, at his betrothal to Philippe of Burgundy's sister, widow of the French Dauphin Louis de Guyenne. This man was as solid as a rampart, as true as tempered steel and as rare as pure gold. Fighting back her tears she smiled and curtsied and placed her hand on his.

"Monseigneur, your welcome has moved and touched me more than I can say. But I beg you to make use of me exactly as you would have made use of my beloved husband had it pleased God to spare him! My only remaining desire on this earth is to avenge him and restore to my son what is rightfully his!"

"It shall be done as you wish. Come!"

Side by side they went up to the throne where Yolande was waiting. She smiled at the young woman.

"Greet His Lordship the Bishop of this good town of ours and then come and sit here," she said, pointing out a velvet cushion on the steps to the throne.

When Catherine was installed there the other men present were introduced to her. These numbered, besides Pierre de Breze whose eyes never left her, the Signeur de Chaumont, husband of the lively Anne, Jean de Beuil, governor of Sable, Ambroise de Lore, Prégent of Coetivy, a personal friend of the Constable, and finally, standing a little apart from the others, a modestly dressed man of a somewhat taciturn expression who was Richemont's squire, Tristan L'Hermite by name. They were all young, the oldest being the Constable, who had just turned forty, and they all came and kissed the young woman's hand respectfully. Breze alone threw in a sigh for good measure and a glance which made Catherine redden to the roots of her hair. She dismissed this embarrassment impatiently. Why was she bothering with this man at a time when so many serious matters were in play? She had come there to find vengeance, not to start flirting with the first pretty youth who came her way. She threw him a severe look and then turned her head away.

The Queen had begun to speak:

"Milords, we are all of us here now since there is no hope of the Captains La Hire and Xaintrailles being present, owing to the fighting in Picardy. At your last meeting, held last September at Vannes, at the funeral of the Duchess of Brittany, Madame Jeanne de Valois, you reached an agreement concerning the liquidation of Georges de la Trémoille. Not content with surrendering Joan the Maid to the enemy, spreading terror throughout the kingdom, reducing the King to poverty while he waxes prosperous himself in the most scandalous fashion, imprisoning and ruining our best men, such as Louis d'Amboise, who is a cousin of you all, and Arnaud de Montsalvy, of surrendering to the English the town of Montargues which belongs to Madame de Richemont, of waging war on our own territory and ravaging and pillaging the Auvergne, Limousin and Languedoc through the agency of his valet Villa-Andrade, this man now has the audacity to try and interfere with the patient and delicate attempts we have been making these past months to effect a *rapprochement* with the Duke of Burgundy. For over a year the Papal Legate, Nicolas Albergati, the Cardinal of Sainte-Croix, has been holding meeting upon meeting with the Burgundian envoys in the hopes of reaching a settlement which would lead to peace. And what has La Trémoille been doing meanwhile? Last October he tried to lay siege to Dijon while simultaneously instigating a clumsy attempt to assassinate the Duke Philippe at the precise moment when the death of the Duke's sister, the Duchess of Bedford, was threatening to turn him away from his English alliance. This must not go on! We will never succeed in getting rid of the English and restoring peace to the kingdom as long as the Lord Chamberlain has the King under his thumb. You have all sworn to help rid France of this troublesome man, milords. I await your proposals."

A silence greeted the Queen's request. Catherine held her breath, secretly turning over all this news and weighing it up. It just proved how cut off from things she had been all this time. She realized, without much surprise, that the news of an attempted assassination against her former lover, Philippe of Burgundy, left her quite unmoved. The bonds which united them had been severed once and for all, and no trace remained of those days she had spent with him. It was as if some other woman had spent those passionate hours in the handsome duke's arms. It all meant no more to her now than an old story told round the fireside of an evening.

Everyone's eyes meanwhile, Catherine's included, turned towards the Constable. He stood with bowed head and folded arms, apparently deep in thought. It was the elderly bishop who broke the silence. His voice piped up like a cracked bell.

"Twice already, Lord Constable, you have rid the King of his unworthy favorites. Why should you fear doing so a third time? What has Messire de la Trémoille got that Pierre de Giac or Camus de Beaulieu did not have? You had the first thrown into the Auron sewn in a sack, and the other you had strangled, so why is it that Messire de la Trémoille still lives?"

"Because he looks after himself better than the other two. Giac believed he enjoyed the protection of the Devil, to whom he had sold his right hand, while Beaulieu's head was as empty as a rattle. La Trémoille's on the other hand is full of dangerous guile. He knows that he is hated and behaves accordingly. We have sworn to finish with him but it seems that this is not so easy to accomplish."

The bishop gave a dry laugh.

"It only needs one blow! I cannot see what holds you back. You do not go to Court much, it is true, but you have enough loyal men . . ."

"And what should one of these loyal men do?" Richemont interrupted dryly. "It is impossible to approach La Trémoille unless you are in his confidence. The King, whose side he never leaves now, is his principal bodyguard. Since the summer he and the King have shut themselves up in the fortress at Amboise, and have never left the place except to make a brief visit together to Sully. It is not the wish to kill which is lacking but the means!"

The Constable's gloomy tone froze Catherine's blood. She saw Yolande's hand clutch nervously at the arm of the throne, and felt her exasperation as if it were in her own body. What use were these statements and these unanswerable questions? What point was there in this council if all it did was emphasize the helplessness of all concerned? But since the Queen remained silent she did not dare speak. Besides the Bishop had plunged agitatedly into the discussion again.

"A skilful archer can hit any target anywhere. When La Trémoille goes out . . ."

"He never goes out. He has grown so fat and heavy that there is not a horse which could carry him. When he travels he goes by closed litter, surrounded by guards, and dressed in chain mail."

"I do not suppose that he wears the chain mail at night. Strike at night . . ."

"He does not sleep in the King's living-quarters, because he does not consider them quite safe. At night La Trémoille allows himself to fall asleep in the keep itself, guarded by no less than fifty men."

"Poison, then, in his food . . ."

Richemont sighed wearily. His friend Prégent de Coetivy answered gloomily.

"His food and drink are sampled by the three Officers of the King."

Monseigneur de Beuil gave a cry of anger, tore off his spectacles and threw them on the ground.

"Is that all you have to say to us, Lord Constable? Are you admitting defeat or is La Trémoille the devil incarnate? In the name of God, milord, we are talking of a flesh-and-blood man, surrounded by mere weak or greedy men who could be bought and who would probably sell their loyalty for gold. . . ."

"I do not trust loyalties which can be bought, Lord Bishop. We need a man who is not only capable of loyalty but prepared to sacrifice his life, because the blow would almost certainly have to be struck under the King's eyes and the murderer would be unlikely to escape with his life. Who among you, gentlemen, would be prepared to go and plunge a dagger into La Trémoille's throat and then be cut down in your turn by the guards?"

A heavy silence greeted the Constable's sarcastic question. The gentlemen looked at each other in embarrassment and Catherine's heart swelled in a burst of anger. These men had no need to prove their courage. They were among the best of the brave, and yet not one was ready to imperil his life to destroy his enemy. They were quite ready to do battle in broad daylight, in the bright beams of the sun and of honor, amid the clash of steel and the silky flapping of pennants, but their pride rebelled at the thought of murdering in the dark, taking the victim by surprise and then falling beneath the valets' blows. Perhaps too they judged themselves too important to the kingdom, too necessary to France's glory on the field to be reduced to committing distasteful and stealthy deeds? . . . Or perhaps they had not suffered sufficiently from La Trémoille. Otherwise surely they would want his blood, at whatever cost . . . and by whatever means? The hatred they felt towards him was without warmth and their struggle was a political one: the noble, but chilly desire to snatch power and the King's person from La Trémoille's unworthy hands. It was not like the hatred she felt, a fury born of her very entrails, the fury of a desperate woman denied her one reason for living. These men were no more than undesirable at Court, and some had seen their close relations suffer under La Trémoille, but they had not seen their castles in flames, or their names vilified, or their very lives threatened or the being most dear to them in the world banished for ever from the land of the living.

A bitter taste rose in Catherine's mouth while a furious gust of anger traveled her veins. And as the Queen's grave voice remarked, with a faint trace of dissatisfaction, "Come, milords, we must decide on something!" Catherine left her seat and came and knelt before the throne.

"If it please, Your Majesty, I am ready to commit the deed from which these gentlemen recoil. I have nothing more to lose but my life . . . and that is a small thing if I could but avenge my beloved husband. All I ask, madame, is that you remember that I have a son, and watch over him for me."

An angry murmur greeted her words. The knights had all gathered round the steps of the throne with their hands on their sword-guards.

"Heaven forgive me!" cried Pierre de Breze in an angry voice. "I believe Madame de Montsalvy takes us all for cowards! Can we allow her to run away with ideas like those, milords?"

Indignant protests arose on all sides, but these were interrupted a moment later by a cold voice uttering these words:

"With the Queen's permission, and that of the Constable, I would like to say, milords, that all this is pointless and a waste of time and breath. It is not a case of debating who would display the most heroism, but of coldly planning a man's death. This is not a competition to prove which among you would behave with the most heroism, but a cold-blooded plan to assassinate a man and work out the best way of doing so. None of the suggestions I have heard here have seemed at all practical or feasible."

The quiet authority of this voice made Catherine turn round. The circle of knights parted to admit the man called Tristan L'Hermite, who occupied the not very distinguished position of squire to the Lord Constable. The young woman looked more closely at him as he came forward. He was a Fleming of some thirty years old, blond with pale blue eyes and the coldest, most impassive face Catherine had ever seen. Not a muscle in it moved. A heavy, even somewhat coarse face in fact, but one which gained a sort of majesty from its extraordinary impassivity. He bent his knee before the Queen, awaiting her permission to continue speaking. Richemont looked at Yolande inquiringly, then:

"The Queen gives you permission to speak. What is it you have to say?"

"This! The Lord Chamberlain cannot be reached outside his castle since he never goes out; therefore any attempt must be made from within, which is to say inside one of the royal palaces now that he has annexed them for himself and takes refuge behind their heavy garrisons."

"That's exactly what we've just been saying," said Jean de Beuil, grimacing; "in other words it's impossible!"

"Impossible at Amboise perhaps," said Tristan coolly, "because the governor there is under his thumb. But it might be possible in a palace or castle where the governor was on our side. Chinon, for instance, whose governor, Messire Raoul de Goncourt, has secretly gone over to Monseigneur the Connétable and is now his loyal servant."

A cold shiver ran down Catherine's back. Raoul de Goncourt! The former governor of Orléans, the man who had once had her put to the torture and condemned her to death! He hated Joan of Arc, and had fought against her blindly. What could La Trémoille have done to him to make him change allegiance so radically? But Richemont now replied, somewhat haughtily, to his squire:

"It is true that we might have a chance if we could persuade La Trémoille, and of course the King, to go to Chinon. But the Lord Chamberlain dislikes Chinon. It smacks too much of the Maid for him and the common people of the village are still devoted to her memory. The King is too easily influenced. La Trémoille is afraid that he might hear Joan's voice echoing still through the Great Chamber. He does not know that Goncourt has come over to us but he would never agree to take the King to Chinon!"

"But he must!" Catherine cried. "Isn't there anyone with influence over him? His reasons for disliking the place are purely sentimental and they could surely be changed? All men in my experience have a weak point which can be exploited if one knows what it is. . . ."

She was interrupted by an angry exclamation from Pierre de Breze.

"And which is the Lord Chamberlain's, pray?"

This time he was answered by Ambroise de Lore, a redheaded Angevin who never smiled.

"He has two: gold and women!" he declared. "His thirst for the former is only equaled by his insatiable desire for the latter. Were we to find a beautiful enough damsel to rouse his blood it might be possible to persuade him to do something foolish!"

As Lore spoke he stared at Catherine with a brutal insolence which made her cheeks flame. The Angevin's meaning was so plain that she felt a hot wave of rebelliousness sweep over her. What did this cynical nobleman take her for? Did he really think he could plant Arnaud de Montsalvy's wife in La Trémoille's bed? But then she paused and bit back the sarcastic retort which came to her lips . . . on second thoughts perhaps it was not such a bad idea? There was a difference between turning a man's head and giving oneself to him . . . and who knew if . . .

But a furious exclamation from Pierre de Breze interrupted her train of thought. He too, like everyone else present, had taken the point of Lore's remarks. Now he turned on him, white with anger.

"Are you mad? What are you thinking of? A noblewoman's misfortunes, beautiful though she may be, should be sufficient defense against thoughts of that kind. You may be my friend but I am sorely tempted to force those insolent words of yours down your throat. . . ."

"Peace, Messire de Breze," the Queen interposed sharply. "After all our friend Lore *said* nothing which could offend Madame de Montsalvy though his glances may have been a trifle bold. Let us forget the incident!"

"In any case," Richemont grumbled, "La Trémoille does not like great ladies. Their eyes are too sharp, and their tongues too barbed, and besides their rank allows them to make invidious comparisons which are rarely to his advantage. The sort of women he likes are strumpets and whores and all the wild sisterhood skilled in the arts of love, or alternatively fair peasant women whom he can ruin and tease at his pleasure!"

"You have left out young pages, monseigneur!" said Tristan L'Hermite sarcastically, "and then there is our Lord Chamberlain's newest craze and passion—a troupe of traveling folk of Egypt and Bohemia who have installed themselves in the valleys round Amboise to escape from the winter cold and the famine which is scourging the countryside round about. The local people are afraid of these folk because they steal and foretell the future and cast spells, but their fear makes them generous. The men are blacksmiths or musicians. The women dance. Some of them are beautiful and La Trémoille has developed a taste for their amber skin. It is not unusual for him to summon some of them up to the château for his private pleasure, and I fancy it is his will rather than shortage of food which keeps the tribe at Amboise."

Catherine had been listening closely to the Fleming's little speech, particularly as it seemed to be addressed primarily to herself. She sensed that there must be some idea behind it but she was not quite clear what it was. Certainly he had brought up the Tziganes for a purpose.

"Are you suggesting," Jean de Beuil asked haughtily, "that we should enter into negotiations with one of these wild creatures! What a dangerous enterprise that would be! We should

105

be betrayed to La Trémoille for the price of a pair of chickens!"

"Certainly not, monseigneur," Tristan replied, looking hard at Catherine. "Rather, I was thinking of an intelligent, brave and resourceful woman skillfully disguised. . . ."

"Just what do you mean?" De Breze cut in suspiciously.

Tristan hesitated, but by now Catherine had seized the point of his discourse. This idea of his which he was nervous of putting forward, no doubt fearing the violent reactions it would provoke from certain of the gentlemen present, had in fact been perfectly plain to her soon after he mentioned the gypsies. And now she would propose it as her own. She smiled encouragement at Tristan and laid a restraining hand on Pierre de Breze's arm.

"I think I catch Messire L'Hermite's meaning," she said calmly. "He is simply saying that if I am ready to do anything to encompass the death of La Trémoille then, clearly, I am the ideal woman to play this role."

The commotion was deafening. All the gentlemen started shouting at once and the Bishop's cracked treble rose louder than any. Ambroise de Lore alone said nothing, but a corner of his mouth twitched in what might have been the ghost of a smile. The Duchess-Queen was obliged to raise her voice to recall them to silence.

"Calm yourselves, gentlemen," she said coldly. "I can understand your dismay at such a bold and dangerous proposition but there is nothing to be gained from shouting. Moreover, we are faced with such a difficult situation that all suggestions, however hazardous or impractical they may seem at first sight, need to be examined with care. And a cool head! As for you, Catherine, are you sure that you have sufficiently weighed up the risks and dangers to which you would be exposing yourself in such a perilous undertaking?"

"I have thought about them seriously, madame, and I do not consider them insurmountable. If I can serve you, and the King, at the same time as avenging my own people I shall consider myself most fortunate!"

The Lord Constable's blue gaze sought Catherine's eyes and held them questioningly.

"You would be risking your life at every moment. If La Trémoille were to recognize you, you would not live to see another sunrise. You realize that?"

"Yes, I do, monseigneur," she said, with a quick bob of a curtsy, "and I accept the danger. Besides there is no need to exaggerate the danger. The Lord Chamberlain hardly knows me. When he saw me I was one of Queen Marie's ladies, all pious and long-faced, and he only saw me two or three times and always surrounded by the other ladies. He would not be likely to recognize me, especially if I were disguised."

"In that case I must say that it seems an excellent plan. You have an answer for everything. I admire your courage!"

He turned away slightly to talk to Tristan L'Hermite and Jean de Beuil spoke up.

"Assuming that we accept Madame de Montsalvy's proposal and allow her to take on this dangerous and distasteful role, how can we be sure that she will be convincing enough to deceive our enemy? These Egyptian folk have strange ways and still stranger customs. . . ."

"I know their customs," Catherine cut in gently. "Messire, my faithful nurse, Sara, is a gypsy-woman. She was sold in slavery to the Venetians."

The next objection came from Pierre de Breze.

"But would these folk agree to become our accomplices? They are wild, fierce, independent people."

A thin smile curled the Fleming's lips, a smile which also contained a threat.

"They too love gold . . . and fear the gallows! The threat of the one together with promises of the other, in alluring quantities, should help to bring them round to our point of view. Besides, this Sara will certainly be warmly welcomed by them, as one of their own people. And, moreover, if it please you, monseigneur, I propose to accompany Dame Catherine among the gypsies. Then I shall be able to ensure her liaison with you, milords!"

"I approve," said Richemont, "and I think the plan is a good one. Has anyone any other objections to put forward?"

"No," said the Bishop, "unless it be the anxiety we all feel at the thought of a noble and virtuous lady risking her soul . . . and body in such a dangerous adventure. The honor of Madame de Montsalvy . . ."

"You need have no fear for my virtue, My Lord Bishop," Catherine said calmly. "I can protect myself."

"But there is one point I should like to clear up," the prelate insisted. "Once you have gained access to La Trémoille, how do you propose to get him to move from Amboise to Chinon? He may have a taste for gypsy-girls but does that mean that he lets them give him advice or influence his behavior? In his eyes you will be no better than any of them. . . ."

Now Catherine began to laugh, a soft ripple of sound which smoothed the anxiety from the knightly countenances as if by magic.

"I have my own plan, monseigneur, but if you don't mind I should like to keep it to myself. I will only say this—I shall be availing myself of the Lord Chamberlain's ruling passion —his lust . . . for gold!"

"May God guard you and keep you, my child! We shall pray for you."

He extended his left hand with its immense sapphire ring towards the kneeling girl, and with his right, traced a sort of benediction on her smooth brow.

Catherine's heart was pounding like a drum. At last, at last she was going into battle herself; she would be hunting the enemy down in his very lair! She had been through many adventures in her life but these had always been ones which fate had inflicted upon her, not of her own choosing. When she left Burgundy to find Arnaud at Orléans she had been obliged to take the hand which destiny dealt her, and make the best of it. But now, freely and deliberately, solely to quieten her conscience and appease the great love she bore towards her lost husband, she was about to bring herself into such a wild and terrible danger that nothing, not even her rank and name, would be of any assistance to her. If she were captured she would be hanged like any one of the gypsy-girls whose coloring she had assumed, and her corpse would rot far from the place where Arnaud moldered in a living death. But even this thought could not shake her resolution.

She was so lost in her thoughts that she jumped when the Queen's clear voices spoke up:

"Before we separate, milords, I would have you swear again, as you did at Vannes, to keep our secret loyally and to seek neither rest nor respite till the man whose loss we have sworn is struck down. Now swear, and may Our Lady and Our Lord Jesus Christ intercede for us!"

With one accord the knights held out their right hands over the sapphire cross which the Bishop had taken from his neck and now held out to them.

"We swear!" they cried in unison. "Either La Trémoille falls or we perish!"

Then, one after the other, they came and knelt before Yolande who gave them her hand to kiss, and then left the room. Only Richemont and Tristan l'Hermite remained to attend to the details of the proposed scheme. While the Queen and Richemont were talking Catherine went up to the Fleming.

"I must thank you," she said. "Your idea has saved us all and I cannot help but see it as a sign from heaven. How could you know that my maidservant . . ."

108

"But I did know, madame," said Tristan, with a thin smile. "Give thanks where it is due. It was not I who put an idea into your head, Dame Catherine, but you who put one into mine."

"You knew? But how?"

"I know everything, everything that I need to know. But you need have no fear, madame. I shall serve you as loyally as I serve the Constable."

"But why? You don't know me."

"No, but I do not have to look twice at a person, male or female, to know their worth. I shall serve you for the simplest and best reason—because I want to!"

The enigmatic Fleming bowed and returned to his master's side near the throne, leaving Catherine plunged in thought. Who and what was this strange man who, though a mere squire, spoke with the authority of a lord and master, and who seemed to know everything about the people he came into contact with through means known only to himself? There was something disturbing about him, Catherine felt, and yet she had no qualms in accepting him as her companion in adventure. Perhaps it had something to do with this stolidity of his, a different sort of stolidity from Gauthier's, but just as reassuring in its own way.

She was longing to get back to Sara to tell her the news and she asked for permission to retire, which the Queen instantly granted. The Queen and the Lord Constable evidently had even more urgent and serious matters to discuss which were not suitable for profane ears, loyal though they might be. But as she was leaving the chamber Catherine ran into Pierre de Breze who was pacing up and down the long gallery which ran alongside the moat. He came swiftly toward her, looking agitated and deeply moved.

"Gracious lady," he said in a flustered voice, "please don't take me for a lunatic if I ask you to spare me a few moments of your company. I have many things to say to you."

"Such as what?" Catherine asked, archly. "I thought we had been through all that last night?"

The mention of their previous encounter made De Breze flush, and Catherine, despite her annoyance, could not help finding something rather charming about this giant who blushed like a girl. He was handsome too, with clear-cut, regular features which reminded her a little of the Montsalvys, but in particular of Michel, because of his blue eyes and fair hair. Realizing this, Catherine felt the last shred of resentment melt away. She looked a little less severely at him and even accepted his hand to lead her to one of the window embrasures. There she sat down on the stone seat and looked up inquiringly at him.

"Very well, then, I am listening. What was it you wanted to say to me?"

"First, I want to apologize for yesterday. I had just returned from a mission in the Haut Maine and I went straight to that room, which is normally mine. I had no idea that it was occupied."

"In that case I forgive you. Are you satisfied?"

He did not answer at once. Nervously his fingers toyed with the long points, lined in gray silk, of his blue tunic, whose only other adornment was the Cross of Jerusalem embroidered on the breast.

"I have one other thing to say," he said gruffly, not daring to look at the delicate face which seemed so fragile and so beautiful framed in its dark veils. Never in his life had Pierre de Breze seen such a beautiful woman. The beauty which he had witnessed involuntarily, the radiance of those incomparable violet eyes, all this agitated him so deeply that he trembled, he, the Queen's Champion, the man before whom Lord Scales and Thomas Hampton had fled ignominiously! He found himself disarmed, helpless, longing only to kneel before her and adore her. Catherine was too feminine, too wise, not to perceive the young man's agitation but she was resolved not to let herself be stirred by it, however delightful such an interlude might prove.

"Tell me then," she said gently.

He clenched his fists, took a deep breath like a swimmer surfacing from a dive, and then burst out:

"Abandon this mad scheme of yours; don't go there! If it is just a matter of killing La Trémoille I swear that I will go to Court myself and strike him down before them all . . . in your name!"

"That would mean certain death. The King would have you seized, imprisoned and almost certainly executed."

"I don't care! I would rather go to my death than see you go to yours! The thought of what you are about to do revolts me. For pity's sake . . . give it up!"

"Pity for whom?" Catherine asked gently.

"Pity for you . . . and me too! What is the use of fine speeches and great words? I am only a soldier and these things do not come easily to me. You already know that I love you without my telling you!"

"And . . . loving me, you are prepared to die for me?"

He fell on his knees and the face he turned toward her was so dark with passion that Catherine felt alarmed. This boy

110

was made of a fine, pure metal; he deserved to be loved and she had no wish to involve him in the sort of impasse which her own destiny represented.

"That is my one desire," he murmured.

"And mine is that you should live. You love me, you say, and your love is such that you would be ready to die for it? Then you will understand the feelings which impel me to sacrifice everything for the memory of the man whose name I bear . . . the only man I have ever loved and will ever love!"

He bowed his head, considering the gentle rebuff these words implied.

"Oh, I never hoped for your love," he sighed. "I often saw Arnaud de Montsalvy when he was a Captain and I was but a page or squire, and I have never seen a man I admired more. I envied him too. He was all I wanted to be: brave, strong, sure of himself! What woman, blessed with the love of a man like that, could ever love another? So you see . . . I have no illusions."

"Nevertheless," said Catherine, more touched than she cared to show, "you are a man whom a woman might be proud to love."

"But I could never count for anything next to him, could I? Isn't that what you were trying to tell me, Dame Catherine? That you loved him as much as that?"

A sudden pain tore at Catherine's heart at this reminder of what she had lost. There was a lump in her throat. Tears rose to her eyes and rolled unchecked down her face.

"I still love him more than anything in the world! I would give my life, messire, and even my hopes of eternal salvation, to have him back again . . . even for just an hour! You see, I have no secrets from you. Just now you spoke of the risks I would be taking. If I did not have a son I would long ago have killed myself so that I might join him the sooner."

"But now you see that you must live! Oh, let me help you and be your friend and champion! You are too frail to go unprotected in these hard times! I swear not to importune you with my love and to ask no more of you than the right to be your champion and defender. Marry me. I have a great name, wealth . . . and ambition!"

Catherine dried her eyes and stared at him thunderstruck, not knowing quite what to say. Then she stood up leaving him still kneeling at her feet.

"What a hot-head you are!" she said softly. "How old are you?"

"Twenty-three."

"And I am several years older!"

"What does that matter? You look like a young girl, and you are the loveliest woman who ever set foot on this earth. Whether you like it or not you shall be my lady, and I shall wear no colors but yours!"

"My colors are those of mourning, messire, silver and sable. Didn't you have a lady, then, before I came?"

To Catherine's astonishment Pierre de Breze made a dreadful face and replied, slowly and reluctantly:

"I had no lady! I have a fiancée, Jeanne du Bec-Crespin . . . but she is too ugly for words!"

All at once Catherine burst out laughing and her laughter was so gay, and young and light-hearted that Pierre found himself, unwillingly at first, joining in. Impulsively she held out both hands and he buried his face in them.

"Keep your fiancée, Messire Pierre!" she said, suddenly serious again. "And give me your friendship. That is what I have most need of, you see."

He looked up at her with renewed hopefulness.

"Then I can watch over you, and wear your colors and be your champion?"

"Of course! On condition that you don't do anything which might interfere with the success of my plans. Do you promise that?"

"I promise," he said, without enthusiasm. "But I shall be at Amboise all the time you are there, Dame Catherine, and if any evil should befall you . . ."

Catherine's face grew solemn all at once. She withdrew her hands and slipped them into her wide sleeves. Her eyes darkened and her lips set in a stubborn line.

"If it should happen that I died before I could achieve my object . . . and if you love me truly, as you so rashly said a moment ago . . . then I accept your offer to die for me. If I die kill the Lord Chamberlain for me! Will you do that?"

Pierre de Breze drew his sword, held it up before him and laid his right hand on the hilt.

"By the holy relics which this sword contains I swear it!"

At this Catherine smiled and then, with a last gesture of farewell, she turned and walked away with a soft rustle of trailing silken skirts. Still kneeling Pierre de Breze watched her go, his soul in his eyes.

CHAPTER SIX

Guillaume the Illuminator

When she got back to her room Catherine was surprised to find Sara and Tristan l'Hermite there, in the midst of a furious argument. The gypsy-woman's angry voice could be heard as far away as the stairs while the Fleming's answers were pitched in a considerably softer key. Catherine's appearance on the scene quietened the belligerents. Sara was scarlet with wrath, and her bonnet all askew. Tristan stood leaning against the mantelpiece, arms folded, and a vexed smile playing about his lips.

"Might I inquire what is going on here?" Catherine asked calmly. "I could hear you shouting from the other end of the gallery."

"You could hear madame shouting!" Tristan corrected her peaceably. "For my part I don't recall raising my voice."

"That still doesn't tell me what I want to know—what you were arguing about? Come to think of it I did not know you had met each other."

"We have only just met," the Fleming replied ironically. "I may as well tell you, gracious lady, that your maidservant does not approve of our plans."

These words revived all Sara's fury, but this time she vented it on Catherine.

"Are you mad? You want to disguise yourself as a Tzigane and then appear before this wretched Chamberlain? What for, may I ask? I suppose you plan to dance for him like Salome danced for Herod?"

"Precisely," Catherine retorted crisply. "With one difference—it's not another man's head I shall claim, but his own! Anyway I must say I'm surprised at you, Sara. I thought you would be pleased to live among your own people for a while."

"We don't know they are my people yet. I don't belong to all the wandering tribes, you know. I come from the mighty tribe of Kalderas who followed the hordes of Genghis Khan, and there is nothing to prove that the gypsies camped round

113

Amboise are from the same tribe as I. They may only be common Djats or . . ."

"The best way to find out is to go there and see for yourself," Tristan interrupted.

"You don't know what you are saying. The Djats would not welcome me. There is rivalry between the two tribes at the moment. I don't want to risk . . ."

Now it was Catherine's turn to interrupt impatiently.

"That's enough! I, and Messire Tristan, shall go among the Tziganes. You are perfectly free to remain here. They will take me in, whatever tribe they may be. When do we leave, messire?"

"Tomorrow night."

"Why not tonight?"

"Because we have something else to do tonight. Might I ask you to remove your head-dress?"

"And why not her dress too while you are about it?" Sara grumbled, offended by Catherine's snub. "A lady's clothing is not something for men to concern themselves with."

"You need have no fear that I plan to usurp your duties, gentle lady," said Tristan with a mocking grin. "I just wanted to make sure of something."

Catherine obediently unpinned her tall head-dress and loosened her hair which floated in red gold waves down to her shoulders.

"Is your hair no longer than that?" Tristan asked in astonishment. "That is going to look strange. All these devilish gypsy-women have long snaky black locks down to their waists."

Catherine just managed to restrain Sara who was on the point of flinging herself at Tristan, shrieking that she too was a "devilish gypsy-woman" and she would soon show him what she was capable of.

"Come now, calm yourself! Messire L'Hermite did not mean to upset you. He spoke without thinking . . . didn't you, messire?"

"Tut, tut!" said Tristan, looking far from convinced. "My tongue ran away with me, that's all. Now to return to *your* locks, Dame Catherine."

"I had to cut them a year or so ago. Is that a great obstacle then?"

"No . . . no. But we will need all the time we have. Would you mind accompanying me this evening, after sundown, on a visit to the town, Dame Catherine?"

"Where she goes I go!" Sara declared. "And I'd like to see who is going to try and stop me!"

114

The Fleming heaved a deep sigh, and gave Sara a sidelong glance.

"If you like. It seems you know how to hold your tongue. Will you come then, Dame Catherine?"

"Of course. Come and fetch us when the time is right. We will wait for you here. But where are we going?"

"Please don't ask questions. Just trust me if you can."

Tristan's backhanded compliment appeared to have calmed Sara who now set about rearranging her mistress's hair, still grumbling a good deal. The Fleming contemplated the gypsy's dexterous hands flying skillfully over the fragile edifice of silver cloth and black mousseline. He murmured, as if to himself:

"It's really very pretty. But tonight I think something a little less eye-catching would be advisable. And for the journey tomorrow I think men's clothes would be the most sensible solution."

At this Sara dropped combs, pins and brushes and planted herself in front of the Fleming, hands on hips. She thrust her face forward till she was almost nose to nose with this enemy and articulated:

"Not for me, my boy! Dress Dame Catherine up in men's clothes if she likes—and it appears she adores them—but no power on earth is going to force me into those idiotic pipestems you call breeches, or those equally ridiculous abbreviated tunics you call doublets. If you want me to dress as a man you will have to find me a monk's robe. At least there's room to breathe in them!"

Tristan opened his mouth to reply, thought better of it, cast an appreciative eye over Sara's majestic person and ended by smiling that strange thin smile of his which did not show his teeth. Then he sighed and shrugged.

"That isn't such a bad idea, after all. This evening then, Dame Catherine. Expect me about the time of compline."

The Angelus had sounded long ago by the time Catherine, Tristan and Sara left the château by the postern gate in the immense ducal gateway, and made their way into the business quarter which surrounded the Cathedral of St. Maurice. Because of the late hour the heavy, iron-barred wooden shutters had been put up over most of the shop windows, but through the cracks there were glimpses of candles burning or the glow of oil lamps. The whole town, crowned by the pinnacles of its cathedral towers, was composing itself for sleep. Behind the silent shuttered fronts one sensed the presence of busy housewives doing the washing-up and tidying the kitchen, while their husbands totted up the day's earnings or discussed the local news with a neighbor.

The three hurried along the narrow streets. The women's heavy cloaks, with their deep hoods, made shadowy, indistinct shapes of them, almost invisible against the black walls. As for Tristan l'Hermite, he had pulled the flopping brim of his enormous black hat well down over his eyes to keep out the rain, one of those fine soft rains which penetrate deep into the earth and make the sap rise. The rain made the large round cobblestones slippery as they hurried up a lane with a conduit hollowed out in the middle of it. The smell of fish from the conduit was so strong and unpleasant that Catherine took out her iris scented handkerchief and held it to her nose. Sara merely grumbled:

"Is there much further to go? It stinks here."

"This is Fishmarket Lane; you wouldn't expect it to smell of amber and jasmine?" Tristan retorted. "Anyway we are nearly there. The Parchmentseller's Street is the next one along."

By way of reply Sara slipped an arm through Catherine's and hurried her steps a little. They soon entered the Parchmentseller's Street which smelled not of fish but of ink and glue. The breeze set the shop signs creaking and there was even less light here than there had been in the other streets. Only one narrow window in the whole street was lit up, and this seemed to blaze with light.

It was in front of this window, or rather the door just below it, that Tristan stopped. Catherine's eyes were so accustomed to the darkness by now that she could make out a little old house, whose overhanging gables reached down so low they gave it the air of a rather tipsy old lady in a bonnet. Unlike the neighboring houses which were made of wood and plaster this one appeared to be of solid stone. And the door might be low but it was stoutly made and banded with iron bars wrought in the shape of flowers, and an immense sign shaped like a piece of parchment hung just above it. A large wrought-iron ring was fixed to the door as a knocker and Tristan knocked three times, slowly.

"Where are we?" Catherine whispered, a little awed by the silence.

"We are about to see the man who can be most useful to us, gracious lady. Don't worry."

"I'm not worried, I'm just frozen," Sara complained. "My feet are soaking wet."

"You should have worn stronger shoes. But quiet, someone comes!"

Just then they heard what sounded like a scurrying of mice behind the door. The door opened silently on well-oiled hinges and a little old lady in a gray dress and white cap and apron appeared, curtsying as deep as her rheumaticky back would allow.

"Messire Guillaume awaits you, sir, and you too, noble ladies."

"Good, we will go up."

A steep, badly lit staircase led up from the far end of the narrow passage whose only door led, presumably, into the kitchen. From the top of the stairs a hearty voice rang out:

"Come up, messire. Everything is ready!"

The loudness of the voice made Catherine jump. It reminded her of Gauthier's, but it turned out that the owner was the complete antithesis of the Norman. He was small, bent, hunchbacked, with a little wrinkled face agitated by constant nervous tics. He seemed to have neither hair nor beard nor brows, and strange bright pink patches disfigured his cheeks, chin and forehead. A black cap was pulled right down till it almost reached his eyes, completely hiding his head and shading his weary reddened eyes. Catherine had to fight against an impulse to recoil before this unappetizing-looking mortal. He stared at her disconcertingly and rubbed his hands together mechanically, licking his lips the whole while. Then the terrifying voice boomed again:

"So this is the lady we are to turn brown! First we must give her a bath. Then we can see about her hair!"

Catherine started back in alarm, and Sara frowned:

"A bath?" Catherine echoed faintly. "But I . . ."

"It is indispensable," said Maître Guillaume faintly. "Your skin must be darkened all over."

Tristan had said nothing hitherto, but he sensed Catherine's repugnance and was perfectly aware of Sara's mounting ill-humor. At this point he hastily intervened.

"It is a bath of herbs, Dame Catherine, which can do you no harm. Sara will help you. But first I feel I should introduce Maître Guillaume to you. By trade he is an illuminator, and one of the best in France. But for some time now he has also been one of the most brilliant members of the Brotherhood of the Passion, who used to present such beautiful Mystery plays at Paris. The art of disguise has no secrets from him. And more than one noble lady of Angers is in the habit of paying a discreet call on him when her hair starts turning white."

The little man went on rubbing his hands, eyes half shut and almost purring with pleasure during the Fleming's flatter-

117

ing little speech. Feeling a little reassured, for she had believed for a moment that she had fallen into the hands of a sorcerer, Catherine took a deep breath and tried to be pleasant.

"Do you no longer present plays?" she asked.

"The war, noble lady, and the great famine which has stricken Paris have dispersed our company. Besides, in my present state, I could not easily perform on stage."

"Did you have an accident?"

Guillaume gave a little cracked laugh which contrasted oddly with his usual voice.

"Alas! One day when I had the honor to play Messire Satan and was capering about the stage amidst the pitch-pine torches which represented Hell, my costume caught fire. I thought I was done for but I survived . . . as you see me now! So I am left with my illuminator's trade, and the advice I am pleased to give on the rare occasions when some play or pageant is put on. But the bath is waiting and it must not be allowed to grow cold . . . if you would step this way."

Sara hurried after Catherine, while she and Guillaume made their way to the far end of the large room where he usually worked on his illuminating. It was a pleasant enough room, full of rolled-up parchments, little pots of colored paints, brushes as fine as human hair, made of hog's hair or sable. A large page from the Gospels stood propped up on an easel. On it Guillaume, with consummate art, was painting a miniature of the Crucifixion. As she passed, Catherine's eye fell on the unfinished work.

"You are a great artist," she said, with genuine respect.

A flash of pride lit up the old man's faded eyes and he made a grimace which might have been intended for a smile.

"Sincere praise always gives pleasure, noble lady. This way, please."

He pulled back a bead curtain and ushered Catherine into a little closet which really did look like a sorcerer's den. It was packed with phials, and horns and stuffed animals; in the center stood a brick furnace on which a large bath filled with smoking dark liquid had been placed.

Catherine looked uneasily at the dark brown liquid into which she was expected to step. As for Sara, she had held her tongue far too long for her own liking.

"What's that in there?" she demanded suspiciously.

"Only plant extracts," the illuminator answered placidly. "You will forgive me if I keep the secret of its composition to myself. I will merely tell you that one of the elements is walnut juice. This lovely lady must immerse herself completely, face and neck included, in the liquid. Fifteen minutes, with as many immersions of the face as possible, should suffice."

"And what will I look like afterwards?" Catherine asked.

"Your skin will be as brown as this majestic person's here."

"And will I stay like that?" Catherine asked uneasily, thinking of the reaction of her mother-in-law and little Michel if she were to return to them disguised as a gypsy.

"No. It will wear off gradually. Two months is the longest it is likely to last, in my opinion. After that you would need another bath, unless you spent a long time lying in the sun. Hurry up now, the bath is getting cold."

He went out almost regretfully, and Sara carefully drew the curtain to behind him and stood with her massive bulk firmly blocking any possible peepholes. Meanwhile Catherine hurriedly undressed and slipped into the bath, taking a deep breath. A soft, slightly peppery smell met her nostrils. The water was hot, but not unpleasantly so, and once in it Catherine's reluctance vanished. She held her breath and closed her eyes and plunged her face in once, twice, ten times.

When the hour-glass next to the bath showed that she had been there for fifteen minutes Catherine stood up. Drops of dark water rolled off her shoulders, now a warm golden brown.

"How do I look?" she asked Sara anxiously as she held out a large towel to dry her with.

"You could be my daughter you are so dark, and the effect is strange with your blonde hair, though that too seems to have gone a little darker."

Guillaume's voice reached them.

"Have you finished? Don't dress yourself again. You might stain your clothes."

Swathed in her towel Catherine went to meet the two men next door. Guillaume had placed a red-cushioned stool next to a pedestal on which stood a bowl full of some thick black paste. Catherine sat down obediently and allowed the illuminator to cover her hair with the paste which had a strong and disagreeable smell. Tristan grimaced and held his nose.

"How nasty! Can a woman be attractive when she gives off a smell like that?"

"We will wash her hair when the dye has taken effect, in an hour or so."

"And what does it contain?"

"Gallwood, rust-water, roman vitriol and ground sheep's flesh, distilled in alembic and mixed with lard."

"Roman vitriol?" Sara burst out. "But you might kill her, you wretch!"

"Calm yourself, woman. Moderation in everything. A poison may kill in large quantities and cure when taken a grain at a time."

The illuminator's long, supple fingers were strangely gentle, light and caressing. As he massaged her hair and scalp he talked as if to himself:

"It is a crime to blacken so bright and beautiful a head of hair. But the beauty of this lovely lady will in no wise be impaired. She may be more dangerous still, I believe."

"And will this wear off gradually too?" Catherine asked.

"Alas, no. Your hair will have to grow and you will have to cut off the black locks."

"I will take care of that," Sara said. Catherine stifled a sigh. Not that she regretted this new sacrifice, but the idea of cutting her hair yet again did not appeal to her.

For a whole hour she sat patiently with this thick paste on her head. It pricked her scalp slightly and weighed as heavy as mud. Guillaume had taken down a viola from a cupboard and he began to sing softly to its accompaniment in an attempt to make the time pass more quickly.

> "The winter wind doth strip the tree
> Till leafy boughs all naked be,
> Like to myself in poverty,
> In poverty, in poverty . . ."

The song was melancholy, the music sweet and the strange little man executed it with a rare talent. Catherine was so charmed and fascinated that she forgot her strange position. Sara and Tristan did the same as her, they listened. And Catherine was almost sorry when her hour of waiting was up, so great was her delight in listening to Guillaume. She told him so, quite simply. The illuminator smiled his quaint smile.

"Sometimes when she is very weary the Queen sends for me to sing to her. I know so many ballads and roundelays . . . and also many of the songs of her native Aragon! I like to sing for her because she is a great and noble lady, and her heart is generous!"

As he spoke he deftly removed Catherine's unpleasant smelling head covering. Her hair, now a glossy black, was washed and rubbed dry with a succession of towels after which Guillaume went to get a small bundle from a nearby coffer. From it he took some long black locks which he compared with the rest of Catherine's hair, and then, satisfied with the result, pinned the hair-piece carefully in among her own curls. He motioned to Sara to follow his movements carefully.

120

"More than one fine lady whose hair is growing thinner with the years has had recourse to this little stratagem as well as a dip in my dye bath."

Then, very carefully, he drew in Catherine's eyebrows with some dark cosmetic from a little silver box and brushed a little more over her eyelashes.

"They are very thick and dark already but I think it might be as well to blacken them still further," he said. "You know you really look very beautiful like this?"

Sara and Tristan gazed open-mouthed and speechless at the transformation. Guillaume fetched a hand miror which lay upon a table in the corner and handed it to Catherine without a word. The young woman gave a startled exclamation. It was her in the reflection, and yet again it was someone quite different. Her black lashes and brows made her violet eyes look darker, dark curls drooped over her forehead and her lips were redder. And her teeth flashed dazzlingly white in her tanned face. She was not more beautiful than before exactly, but it was a different sort of beauty, more perverse, more dangerous too perhaps, and Tristan contemplated the change in her with undisguised satisfaction.

"He will find it hard to resist her!" he said calmly. "You have worked well, Maître Guillaume. Take this . . . and remember to hold your tongue."

He held out a fat purse, but to his great surprise the little man gently refused the proffered payment.

"No," he said quietly.

"What? Don't you expect any payment for your trouble?"

"Yes . . . but not that sort of payment!" He turned to Catherine who was still looking at herself in the mirror.

"I have enough gold already. If this lovely lady would grant me the pleasure of kissing her hand I should consider myself repaid a hundredfold."

Impulsively, quite forgetting her earlier repugnance, Catherine held out her hand to him.

"Many thanks, Maître Guillaume. You have done me a service I shall not readily forget."

"A little place in your memory will make me the happiest of men. And in your prayers too . . . for I have great need of them!"

Before Catherine went to dress he presented her with a little silver box containing the black cosmetic, also another containing a sort of thick creamy substance colored bright red, and a little bottle.

"The red ointment is to darken your lips with. Those gypsy girls look as if fire ran in their veins, and your own lips are too soft a pink. This little bottle holds a scent which is strongly impregnated with musk. Be careful how much you use of it; it only needs a little to set a man's blood aflame."

It was close on midnight by the time Catherine and her two companions reached the little postern gate of the castle. They had traversed the narrow streets and alleys of the town without meeting a living soul, only a black cat which slipped mewing across their path and set Sara crossing herself vigorously.

"A bad omen!" she mumbled. But Catherine had resolved to close her ears to this sort of pessimistic talk. Ever since leaving Guillaume's house she had felt like a new woman. In this new guise of hers she was no longer a Montsalvy whose name might risk being sullied in the dangerous paths which she must soon enter, but a new person whose name did not matter. She would not be Catherine de Montsalvy again till her revenge was complete. Then she could remove the last traces of her disguise with spirits of wine, as Guillaume had instructed her, cut off the black curls which felt as artificial as the false ones he had given her, and then return to her deep mourning and her own country of Auvergne, there to live the rest of her days as close as possible to her beloved husband.

But the first thing she did when she got back to her room was to strip off her clothes and stand in front of a tall mirror of polished silver where she could see herself reflected from head to foot. Her skin was now the same dark tone as Sara's, though a little more golden. It was smooth and shone faintly in the glow of the oil lamp like bronze satin. Her dark skin made her figure look more slender and supple. The long black locks undulated like fine serpents down below her waist. Her crimson lips burned in her brown face and her eyes shone, dark stars glowing beneath black, arched brows.

"You look like a she-devil!" Sara murmured.

"And a she-devil I shall be till the man I hate is brought down!"

"Have you thought of all the other men you are going to attract, who will stop at nothing now that you have no name and rank to protect you. Now you are nothing but a common gypsy girl, a creature to rape or hang as one sees fit, or send to the stake for the treacherous, accursed wretch that she is!"

"I know. And I shall defend myself with such weapons as I have. I am prepared to stoop to any means to achieve my ends."

"Would you give yourself to a man if it were necessary?" Sara asked her solemnly.

"To the executioner himself if necessary. I am Catherine de Montsalvy no longer. I am a girl of your race. And my name . . . what *is* my name to be?"

Sara thought for a moment, with her eyes shut. Then she gave her verdict.

"I shall call you Tchalai . . . which means 'star' in our tongue . . . but until we get there you are still Catherine, as you always were! Oh dear, I don't like this adventure of yours at all!"

Catherine turned away and cried fiercely:

"What about me! Do you think *I* like it? But I know that until I do what I have set out to do I shall have no rest, either in this life or the next! I must avenge Arnaud, avenge the destruction of Montsalvy, avenge my impoverished son! Otherwise what point will there be in living?"

The next morning Catherine was sitting quietly on a stool while Sara pinned on her false curls and plaited them when there was a knock at the door. Sara went to open it. Tristan L'Hermite appeared on the threshold. He took several paces forward into the room, till the pale rays of sunlight fell upon him through the tall windows and showed that he was terrifyingly, deathly pale. The two women instinctively drew closer together.

"You are as white as a sheet!" Catherine stammered. "What is the matter with you?"

"Nothing is the matter with *me!* But Guillaume the Illuminator was strangled during the night in his house. His maid found his body this morning . . . and it seems he was tortured before he died!" A terrible silence fell when he had spoken. Catherine felt the blood drain away from her face and limbs but she recovered enough to ask faintly:

"Do you think it was . . . because of us?"

Tristan shrugged and collapsed unceremoniously on to a stool. His face was so haggard with doubt and anxieties that he seemed to have aged ten years. Without a word Sara went to the dresser, poured out a goblet of wine and handed it to him.

"Drink this. You need it."

He took the goblet gratefully and drained it at a gulp. Catherine had clasped her hands round her knees to stop them trembling and now she fought hard to stem her rising panic.

"Tell me honestly," she said in a voice which she forced to remain calm. "Do you think it was because of the work he did for us?"

Tristan L'Hermite flung up his hands in a gesture of ignorance.

"Who knows? Guillaume undoubtedly had enemies, for not all his activities were above board. More than one young woman in childbirth must have been discreetly delivered by those dexterous hands you admired yesterday. It is possible that this is just a case of coincidence."

"But that isn't what you think, is it?"

"To be frank I don't know what to think. But I wanted to warn you first and find out what you feel. You might decide to change your plans, and in that case I must convoke the council again."

He was about to get to his feet but Catherine stopped him with a quick movement.

"No, wait! I admit I was frightened just now! But I'm all right now. You were so pale, you know! I don't want to go back now. It's too late. The plan is a good one and I shall go through with it as we agreed. But you can give it up if you like. . . ."

The Fleming's stolid face twisted into an appalling grimace.

"What sort of coward do you take me for, Dame Catherine? When I take something on I always see it through, whatever the consequences. And I have no desire to find myself thrown into a dungeon on the orders of Milord Constable. If you agree I think we should set out tonight. I have a safe-conduct which will open the town gates for us. It would be as well for no one to see us leave. And it would be best if you stayed in your room all today. Rest . . . you will need all the strength you can muster. The Queen will be coming to see you here tonight, after vespers. . . ."

"Very well. I had no intention of acting otherwise."

"In that case . . . may I tell Monsieur Breze that you are unwell and cannot see anyone?" Tristan gestured with his thumb towards the door. "He is out there in the corridor, pacing up and down."

"Tell him anything you like . . . say that I'll see him tomorrow."

The Fleming smiled thinly in reply to her chuckle and the atmosphere seemed magically lightened all of a sudden. Sara alone remained sunk in gloom.

"We are walking straight into a trap, Catherine," she said. "Surely you realize that?"

But Catherine merely shrugged impatiently and picked up her mirror again.

"Well, what of it?" she said harshly.

CHAPTER SEVEN

The Gypsies

"And that is the lair from which we must flush our prey!" Tristan said, using his whip to point out the castle on the other bank of the river.

The three riders had halted on the right bank of the Loire, near the old Roman bridge, to examine the lie of the land. Catherine, tightly buttoned into a boy's costume in brown frieze which left only her tanned face showing under the hood, stared hard and long at the rocky spur, which crouched alongside the river like a sleeping lion, and the fortress on its summit. Black walls, ten or so massive towers encircling a formidable keep, war engines and machicolations which had the air of being put to frequent use: all this was in strange contrast to the riverside scenery in its tender green spring verdure. The only note of gaiety in the whole somber edifice was a cluster of banners streaming out over the walls, surmounted by the brilliant colors of the royal standard.

Sara threw back her friar's hood and stared mistrustfully up at the castle.

"If we ever get in there we shan't be allowed out alive."

"We have escaped from worse places than that! What about Champtoce and Gilles de Rais!"

"Thank you! Small danger of forgetting that Milord Bluebeard who wanted to roast me alive!" said Sara, shuddering. "The whole time we were at Angers I kept reminding myself that we were no distance at all from there. But now that we have reached our destination what do we do next?"

Tristan wheeled round in the saddle and pointed out a small inn which stood facing the bridge some way down the road. Its green, yellow and red sign proclaimed that the Royal Wine-Press served the best Vouvray wine in the province.

"Go in there and wait for me. I have to speak to the leader of the tribe. Make yourselves comfortable there, rest, order a meal if you wish, but don't drink too much! Vouvray wine is pleasant but it goes to your head."

"We aren't drunkards!" Sara protested.

"Heaven forbid . . . reverend sir! But monks have such a bad reputation! Whatever you do don't leave the place before I get back."

While the pseudo-monk and pseudo-squire went to tether their horses in front of the Royal Wine-Press, Tristan set off across the bridge and was soon lost from sight. The little inn was empty and the innkeeper hastened to attend to these unexpected guests. There was still some pork left in the salt-press, and besides that he could offer them some cabbage soup which, washed down with some of the celebrated wine, made a very adequate meal. It was midday and the two women were ravenous. When they had eaten they felt much restored, and Sara was able to look at things in a more optimistic light.

Tristan returned at nightfall. He seemed weary and anxious, but there was an encouraging glow in his blue eyes. He refused to say a word till he had drunk a cup of wine because, he explained, his "throat was as dry as tinder and it only needed a spark to set it alight." Catherine watched him drink, positively consumed with impatience. At length she burst out:

"Well?"

Tristan set down his cup, wiped his mouth on his sleeve and darted her a mocking look.

"Are you in such a hurry to walk into the lion's jaws then?"

"In a great hurry," the young woman said dryly. "And I want an answer."

"Be of good cheer then; it is all arranged. In one sense you are lucky . . . but only in one sense, because, to put it mildly, relations are pretty strained between castle and gypsy camp just at present."

"What tribe are these gypsies from, first of all?" Sara asked. "Did you think of asking?"

"You are lucky there . . . they are Kalderas, so you should be delighted. They call themselves Christians and claim to have a Bull from Pope Martin V, who died two years ago. That does not, however, prevent their leader, Fero, from calling himself Duke of Egypt."

As he spoke Sara's eyes brightened and when he had finished she clapped her hands delightedly.

"They are my own people! In that case I am sure of a welcome!"

"You may rest assured of that, Dame Sara. The chief is the only one who knows the truth about Dame Catherine. As far as the rest of the tribe are concerned she will be your

126

niece, who was sold into slavery with you when she was but a child."

"What does the chief think of my scheme?" Catherine asked.

Tristan's face clouded.

"He will give you all the help in his power. Hate consumes him. La Trémoille's caprice keeps him cooped up in his camp by the castle walls, because it so happens the Lord Chamberlain enjoys watching the gypsy girls dance. Yesterday, however, one of his men was caught stealing from a hen roost and he was hanged this morning. If he were not afraid that his people would be pursued and put to death along the highway, Fero would flee tomorrow. To that extent then, you are in luck but in another way you will find yourself less well off. . . ."

"Never mind. I must go there whatever happens!"

"The weather is cold still. You will have to go barefoot, sleep in the open or at best in a rude cart, live rough and . . ."

Catherine burst out laughing so abruptly that he broke off.

"Don't be silly, Messire Tristan. If you knew more about my life you would know that none of that frightens me at all. Enough talk now! Let's get ready!"

As soon as they had paid their bill the three conspirators left the inn and set off towards the bridge. The weather had grown milder during the past two days, and though the night was damp it was not cold. Catherine flung her hood back and shook her plaits free. Her old fighting spirit was returning to her. The silence of the night was broken only by the silken rustling of the water in the reeds and the plodding hoof-beats of their own steeds. A heartening smell of damp earth met Catherine's nostrils and she breathed in once and then again. The bridge took them first of all to a small wooded island where a faint light glowed. During the day Catherine had observed the little chapel of St. Jean which stood there, and the little hermitage which stood leaning against it. This chapel must belong to the hermit. On the far side of the island another bridge led as far as the foot of the castle mound and now Catherine could discern the glow of firelight in the trenches around the castle: the gypsy camp must still be wide awake.

Occasionally a lighted torch passed along the battlements like a shooting star, carried aloft by a sergeant of the watch making a tour of inspection, and as they drew nearer they could hear the cries of the sentinels calling from tower to tower. All Catherine could see of the little town of Amboise, enclosed within its walls in the shadow of the rocky spur, was a dim shadow stretching southwards. Up above the cloudy sky shone lighter here and there indicating the moon.

The three riders halted by the trench, and for a moment Catherine stared down wide-eyed, half believing herself looking into the pit of hell. A fire blazed in the middle of the camp and the whole tribe sat round the fire, squatting on the ground. They sat in a strange sort of immobility, but a weird lament issued from all those closed mouths, a dull, monotonous sound, emphasized from time to time by the dry staccato rhythm of tambours held by some of the men of the tribe.

The red-gold flames flickered over bronzed countenances, some of them tattooed. The women, most of them dressed in rags, had greasy, shining black hair, full lips, thin aquiline noses and blazing eyes, even the old women whose skins were wrinkled into more furrows and folds than an old parchment. Some of them wore turbans, primitive jewelry . . . some were beautiful, as their loosely fastened chemises of coarse cloth generously testified. The men were terrifying.

They were filthy, ragged, with crinkly, woolly hair and long mustaches where their teeth flashed brilliantly white. They wore tattered hats or dented helmets—pillaged off corpses or discovered along the highways—on their heads. They all wore heavy silver rings in their ears. Those motionless faces, those glittering eyes fastened on the glowing heart of the fire, that incessant keening noise of theirs . . . all this sent a shudder along Catherine's spine. She glanced round at Sara and seeing she was about to speak the gypsy put her finger swiftly to her lips.

"Don't say a word," she whispered so softly that Catherine could only just hear, "or move just yet!"

"Why?" Tristan asked, equally softly.

"This is a funeral rite. They must be waiting to receive the body of the man who was hanged this morning."

Just then, in fact, they saw a small procession wending its way down the mound from the castle towards the camp. A tall thin man went on ahead holding a torch aloft to light the way for his four companions who bore a motionless body on their shoulders. The man with the torch was dressed in tight, scarlet hose and a doublet of the same color, though considerably stained and torn, which still bore traces of gold embroidery. The broken laces of the doublet gaped open displaying a brown torso naked to the waist, whose glistening, rippling muscles testified to considerable strength. The man was young and arrogant looking. The long, fine black mustache which outlined his red lips accentuated their cruel curve, and his dark eyes slanted up towards the temples, indicating his Asiatic origins. He had thick black hair falling to his shoulders.

"That is Fero, their chieftain," Tristan whispered.

The funeral lament ceased when the four men deposited their burden in front of the fire. The gypsies were on their feet now. A few women came and knelt by the body. One of them, so aged and wrinkled that she seemed only skin and bone, began to sing in a ghastly cracked voice. It was a sort of dirge whose melodic line kept being interrupted. When the old woman stopped another woman, this time a young one, took it up.

"The dead man's wife and mother," Sara whispered. "They are extolling his virtues. . . ."

The ceremony after that was brief. The chief bent and slipped a coin between the dead man's teeth, then the four men shouldered their burden once more and clambered down to the river. A moment later the corpse was floating away on the dark water.

"It is over," Sara said. "The man has gone, along the river road, to join his ancestors. . . ."

"We can approach then," said Tristan, "because . . ."

But then he broke off. For without warning Sara had begun to sing. Catherine was so startled she jumped. It was a long time since she had heard Sara sing, at least the way she was singing now. Of course she had often hummed old ballads to put little Michel to sleep, but these weird, ancient chants, which seemed to be handed down from earliest times, with their wild, incomprehensible rhythms and cadences, Catherine herself had only heard twice before on Sara's lips. Once in the tavern of Jacquot-de-la-Mer in Dijon, and once again by the camp fire of the gypsy tribe who had taken Sara away with them for a while, long ago. A lump rose in her throat as she listened. Sara's full, powerful voice seemed to fill the night and carry with it echoes of the faraway land from which this strange woman had come. . . . The whole tribe had turned to listen, entranced. . . .

Slowly, and without stopping her song, Sara started off down the slope towards the camp fire. Catherine and Tristan followed, the latter leading their horses by the bridle-reins, and the ranks of gypsies broke to let them pass. It was not till she reached the leader himself that Sara fell silent.

"I am Black Sara," she said simply, "and I am your blood-brother. This is my niece Tchalai and this man here has led us to you through many perils and dangers. Will you take us in?"

Fero slowly raised his hands and laid them upon Sara's shoulders.

"You are welcome, sister! The man who brings you did not lie. You are one of us, your blood is pure, for you know the old ritual songs which are known only to the best among us. As for her . . ." his black eyes fell upon Catherine who felt suddenly as if she were being consumed by their brilliance, "her beauty will be the jewel of our tribe. Come, the women will attend to your needs. . . ."

He bowed before Sara as if she were a queen, and led Tristan towards the fire, while a chattering ring of women closed around the two new arrivals. Catherine was bewildered and deafened by the noise and she allowed herself to be led towards the few caravans grouped round the foot of one of the towers. An hour later she was lying between Sara and old Orka, mother of the hanged man, trying to get warm and at the same time to put some order into her thoughts. Tristan had gone back to the inn of the Royal Wine-Press where he planned to remain, in easy reach of his accomplices, but not connected in any obvious way with the gypsy camp. He took Catherine's and Sara's clothes with him. The two women's first move had been to dress themselves anew in such clothes as could be found for them in the gypsies' caskets and chests. Now Catherine was dressed in nothing more than a long chemise of rough linen, which chafed her skin, and a curious striped length of cloth which she wore draped round her in the style of a Roman toga. It was not too tattered, and passably clean. Catherine's feet were bare. She huddled closer to Sara and folded her feet under herself, trying to get warm. She would have given anything for a straw mattress, but the best this crude shelter with its leaky roof could offer was a thin layer of rags on the floor to keep out the draft. She sighed. Sara felt her moving about and whispered:

"No regrets?"

Catherine could hardly ignore the irony of this question. She clenched her teeth.

"No regrets . . . but I'm cold!"

"You'll soon get used to it. Besides the fine weather will be here again soon."

Catherine said nothing. She couldn't help feeling that Sara was not as sympathetic as she might have been. She was probably not finding it all that easy to adapt herself to the hard life of a gypsy encampment either. But there was a sort of tranquil contentment in her voice, the peace that comes of returning to one's deepest origins. Catherine vowed that she would not fail in this task she had assigned herself. She did not want to lose face in front of Sara. So she rolled herself a little more tightly in her coverlet, taking good care to wrap her icy feet up, and murmured a vague good night. Old Orka slept beside her as motionless and silent as if she were dead.

The following morning Catherine had to mingle with the tribe and this gave her a chance to measure their poverty. The camp fires of the night before had given a sort of flattering glow to the shabby caravans and filthy clothes and faces. Daylight exposed the half-naked children and skinny animals —dogs, cats and horses—wandering about the encampment in search of a morsel of food, and it also showed up the gypsy life for what it really was.

In order to live, some of them wove baskets of rushes from the river-bank, but most of them were tinkers by trade. Their equipment was as rudimentary as could be imagined: three stones roughly shaped into a hearth, a pig-skin bellows and another stone as anvil. As for the womenfolk, they read palms and cooked and swaggered about the place, rolling their hips in a provocative manner. The mode of dress astonished Catherine. It was not unusual to come across a woman going about her chores with her breasts quite bare, but they all hid their legs right down to their toes.

"Modesty, in our tribe, means hiding the legs," Sara remarked, with dignity. "The breasts mean only one thing to us —feeding babies!"

Be that as it might, Catherine thought, the men all looked like demons with their wild eyes and white teeth and their women were shameless she-devils when young, and sinister old crones when they grew old. She admitted to herself that she was afraid of them.

And most of all, perhaps, of tall Fero. The chieftain's fierce face seemed to grow fiercer still when he looked at her. His black eyes gleamed like a cat's then, and he bit his lips nervously. But he never spoke to her and when he crossed her path he walked slowly by, turning round occasionally to watch her go.

Catherine felt completely out of her element, and in desperation she clung to Sara who moved about the encampment with regal confidence. Everyone treated her with awe, and Catherine benefited from this, realizing that without Sara there to protect her she would have met with scant respect, belated gypsy that she was, unable even to speak their common tongue. To put a stop to questions Sara had the forethought to imply that Catherine was a little touched in the head. . . .

This was obviously a sensible move, but all the same Catherine grew a little weary of seeing the gypsies fall silent as she came near and then follow her with their eyes as she went by. She felt as if she were hedged round by glances, in which she could read many things: envy and mockery in the women's, sly desire in most of the men's.

"These people don't like me," she told Sara after three days had passed. "They would never have accepted me if you had not been here."

"They sense something foreign and strange about you," the gypsy explained, "and this surprises and alarms them. They think you may be some kind of supernatural being, but they don't quite know what. Some of them think you might be a keshalyi, a good fairy, who will bring them good luck—that is what Fero is trying to convince them—but others say you have the evil eye. The latter are mostly women, and it is because they know their men want you and this frightens them."

"What can I do about it?"

Sara shrugged and nodded towards the château whose black bulk loomed over them.

"Wait. I dare say it won't be long before the Seigneur de la Trémoille sends for more dancing girls. Two of the tribeswomen have been up there more than a week now. Fero says it is not customary for them to remain there that long. He thinks they may have been killed!"

"And he . . . just allows that to happen?" Catherine protested, her mouth suddenly dry with fear.

"What can he do? He is afraid, like everyone else here. All he can do is obey and give up his women, however much he may hate it. He knows quite well that if the Lord Chamberlain took it into his head to line a company of archers up along the battlements and order them to shoot at the camp no one would try to stop him, particularly not the townspeople, who fear the gypsies as much as they do the devil!"

Sara's voice was bitter. Catherine realized that Sara shared Fero's anger that the women sacrificed to La Trémoille's pleasure should be of their race. She longed to comfort her.

"It won't last long now! Let's pray heaven that they send for me soon!"

"Do you think I'd pray for something that would endanger you?" Sara said sadly. "You must be mad!"

But Catherine thought continually of the moment when the Lord Chamberlain's caprice should finally bring them face to face. Every evening while they sat round the camp fire after their communal meal, she watched carefully as the gypsy girls danced so that she would be able to imitate them when the time came. The chief never spoke to her, but she knew that it was for her sake that he made them dance every night and sometimes, often, she felt his heavy, dark, inscrutable gaze fasten upon her.

She had, however, made two friends among the women of the tribe. There was old Orka first of all, who never spoke but would sit for hours at a time staring at her, nodding her head. They said that her son's death had started her mind wandering but Catherine found it comforting to look at this friendly old face. The other friend was Fero's own sister, Tereina, who must have been about twenty. But unfortunately she had been left crippled and hump-backed as the result of a fall when she was a child and she looked little more than twelve. Her face was unattractive, but one forgot this looking at her eyes, two huge, luminous black lakes which seemed to see further and deeper than anyone else's.

Tereina came to Catherine the day after she arrived in the camp. Silently, with a shy smile, she held out a duck whose neck she had wrung with her own hands. Catherine realized that this was a gift to welcome her into the tribe and she thanked her. But she couldn't help adding:

"Where did you get it?"

"Over there," the girl said, "near the abbey pond."

"It is kind of you to give it to me but do you know what you risk in taking other people's property?"

Tereina's eyes widened in astonishment.

"What other people? Didn't the Lord create animals to feed men? Why should some men keep them for themselves alone?"

Catherine found her logic unanswerable. She shared the duck, when it had been roasted, with Tereina. Since then the girl had attached herself to her, and she was a great help to Catherine in her new role. The chief's sister had a special place in the tribe. She knew about herbs and simples, and because of this skill of hers she was the drabarni, the herbalist, who knows how to cure illness, take the sting from death, and make people fall in love. This earned her the slightly nervous respect of the whole tribe.

The fourth day, at dusk, Fero did not summon the two women to his camp fire to share his meal as he had done on the other evenings. They stayed sitting round old Orka's cooking-pot, eating the stew of barley and bacon strongly flavored with wild garlic which she had prepared. The camp was silent and dreary for there was still no news of the two girls who had gone up to the château. And ten of the men had gone off to fish in the Loire some distance away, so that they would not run the risk of falling into the royal forest wardens' hands. They would not be returning for two or three days. Fero had withdrawn into his own caravan, where he remained invisible. This night there would be neither singing nor dancing. All that day the sky had been covered with black clouds. It had been unusually hot for the time of year. A thunderstorm seemed to be on the way and Catherine found it hard to breathe. She had barely touched the greasy stew whose powerful smell made her feel slightly sick. She was about to climb into her caravan to sleep when Tereina appeared by the fire. Her twisted body was swathed in a length of crimson cloth and her pale face looked almost ghostly in the darkness. Sara pointed to a place beside her but the girl's eyes were fixed on Catherine.

"My brother wants to see you, Tchalai! I am going to take you to him."

"What does he want?" Sara said quickly, rising to her feet.

"How would I know? The chief commands and must be obeyed."

"I go with her."

"Fero sent for Tchalai, not Tchalai and Sara. Come, sister. He does not like to be kept waiting."

The girl stepped back into the shadows. Then Catherine followed the little red phantom without a word. One behind the other they crossed the silent camp. The fires were burning low by now and the Tziganes were preparing for sleep. But suddenly, as the chief's caravan with its large wheels appeared before them, an oil lamp glowing inside it, Tereina stopped and turned towards Catherine. She saw the gypsy-girl's huge eyes glitter in the darkness.

"Tchalai, my sister, you know that I love you," she said gravely.

"I believe you do. You have always been kind to me anyway."

"That is because I love you. But tonight I want to prove it to you. Here . . . take this and drink it!"

She took a little flask from her dress and handed it to Catherine. It was still warm where she had been holding it.

"What is it?" Catherine asked, suddenly suspicious.

"Something you badly need. I see that your heart is as cold as a dead woman's heart, Tchalai, and I want your heart to come to life again. This will do it. Drink without fear . .

unless of course you don't trust me," she said, and so sadly that Catherine's suspicions melted.

"I trust you, Tereina," she said, "but why tonight?"

"Because you will need it tonight. Drink without fear. It is made of health-giving herbs. You will feel neither weary nor sad. I made this mixture for you . . . because I love you."

An impulse stronger than herself made Catherine put the little flask to her lips. It gave off a strong but not unpleasant smell of herbs. She was no longer afraid. One does not offer poison to someone in that tender tone of voice. . . . She drank the contents down in a single swallow and then coughed. It felt like a perfumed flame coursing through her, and she felt stronger and happier in an instant. She smiled at the girl's anxious face.

"There. Now are you happy?"

Tereina squeezed her hand gently and smiled in her turn. "Yes . . . go now! He is waiting for you."

Just then Fero's black shape loomed up darkly in the door of the caravan. Tereina disappeared as if by magic and Catherine, feeling suddenly twice as brave, went up to the chief's caravan. He held out a hand without speaking and helped her up into the caravan, and then let down the cloth flap behind them. Just then a flash of lightning lit up the sky as far as the horizon, and there was a crash of thunder. Catherine gave a little start of surprise, and Fero's white teeth glittered between red lips.

"Are you afraid of the storm?"

"No, I was just surprised. Why should I be afraid?"

Another, still louder, crash of thunder interrupted her. And almost at once the rain started falling, torrential rain which rattled on the caravan's roof like a tattoo on a drum. Fero went and lay down on the folded blankets where he slept. He had taken off his red doublet and wore nothing but his scarlet hose. The light from the oil lamp made his brown skin and long black hair gleam. His eyes never left Catherine who stood near the doorway. He smiled again, slowly, and somewhat mockingly.

"Truly I think you cannot be afraid of much, since you have come here tonight. . . . Do you know why I sent for you?"

"I imagine you will soon tell me."

"Exactly. I wanted to tell you that five of my men have already asked for your hand in marriage. They are ready to fight for possession of you. You will have to choose which man you want to take bread and salt and break the betrothal bowl with."

Catherine drew herself up, and instantly reverted to a more formal manner.

"You must be out of your mind! Have you forgotten who I am and why I am here? I want to get into the château; that's the only thing I'm interested in."

A cruel light flared in the gypsy chief's eyes and he shrugged.

"I have not forgotten anything. You are a great lady, I know that! But you wanted to live amongst us and willy-nilly you must abide by our customs and rules. When many men desire one woman she must make a choice between them, unless she prefers them to fight, in which case she will belong to the victor. My men are all brave and you are beautiful: the fight will be fierce."

An angry flush rose to Catherine's cheeks. This insolent boy, outstretched half-naked before her, was disposing of her person with outrageous cynicism.

"You can't force me to make this choice! Messire Tristan . . ."

"Your companion? He would never dare interfere in my people's customs. If you want to remain here you must live like a real gypsy-girl, or at least appear to. None of my subjects would allow a gypsy in this tribe to evade the tribal laws."

"But I don't want to do this," Catherine cried tearfully. "Can't you spare me this? I will give you money . . . anything you like! I can't belong to any of those men. I don't want them to fight for me, I don't want them to!"

She wrung her hands together in unconscious supplication and turned huge tear-wet eyes upon him. Something softened in the chief's fierce countenance.

"Come here," he said gently.

She didn't move, but went on looking at him uncomprehendingly. He repeated, more harshly:

"Come here!"

When she remained petrified, he leaned forward and stretched out an arm. His hand seized Catherine's arm and with a quick jerk he pulled her down on her knees beside him. She gave a cry of pain and he laughed:

"For someone who is never afraid you are a pretty spectacle now! But I won't hurt you. Listen to me, beautiful lady, noble lady . . . I too am noble! I am the Duke of Egypt and in my veins flows the blood of the Master of the World, the conqueror before whom even kings bowed down!"

His hand moved slowly up Catherine's bare arm till it reached her shoulder and held it. She could see him very

136

close to her now and she was amazed by the fineness of his brown skin, and the glitter of his black eyes fascinated her. His hand was warm against her arm and suddenly her own blood took fire. . . . Her eyes clouded, and waves of hot desire rolled over her body. Suddenly she found herself longing for this hand, now caressing her shoulder, to go further. . . .

Appalled by this imperious, primitive longing for love which surged through her she started back, and would have fled, but the imprisoning hand held her fast.

"What do you want?" she murmured with a catch in her voice.

The hand slid down her arm again and pulled her closer. The chief's hot breath burned on her lips.

"There is one way for you to escape belonging to my men, and one way only. The chief's property is sacrosanct!"

She tried to laugh scornfully but was dismayed by how unconvincing she sounded.

"So now we get to the point!"

"Well, and why not? But my men's demands are real enough. And I might add that if you insist on the combat I shall fight for possession of you myself."

The gypsy's grip forced her down, till she was almost lying across his chest. He leaned forward and his lips brushed across her face.

"Look at me, beautiful lady! Tell me where I'm so different from those lords and nobles you go with? The Lord Chamberlain, to whom you may have to give yourself, is fat and repulsive. He is aging now and love is a difficult game for him. But I am young and my body is strong. I can make love to you night after night without wearying. So why not choose me?"

His hoarse voice had a hypnotic effect. Catherine's trembling body was burning and raging with desire. She discovered with horror that she didn't want to resist, that she wanted to hear more, that she was hungry for love. . . . The urge she felt to fling herself on to this man was so violent, and so animal, that Catherine's blood ran cold. In a flash she realized what Tereina had given her to drink. A love potion! Some hellish concoction designed to make her submissive and consenting to the gypsy chief's demands!

A surge of pride came to her aid. She tore herself out of his arms and staggered across the caravan, gripping hold of anything she could find to steady herself with. She leaned against the wall. The wood felt rough against her skin, and the wet canvas roof smelled unpleasantly damp. She was shaking violently and she had to clench her teeth to stop them

137

chattering. A prayer rose up from the depths of her desperate heart, while her hand sought feverishly at her waist for the dagger with the sparrow-hawk, Arnaud's dagger, which she usually wore. But Tchalai the gypsy girl did not wear a dagger and her hand found nothing but a handful of coarse cloth. Fero watched her from where he still crouched in the shadows, like a wild animal, and his eyes were bloodshot.

"Answer me!" he growled. "Why not choose me?"

"Because I don't love you! I can't stand you. . . ."

"Liar! You want it as much as I do. You don't know how wild and cloudy your eyes are, you can't hear yourself panting. . . ."

Catherine cried out angrily:

"It's not true! Tereina gave me some diabolic mixture to drink, and you knew that and you were counting on it! But you won't have me. I don't want you!"

"Do you really believe that?"

He crossed the wagon in one lithe movement and forced his body up against hers, imprisoning her between himself and the wagon wall. She tried to slip sideways but she could scarcely breathe let alone move. And still this fire burned deep down inside her. It was primitive and degrading, this hunger of hers, but at the touch of this man it became uncontrollable. . . . Catherine clenched her teeth and tried to push him away with both hands against his chest.

"Let me go," she panted. "I order you to let me go!"

He laughed softly, his mouth almost on top of hers in spite of her efforts to move her head away.

"Your heart is beating like a drum. But if you 'order' me to let you go, I might obey you . . . I might even summon all the men who want to fight for you; and, since I have no desire to see them lose their lives for the sake of your big eyes, I might tie you up in this chariot and tell them to take their pleasure of you. When they have all had you, at least they would know whether they still wanted to fight for you. I would take you last. . . . Do you still 'order' me to release you?"

A red cloud of fury crossed Catherine's field of vision for a moment. So this man dared to speak of her as a worthless object, no sooner possessed than scorned? Catherine's pride was wounded, and the alternative which Fero painted for her made her blood run cold. All of a sudden Catherine found herself relenting towards her clamoring body. She felt a savage need to tame this insolent savage and reduce him to the passionate slavery to which she had reduced so many men. Besides it was the only means of escape. . . .

138

Abruptly she stopped trying to escape his lips. Fero was surprised at first to find her mouth offering itself to him, then he seized on it avidly. . . . His lips were soft and smelled of thyme. Triumphantly, Catherine felt them tremble slightly, but her triumph was short lived. That damned philtre had unloosed all the powers of hell within her. She could hold out no longer. Her heart banged wildly against her ribs. The fury in her blood seemed to be choking her, and her hips were already vibrating under the gypsy's touch. Nothing would have checked Fero's frenzy now; he was deaf and blind to everything but this woman's body he clasped against his own.

Catherine closed her eyes and gave herself up to the storm. But she gripped the gypsy's damp shoulders with both hands and murmured:

"Love me, Fero, with all your strength . . . but make me forget everything, even who I am . . . or I'll never forgive you!"

He dropped down to the floor by way of answer, pulling her down with him. The two of them rolled together, clasped in each other's arms, across the filthy floor.

All that night the storm raged, buffeting the caravans, tearing at the trees, snatching tiles from roofs and forcing the archers on guard round the battlements to crouch for shelter behind the merlons. But in their caravan neither Catherine nor Fero heard a thing. The man's passion was ceaselessly renewed, and the woman met it with this strange madness of the blood which had made a shameless bacchante of her, a creature crying out for very passion in the frenzy of her desire.

When the first light crept stealthily along the river, touching the storm-swept banks with its wan, misty glow, the damp freshness of the countryside at dawn seeped through the entrance to the caravan and bathed the sweaty bodies of the two lovers. Catherine awoke with a shiver from the heavy slumber into which she and Fero had both fallen a few moments before. She felt deathly tired. Her head was spinning and her mouth was as bitter as if she had drunk too much. With a colossal effort she managed to push her lover's tall body away without even waking him, and got to her feet. Everything seemed to whirl round her and she had to clutch at the sides of the caravan to stop herself falling. Her legs trembled and her stomach was cold with nausea. A cold sweat beaded her temples and she closed her eyes for a moment. The sickness passed but the craving for sleep returned and it was almost impossible to fight it off.

She groped about for her chemise and struggled into it,

then she snatched up her striped outer garment and stepped out of the caravan. The rain had stopped but long scarves of yellow mist lay along the river. The ground was soaked, and tree-branches which had been wrenched off by the storm were strewn about everywhere. Catherine's bare feet sank into soft squelching mud. She took three steps forward, and became dimly aware, through half-shut lids, of a reddish shape crouched beneath a caravan. As she came nearer it stirred and sat up. She recognized Tereina. The girl watched her approach and her face was alight with triumph. Then Catherine remembered all that had happened to her and that this girl was responsible. . . . Her anger shocked her into wakefulness. She flung herself on the gypsy girl and seized her red shawl:

"What did you make me drink?" she cried. "I command you to tell me. What did you make me drink?"

Tereina's ecstatic smile did not show the slightest trace of fear.

"It was love you drank. . . . I gave you my strongest love potion to make your heart warm to the fire which burns in my brother's breast for you. Now you belong to him . . . and you will be happy together! You are really my sister now."

With a sigh Catherine let go of the shawl. She bit back the reproaches which crowded to her lips. What was the good? Tereina had no idea of her real identity. To her she was simply a gypsy-girl like herself, a refugee whom her brother desired, and she had hoped to make them both happy by flinging her into Fero's arms. She did not know that love and desire can be hostile brothers.

The gypsy-girl took her hand and laid it against her cheek in an adoring gesture.

"I know that you were happy . . ." she whispered. "I listened all night long . . . and I was happy, too!"

Catherine felt her face crimson. The recollection of all that had occurred during that diabolical night filled her with burning shame. She saw herself again, Catherine de Montsalvy, delirious with pleasure under the lips of a vagabond. And she hated herself for it now. Certainly the love potion had played an aphrodisiac part in the affair. But Catherine was none the less aware of a strange duality in her nature. This wanton creature whom the philtre had roused to such abandon must really exist somewhere within her. It was she who had found such pleasure in the arms of Philippe of Burgundy, who would have yielded herself to MacLaren if Gauthier had not intervened, she who felt these strange, troubled reactions at

140

the touch of certain men, she, finally, who silenced the cries of a heart that belonged to her husband alone to gratify an urgent, overmastering desire for physical love. . . . The mud her feet was sinking into now was no thicker or slimier than the wretched clay which human nature was composed of.

Gently she laid her hand on Tereina's head as she knelt at her feet.

"Go to sleep now," she said softly. "You are wet, and cold . . ."

"But you are happy, aren't you, Tchalai? Are you really happy?"

One last effort to spare the heart of this poor innocent. "Yes . . ." Catherine murmured, "very happy."

Fighting back her tears, Catherine went heavy-hearted on her way, losing herself in the mist as if she wanted to hide her shame. She went down to the river oblivious of the pebbles cutting into her feet, and did not stop till the water was lapping round her bare feet.

The Loire was gray and merged into the swollen sky, but here and there were streaks of almost imperceptible golden light. The water seethed and swirled past, swollen by the night's rain, bursting with renewed vigor. Catherine suddenly longed to plunge into the water. The river-king had always been her friend, and in this sad dawn it seemed quite natural to come to him, to ask him to soothe her stricken heart.

With automatic gestures she let her clothes slide off and stepped deeper into the water. The current was strong and swift and she found it hard to walk along the bottom. The water was cool. When it reached her belly she shivered. Gooseflesh appeared all over her but she pressed on. Soon it reached her shoulders and she closed her eyes. The water seemed to be massaging her body. All that was holding her were her feet which wriggled down into the river-bed. All of a sudden there was a great silence inside her. Perhaps the best thing would be to finish with everything there. Make an end of this hopeless life of hers. So long as she had been pure the struggle had been easy and the victory worth while. But now? She had given herself to a stranger like a common whore, and it was as though she had dug an immense, unbridgeable gulf between herself and her husband's memory. If God ever allowed her to see him again, even once, would she be able to look him in the face without dying of shame? A great sob rose in her throat and two tears squeezed out of her closed lids.

"Arnaud!" she murmured. "Would you forgive me if you knew . . . if you knew . . ."

No, he never would! She was sure of that. She knew his fierce jealousy and passion too well to have the least doubt of that. How could a man who had gone through torture rather than betray her ever understand or accept or forgive? . . . And if that was so, what point was there in struggling further? Even her little Michel did not need her so badly. He had his grandmother's love and when he grew up he would know how to rebuild the Montsalvy fortunes. And it would be so pleasant to abandon herself to this great rushing river, and become a part of it for all eternity . . . so pleasant and so easy! All she had to do was let go of her foothold. Ah yes, it was so easy . . . it was . . .

Catherine's legs were beginning to give. A moment more and the current would have borne her slender form away to that dark, mysterious bourne from which no traveler returns. But then from the river-bank, a frantic, loving voice cried out:

"Catherine! Catherine! Where are you . . . Catherine?"

It was Sara's voice, half-choked with terror. It came to her out of the mist, a heartbreaking call from the very life which Catherine had been so eager to abandon, and it conjured up so many memories that, automatically, Catherine's feet scrambled for a foothold on the bottom. For a fleeting moment she saw her old Sara kneeling on the wet sand, winding a shroud about the body which the river had returned to her. She almost seemed to hear her crying . . . and, brusquely, all her old instinct for survival revived again. She fought against the powerful current with the spirit she thought she had lost forever, and struggled back to the bank, half-swimming, half-walking. As she gradually made her way back to life she caught sight of Sara standing on the river-bank, still calling her.

She stood there, pale with anxiety in her gray cloak, holding Catherine's clothes in her hands, with great tears rolling down her cheeks. When she saw Catherine's dripping form emerging out of the mist she gave a hoarse cry. Catherine stumbled and Sara darted forward and would have held her up but the young woman drew aside.

"Don't touch me!" she cried wearily. "You don't know how I hate myself. I am dirty . . . I make myself sick!"

Sara's broad face softened with pity. In spite of Catherine's protests she took her by the shoulders and rubbed her dry in her own cloak. Then she dressed her again and led her back to the village.

"And it was for that you wanted to die, poor little one? Because a man possessed your body last night? Is it spending

142

a night with Fero which has put you in this state? Must I remind you that all this is only a beginning? You still don't know what awaits you at the château. . . . In thought you were ready to endure anything to bring this wild scheme of yours to a close!"

"But I gave myself of my own free will last night . . . I drank some devilish potion of Tereina's," Catherine cried in anguish. "And I found pleasure in Fero's arms. Pleasure! Do you understand?" she shrieked.

"And what if you did?" Sara interrupted coldly. "It wasn't your fault. You didn't ask for this to happen. What happened to you last night is no more important than a temporary attack of madness . . . or even a cold."

But Catherine would not be consoled. She flung herself down on the hard bed she shared with Sara and sobbed till she was worn out. The weeping did her good. The tears washed away the last fumes of the drugged drink as well as the agonizing shame which had made her break down. At last she was exhausted and fell asleep and slept peacefully until midday. She emerged feeling mentally alert and physically refreshed. Alas, only to learn from old Orka that that very night she was to be wedded to Fero according to the strange rites of the gypsies.

Fortunately for Catherine old Orka disappeared as soon as she had announced what she called "the great news," because the young woman flew into a terrible fury. It was bad enough that Fero should have made her his mistress, but that he should now propose to marry her was a suggestion she rejected so violently, with such a wealth of picturesque epithets, that Sara had to silence her forcibly. Her cries were becoming dangerously audible. Sara seized her and clapped a hand over her mouth.

"Don't be silly, Catherine! It makes no difference at all to you that Fero should want to marry you. If he does not bind you to him, one of the others will have the right to insist that you are given to them. If you refuse, we shall have to flee, and flee at once. But where? How?"

Catherine was growing a little calmer now in Sara's restraining grasp. Now she disengaged herself and asked:

"Why do you say that it makes no difference to me?"

"Because it would not be a real marriage at all, at least not in the way you understand it. The wandering tribes do not bring God into such a simple matter as the coupling of human beings. And besides it is not Catherine de Montsalvy Fero would be taking for his wife, but a phantom, an imaginary creature who will vanish one fine day, a gypsy-girl called Tchalai. . . ."

Catherine shook her head and looked despairingly at Sara. She could not understand how anyone could be so insensitive! She seemed to think it was almost natural. But this marriage made Catherine feel sick with dismay!

"I can't help it," she said. "I have the feeling that I am betraying a trust . . . being unfaithful to Arnaud a second time!"

"Not at all, since you are no longer yourself! Besides, this marriage will give you a secure position in the tribe; no one will mistrust you now!"

In spite of these arguments and exhortations Catherine still had a feeling of sacrilege when she went to join Fero before the great fire where the whole tribe had assembled for the celebrations. The previous day's storm had purged the weather, leaving a great dark blue heaven as soft as velvet. The men had come back from their fishing expedition with full baskets, and the whole camp smelled of fish grilling over hot coals. The muffled beat of drums and tambourines arose. Children danced joyfully round the cooking-pots, and even the babies crowed in their baskets.

All these preparations, and all this joy which followed in her wake, only contributed to Catherine's repugnance. Every fiber of her being cried out in protest against this false ceremony they were leading her into, and she had every reason to fear that the marriage would be followed by a life together, and possibly many shared nights. She found it hard to imagine herself in Fero's caravan serving him the way the other women tended their men, belonging to them body and soul . . . even if God was not a party to the contract! She had a wild desire to flee from this impossible situation, especially now as she no longer trusted Fero. He knew her identity and she had thought him an ally. But he seemed to want to take advantage of the situation. What guarantee was there that he would let her go when they sent for her to come and dance at the château? . . .

Paradoxically, however, in view of her fears, it was her belief in her mission which held her back. For a moment her life was not in danger and she was determined to see the adventure through. But that did not prevent her casting about frantically for a way of escaping from this odious marriage.

The women had dressed Catherine in the most flamboyant finery which the tribe could muster. A length of green silk, slightly frayed but woven with silver thread, was rolled several times round her body which had been stripped of its rough chemise for the occasion. There were silver rings in her ears and they had fastened rows of silver necklaces, some of coins and others of engraved plaques, round her neck and shoulders, one of which was left bare. More coins had been bound round her head in a sort of crown and the women's eyes told her that she was beautiful in this bizarre outfit.

Catherine read further proof of her beauty on Fero's radiant face, in the proud way he looked at her when he came to fetch her and lead her before the phuri dai. This was the oldest woman in the tribe, and because she was also the wisest and the keeper of the old customs, she enjoyed a power almost equal to the chief's. Catherine had never seen a woman who looked so much like a toad, but the phuri dai's small round eyes were as green as spring grass. Black tattoo marks could be seen on her gaunt cheeks and under the straggling gray locks which escaped from her red turban. Catherine could not help looking at her with revulsion, because to her this woman symbolized the marriage which she was being forced into.

The old woman stood in the midst of the tribal elders, and the dancing flames lit up the sharp planes and folds and hollows of her face. The music of fiddle and drums made a sort of circle of sound round the fire, and women's cries and men's singing joined in from time to time. The noise was deafening. When the couple stopped before her, the phuri dai extended two hands, as fragile as birds' claws, from her ragged clothes and took a piece of black bread from a huge bearded gypsy. There was a sudden silence, and Catherine realized that the decisive moment had come. She had to grit her teeth not to cry out and scream with panic. Was she really condemned to see out this sinister farce?

The old crumpled hands broke the bread into two pieces. Then the old woman took a little salt, which was offered to her in a silver cup because this was a rare and highly valued luxury. She sprinkled a little on both pieces of bread and gave one to Catherine and the other to Fero.

"When you weary of this bread and salt you will be weary of each other. Now exchange your pieces of bread."

Catherine was reluctantly impressed by the old woman's solemn manner and she took the piece of bread from Fero, mechanically and they both took a bite from the hard crust. Fero's eyes did not leave the young woman's for a moment, and she had to close her own eyes for a moment to shut off the brutal, primitive passion which stared out at her. . . . Soon she would have to belong to him again, but this time there would be no inclination on her part. She not only did not desire Fero—but her body was already rebelling against what was to follow.

"And now the cruche," said the beldame.

They passed her an earthenware cruche which she broke above their heads with the help of a stone. Several grains of corn fell upon them. And instantly the old woman crouched down and counted them.

"There are seven grains," she said, looking up at Catherine. "For seven years you belong to Fero."

The gypsy-chief sprang forward with a triumphant cry and took Catherine by the shoulders to embrace her. She allowed him to pull her against him while all around triumphant and joyful cries rose up from the tribe. But Fero's lips did not touch Catherine's. In the space of a second it seemed, a girl with night-black locks sprang out of the shadows and tore Catherine from Fero's arms.

"One moment, Fero! I am still here, and you swore to me that I should be your rommi . . . your only wife!"

Catherine almost cried out loud with relief. She was standing several paces away from Fero now, separated by this girl whom she was inclined to look upon as miraculous. The girl had a haughty face; she was copper skinned, with a little aquiline nose and slightly slanted almond eyes, long smooth plaits and a red silk dress, which looked strangely elegant amidst so much raggedness. A gold chain gleamed at her neck. But Fero's stupor was not feigned.

"Dunicha! You disappeared so long ago! I thought you were dead!"

"And that must have made you very sad? Who is this creature here?"

She indicated Catherine with a contemptuous gesture, which did not augur well for their future relationship. Catherine, for her part, was delighted by her appearance and was examining her with intense curiosity. She must be one of the two girls La Trémoille had had brought to him at the château two weeks earlier. But why must the gypsy-girl look at her like an enemy when all Catherine wanted to do was ask her hundreds of questions about what went on in the château.

Meanwhile the dispute between Fero and Dunicha was growing more bitter. The gypsy-chief defended himself fiercely from the charge of infidelity. If his bride-to-be had not been murdered in the château, he said, she should have found means to let them know that she was safe. Anyway he was now married properly to Tchalai and he could not get out of it.

"You mean it would have been more convenient if I had

died!" the girl cried. "But that makes you no less of a perjurer, and I Dunicha say that your marriage is not valid. You had no right to wed!"

"But I've done so," the chief roared, "and nothing can change that!"

"You think so?"

Dunicha's slanting eyes flickered from Catherine to Fero and back again.

"You remember our customs? When two women dispute the same man, and both have right on their side, they must fight till one of them is killed. I claim the right to invoke the old law. At sundown tomorrow you and I will fight!"

And without another word Dunicha turned on her heel. Haughtily she stepped through the ring of gypsies and went off into the shadows, with four women following her. The old phuri dai who had wedded Fero and Catherine now came up and gently disengaged Catherine, whose arm Fero had seized, and led her away.

"You must take leave of each other till the combat tomorrow. Tchalai is in the hands of fate. According to our laws four women must watch over her till then and four over Dunicha! I have spoken!"

There was a deathly silence. As if by magic Sara had appeared beside Catherine, whom Fero gazed at now despairingly. He no longer even had the right to speak to her. . . . The celebrations were cut short and the drums were silent, so that the only sound to be heard was the fire crackling under the cooking-pots. It was as if the angel of death had suddenly passed over the camp, and Catherine could not help shivering. Sara laid a hand on her bare arm.

"Tchalai is my niece," she said solemnly. "Orka and I will look after her. You can pick two other women. . . ."

"One other!" cried Tereina, leaping to her friend's side. "She may be Sara's niece, but she is also my sister!"

The phuri dai nodded. A skinny finger beckoned another old crone to join them—her sister. Guarded by her escort Catherine walked silently back to Orka's caravan where she was to remain till the hour of the contest.

The relief she felt earlier at Dunicha's timely appearance had quite gone. An hour earlier this mockery of a marriage had seemed the worst that could befall her. But now she found herself threatened with death itself. The customs of this tribe were the strangest and most barbaric she had ever known. They seemed to dispose of her quite arbitrarily without asking her consent, or even consulting her wishes. First the gypsies had decided that she must marry Fero, now that

147

she must fight this young tigress. And all because of a man she did not even love!

"I'm warning you now," she whispered to Sara. "I won't fight. I don't even know how to set about it. I have never fought with anyone before and I am not going to start now, . . ."

Sara took her hand and squeezed it warningly.

"Be quiet, for heaven's sake!"

"Why? Because of these women? I don't care if they do hear. In fact I . . ."

"Be quiet!" Sara repeated, so fiercely that Catherine reluctantly obeyed. "Don't you realize that your life is in danger if you refuse to fight?"

"And I suppose it won't be in danger if I do fight?" Catherine retorted. "You know very well that I haven't a chance. She will kill me. . . ."

"Yes, I know. But for God's sake calm down. When the others are asleep I shall slip out of the camp and go to warn Messire Tristan at the inn. He will think of a way of getting you out of this trouble. But, I beg you, don't let them see that you are afraid. My brethren cannot forgive cowardice. You would be whipped out of the camp and left to starve to death. . . ."

Catherine's eyes were round with horror. She felt as if some dreadful snare was closing about her, and she would never manage to struggle free unaided and alone. Sara sensed her terror and folded her in her arms.

"Courage, little one. Messire Tristan and I will find a way of rescuing you."

"It is high time he did something," Catherine cried bitterly. "After all that talk of keeping a close watch over me!"

"He was not supposed to intervene except in case of real danger," Sara reminded her. She looked around. The two old women were asleep. Only Tereina was still awake. She sat near the oil-lamp, wrapped in her red shawl, staring into the fire with the look of a sleepwalker. She did not move a muscle.

"Now," Sara whispered. "This is the moment. I am going."

Sara slipped out of the caravan as noiselessly as a snake, and Catherine, heavy-hearted but full of confidence in her old friend, tried to get a little sleep. But sleep eluded her. Her eyes stared at the stained walls of the caravan while she tried vainly to still the wild beating of her heart. The silence was oppressive and suddenly she couldn't bear it any longer. She called softly:

"Tereina!"

148

The little gypsy turned slowly towards her and then slipped to her side.

"What do you want, my sister?"

"There's something I must know. My rival, Dunicha, is she used to this sort of combat? What weapons must we use?"

"The knife. And I'm afraid it isn't the first time for Dunicha. She's like a tiger cat when she fights. Two women whom Fero liked have already fallen victim to her!"

This revelation sent a terrible cold chill running down Catherine's spine. She was furious with herself for throwing herself into this impossible situation. If Tristan did not intervene she would be carved up by the gypsy-girl without a soul lifting a finger to help. Even Fero, who appeared head over heels in love with her, had not so much as lifted a little finger to check this madness. Respectfully, he had submitted himself to the laws of the tribe. And, Catherine thought bitterly, he would probably not be too reluctant to console himself, on the very same night, with the victorious Dunicha for the death of the unfortunate Tchalai.

"The only thing I can do for you," said Tereina in a stricken voice, "is to give you a drug which will increase your strength and courage a hundredfold. But now, you must try and rest."

Catherine grimaced in her dark corner. She was a bit disgusted by the gypsy pharmacopoeia, and besides she had not the slightest desire to sleep. All she wanted to do was run away, run as fast as she could go from these bloodthirsty people with whom she had so rashly become involved. She was trapped in a nest of vipers and she had no idea how to get out. She was suffocating in the caravan and the regular breathing of the sleeping women made her feel like screaming out loud.

Then she reminded herself that her life was too precious to the conspirators of Angers, and therefore to Tristan l'Hermite, for him to allow her to be foolishly murdered! There must be a solid hope there.

In spite of these reassuring thoughts which she tried to cheer herself with, Catherine did not sleep a wink that night. She lay there, her mouth dry, her temple throbbing, listening to the hours slipping by as the night watchman proclaimed them from the castle battlements. It was all very well knowing that Sara was looking after her, her absence still weighed heavily upon her. She felt desperately lonely and nothing she could do would dispel this feeling of hopeless absurdity. Daybreak did nothing to alleviate her anguish. Why hadn't Sara come back yet? What could be keeping her so long with Tristan? Could she have been discovered leaving or re-entering the camp?

When a cock crowed somewhere in the countryside, Catherine's impatience knew no bounds. The others were sleeping deeply. She slipped towards the caravan door. Just then Sara reappeared.

A huge sigh of relief broke from her.

"At last!" she whispered. "I was too worried to sleep."

"I was afraid you might be tormenting yourself, that's why I came back. But I shall have to leave again."

"Why?"

"Because Tristan l'Hermite has disappeared!"

The blow struck home. Catherine had to struggle for breath for a moment, and her voice was no more than a whisper as she asked:

"Disappeared? But when? Where?"

"Two days ago. He left the inn and didn't return. I have already searched through most of the town in the hope of finding something out. I must find him before the sun rises . . ."

"And what if you don't find him?" Catherine asked.

"I prefer not to think of that. The best thing might be to reveal your real identity. But that would mean risking your life, and Fero's too, for he has introduced a stranger—a gadji —into the tribe."

"What do I care about Fero? I don't want to die for him. Wouldn't it be easier to tell Dunicha that I have no desire to take her rightful place, and that I willingly renounce all claims to Fero?"

"That would be a mortal insult to Fero. The chief cannot allow himself to be disdained. Your death would not be an enviable one but you would not live long enough to remember it. Anyway the others would never understand. You would be accused of cowardice. Then it would be a case of the whip . . . and the rest!"

Catherine gave an angry exclamation. Every way she turned she seemed to be running up against a brick wall. Everything seemed to drive her towards this death she desperately wanted to avoid. She had forgotten that a short while before she had been longing to die. Now she wanted to live with all the ardor and strength of her young body. Life seemed precious to her now that people were trying to snatch it away.

"Let me go now," Sara begged. "I simply must find Tristan again. Don't worry. I shall be there if . . ."

She said no more. Then she softly brushed Catherine's forehead with her lips and vanished again into the morning mists, leaving Catherine more heavy of heart than before. . . . Her impulse was to slip out and follow her old friend, but she managed to stop herself by a deliberate effort of will. If she fled their whole plan would be spoiled, and she would have to return to Angers knowing that she had failed when the prize was almost within reach. Besides she had always known, in accepting this role, that she would have to risk her life more than once. Now she must simply accept that she was about to risk it for the first time. A surge of pride steadied Catherine a little. If it came to the point she would fight Dunicha with a knife in her hand. It was not in her character to back out. She was even ashamed of the abject fear which had gnawed at her stomach a moment before.

The thing to avoid was thinking of her little Michel. Otherwise she would lose heart for the enterprise at the thought that she might never see him again. But she would think of her beloved husband, her Arnaud, so that death might lose some of its sting.

All the same when the sunset came and there was still no sign of Sara, Catherine had to fight against the panic fear which seized her. The other women had not seemed surprised by Sara's absence. Tereina had summed up their feelings when she murmured with tears in her eyes:

"A bad omen! Black Sara did not want to see her niece die!"

Catherine began to wonder, with a sinking heart, whether there was not some truth in this opinion. Nevertheless, when the appointed time came and the three women led her outside, Catherine set her jaw and held her head up high. Now her only hope lay in herself, and oddly enough she derived a sort of fatalistic calm from this thought. Besides, she had too often looked death in the face to turn her back on him this time!

As she left the caravan Tereina handed her a goblet and this time she drank the contents unhesitatingly. She even smiled faintly. If this potion, intended to increase her courage, was anything like as effective as the one she had been given the other night, she would be able to fight like a lion!

Once outside she saw that a great space had been cleared in the center of the camp, in the part usually reserved for the tinkers. The whole tribe had gathered round it in silence. In the rays of the setting sun they looked like a mass of copper statues. Fero and the old phuri dai were in the middle seated on a fallen tree-stump which had been covered with an animal skin. As Catherine entered this human circle she saw that Dunicha too was approaching, from the opposite end, still accompanied by her four companions. An old gypsy called Takali, who appeared to be the chief's principal adviser, stood in the middle of the empty space. He wore a sort of cape composed of innumerable tiny scraps of cloth which fell to his feet and gave him a slightly priestly air. On his head, which had the appearance of an old oak carving, he wore a bonnet of motheaten fur from which a long black feather drooped. And in each hand he held a dagger.

When the two women were standing near by him their shawls and dresses were taken away, leaving them dressed only in their chemises which they belted round their waists with leather thongs. Then without a word Takali handed them each a dagger and retired among the rest of the tribe. Catherine found herself alone facing Dunicha. She stared with a sort of horror at the knife in her hand. How did one use it? Wouldn't it be better to let herself be killed rather than plunge this blade into the other girl's body? The mere idea of shedding blood made her feel sick.

The gypsy-girl's eyes glowed like coals in her dark face, but to Catherine's surprise there was no hate in them, only a sort of savage joy as though Dunicha was already enjoying the thought of what was to come. Bitterly the young woman reflected that her rival was already savoring her victory and thinking gleefully of her death.

She looked round at the silently watching crowd, still hoping to see Tristan or Sara, whose absence she found inexplicable, appear suddenly and save her. Something must have happened to her loyal old friend for her to abandon her at this dreadful time . . . something bad. Nothing else would have kept her away.

With her eyes fixed on her adversary's Catherine mumbled a rapid prayer, then she bent forward slightly, waiting for the first blow to strike. Over there on his tree-trunk Fero raised his hand and Dunicha moved. Slowly, very slowly she began to circle sideways round Catherine. She was smiling. . . . Catherine felt her legs tremble for a moment, then her fear lessened slowly. A new warmth stole through her tense muscles and she realized that Tereina's drink was having its effect. But she kept a close watch on Dunicha's movements.

And suddenly the blow fell. With an animal spring the gypsy-girl bounded forward, dagger held high. Catherine, who had been watching her, ducked swiftly and the long blade only took a scrap of her chemise with it. Dunicha lost her balance and rolled a little way off. Then Catherine leaped upon her. She flung her own dagger away at the same time.

Two blades were more dangerous than one in this sort of close fighting and now Catherine was bent on disarming her adversary. She managed to seize the gypsy round the wrist and began to squeeze it with all her might. She was conscious of murmurs of approval from the crowd.

But the gypsy was stronger and bigger than she was and she was difficult to hold down. Catherine saw her face from close to, grimacing with effort. She gnashed her teeth and her nostrils flared like an animal's scenting blood. With a violent effort she flung Catherine backwards. She gave a cry of pain. Dunicha had bitten her arm to force her to let go. Now she found herself lying on the ground with the gypsy's full weight on top of her. A reflex movement made her seize the hand which held the dagger but she knew that the other girl had the advantage now and that it was useless trying to defend herself. She was certain to be killed in a minute or two. She saw this clearly in the other woman's triumphant gaze. Slowly, with a breathless laugh, she began to twist Catherine's arm to free her dagger and at the same time she seized her by the throat, looking for the best place to strike. . . .

Then an anguished supplication rose from Catherine's stricken heart. It was all over for her; her strength was gone, she could do no more. And she knew that no help would come to her from the impassive circle standing round. Not one voice would be raised to halt Dunicha's hand. She closed her eyes.

"Arnaud!" she murmured. "My love."

Her arm was beginning to weaken in Dunicha's cruel hold. But suddenly a loud voice spoke out, almost beside her.

"Separate these women immediately!"

For Catherine it was like hearing Easter bells peal out the Resurrection. She heaved a huge sigh of relief which was echoed almost at once by Dunicha's howl of rage as two archers tore her roughly off her prey. Two more snatched Catherine up, not much more gently, and set her on her feet. Catherine still couldn't believe her good fortune. The two women stood face to face, but they were firmly held in the grip of the archers. Between them, with a contemptuous smile on his lips, stood a tall man sumptuously dressed in green velvet and black brocade. And at once Catherine's joy was extinguished and the sun itself grew black. Then she was seized by wild terror. Safety seemed still worse than danger. For the man who had rescued her was none other than Gilles de Rais!

In a sudden vision she beheld the towers of Champtoce, and the dark horrors of that accursed castle—the abominable man-hunt which had almost cost Gauthier his life, the immense pyre where Gilles had wanted to burn Sara alive and lastly old Jean de Craon's disgusted expression, the heartbreaking tale of his crushed pride and humbled heart, when he found what a monster his grandson had become. . . .

Catherine was sure that she must be unrecognizable in her ragged disguise, but as the Marshall's eyes dwelt ironically and insolently on her dusty face, she hung her head as if ashamed of her seminakedness. Her chemise had been badly torn during the fight . . . Dunicha was still struggling in the archers' grasp. Gilles's voice rapped out:

"Let that one go, and whip this Egyptian rabble here back into their lairs!"

"And what about this woman, monseigneur?" said one of the men who had hold of Catherine. Her heart skipped a beat as the disdainful voice commanded:

"Bring her along!"

CHAPTER EIGHT

Among the Wolves

Night was falling like a black curtain when Catherine found herself being pushed, none too gently, by her escort into a room in the keep. She had started back in terror when she found that they were leading her towards the massive central tower, from whose battlements one could see as far as the rooftops of Tours, fearing at first to be thrown into one of the terrible dungeons like the one where she had been imprisoned in Rouen. But as it turned out the room was huge and well furnished. The walls were almost hidden by embroidered hangings and oriental silks, in dark crimson and silver, and there were cushions scattered about the floor, which was tiled with the arms of the Amboise family, who only a short while before had been dispossessed of their domain by the King's command.

Catherine resisted the temptation of the immense square bed which stood in one corner of the room and offered a tempting glimpse of white linen sheets and velvety covers. Sleep! How delicious to stretch her poor, bruised and battered body out there! But the great sword placed on a table, the armor standing in one corner, the masculine garments flung over chairs and coffers, from which precious materials, furs and toilet articles spilled in profusion: all this indicated only too clearly that this was Gilles de Rais's own room.

She was too bewildered to think very clearly but one thing she was sure of, and that was that her fear of him was as tenacious and paralyzing as ever. Her memories of the time she was imprisoned in his castle were too horrifying for it to be otherwise. It seemed as though she had merely jumped from the frying-pan into the fire in escaping from Dunicha only to fall into his hands. What tormented her was not knowing what he wanted of her. Why had he brought her here? He could not possibly have recognized her. In that case . . . ?

If her disguise were penetrated her death was assured. But if not? She knew this blood-lust too well not to know that he would not hesitate to kill a gypsy-girl if he felt like it. He

155

might rape her too, then kill her. . . . Whichever way she looked at it the end seemed the same! Death! For what other reason except to amuse himself would a man like Gilles de Rais have a gypsy-girl taken to his room?

She crossed the room barefooted to where a great fire leaped in the chimney and sank down on a bench strewn with cushions. She held her frozen hands out gratefully to it. Her body shook with cold under the torn chemise of coarse linen which was the only garment she wore, but the fire soon prevailed over the dampness from the river and the coolness of the night. Almost without realizing it her eyes had filled with tears. One by one, they splashed down her chemise. Catherine was so hungry! She had been hungry ever since she arrived at the gypsy camp. She was weary too, and morally even more than physically. And in truth the résumé of the last few hours' events was far from encouraging: she had fallen into the hands of her enemy, Gilles de Rais, Sara had mysteriously disappeared, not to mention Tristan l'Hermite, whose behavior she preferred not to even try to explain. It looked too much as though he had abandoned her. . . .

In her misery she hardly gave thought to the fact that here she was at last inside the château she had been so determined to enter. Oddly enough it was the noises outside which gradually brought this fact home to her. The immensely thick walls of the keep kept out most of the noise, but through the narrow window she could hear the refrains of a song. Over there in the King's lodgings, on the far side of the courtyard, a man was singing to the accompaniment of a harp.

"Fair lady, what thinkest thou of me?
What is in thy heart? Hide it not from me . . ."

Catherine raised her head, flinging back the black curls which tumbled over her brow. That song was the favorite song of Xaintrailles, and through the singer's beautifully modulated voice she seemed to hear her old friend's nonchalant, slightly tuneless singing. That song was the one Xaintrailles had sung during the tournament at Arras, and these beloved memories gave Catherine new courage. Her mind cleared. The blood began to flow through her veins again, and little by little she regained her self-control.

Some remarks made by the Connétable de Richemont came back to her: "La Trémoille does not even share the King's quarters. He spends the night in the keep, guarded by fifty armed men. . . ." The keep? But that was where she was! . . .

Instinctively she gazed up at the stone-vaulted ceiling,

whose pointed arches were lost in the shadows. This room was on the first floor. The man she was searching for must live just above . . . almost within reach! At this thought the blood leaped in her veins.

She was so lost in her thoughts that she did not hear the door open. Silently Gilles de Rais went up to the fireplace. Catherine did not notice him till he was standing beside her. To remain in character she jumped to her feet, with a startled and frightened look on her face, which in fact she had no need to feign. The mere presence of the man was terrifying enough.

"Seigneur," she stammered, "I . . . I . . ."

Her frightened heart was beating like a drum, but she did not have a chance to say another word. Roughly he seized her shoulders and crushed his lips on hers. But he thrust her away almost at once.

"Ugh! You stink, my beauty! You must be filthy!"

She had expected anything but that. The curious thing was that she felt quite mortified! She knew she was dirty but it was intolerable to be told it! Gilles stood aside and clapped his hands. A guard appeared, armed to the teeth. He commanded him to go and fetch two chambermaids. When the man returned with two servants Gilles de Rais pointed to Catherine who was crouching nervously on the bench.

"Take this charming person to the bath-house. And take good care of her. You, archer, are personally responsible for seeing that my prisoner does not escape!"

There was no help for it but to follow her guards. Catherine was furious, and infinitely more humiliated than she would have liked to admit. But a trace of humor lightened her bad temper. She had seen one of the serving-girls make a superstitious gesture behind her back as if to ward off the evil eye. These two maids must be blue with fright at having charge of this gypsy-girl! It spoke well for the efficacy of her disguise. But then a new worry came to trouble her, and spoil her pleasure in shedding the layer of dirt all over her: what if Guillaume the Illuminator's dye did not stand up to the bath-water? Her hair was still a glossy black, though thick with dust, and she had her two little pots of cosmetics in a pocket Sara had stitched into her chemise, but what about her skin?

She was soon reassured. The color was fast. The bathwater might have taken on a faintly yellow tinge perhaps, but that was all. Catherine abandoned herself to the voluptuousness of hot water and delicious perfumes. Her bruised body felt wonderfully restored by it, and her mind too felt refreshed. She shut her eyes and tried to infuse a little order into her thoughts, and calm the anxiety which knotted her throat. This bath was an unexpected pleasure, and it was anyone's guess what might follow. She stretched herself out full length and tried to empty her mind. This moment of respite might be the last. She must take full advantage of it. Afterwards . . .

Catherine could willingly have stayed for hours in that warm scented water which soothed her sore body and eased her scratches. But it seemed that Gilles de Rais was not prepared to let her too long out of his sight. The chambermaids finally helped her out of the bath and dressed her in a fine silk chemise and then in a wide-sleeved garment made of green and white striped heavy silk.

But as the two women made to dress her hair she thrust them away and showed them the door so imperiously that they shrank away timidly and hurriedly obeyed, no doubt fearing that she might cast some spell over them. The truth was that Catherine had no desire to show them that her abundant black hair was not all her own.

When she was alone she unplaited her hair, and brushed and combed it for a long time. Then she calmly rearranged it again, twining some white ribbons among it to make it more secure. Then she darkened her eyebrows, smoothing them carefully, and reddened her lips. If she were going into battle, however desperate, it was as well to make sure of being well armed, and Catherine liked to be in full possession of all her womanly weapons. Now that she was clean and well dressed, and confident of her beauty in spite of her strange appearance, she felt like the old Catherine de Montsalvy again. She had to admit to herself that she was finding it difficult to play the role in which she was cast. Still, having flung herself into the water, there was nothing for it but to swim! If only she could silence the pangs of her hungry stomach!

She flung back the bath-house doors and found herself face to face with the chambermaids and the guards. Her appearance brought a gleam to the men's eyes but she paid no attention.

"I am ready now," she said briefly. And she set off with firm, measured footsteps like someone going into battle.

A few moments later she found herself back in Gilles de Rais's room. Only to discover, with relief, that a whole table had been set and laid with food in her absence. She noticed this fact with some satisfaction. Usually, when one wants to kill a person, one does not begin by feeding her!

The owner of the room was there too of course, lounging in a tall chair of carved oak, but Catherine forgot her terror of him for once in contemplation of the delectable-looking fowl, juicy and golden, which lay steaming on silver platters and giving off the most delicious smells. Pâtés, bowls of sweetmeats and flagons of wine stood around it. Catherine's nostrils quivered. . . . Gilles de Rais had been observing his prisoner. Now he beckoned her across to him with a pale hand.

"Are you hungry?"

She nodded, without speaking.

"Sit down then . . . and eat!"

She needed no further telling. She pulled up a stool and sat down at the table. Then she snatched up a pâté and cut a large slice off it, wolfing it down avidly. She had never tasted anything so good! After those disgusting messes they prepared in the gypsy camp this was a real delight! She ate a second slice, then half the bird, while Gilles poured her out a great cup of thick, sparkling wine. Catherine accepted the wine too and drained it off at a gulp. She felt so much better after this that she failed to notice the sharp glances her host was darting at her: like the measuring way a cat looks at a mouse. She felt equal to taking on Satan himself now! False courage lent by the wine, no doubt!

Gilles leaned on the embroidered cloth the better to watch her nibble at some sugar plums. Now that her hunger was appeased Catherine looked sharply at him, waiting for him to speak. But he did not, and the silence was growing intolerable. So she spoke first. She wiped her hands and mouth on a silk napkin, gave a sigh of satisfaction, and somehow managed to smile at her sinister table-companion. She knew that to show her fear would be to give herself away for sure.

"Many thanks for the meal, kind lord! I think I have never eaten such good fare before, in all my life!"

"Never . . . really?"

"Really! Our poor camp fires are not capable of producing such dainties! We are but poor folk, my lord, and . . ."

"I was not referring to the wretched gypsy cooking-pots," Gilles de Rais broke in coldly, "but rather to the kitchens of Philippe of Burgundy, known as the Great Duke of the West. I had imagined them more refined!"

Catherine was too thunderstruck to reply. He came across and bent over her.

"You are playing your part superbly, my dear Catherine, and I have found it dazzling to watch . . . particularly your fight! I would never have believed that the Dame de Brazey could fight like a common wench! But don't you think it would be better to drop the pretense with me?"

Catherine's lips curved in a bitter smile.

"You recognized me then?"

"It wasn't too difficult. I knew you were here disguised as a gypsy girl."

"How did you know that?"

"I have spies wherever I need them. Among other places I have some in the château of Angers. One of them recognized you after having seen you at Champtoce. He followed you when you went to see Guillaume the Illuminator. I may say that that repulsive little creature put up quite a struggle when we asked him about you and your disguise, although I think we were very persuasive . . ."

"It was you who had him tortured . . . and strangled!" Catherine cried in horror. "I might have recognized your touch!"

"It was I, as you say. Unfortunately he refused to tell us the reason for this masquerade of yours, despite our entreaties."

"For the very good reason that he didn't know it!"

"I had already come to the same conclusion. Anyway I am counting on you to supply it. I want you to realize though . . ."

This tall form bending over her was beginning to get on Catherine's nerves. She stood up and went across to the open window. She leaned against it, and her eyes met Gilles's without flinching.

"And why do you suppose I have come here?"

"To get back your property. That is reasonable enough and the sort of action I can understand."

"My *property?*"

Before Gilles de Rais could answer there was a knock at the door and a man entered without waiting for permission. Two guards, armed with halberds, preceded him and stationed themselves either side of the archway. The man who appeared was as broad as he was high, a veritable mountain of fat draped in swathes of gold-embroidered velvet, topped by an arrogant red, swollen countenance with a short dark beard.

"Cousin!" cried the visitor. "I have come to sup with you. It's deadly boring with the King!"

Catherine stepped back instinctively on recognizing Georges de la Trémoille! A wave of blood rushed to her face: joy, anger and hatred all mixed up together. She had not expected to cast eyes so speedily on the man she had come to find through so many trials and dangers. She felt a fierce joy as she observed that he was fatter than ever. His skin was yellow and unhealthily puffy and his labored breathing indicated that his health was becoming undermined by debauchery. But then, as she went on studying her enemy carefully, she stopped in open-mouthed amazement, gazing at the Lord Chamberlain's curious headgear. It was a sort of turban of cloth of gold which emphasized his look of an oriental satrap, and among its folds there glittered a black diamond . . . the unique inimitable and easily recognizable black diamond of Garin de Brazey! .

The walls and floors began to spin round and Catherine thought for a moment that she must be going mad. She groped about in the dark corner where she had withdrawn on La Trémoille's entry, found a stool and collapsed upon it without paying attention to the remarks exchanged by the two men. She was desperately trying to work out how the diamond could have fallen into the Chamberlain's hands. She recalled the scene where she had placed the diamond in Jacques Cœur's hands in the inn at Aubusson. What was it he had said then? That he was going to raise money for the stone from a Jew in Beaucaire, whose name she even remembered: Isaac Abrabanel! How, in that case, did the diamond come to be flashing in La Trémoille's turban? Had Jacques been captured on the road between Aubusson and Clermont? Had he fallen into a trap? And what if he were . . . She could not bring herself to utter the dreaded word, not even to herself. A sudden urge to weep tore at her. Yes, there was no getting away from it . . . for the Lord Chamberlain to have acquired that jewel must mean that Jacques Cœur had ceased to live. He would never have given up Catherine's treasure of his own free will . . . particularly not to this man he loathed almost as much as she did herself.

She closed her eyes for a moment and did not notice that La Trémoille had observed her and was coming toward her. When a fat flabby forefinger, loaded with rings, lifted up her chin she gave a startled jump.

"Zounds! What a beauty! Where did you find this marvel, cousin?"

"In the gypsy camp," Gilles answered reluctantly. "She was fighting with another she-devil. I separated them and kept this one because she pleased me."

La Trémoille condescended to smile, revealing unwholesome teeth whose color fluctuated between green and black. He laid his hand possessively on her head in a gesture which made her tremble with revulsion.

"It seems you did well, cousin! It was intelligent of you to

161

keep this wild doe! Get up, little one, so that I may see you better."

Catherine obeyed uneasily, wondering what was to happen next. If Gilles de Rais revealed her true identity, she was lost. La Trémoille and he were not only cousins but allies, united by a signed and solemn treaty. Gilles himself had spoken of this pact at Champtoce. However, she took a few paces round the room followed by the Lord Chamberlain's greedy eyes. He spoke of her exactly as though she had been a mere *objet d'art.*

"Very beautiful in truth! A jewel fit for a prince's bed! Her bosom is round and high, her shoulders are superb . . . the legs look long . . . and the face is exquisite! Those great dark eyes . . . and delicious lips!"

La Trémoille's asthmatic breathing grew shorter still and he kept passing the tip of his tongue over his lips. Catherine realized that this was the decisive moment, and that an overly modest manner was hardly in keeping with her gypsy role. With a great effort she forced herself to smile flirtatiously at her enemy. Her walk became undulating, and she threw him a sultry look which turned the Chamberlain's face purple.

"Exquisite!" he breathed. "How is it I never noticed her before?"

"She is a refugee," Gilles growled. "It's only a few days since she joined Fero's tribe, with her aunt. They are escaped slaves. . . ."

Catherine sighed with relief. Well, it seemed as though Gilles was not prepared to reveal her true identity after all! She felt much more comfortable in her assumed role all of a sudden. But La Trémoille silenced his cousin with a raised hand.

"Let her answer for herself, so that I may hear her voice. What is your name, my pretty?"

"Tchalai, lord! In our language it means star. . . ."

"It suits you perfectly! Come with me, lovely star. I am eager to know you better!" He had already taken Catherine's hand and now he turned to De Rais: "Thank you for the present, cousin! You have always known how to please me!"

But Gilles de Rais stepped across and barred the door. The curl of his lip was ominous, as was the dark fire which glowed in his black eyes.

"One moment, cousin! I do not deny that I carried her off for you, but I do not intend to give her to you till after tonight!"

Catherine glanced at Gilles in astonishment. She had believed him the willing tool of his unattractive cousin. And

162

now it appeared they were not so united as she had supposed. Far from it in fact! Gilles's insensate pride made him a poor vassal, it was true. It was not easy to imagine him humbling himself before anyone, but right now, yes . . . right now the light of murder shone in his eyes. How would this duel between tiger and jackal end?

La Trémoille's small eyes narrowed in their holes of fat, while an ugly pout twisted his thick lips. But he did not let go of Catherine. She noticed, however, that the hand gripping her wrist was damp with perspiration. La Trémoille must be afraid of his dangerous cousin. But strangely enough there was no anger in his voice as he asked:

"And why not tonight?"

"Because tonight she belongs to me! I found her and saved her from the other gypsy who was about to kill her; I brought her here and washed her. I will give her to you tomorrow, but tonight I intend to have her to myself!"

"Everyone obeys me here," said La Trémoille in a dangerously soft voice. "I have only to raise my hand for twenty men . . ."

"But you won't raise your hand, my fine cousin, because if you did you would lose the girl. I would kill her first. And besides I know too much for it to be safe for you to attack me. For instance, what would your wife, my fair cousin Catherine, say if she knew that that fine gold and enamel necklace she coveted had been given to the wife of a vintner in this town, in return for a night of love. . . ."

This time La Trémoille did let go of Catherine who had been following this scene with shining eyes. She could only conclude that the all-powerful La Trémoille, scourge of the kingdom, was truly afraid of his wife. That was a useful thing to know. De Rais appeared to have won his battle. And she didn't know whether to be relieved or not. The fat Chamberlain went toward the door, casting a lingering look of regret at Catherine.

"Very well then," he mumbled, shrugging his shoulders. "Keep her tonight. But I shall send for her tomorrow. And take good care not to spoil her for me, cousin, or I might be tempted to forget the . . . tender affection I feel toward you."

One last look, and a grimace which might have been intended as a smile for Catherine, and he had gone. The impassive soldiers closed the doors behind him. Catherine and Gilles de Rais found themselves alone together once more.

Catherine's throat was dry. Her danger was acute. In her eagerness to try and draw La Trémoille out of this closely

163

guarded castle, she had merely thrown herself between hammer and anvil. She had hoped to be summoned to dance for the Chamberlain's amusement, and thereby to lure him into making a stay at Chinon, by means of a plan she had devised. But now, trapped between the terrifying Gilles de Rais and the fat Chamberlain, she sensed that her life was worth nothing. Gilles merely wanted to amuse himself with her, after which he would fling her unceremoniously into La Trémoille's bed. What would become of her then, when she had ceased to please? Would she even have time to carry out her plan? Gilles was not the man to set his prisoner free!

Milord Bluebeard meanwhile had run to the door and thrust home the massive bolts. Then he went to the window and leaned out and took two or three deep breaths, presumably to calm his rage. Muffled sounds of lutes and viols reached her from the darkness outside, frail, melodious sounds.

"They are holding a concert in the King's chambers," he murmured in a voice from which every trace of anger had vanished so that it struck Catherine as strangely altered. "How lovely that music is! There is nothing as divine as music . . . especially when sung by a choir of children! But the King does not like children's voices . . ."

He was talking to himself, as if he had forgotten Catherine. She felt a cold shudder run down her spine remembering those terrible nights at Champtocé, and old Jean de Craon's heartbroken confession to her. She clasped her hands together. She must not let her jailer know how frightened she was of him. If she was to carry the day she must keep her wits about her and not let herself be haunted by nightmares.

She took a step towards him as he stood leaning against the window.

"Why didn't you tell your cousin who I really am?" she asked softly.

He answered without looking at her.

"Because it is not to my advantage to have Dame Catherine de Brazey moldering away in some dungeon or other! Whereas the gypsy-girl Tchalai could be very useful to me!"

Catherine decided to be frank if only to see what Gilles's reaction would be.

"I am no longer Catherine de Brazey," she said. "Before God and before men, I am now the wife of Arnaud de Montsalvy."

Gilles de Rais leaped as though a bee had stung him. He turned and stared at Catherine in astonishment.

"How can that be? Montsalvy died in the dungeons at Sul-

164

ly-sur-Loire almost two years ago! La Trémoille is a good jailer. His dungeons never yield up their prisoners."

"I am afraid you have been misinformed. I married Arnaud de Montsalvy at Bourges, in the Church of St. Pierre la Guillard, on the night of the 24th of December 1431. It was Brother Jean Pasquerel who married us. You remember Brother Jean, Messire de Rais? He was chaplain to . . ."

Gilles silenced her with a horrified gesture.

"Don't mention that name!" he gasped, crossing himself hurriedly more than once. "Not in front of me! Never in front of me! God . . . if she were to hear you!"

"She is dead," Catherine said scornfully, contemptuous of such abject terror. "What have you to fear?"

"She may be dead but her soul lives, and a witch's soul is a terrible thing. You might only have to say her name to summon it up! I don't wish to hear that name spoken ever, ever!"

"As you wish," Catherine said, shrugging. "But it still doesn't alter the fact that I am the Dame de Montsalvy, and that I even have a son."

Gilles de Rais grew calmer when Catherine stopped talking about Joan of Arc. A little color returned to his ashen face. "How comes it that you are here now in that case? Where is Montsalvy?"

Catherine's face turned to stone. She lowered her eyes so that he should not see the grief they held every time she had to say the dreadful words.

"My husband is dead too! That is why I am here, alone."

A silence fell, which threatened to become intolerable. To lighten the atmosphere somewhat Catherine inquired, in an almost social tone:

"Might I ask after the health of your grandfather, Messire Jean de Craon, and also of Dame Anne, his wife; who was very kind to me while I was staying with you."

She instantly regretted her remarks. Gilles's face twisted into a mask of maniacal hatred. He glared at her with crazed eyes.

"My grandfather died last autumn, on the 15th of November . . . cursing my name! And he left his sword to René, to that feeble half-witted brother of mine! How dare you ask for news of him? I hope his soul is suffering the tortures of the damned! I hope . . ."

A cry from Catherine interrupted him. Her fear of him was too strong for her.

"Let us change the subject, messire," she said curtly. "Forget your relations and the grudges you appear to hold against

165

them . . . tell me how the gypsy-girl Tchalai can be so useful to you?"

"Because I want the very thing you came here to find: I want the black diamond! A gypsy-girl now . . . she knows how to cheat and steal and bewitch!"

"I am not a real gypsy-girl. . . ."

Abruptly Gilles dropped the courteous manner he had forced himself to maintain until now. He strode towards Catherine and seized her so roughly by the shoulders that she cried out.

"No, perhaps not, but you are twice as artful. You may not be a child of Bohemia, but you are a child of the devil! You are a witch, you too! You bewitch men, lords and peasants alike, till they come and eat out of your hand like frightened birds. You escape from danger after danger and every time you reappear you are stronger, more beautiful! You are better than a gypsy! Weren't you reared by that she-devil I wanted to burn?"

Sara? Catherine had no sooner thought of her than she began to reproach herself passionately. How could she possibly have forgotten Sara all this time? . . . And this was the man who had mentioned, a little while earlier, that she had joined the gypsies with her aunt.

"I've lost my old Sara. I don't even know where she is. She has not been seen since this morning."

"I know where she is. One of my men recognized her when she was searching the town for that man called Tristan l'Hermite. She is under strong guard now . . . no, don't worry, she has nothing to fear! Nothing for the moment anyway. Her fate depends on your obedience."

"I should be grateful if you would tell me what has happened to Messire Tristan," Catherine said harshly.

"I don't know anything about him," said Gilles. "When I sent my men to arrest your accomplice at the inn, he managed by some trick or other to escape by jumping through a window. Since then no one has clapped eyes on him!"

Catherine tried to free herself from the nervous grip of his two hands which were bruising her shoulders. But he held her fast. Then he pushed his face up close against hers. His breath was laden with wine and the smell made her grimace.

"Let me go, sire," she ordered, through clenched teeth. "And let us be frank with each other since we seem to be laboring under a gigantic misunderstanding. I did not come here with any intention of taking back the black diamond, whatever you may think. I didn't even know your cousin had possession of it!"

Gilles seemed impressed by her decisive tones. He let go of her and she went and calmly sat down in the tall carved chair where he had been sitting earlier. He stared at her in astonishment for a moment as if he didn't quite understand what she meant, and did not speak.

Then he put his head on one side and asked, incredulously:

"You didn't come for the diamond?" He murmured: "What did you come for then?"

"Reflect, monseigneur. I am a widow and I have a son. Our family, the Montsalvys, are banished, ruined, in danger of our lives if we are captured. And who is responsible for our fate? Your cousin La Trémoille. That is why I wanted to enter this place—so that I might see him, and seduce him if I can, and thereby obtain a pardon for me and my family and some land which will give my son some property when he grows up. Doesn't that strike you as a sufficient reason?"

"Why this disguise in that case?"

Catherine shrugged.

"Do you suppose I should even have crossed the outer drawbridge without being arrested if I had come undisguised." As Gilles shook his head she went on: "I came to know, by chance, of the Lord Chamberlain's liking for gypsy songs and dances. With Sara's help it was an easy matter for me to introduce myself among them. You know the rest. . . . Now, I should like to know, in my turn, what you propose to do with me."

Gilles did not answer at once. His face was somber. He picked up a dagger with a gold hilt and started playing with it nervously. Catherine hardly dared breathe, afraid to disturb this threatening silence. Suddenly she jumped. Gilles had just plunged the dagger into the carved wooden chest, and now he cried:

"I want you to steal the black diamond for me, and then bring it to me. . . ."

"You seem to forget that it belongs to me. Anyway I still want to know how it came into your cousin's hands."

"An innkeeper somewhere or other appears to have overheard the man to whom you gave the stone, a certain furrier of Bourges, saying that he would raise money against it with a Jew in Beaucaire, called, if I remember rightly, Abrabanel. Hoping for a fat reward the innkeeper came and told his story to the Lord Chamberlain. After that it was easy . . ."

"You mean he had Maître Cœur killed?" Catherine cried dolorously.

"No, of course not. Your own man had already got hold

of his money and left. The Jew had the diamond. He refused to hand it over to my cousin's messengers . . . and that cost him his life!"

Catherine gave a horrified exclamation which turned into a laugh, a tragic, ironical laugh which grated on the ears.

"Death . . . once more! And you still want to get your hands on this accursed stone? For it is a jewel of ill-omen, believe me. It brings misery, bloodshed and suffering. Whoever possesses it meets with a terrible fate, or quite simply, dies. And I hope the same thing happens to your fine cousin. If you want that diamond, which appears to have come straight from hell itself, you have only to take it!"

In her anger her voice had risen almost to a shout. Now Gilles seized her brutally by the shoulders and forced his face, twisted by anger and fear, closer to hers.

"I fear Satan less than your curses, evil witch! But you have no choice. Tomorrow I shall hand you over to La Trémoille: either you steal the diamond for me or you and your gypsy-woman shall be left to rot in the dungeons and torture chambers. You are a person of no importance here, a trollop one can dispense with if one chooses. The good people of these parts are never so happy as when they see one of your fellow-countrymen swinging from the gibbet!"

"In that case you would have to cut my tongue out," Catherine said icily. "I would talk in the torture chamber. I would tell them who I am and why you brought me here. I may in any case," she added bitterly, "since you would never let me out of the place alive. So I've nothing to gain from stealing your jewel for you."

"Yes, you have! Once I had the stone I would set you free. The theft would have to take place at night. La Trémoille lives in this same tower. Once you have possession of the jewel all you need do is bring it to me. Then I will help you escape from this place. All you would need to do then is make your escape, with the rest of your tribe, as fast as possible. Your safety would depend on your speed. You would have all the rest of the night in which to do it . . . because of course, *you* would be the suspect, you and the rest of your tribe!"

"The soldiers would soon catch up with us," Catherine said. "Your talk of setting me free is just a way of getting me to put my head into the noose, and not only mine but those of many other innocent people too."

"That's not my affair! It's up to you not to let yourself get caught. If you *are* caught, incidentally, it is no use thinking it would help you to tell the truth. No one would dream of believing a gypsy-girl rather than a King's Marshal. People would just laugh at you!"

"And . . . if I refuse?"

"Your precious Sara will presently be conducted to the torture chamber. You will be allowed to watch the entertainment before being invited to take part yourself!"

Catherine turned her head away in disgust. Gilles's features were twisted into a diabolic mask which made them hideous to behold. She shrugged and sighed:

"Very well, I will do as you say . . . it doesn't appear that I have much choice."

"You will steal the diamond and give it to me?"

"Yes," she said wearily. "I will give it to you, and I hope it brings you bad luck as it does all the others . . . anyway I haven't much desire to keep a . . ."

The blow Gilles struck her across the face cut her short with a cry of pain. It was so violent she felt as if her head had been knocked off.

"Keep your curses to yourself, wench! All I want from you is obedience. Obedience, do you hear, *humble* obedience!"

The pain had forced smarting tears into Catherine's eyes. She swallowed them back bravely, though her head was ringing like a bell. She stared with undisguised hatred at the man who stood before her.

"Help me undress!" he commanded.

He sat down and extended a booted leg for her to deal with. She hesitated for a second but she knew him too well to argue. What was the point? She would only risk being stabbed in a fit of rage. It appeared that he was bent on humiliating her. . . . Sighing, she got to her knees.

While Catherine removed his different pieces of clothing Gilles snatched up a flagon of wine from the table and drained it in long, thirsty swallows. When it was empty he flung it aside and picked up another which he drank off equally thirstily. And then a third. Catherine watched in alarm as his face grew red and puffy and his eyes bloodshot as if the wine itself were flowing directly under his skin. When he was naked he snatched up a long black velvet robe and knotted the belt round his hips. Then with a wicked glance towards Catherine he walked across to a dresser covered with bottles and flasks.

"Now, take your clothes off!" he ordered.

Slowly, Catherine's cheeks crimsoned. A gleam of anger flashed in her eyes and her lips folded obstinately.

"No," was all she said.

She expected a furious outburst. But all Gilles did was

169

sigh, and stroll across the room where he picked up a long hunting-whip.

"Very well then," was all he said. "I'll do it myself . . . with this!"

He lifted up the whip and struck. The long supple thong hissed as it snaked through the air. It curled round a floating sleeve and wrenched it off, at the same time stinging Catherine's arm so painfully that she almost cried out. She realized that she was defeated. If she didn't give in this monster would tear her to pieces with his whip.

"Stop," she said dully. "I will do as you say."

A moment later her silky tunic and fine chemise fell in a heap round her feet. . . .

By the next morning Catherine felt she could weep no more tears even if she tried. She had had her fill of horror and pain, and she had reached the limits of her endurance. That night spent in the bed of the Sire de Rais was to leave an indelible and terrible imprint on her mind. . . .

The man was mad, there could be no other explanation. He was a maniac who craved blood and vice and perversity, and for hours on end the unfortunate creature had been forced to submit to the disgusting whims which Gilles's morbid imagination and declining sexual powers suggested to him. Her poor bruised, scratched, maltreated body hurt too much for her to sleep and the blood was still flowing from her shoulder where the madman had bitten her. . . .

During that whole nightmarish night he had never stopped drinking. He drank till he was almost delirious and more than once Catherine believed her last moment had come; but Gilles had been content to rain blows on her till she moaned aloud, calling her every foul name under the sun meanwhile.

Seeing the enormous quantity of wine her tormentor had drunk Catherine had hoped that he might at length fall asleep, but when dawn broke and the watchmen sounded the opening of the town gates, Gilles had still not closed his eyes. He got out of the bed and stretched his naked body in the fresh morning air. Then he dressed and went out to hunt, as he did every morning, without so much as a glance at the young woman who lay motionless in the rumpled bed. From the spot she had found screened by the bed hangings, Catherine heard the huntsmen's horns, the barking of impatient dogs, the creaking of the drawbridge being slowly lowered.

Outside a fine spring day seemed to be on the way but not much sunlight filtered through the narrow windows with their little gray leaded panes. The fire had gone out though the candles were still burning. Catherine's shoulder hurt her so much that she got out of bed, despite her exhaustion, to look for some water to bathe it in. But she had no sooner set foot on the ground than the room started to spin round, and her mind went blank. She groaned and fell back, half-fainting, on the bed. She felt dreadfully weak and miserable. Her body was racked by shuddering. She pulled the covers up over herself. Perhaps she should call? One of the maids might come and look after her. . . .

Just then the door opened softly. First the bearded head, then the immense body of the Lord Chamberlain stole into the room. Before entering La Trémoille threw a quick look round to assure himself that Gilles was not there. Then he shut the door gently and tiptoed across to the bed. Catherine watched him approach wide-eyed with dismay. As was his wont, La Trémoille wore a vast dressing-gown of apple-green silk lavishly trimmed with gold, and a night-cap draped over his almost bald head. This outfit alarmed Catherine—was the Lord Chamberlain's intention to immediately fill the place Gilles had just vacated? She could have screamed, and bit on the sheet to stop herself becoming hysterical. . . .

Meanwhile La Trémoille bent over her with a broad smile, seeing that she was awake, and said:

"I heard my cousin leaving and I thought it was time I paid you a little visit, my pretty doe. I didn't sleep a wink last night for thinking of you! Happily the night is over now and from now on you belong to me."

His fat hand felt for the outline of a round shoulder, hidden by the sheet, and impatiently pushed the cover aside in search of soft skin. This was Catherine's lacerated shoulder, and she moaned involuntarily, while La Trémoille snatched his hand away and stared at it in astonishment, finding it stained with blood.

"For pity's sake, don't touch me, messire," Catherine moaned. "It hurts so much!"

By way of reply La Trémoille seized the covers and flung them back revealing Catherine's naked body, bruised, scratched and streaked with blood, some fresh, some congealing. The fat Chamberlain grew purple with rage.

"The stinking swine! How dared he spoil it when it was reserved for me? Ah, he will pay for this! Oh yes! I'll make him pay!"

Even in the midst of her suffering Catherine could not take her eyes off this vast bulk which anger set quivering like a jelly. La Trémoille mistook this astonishment for terror. With

171

unexpected gentleness he pulled the silk sheet up over her lacerated body.

"Don't be afraid, little one. *I* shan't hurt you! . . . I am not a monster. I worship beauty too much to treat it in this barbarous fashion! You belonged to me, and he dared to whip you and hurt you, knowing that you were to come to me this morning. . . ."

It was that he found hardest to forgive, Catherine thought: that Gilles should have dared lay hands on something which he thought of as his own property. His indignation would doubtless have been as strong over a dog, or a horse, or a bit of jewelry. But she decided to take advantage of it all the same.

"Milord," she begged, "could you send a maid to tend my shoulder? It hurts terribly and . . ."

"I shall send not only maids but valets too. I shall have you taken to my own quarters immediately, my lovely Tchalai . . . that is your name, isn't it? You shall be tended and comforted and I shall watch over you myself till you are quite better."

"But . . . Monseigneur de Rais?"

The moist fleshy lips set in an ugly line.

"You will not hear him mentioned again. No one comes into my quarters without permission, and that includes him as much as the rest! He knows very well that if he were to take the liberty I should send him straight back to his manor in Anjou. Wait here for me . . . I will be back!"

He was on the point of leaving when suddenly, driven by an uncontrollable desire, he laid one hand on Catherine's thigh and caressed it gently.

"The sooner you get well, my dear, the sooner I shall be happy! Because, afterwards, you'll be very nice to me, won't you?"

"I am your slave, lord," Catherine stammered, alarmed at the way his breathing was thickening, "but just now I feel so ill, so dreadfully ill. . . ."

He removed his hand reluctantly, and then tapped her cheek. "Ah well, we will just have to control ourselves! A little waiting only makes desire the keener, eh?"

This time he really did go out, with a speed which astonished Catherine in so vast a bulk. The door slammed behind him like a thunder-clap. She was too weak to think any more. She lay with her eyes closed, waiting for the servants to come and tend her. She was not in the least afraid of going to La Trémoille's quarters. Nothing could be worse than the night she had just lived through . . . and besides, wasn't that what she had come here to find: a way of getting at her enemy?

A few minutes later two old women, so old and wrinkled they reminded Catherine of the ancient phuri dai, came to minister to her. They washed her wounds and covered them with ointment and bandaged them, all without uttering a word. They were extraordinarily alike to look at, and in their black clothes they looked like figures at a funeral. When they had finished with her, Catherine already felt better. She tried to thank them and the two old women bowed without a word and went to the foot of the bed where they sat as motionless as twin pillars. After a while one of them clapped her hands and some valets appeared, carrying a sort of litter on which the two women laid Catherine, dressed in her chemise and white gown, and covered her with a blanket.

The procession started up the narrow stairway towards the floor above. Two valets stood carrying torches at the door. One of them bent over her for an instant as the stretcher passed by him, and Catherine stifled an exclamation of surprise.

The valet dressed in La Trémoille's livery was none other than Tristan l'Hermite in person, with a beard and wig!

She did not even try to understand what he was doing there. A great wave of relief swept over her and she closed her eyes as they carried her into her new prison.

CHAPTER NINE

The Dame de la Trémoille

The style in which Catherine was installed gave her some
idea of the value the Lord Chamberlain attached to her person. They carried her into one of the turrets leading off the
central tower, which was almost entirely taken up by a huge
bed with red woolen hangings. The room itself was lit by a
single narrow window. Catherine was carefully laid on the
bed, on a pile of soft mattresses, and then left in the care of
the two old women, which did not please her quite so much.
There was always one of them in her room, sitting hunched
up at the foot of the bed, silent and still as a stone.

The young woman soon discovered the reason for the silence. The two women, twins, were both dumb. A long time
before their tongues had been cut out to make certain of
their entire discretion. They were of Greek origin, La
Trémoille told Catherine, but without informing her of the
curious twist of events which had brought these two women
from the slave markets of Alexandria to King Charles VII's
Court. The Lord Chamberlain had won them at chess some
years earlier from the Prince of Orange. Since then Chryssoula and Nitsa had served him faithfully and had followed
him into the darkest twists and turns of his existence. They
were always given charge of the women La Trémoille pro-
cured. They were so alike that after five days Catherine still
could not tell them apart.

The continual presence of these two women unnerved her.
She would have far preferred complete solitude to these silent
shadows, in whose impassive faces the eyes alone flickered
with life. Catherine still felt uneasy whenever their eyes slid
round and contemplated her . . . and the joy she had felt
when she recognized Tristan in the valet's disguise had worn
off. She had hoped that he would come to see her before
long, but apart from La Trémoille not one man had crossed
the threshold of her little room. The two old Greek women
seemed to be the only other people with permission to enter.

The twice-daily visits from the Lord Chamberlain were a
considerable trial too. He was sweetness itself to her, and she

found this nauseating, especially since she was obliged to be sweetness itself in return, as well as a little humble: the sort of behavior one might expect from a poor gypsy-girl. She shrank into the depths of the bed and pretended to be a great deal more ill and feeble than she really was, because she was terrified that he would soon be expecting her to be "nice" to him. The mere thought of intimate contact with that mountain of yellow fat made her feel sick. She wanted his death, she wanted with all the strength of her hatred to revenge Arnaud's living death, and the sufferings of herself and her own people on this ignominious tyrant, who had reduced them to beggary and was now bent on doing the same to the kingdom itself. It required an almost superhuman effort every day to conceal these passionate feelings of hers, and appear smiling, normal and grateful. To help herself on these occasions she had to conjure up in her mind's eye that moment, the moment she had lived all these months for, when she would have her enemy at her mercy. This thought gave her new energy. But, the morning after that infernal night with Gilles de Rais, she had sworn one thing to herself: not for anything, whether it was luring La Trémoille to Chinon or bringing her plans to a successful conclusion, would she give herself to this creature whose corruption was so total and profound that it had even tainted his physical appearance. If it were really not possible to deter him until she had persuaded him to leave Amboise for Chinon, Catherine had resolved to kill him and have done with it, even if it meant being executed herself immediately afterwards. At least they wouldn't kill her without talking to her first.

But to kill him she would need a weapon, and this she did not have. She was counting on Tristan to provide her with one. But first she would have to get into communication with him. . . .

All these ideas wheeled through her head as she lay motionless for long hours behind her red hangings. The sounds of the château were her only distraction—the cries of the watch, changing of the guards, horses galloping, distant strains of music. Catherine was almost dead with boredom. The rest of the time she gazed at a little figure of the archangel Michael which stood on a little altar opposite the bed. She was surprised to find a holy figure in the room which La Trémoille kept for his changing population of mistresses. All the same this vegetative existence of hers, was doing Catherine a great deal of good. It gave her time to get back all her strength. Well fed, well cared for and obliged to rest, as she was, she was soon in the best of health again.

By the sixth day, however, she decided the time had come to take action. A slight incident occurred which emphasized the importance of hurrying events along a little. That morning, as she usually did when the rest of the château were taking their first meal of the day, old Chryssoula (or was it Nitsa?) had brought Catherine something to eat: a plate of roast larks, a pitcher of wine and some bread . . . in which the young woman discovered a thin scroll of parchment, folded very small.

She hurriedly hid it from her keeper's sharp eyes and did not look at it again till the old woman had taken the empty plates away. It contained only three words, but such threatening ones that Catherine was stung back to life. "Don't forget Sara" the note said, and she realized that it came from Gilles de Rais, that Milord Bluebeard was growing impatient, and that in his eagerness to acquire the fabulous diamond he was capable of doing something savage. But how was she to get Sara away from him? By stealing the diamond? Catherine would willingly have done so if it were simply a question of freeing Sara. But it was necessary for her to remain in the château, and, besides, she had no idea where La Trémoille kept the jewel. Should she ask La Trémoille to set Sara free? That would probably not be too difficult to do, since the fat Chamberlain seemed bent on pleasing her. Had he not brought her a fine and massive gold chain the day before, implying at the same time that her favors would be recompensed in future by even more desirable gifts? But if she were to snatch Sara away from Gilles de Rais, he might easily revenge himself by revealing Catherine's true identity, and nothing would save her then.

She suddenly found this imprisonment of hers unbearable. She could not spend any more time lying in bed. When the old crone returned she found her standing up.

"Dress me," Catherine commanded. "I want to go out!"

The old woman looked at her incredulously. Then she shook her head, pointing to the room's only door which opened into the immense round chamber which housed La Trémoille. Catherine realized that her guardian would do nothing except at his command.

"Go and fetch the master, then," she said curtly. "Tell him I want to see him."

The woman's look of consternation left Catherine unmoved. She stood over her threateningly.

"I am stronger than you are," she said menacingly. "If you won't go and fetch the master I swear to you I'll get out of

176

here whether you like it or not. And in my nightgown too, if necessary!"

Catherine's determined air seemed to convince the old woman, who gestured to her to wait and went out of the room, carefully shutting the door behind her. Meanwhile Catherine went across to the window and stood on tiptoe to try and see out. From her bed, across which a long ray of sunshine now slanted, she could see a corner of deep blue sky and the air which entered through the narrow slit was warm and balmy.

From where she stood she could see a glittering stretch of river, a swath of green grass and a few trees on the Ile St. Jean. A bird went winging across the sky, and Catherine felt a wild longing to escape from this dour fortress and plunge into the very heart of this glorious springtime. All her youth, suddenly reawakened, clamored to be heard, sweeping aside for an instant all thoughts of vengeance, ambition, worries about the future. Oh, if she could but have a cottage with a garden full of flowers next to the great river, where she could live sweetly and simply with her son and the man she loved! Why was this modest wish, which was the lot of so many women, denied to her alone?

The old woman's return interrupted Catherine's sad thoughts. She had brought some clothes folded over one arm. A valet was with her and Catherine's heart leaped joyfully when she recognized Tristan.

"The master cannot come," he said in an expressionless tone of voice, not even looking at her. "He says you may dress and take a short walk round the courtyard. But Chryssoula is to accompany you. And you are to obey her, and return as soon as she commands you." The Fleming's slow voice grew threatening: "Take care that you obey her, Egyptian girl, because it is not good to disobey the master!"

Catherine put as much humility as she could into her reply, and answered modestly:

"I will obey, messire. The master is good to me. Did he not say anything else?"

Her questioning violet eyes met Tristan's cold gray ones, and she saw a quick gleam flash through them.

"Yes. He was much pleased at your desire to take up a normal life once more. He asked me to tell you that there would be a banquet in the King's quarters tonight but that you would doubtless not be strong enough yet to dance for the Court. However, the master promises that he will come tonight after the feast . . . and assure himself personally of this welcome return to health!"

177

Catherine's skin prickled disagreeably. She had understood. La Trémoille would be coming that night to claim his rights over her. And as he would be coming after a long evening's entertainment, he would certainly be drunk, and consequently quite deaf to the appeal of reason. The prospect was not a pretty one, and Catherine felt her throat grow tight. Meanwhile Tristan, whose bearing was stiff and haughty, as one would expect from the servant of a great house in conversation with rabble like herself, had gone over to the door. He turned at the threshold and added almost casually:

"Ah, I was forgetting! Your personal belongings have been placed in the pocket of your dress. Monseigneur has really been uncommonly kind to a girl of your sort. He asked that all your own belongings should be returned to you!"

Chryssoula's presence prevented Catherine from leaping at her clothes and burrowing in the pocket. All her belongings? But she had had nothing on her when she arrived, except a torn chemise. Apart that is, from the two little boxes of cosmetic which Guillaume the Illuminator had given her, and which she had transferred after her bath to the heavy green and white robe she had been given, and which she still had with her now. What could Tristan be talking of in that case?

After some rather careful ablutions—because she had the impression lately that her skin was growing paler and a lighter color appearing at the roots of her hair—she put on the clothes Chryssoula gave her, which were clean and simple but not luxurious. There was a gray fustian dress, a chemise of fine cloth, a pleated bodice and white starched cap, and a leather belt and purse—the latter strangely heavy. Clearly La Trémoille was anxious that no one should notice her. She must blend in with the other servants, and not attract the attention of the other people in the château. . . .

As she buckled the belt round her hips her hands shook a little. She was burning with curiosity, particularly since the leather was too thick for her to tell what might be inside. But she managed to restrain herself from opening it. Then she noticed that a black woolen cape was among the clothes and she threw it round her shoulders and signed to Chryssoula that she was ready to go. The old woman opened the door and preceded Catherine across the Lord Chamberlain's huge and sumptuously furnished chamber, a veritable temple of gold where even the bed hangings and cushions glittered with the magical metal, and then down the tower stairs.

It was dark there and Catherine hurriedly explored her purse under cover of her cape. There was a handkerchief, a rosary, a few coins, then her fingers closed upon a little roll

178

of parchment, and lastly an object which made her tremble with joy as she felt it with her finger-tips—a dagger! *The* dagger, the one with the Montsalvy's sparrow-hawk crest upon it, which she must have left in her boy's disguise! Catherine sent up a fervent prayer of gratitude to Tristan. He had thought of everything! He really was watching over her, and he had realized that she would rather kill the Lord Chamberlain than submit to his advances!

She ran lightly down the last stairs behind Chryssoula who scurried along like a mouse. She was free! Free to live or to die, to kill or have mercy on her victim! As they went out into the great courtyard she raised a happy, triumphant look towards the sunlit sky. Now she had the weapon she needed to bring down her enemy and achieve her revenge. What did it matter what happened to her afterwards?

But she was not so detached from earthly things not to be consumed with curiosity to know what was written on the scroll of parchment. Tristan must have written an important message upon it. But how was she to get an opportunity to read it? Say she wanted to go back to her room? That might look strange, when she had been outside only a few minutes. It might be better to wait a while—a half-hour one way or the other could not make much difference. . . .

There were many people in the castle courtyard, and a great deal of bustle and movement. A company of archers were going up to the battlements and their steel hats glinted in the sunshine. A procession of carts laden with faggots of wood toiled slowly up the steep slope, leading from the hollow where the portcullis stood to the courtyard which was raised up like a platform. Washerwomen were going downhill towards the river, with baskets of dirty linen proudly balanced upon their heads. Some huntsmen were grouped near the entrance to the imposing but plainly constructed royal lodging, with hooded falcons perched on their thickly gloved wrists. They appeared to be waiting for another huntsman, doubtless one of high rank. A group of Court ladies meanwhile were strolling towards the orchards, chattering like magpies below the long floating veils on their tall headdresses. Catherine wandered for a little while amid the crowd, with old Chryssoula at her heels, enjoying the simple pleasure of feeling the sun warm on her shoulders. The month of May displayed all its freshly budded beauty in the flower-enameled orchard which could be glimpsed beyond a low archway, and which stretched the whole length of the walled terrace overlooking the Loire. It was as if the summer were declaring its belated victory over nightmare winter and tardy spring, as

179

though the beleaguered land itself were taking its revenge on so much ravaging, and blood and tears. And Catherine discovered to her delight that there were roses growing in the shadow of this vast fortress. It was such a long time since she had last seen a rose!

She was drawn to the greenness of the orchard and was just making her way quietly towards it when a party of ladies and pages came out, most of them young girls wearing wreaths of flowers on their long loose hair and identical pale blue silk dresses. They clustered round a tall, haughty and imperious beauty whose proud looks were enhanced by a sumptuous gown of orange and gold brocade, whose colors almost matched those of her flowing auburn locks. There were emeralds gleaming round her bared throat and on the immensely tall head-dress—almost as high as a church steeple —which formed a regal crown for this striking personage. As she passed by, everybody drew back and bowed respectfully. Catherine would no doubt have taken this woman for the Queen herself if she had not known her, and had not felt her heart swell with bitterness. Her feet suddenly seemed rooted to the spot. She stood staring with burning eyes at the pretty little fleet of pale blue maids-in-waiting escorting the Dame de la Trémoille, the woman who had dared to love Arnaud and have him tortured because he spurned her, the woman whom she, Catherine, had sworn to kill!

She felt Chryssoula plucking anxiously at her sleeve, but she was unable to move. Never before had Catherine felt the urge to kill so strongly and nakedly. She stood so petrified that the great lady noticed her. She frowned and beckoned haughtily to her.

"Here, you girl, come here!"

Catherine could not have moved a step for all the gold or silver in the world. She stood as if petrified. The only thing alive about her were those huge, blazing eyes. Behind her she could feel Chryssoula trembling. One of the young ladies-in-waiting must have recognized the old Greek woman because she murmured something in her mistress's ear. The Dame de la Trémoille's shapely lips curled in a contemptuous smile and she shrugged.

"Ah, I see. Yet another of the common whores my husband finds his pleasure with! Much good may it do him, mixing with the riff-raff of the streets!"

And the colorful procession moved on into the royal lodging without paying any more attention to Catherine. The old woman pulled at her sleeve so vigorously that at last she allowed herself to be led away, back to the keep, thinking angrily to herself that the day she destroyed La Trémoille she would find time to dispose of his wife too.

She was on the point of entering the low doorway when she suddenly felt herself seized by a pair of powerful hands which swung her round again. In spite of the shabby, dirty peasant clothes he was wearing she had little difficulty in recognizing Fero, and she gave a cry of alarm at seeing the chief's face so radiant with relief.

"For days now I have been prowling round this castle, and I finally came in to see if I could find news of you . . . and here you are!"

"Go away, Fero," she cried. "You mustn't stay here. Gypsies are not allowed in here. If you are caught . . ."

"I don't care! I couldn't live without seeing you! The poison of love has taken hold of me, Tchalai; it consumes my blood and my spirit . . . and it is you who put it there!"

There was no mistaking the passion which flamed in the young gypsy's eyes. It was all the more alarming to Catherine now that old Chryssoula was struggling vainly to drag her from Fero's clasp and uttering inarticulate cries for help.

"Go, for heaven's sake; if the guards . . ."

No sooner had she spoken the word than a whole swarm of archers came running up, summoned by the old woman's cries. They must have known Chryssoula well because they unhesitatingly obeyed her orders expressed by means of one arm pointing towards Fero, and the other flung towards the castle gates. The gypsy-chief was seized by four stout men and dragged by main force towards the gates, shouting to Catherine as he went:

"I love you!! You are my wife! I shall return . . . !"

A moment later he had disappeared and Catherine, feeling somewhat relieved in spite of everything, followed Chryssoula docilely. The old woman seemed considerably agitated. The short walk had obviously been too full of incident for her taste. A few moments later Catherine found herself back in her tower room, with the door double locked . . . but alone, thank heaven, alone! She instantly forgot about Fero and emptied out her purse on the bed, snatching up the little scroll on which Tristan had written: "Don't worry about Sara. I know where she is and I am watching over her as I watch over you."

Catherine let out a huge sigh of relief. Those few lines were enough to blot out Gilles de Rais's threatening note. She did not doubt Tristan's word for a second. That strange squire of the Constable de Richemont had a strength of will, and tranquil power about him, which set her fears at rest. She had complete faith in a man who had not only managed to escape De Rais's men but had even succeeded in getting himself taken on as valet to the Lord Chamberlain. If Tristan had Sara under his protection, Catherine need not torment herself further about her. . . .

Feeling somewhat easier in her mind she allowed the remaining hours of daylight to slip by. Her door did not open again till dusk had shadowed her room. Chryssoula entered to light the candles and bring her another tray of food, but this time it contained no message. When Catherine had finished her meal the old slave woman was joined by her sister. The two of them took charge of Catherine's toilette. They bathed and perfumed her, and dressed her in a nightgown of fine white lawn which veiled her body in a gauzy cloud, then she was carefully installed in the bed whose linen sheets had been changed for ones of crimson silk.

All these preparations made her shudder. Their object was only too clear. She was being prepared in this fashion to appear more pleasing to her new master's oriental tastes. In a little while this door, through which the two women were now departing, would open to admit the immense, sumptuously attired figure of the Lord Chamberlain. At the thought of that huge flabby body stretched out on top of her Catherine felt a wave of nausea, and she had to shut her eyes. She could see that loose mouth, those rotting teeth and the over-perfumed beard. She sprang out of bed and fetched the dagger out of the purse and slipped it under the mattress, close at hand. And all at once she felt calmer. What was there to fear now? When La Trémoille flung himself upon her she would strike him with Arnaud's dagger and that would be the end. Undoubtedly she would not escape from there with her life . . . unless Tristan, who must have given her back the dagger for a specific purpose, had arranged for her to flee? If only she had been able to talk to him, even for a moment. Perhaps he was not far away, waiting, like herself, for something to happen in that little room. . . .

Hours went by and nothing happened. Lying motionless in the immense bed Catherine was vaguely aware of the distant sounds of the royal feast: cries, laughter, drinking songs. The devout Queen Marie was expected to arrive shortly from Bourges. The King, apparently, was taking advantage of her absence to amuse himself with his usual companions . . . Catherine heard midnight strike, and the sounds of the changing of the guards. How much longer must she wait? The candles were burning low, and soon they would be out. . . . Was La Trémoille too drunk to remember his tryst?

182

She was just beginning to relax under the influence of this soothing reflection when she jumped, and stifled a scream. The door of her room was opening gently. . . .

A silent, instinctive prayer rose from her heart to her lips but went no further. It was not the Lord Chamberlain but a young girl in pale blue silk with a wreath of flowers in her hair, one of the Dame de la Trémoille's ladies, who entered. She carried a candle in one hand which she set down on the chest.

They stood looking at each other for a moment, the beautiful girl at the foot of the bed, and Catherine sitting up in it, with disdainful curiosity on the one hand and unfeigned surprise on the other. At length the girl spoke.

"Get up," she said; "my mistress wants to see you!"

"Me? But I have to wait here. . . ."

"For Monseigneur to come? I know. But you should know, gypsy-girl, that when my mistress commands the Lord Chamberlain himself obeys. Dress yourself and follow me! I shall be waiting next door. But hurry up! Unless you want to be beaten. My mistress is not a patient woman," she added insolently.

The girl went out leaving Catherine astounded, and uneasy. What did the Dame de la Trémoille want with her? What could be the meaning of this order which came in the middle of the night and threatened to disrupt all her plans? Should she obey? And if not how should she refuse?

Catherine decided that she had no choice, and that after all she could not be taking such a risk in finding out what was wanted of her. As far as the haughty countess was concerned she was nothing more than a gypsy-girl destined for her husband's bed, less important even than a dog or a thing. A creature of whom she certainly would not be jealous. Catherine de la Trémoille's innumerable lovers should protect her from feelings of that sort. Could anyone be jealous of a mountain of fat? That couple was united only by a common love of gold, power and debauchery. And of these it was gold the lady preferred.

Catherine remembered hearing how, when they came in the middle of the night to arrest her second husband, the devilish Pierre de Giac, dragging him out of his own bed, the beautiful countess's only anxiety had been for her gilded toilet articles, some of which had been appropriated by the soldiery who arrested her husband. While her husband was being taken off to his tragic fate the Dame de Giac sprang out of bed, naked as mother Eve, and pursued the thieves in this wise through the passages of the castle of Issoudun!

Catherine was ready in a few moments. She fastened the purse to her belt but slipped the dagger into her bodice. She had burned Tristan's note hours before in the fire. She flung her cape round her shoulders and opened the door.

"I am ready," she said.

Without a word, the girl, who had been waiting stretched out nonchalantly on a cushioned bench, stood up, picked up her candlestick and went towards the staircase where the usual guards stood at attention. Catherine followed her across the courtyard which was lighted by the glow from the windows of the royal lodging, whither her guide seemed to be leading her now. As she crossed the threshold, guarded by two mailed statues, Catherine felt as though she were stepping into a huge hollow shell reverberating with the sounds of merrymaking. In spite of the thickness of the walls the air was loud with music of violins, rebecs and lutes, dominating the noise of voices, laughter and joyful cries. There were torches and immense candles everywhere, and the place was full of bright, warm golden light. Catherine grew anxious.

Could they be planning to plunge her headlong into the midst of the banquet like a night bird suddenly snatched from its shady perch and flung towards the sun? But no . . . her guide crossed the ground floor, where the great hall took up almost all the available space, and led her up towards the upper story of the castle. The girl suddenly pushed open a low door and Catherine stepped from the darkness of the corridor into a room which was not very large, but had the air of a jewel-case, hung with green velvet round all the walls. The floor was covered with thick, brilliant carpets. In spite of the balminess of the night there was a great fire blazing in the hearth, whose flames seemed oddly to be leaping round the walls too, because there were great gold flames embroidered on the velvet hangings.

In the middle of this strange but luxurious room, stuffed with rich and rare objects, stood the Dame de la Trémoille encircled by her ladies, a few of whom lay indolently among the cushions on the floor plucking at the strings of a lute or eating sweetmeats. The beautiful countess now wore nothing but pale blue silk of extraordinary fineness and transparency, and her fiery hair hung loose about her shoulders. The cloud of material all but revealed the lush contours of her body but this did not seem to embarrass her in any way. Catherine could see at a glance that she was in a state of great agitation, biting her lips and twisting her hands together as she prowled the length of her room.

"Here is the girl, gracious lady," said Catherine's guide, as they stood in the doorway.

The Dame de la Trémoille gave an exclamation of satisfaction. Then with an imperious gesture she showed her ladies the door.

"Out all of you! Off to bed! And no one is to disturb me under any pretext whatsoever!"

"Not even *me?*" said the girl who had brought Catherine there and who appeared to be the favorite, pouting sulkily.

"Not even you, Violaine! I want to be left alone with this girl. Keep watch outside to make sure no one comes in. I shall call you when I need you."

Violaine went out unwillingly and closed the door. The others had already vanished. The two enemies, great lady and pseudo-gypsy, were left face to face, looking at each other. . . . With a fierce, but very feminine, delight, Catherine noted that her rival's beauty was beginning to fade. Little lines at the corner of her eyes and full red lips creased the snowy whiteness of a skin like velvet, and there were purple shadows round her gray-green eyes. Fat had thickened her hips and long thighs, and coarsened the outline of her full breasts which were beginning to droop a little. The beautiful redhead lived too pampered, too sumptuous and rich a life. Pleasure and debauchery had left their indelible stigmata upon her. . . . But Catherine took care not to let her satisfaction show. She was only too aware of those eyes examining her, insolently undressing her.

She flushed as she heard the lady's dry voice crying:

"Why don't you kneel before me? Is your spine so stiff it forbids you to salute your masters properly?"

Catherine bit her lips and told herself that she was an idiot. She had forgotten her assumed role for a moment, and had even been on the point of greeting the countess as an equal. She hastened to obey, hanging her head humbly and hiding her embarrassment with a bit of hasty invention.

"Forgive me, noble lady, but I forgot where I was for a moment. My eyes were dazzled! I thought I must be in the palace of the Queen of the keshalyi, the fairies of our people."

The lady's sullen face broke into an arrogant smile. Flattery, however crude, and from whatever source, still had the power to please her.

"Get up," she said. "Or rather sit down on a cushion. What I have to say may take time."

She pointed at a cushion placed on the steps to her bed. Catherine sat down upon it while the countess stretched out upon the bed. Her eyes never left Catherine's face, and this unwinking scrutiny was beginning to make her uneasy. After a moment, which seemed an eternity to Catherine, the beautiful countess murmured:

"You are indeed beautiful . . . too beautiful! You will not go back to my lord again! You could prove dangerous in the long run, because he is stupid with women. And you . . . you look intelligent."

"What shall I do then?" Catherine asked. "If I don't go back . . . I shall risk . . ."

"You will risk nothing. If you are useful to me I may keep you myself and you would have nothing to fear. Unless . . ."

The unfinished phrase was menacing enough, and Catherine did not ask to hear the rest. She must bide her time if she was to avoid making mistakes. So she drooped her head humbly, and waited to hear what would follow.

"I will do my best," she murmured.

The Dame de la Trémoille took her time. Dreamily she stretched out a bare arm for a goblet of wine which stood on the steps close to her bed, and drank it slowly. Catherine saw her opulent throat swelling. Then she flung the cup aside and bent closer to Catherine. The wine had flushed her face a little and her eyes shone.

"They say the girls of your race are skilled at telling fortunes and weaving spells and preparing strange potions. They say the future is an open book to you, and that you know how to summon up death, misfortune . . . and love. Is it true?"

"Perhaps," Catherine answered cautiously. She was beginning to glimpse what was wanted of her, and she thought that there might be an opportunity for her if she played her cards carefully. If this greedy, spoiled woman could be led to believe in her skill or loyalty she might be able to put her, and her husband with her, where she wanted them.

"Do you know of a philter," the countess asked in a lower voice, "which makes people fall in love, and sends fire coursing through their veins, which overcomes modesty, wisdom, even antipathy? Do you know of this magical draught which puts one being in the power of another?"

Catherine looked up and forced herself to look the countess in the eyes. She remembered her experience with Fero only too well, so she was hardly lying when she said:

"Yes, I know it. It gives one such a need of love that the whole body writhes in torment until it is satisfied. There is no one, man or woman, who can resist it."

186

A triumphant gleam lit up the avid face bending over her. The countess sprang up suddenly, ran across the room, opened a small coffer and plunged her hands into it and brought them out again dripping with gold.

"See, Egyptian girl! All this gold will be yours if you get this potion for me!"

Catherine slowly shook her head. Seeing her scornful smile the Dame de la Trémoille slowly let the rain of gold fall back into the coffer.

"You don't want it?" she asked incredulously.

"No. Gold melts and vanishes with the wind. Your protection, noble lady, is of greater value to me. Trust me, let me serve you . . . and I will be much more richly rewarded!"

"Holy Mother, but you speak with spirit, Egyptian girl, and that pleases me! What is your name?"

"They call me Tchalai. It will sound strange to you."

"A strange name indeed! Listen, you please me as I said. Give me this philter I asked you for."

"I do not have it on me, and to make it I shall need two things."

"Speak! You shall have whatever you want!"

"I shall have to go back to my tribe; oh, not for long," she added hastily, seeing the reddish brows knitting doubtfully, "just long enough to get certain things. . . ."

"Agreed! At day-break, when the gates open, I shall have you escorted to the camp; the archers who take you will have orders to shoot!"

Catherine shrugged disdainfully.

"What for? I like it here in this castle. . . ."

"Excellent. The other condition?"

"I must know the name of the one for whom this drink is intended. For it to work properly one must say certain spells over it mentioning the name of the person who will drink it!"

There was a silence. Catherine guessed that this last request of hers was displeasing but, knowing her adversary, she was curious to know who the man could be who had inspired the countess with such a wild passion that she was even prepared to ask help of a gypsy-girl. It was possible that it might prove a valuable weapon.

At length the Dame de la Trémoille rummaged in a coffer and took out a black velvet cape which she put on. She twisted her hair up hurriedly, and covered it with a silver veil. Then she turned to Catherine.

"Come with me. I will show you."

She seized a torch and left the room, followed by Catherine. The countess found Violaine in the passage, waiting

187

faithfully at her post, and packed her off to bed. Then she started down the stairs, but instead of continuing as far as the great hall she pushed open a little door in the wall and slipped through, with Catherine at her heels, into a narrow tunnel which appeared to have been hollowed out within the thickness of the wall itself. It seemed to go on forever. It must have completely encircled the domed roof of the great hall. It was cold and damp in there and the torch the countess was holding started to smoke. At length she stopped, passed the torch to Catherine, and slid her hand over the wall. A little panel slid aside and revealed a narrow opening in the ceiling of the room itself—no doubt artfully concealed from the sight of those below. The din of the feast, which was already loud enough, grew quite deafening. The countess took Catherine's arm.

"Look there by the fireplace. Can you see King Charles?"

Catherine leaned forward and saw a man wearing a golden circlet on his brown hat sitting in a high gilded chair below a blue canopy. It was the King. He did not seem to have altered much since the time of Joan the Maid. He still had the same long gloomy face, with dull popping eyes, but he was not as thin as he used to be. His face was fuller and his expression had lost that hunted look so tragically unsuited to a King.

At that moment he was smiling at a very handsome young man of about eighteen or nineteen, who sat at his feet, half reclining on the cushions which were heaped upon the steps to the throne. Catherine recognized that the boy was exceptionally beautiful, but she found something a little feminine in his perfection. This was no doubt due to his extreme youth, since he appeared to be tall, strong and well-built, though perhaps a little too graceful. His smile was a miracle of charm. . . .

Behind her she heard the countess whispering:

"Do you see the one at His Majesty's feet?"

"Yes. Is that . . ."

"Yes, that is the one. He is the Queen's brother, and his name is Charles d'Anjou, Comte du Maine."

Catherine had to retain a cry of astonishment. The Queen's brother? The youngest of Queen Yolande's sons in that case? That famous Comte du Maine whose charm and courage had so often been extolled to her at Angers! And it was of this stripling, barely out of his adolescence, that the Dame de la Trémoille was enamored? She must be at least twenty years older than him. . . .

A troupe of dancers in brilliant, multi-colored costumes suddenly overran the steps to the throne but the little panel had been closed now, and the banquet vanished from sight. She had not even seen La Trémoille. She found herself alone in the narrow passage with the countess. Under the influence of passion the woman's face suddenly struck her as hideous. She had a startling vision of what she would look like when age had completed its ravages upon her. Like a hideous witch. . . ! But the die had been cast now, and there was nothing to do but play the game through till the bitter end. She looked ingenuously at the countess.

"And . . . he does not love you?" she asked in an innocent voice which allowed the countess to infer how incredible this seemed to her.

"No. He gives me the drama of high-flown sentiments and knightly honor, and cites my husband . . . as if I did not know that all these people of Queen Yolande's hated him passionately! . . . I am afraid, myself, that he must have some young girl in mind. And I want him to love me, do you hear, Tchalai? I want him to be mine . . . for one night at least. After that I will know how to hold him!"

Catherine did not answer. Undoubtedly that hellish concoction of Tereina's would procure the Dame de la Trémoille this night of love she desired, but she felt a certain repugnance at conniving at it. It was only with horror that she could imagine the gay, innocent young sprig, with his fresh, charming good looks, in the arms of this ripe woman of the world. It seemed to her that it would be sacrilege, profanation. . . .

But now the countess was returning to the charge.

"I've done what you asked, Egyptian girl. Tomorrow at dawn the men will take you to the camp to get you what you need. Take care that you keep your promise."

With an effort Catherine shook off the depressing effect of her previous reflections. After all what did it matter to her if the boy spent a night with this woman? It must be the countess's love which had protected him hitherto from La Trémoille's displeasure, because the young count's presence near the King was a nuisance to the Lord Chamberlain. Had it not been for her, a cunningly contrived accident would no doubt have left the place clear. . . .

She threw back her head and looked the lady in the face.

"I will keep my promise," she said.

"Very well then, let us go back. You will sleep on the velvet cushions at the foot of my bed tonight."

One behind the other they left the tunnel in the wall.

Catherine slept badly on the pile of cushions which served as her bed until something more permanent could be installed in the countess's wardrobe room. She was nervous, anxious about the way La Trémoille would react when he found she had disappeared, and anyway it was too hot and stuffy in the room, which was drenched in strong perfumes. She dozed off at last, but when Violaine came to wake her in the small hours she felt deathly tired and her head ached. It was a moment or two before the previous day's events came back to her.

"Come on now," said the maid-of-honor curtly, "get up! There is a sergeant and two archers down below waiting to escort you to your camp."

Catherine got up and splashed a little water over her face. Violaine's insolence annoyed her, but how was she to put her in her place? Clearly the countess's favorite had little use for her. This newcomer, this very lowly newcomer especially, excited her wrath. The Dame de la Trémoille still slept and Catherine did not want to risk waking her with the sound of quarreling, so she hurried as much as she could. . . .

A moment later, at the side of a huge, bearded, and thoroughly disgruntled sergeant, escorted by two archers, she was hurrying across the great courtyard towards the castle gates. The sky was flushed with dawn towards the east, and a damp smell rose from the earth. Catherine felt better at once. Her mind was clearer, and her heart lightened. The early morning breeze was good after so many days of imprisonment. . . .

But there was one problem on her mind. Would she be able to see Tereina without Fero observing her presence? It seemed highly unlikely, and in that case she would have to speak very convincingly to him. The gypsy chief's madness in seeking her out within the castle walls the previous day seemed to suggest that he would be capable of other equally rash actions. What if he were to try and tear her away from the men who were guarding her?

It was not far to the gypsy camp. Once under the portcullis and over the drawbridge it was simply a matter of going down into the castle fosse, and Catherine did not have much time to think. Moreover, she was soon distracted from these thoughts by an unexpected development. She had expected to find the camp asleep at this early hour. But in fact the place was in an unusual commotion.

The women were already busying themselves lighting fires and fetching water from the river, but the elders and the menfolk were all grouped round the caravan of the phuri dai. It was a silent, somber group, from which an oppressive feeling of sadness arose. For a moment Catherine thought the old woman was dead but then she caught sight of her sitting on the ground, wrapped in a heap of tatters. Everyone stood gazing up at the castle with a sort of terror. Fero was not among them.

The arrival of Catherine, warmly dressed and escorted by soldiers, filled the gypsies with astonishment and dismay. What had this stranger whom they had adopted out of charity come to seek from them now, and how dared she come escorted by soldiers? Some of the men started towards her with threatening expressions on their faces but Tereina, who had been sitting brooding by one of the cooking-pots, had likewise recognized the one she called sister, and now she came running up, her small face radiant with joy.

"Tchalai, you are back! I never expected to see you again!"

"I have only come back for a minute, Tereina! And only to see you. There is something I must ask you about . . . and you see, I am under guard."

It seemed as though the agitation which reigned in the camp had alarmed the sergeant who stood looking at all these swarthy faces with visible mistrust, one hand on his sword-hilt. The two archers had already drawn their bows in readiness and their sharp eyes did not miss a single move in the crowd. Tereina looked at them in terror and exclaimed sorrowfully:

"Alas! I hoped you were bringing us news of Fero!"

Despite the threat of the soldiers some of the gypsies had ventured close enough to hear what the two women were saying. Now one of them cried:

"Yes, Fero, our chief! Tell us what has become of him or . . ."

"Be quiet," Tereina interrupted angrily. "Don't threaten her! You seem to forget that she is his wife according to the law!"

"My men shoot straight," the sergeant cut in threateningly. "Stand back, you lot! No harm is to come to this woman—unless she tries to run away!"

He drew his sword and the gypsies retreated, baring their teeth like whipped curs. The circle round the two women and the soldiers grew larger.

"I don't know where Fero is," said Catherine. "I saw him yesterday in the courtyard of the castle disguised as a peasant. The guards threw him out."

"He went back there last night. He knew there was a banquet at the castle. He went up with one of the bears, hoping they might let him show the animal's tricks during the feast.

The bear came back during the night . . . alone . . . and wounded!"

"I swear, Tereina, I had no idea Fero had returned to the castle. But what madness to do such a thing!"

The girl hung her head. A great tear rolled on the red shawl.

"He loves you so much! He was determined to get you back at all costs. . . . And now I want to know what has become of him?"

The tear-filled eyes of the little gypsy-girl must have touched the sergeant's heart because he mumbled something gruffly:

"The man with the bear? They caught him trying to climb up the keep and break in at a window. He fought like a devil when they seized him and the animal went mad. There was a scuffle. And then the bear got away. . . ."

"And Fero? My brother?"

"They put him in the dungeon to await sentence."

"Why must they sentence him?" Catherine cried. "Is it such a crime to be caught climbing up the keep as to need dungeons and judgments? Why couldn't they just throw him out?"

The man's face hardened and his eyes were cold.

"He was armed. He killed one of the pikemen! It is right that he should receive judgment. Now, my girl, get on with what you have to do here and let's go back! I don't like hanging about here. . . ."

Catherine did not answer and led Tereina away, sobbing bitterly. The girl had realized, like Catherine herself, what fate awaited her brother. The gypsy had murdered a man, he would be hanged . . . or worse! Catherine's own eyes misted with tears as she coaxed the little gypsy back into her caravan. What she had to say to her could not be said in front of everyone. The soldiers stationed themselves at both ends of the caravan.

Tereina was still weeping, deep convulsive sobs. Catherine searched desperately for something to say which might lessen this anguish of hers. The thought of Fero's impending death upset her more than she cared to admit. This man had loved her to madness, and in return for one night of love which she had given him, almost involuntarily, he had risked all, even life itself, for her sake. And now this crazy passion of his was to be the cause of his death! . . . Something must be done! If she took back the love philter the Dame de la Trémoille might grant the gypsy chief his life. But she would have to be quick about it.

She seized Tereina by the shoulders and shook her hard.

"Listen. Stop weeping! I shall have to go back there and try to save him. But first you must give me what I came for."

Tereina wiped her eyes and smiled a weak little smile.

"Everything I have is yours, sister. What is it you want?"

"I must have that love philter you made me drink the night when . . . You remember? The night Fero sent for me? Show me how it is made. All our lives may depend on this drug. I must have it at all costs, and the sooner the better. Can you show me how to make it?"

The girl looked at her in surprise.

"I don't know why you should have asked me this, Tchalai, but if, as you say, human lives depend on this drink I won't question you further. I must tell you though that the philter takes a long time to make, and the recipe for it cannot be passed on. It requires more than just the knowledge to make it . . . it needs an extra gift, otherwise it is not fully effective. There are spells one must say and . . ."

"Could you make me just a little then?" Catherine interrupted. "It is very serious . . . very urgent!"

"Do you need much? Do you want to try it out on many people?"

"No, only on one."

"In that case I have what you need!"

Tereina went to the back of her caravan, rummaged in a box hidden under some clothes, and drew out a little earthenware bottle which she came and placed in Catherine's hands, tenderly closing her fingers over it.

"Here! I made this for you . . . for your marriage night! So it belongs to you. Do what you want with it. I know that you will only use it for the best in any case."

Moved by a sudden impulse Catherine threw her arms round the little witch and embraced her warmly.

"Even if some evil befalls Fero I shall still be your sister, Tereina. . . . I would like to take you with me, but for the moment, I cannot."

"And I must stay here. They need me, you know."

The sergeant was growing impatient outside. He thrust aside the cloth draped over the door and poked his head in.

"Hurry up, woman. I have my orders. That's enough talk!"

By way of reply Catherine embraced Tereina again, and slipped the phial into her purse.

"Thank you, Tereina. Look after yourself. Adieu."

Swiftly she slipped out of the caravan and joined the soldiers. "Let us return. I have finished."

They surrounded her once more, then they passed through

the silent tribe and climbed up the mound to the entrance. On the way Catherine recognized Dunicha, the girl who had forced her to fight, and looked the other way. But not soon enough to escape the gypsy's look of deadly hatred. Dunicha no doubt held her responsible for Fero's capture, and probably hated her a hundred times more now than at the time of the combat. Catherine did not hold this against her. Dunicha loved Fero, and therefore she must hate the woman who had taken him from her, and for whom he was going to die! She vowed to be careful however; Dunicha was not the sort of girl who would let her hate lie fallow and not seek revenge.

The sound of a trumpet behind her made her turn. It was broad daylight now. . . . The Loire shone between reeded banks like a river of gold, and against this glowing background a vivid cavalcade went riding by, across the bridges that spanned the river. There were knights in armor, contrasting strongly with a group of ladies in pale dresses, mounted on gentle palfreys, who surrounded a great litter. The blue silk curtains were drawn back, and inside could be seen a lady muffled up in white veils, a nurse carrying a baby, two servants and three little girls aged somewhere between three and eight years old. A company of archers, pages and heralds preceded the cumbersome vehicle, and foremost of all rode a standard bearer carrying a massive banner on which Catherine was able to make out, her heart beating a little faster, the arms of France joined to those of Anjou. She had stopped instinctively but the sergeant was already pushing her up the grassy bank with the archers.

"The Queen! Make way! And don't forget to kneel, Egyptian girl, when our Good Lady goes by."

Catherine was not likely to forget that instruction. Marie d'Anjou, Queen of France, might be a timid and retiring woman but she had an excellent memory, and Catherine had been one of her ladies-in-waiting for many long months. It was unlikely that she would recognize her in her gypsy disguise, but dressed as she was now, like the servant of a good house, with this linen coif over her hair, there was little to disguise her appearance except the slightly darker skin and black brows. Only the night before as the Dame de la Trémoille was getting ready for bed, she had stared at her new servant with a reflective look in her eyes.

"It's funny," she said. "It seems to me that I've seen you before somewhere. You remind me of someone . . . but I can't think who."

Catherine had blessed this fortunate gap in her memory and had hastened to reply that, doubtless, the noble lady was

194

thinking of one of her sisters who had come to dance at the château. The countess must not be left to think too long about the matter. And as it happened she did not seem to give it another thought. It would be disastrous if the Queen were to recognize her now. . . !

So when the royal cavalcade, followed by the joyful acclaim of the people of Amboise, went past, she knelt down and hung her head very humbly . . . all the more so as just then a band of horsemen rode out of the château to greet the Queen, with Gilles de Rais at their head.

Luckily he did not pay any attention to her and once the litter had passed under the archway Catherine felt it was safe to raise her head. When she did so she found herself looking at a horse's legs while a juvenile, dry voice rasped:

"What has this woman done, sergeant? Where are you taking her?"

The haughty tone made Catherine blush for some reason and feel suddenly guilty, although the speaker could not have been more than ten years old. This young boy was skinny, sallow, with straight black hair, large bony shoulders, a big nose and strangely bright and perspicacious eyes for one so young. There was nothing charming about him, but something about the proud carriage of his head, the beauty of the horse whose reins he managed with supreme assurance, and the part red, part black and white costume he wore, appanage of the princes of the blood, made her realize that she was face to face with the Dauphin Louis, the King's eldest son.

Meanwhile the sergeant, red with pride, announced hastily: "I am not taking her anywhere, monseigneur. I am merely escorting her by order of the most high and noble Dame de la Trémoille."

Catherine watched open-mouthed as the Dauphine shrugged, crossed himself and spat unceremoniously.

"Some Moorish slave no doubt! I hate their damned tribe, but nothing that lady does would astonish me! Birds of a feather . . ."

He did not get to the end of his sentence because another rider had come up to him and was speaking rapidly to him in an undertone, no doubt counseling him to be more cautious about what he said. The sight of this newcomer made Catherine blush to the roots of her hair, and changed her alarm to panic. In spite of the suit of armor which concealed most of him she had recognized the Cross of Jerusalem on his coat-of-arms, and then the handsome blond face under the raised visor—it was Pierre de Breze! The man who had fallen in love with her at first sight at Angers, and had even asked her to marry him. He was party to the plot against La Trémoille

195

and would not denounce her. But he might well show some reaction at coming upon her so unexpectedly by the side of the road.

All the same she felt a sudden, inexplicable joy at seeing him again, and she could not help looking at him admiringly. He really was very handsome, this Pierre de Breze, and he cut a noble figure mounted on his tall gray warhorse. His heavy suit of armor seemed to weigh no more than a feather on those broad shoulders, and he dandled his long ash lance lightly against one thigh. The young man's voice broke into her thoughts.

"Monseigneur," said De Breze, "we shall be late and the Queen is waiting for us!"

As he spoke his blue eyes met Catherine's and a faint smile hovered about his firm mouth. It was only a brief glance, lasting no more than a second, but in it she was able to read all the passion he felt for her. As escort of the Queen he would be entering a castle where his presence was not welcome. He had come there for her sake alone braving the displeasure of the King and the hatred of La Trémoille. He had not only recognized her, but found a way of declaring his love anew without a word or gesture. Nevertheless his faint smile had not escaped the Prince's sharp eyes, and he darted a mocking glance at the knight.

"Hum! It seems to me, sir knight, that your tastes are as questionable as the lady's herself!"

He paid no more attention to Catherine but spurred on his horse, and De Breze was obliged to follow him. He did not look back but Catherine stood gazing after him till his proud silhouette had disappeared. When she set off once more, a moment later, her heart was warm with renewed confidence and courage. She had seen a black and silver scarf hanging from De Breze's arm, and were these not her own mourning colors which he wore so faithfully?

He had declared himself her knight and protector and evidently intended to remain so. Henceforward she could be sure of his comforting presence in this château where she had good reason to fear everything and everyone. And she could die without fear, if it were needful, because he would avenge her as he had sworn a solemn oath to do. If she failed, he would kill La Trémoille himself with his own hands, even though his own head would roll for it later.

However, as they crossed the drawbridge, Catherine forced herself to chase these comforting reflections away, pleasant though they were. There was another man in this same château who might have to die for her. . . .

CHAPTER TEN

At the Bottom of the Hole

When Catherine and her guards entered the courtyard they found it full of people. As well as the Queen's cortège there were now all the castle servants who had come out to unpack the baggage, as well as officers and dignitaries of one sort or another. She even saw the King's thin figure leading his wife into the royal lodging. She could not resist looking about in the crowd of lords and ladies for a certain proud profile and burning glance, but by now the archers were taking her across to the little stairs which led up the turret to the Dame de la Trémoille's quarters.

She found the door closed, and Violaine standing outside, wrapped in a long cloak. The girl dismissed the soldiers with a single gesture but did not move aside to let Catherine pass.

"You cannot enter, Egyptian girl!"

"Why not?"

Violaine did not deign to reply but merely shrugged. And then Catherine heard loud, angry voices from within, so loud they could be heard through the massive oak doors. She recognized the countess's shrill voice.

"I shall keep this girl as long as I like. And I advise you not to try and stop me!"

"What has put it into your head to try and interfere in my affairs? What do you want with this girl?"

"That is my business. Be patient . . . I will give her back to you when I have finished with her. . . ."

The voices dropped, but Catherine had grasped the situation. Husband and wife were quarreling on her account . . . and she need expect no gratitude from this woman whom she had thought to dominate. Violaine guessed where her thoughts were leading her; she gave a spiteful laugh and then whispered:

"Does that surprise you then? But what did you expect? To become a lady-in-waiting?"

Catherine shrugged, with assumed nonchalance: "I had imagined that great ladies knew how to reward folk for the

197

services they rendered them . . . but still, what does it matter?"

Her apparent calm must have impressed the maid-of-honor, because she stopped laughing, cast a quick mistrustful glance at Catherine and crossed herself as precipitately as if she had just encountered the devil. The conversation ended there. Almost at the same instant the door opened and La Trémoille burst out, his red and gold mantle flapping in the wind of his wrath. He stopped dead on seeing Catherine and darted a glittering eye over her, then plunged on down the stairs without a word.

Catherine's eyes met Violaine's, and it was like steel crossing steel. The sound of the Lord Chamberlain's steps died away, and with a disdainful smile the maid-of-honor gave the oak door a little push.

"You can go in now."

Catherine marched past, head held high, and had the satisfaction of hearing the door slam behind her.

"Not so much noise, Violaine," cried the Dame de la Trémoille irritably. "My head aches abominably!"

Dressed, but with her hair undone, she was pacing furiously up and down her room which was in an appalling state of untidiness. Catherine guessed that the chambermaid and ladies must have fled when the Lord Chamberlain entered, dropping everything, combs, pins, cosmetics and perfumes, in their haste. And the quarrel between the two had sent everything flying into all four corners of the room. She could not help smiling inwardly as she reflected that it was like entering the cage of one of the wild beasts the great noblemen and princes kept so luxuriously in captivity. The jackal had gone, leaving her alone with his angry female, who was a hundred times more dangerous. But Catherine had vowed never to let this woman see her flinch. All at once the countess rounded on her.

"My noble lord is more enamored of your dark skin than seems wise! My word, he behaves like a dog in heat!"

"If he fancies my skin," said Catherine coldly, "it is not for having sampled it. Your summons, noble lady, saved me. . . ."

"*Saved* you? What talk is this? What more can a girl like you hope for than the notice of a great lord? Have you forgotten that I am his wife?"

"I am your servant. And in truth the commands you gave me did suggest that I might forget the fact."

The lady's anger subsided instantly, deflated by the coldness of Catherine's manner. In the grip of anger she had

198

sought to draw blood from the first person who came within reach of her claws. But the woman standing there so proudly was unafraid, and all at once she remembered the need she had of her services. She questioned her feverishly:

"Have you the thing I asked you for?"

Catherine nodded, but crossed her arms as if to protect the little bottle she had slipped into her bosom.

"Yes, I have it, but there is something I must say to you . . ."

The countess's hand was already outstretched and her eyes shone greedily between their heavy lids.

"Say what it is you have to say . . . and be quick about it. I am in a hurry."

"Yesterday you offered me gold for this love potion . . . and I refused it. I still refuse it . . . but there is something else I want!"

A thin smile stretched the lady's lips but there was a dangerous light in her eyes.

"I already know: you want to serve me. Now give it to me!"

"That is what I said, it is true, and I still say so, but things have changed this morning. The leader of our tribe is imprisoned in the castle. He is in danger of his life. I want him set free!"

"What do I care for the life of a barbarian? Give me that phial unless you want my women to take it from you by force."

Catherine took the bottle slowly from her purse and held it in one hand. Her eyes met the countess's boldly, and she smiled faintly.

"Here it is! But if anyone comes near me I will throw it on the floor and break it. We don't have gold and silver bottles, we gypsies . . . only pottery ones! And pottery is fragile. Your women would not have time to seize it. I will break it . . . just as I will destroy it if Fero is not returned to his people."

It was easy to read, on her adversary's contorted face, the battle that was going on between fury, passion and greed. It was the latter which won.

"Wait here a moment. I will go and see what can be done."

The countess did not even bother to knot up her hair but threw a silk scarf over it and went out. Catherine sank down on some cushions heaped up near the fireplace. The atmosphere of this room was stuffy and oppressive. All these heavy scents were like the emanation of the poisonous woman who lived here. She felt about feverishly under her dress for the hard outline of the dagger, and caressed the shape of the sparrow-hawk carved upon its hilt as though to draw strength from it. Arnaud's hand must have closed upon it so many times—surely a little of his force must have clung to it. . . . But at the recollection of her proud, tall husband, tears sprang to her eyes, hot, bitter tears. What would be left now of that strong body, and handsome face? How badly had the leprosy ravaged them? She shuddered with horror at the thought of some of the lepers she had met on her journey, dreadful ruins of gray flesh with nothing human about them. And yet many of them came hopefully to seek a miraculous cure from one holy place after another. That woman who had just gone out was the whole cause of the evil which devoured Arnaud alive, and broke her heart. How gladly she would have plunged this dagger into the woman's breast! But she must wait . . . still wait! Wearily Catherine let her head fall into her hands, trying to drive out the painful images which were sapping her courage. Another figure suddenly appeared before her mind's eye, a tall blond man whose pale eyes gazed tenderly and who wore a black and silver scarf on his arm. It was a beautiful, gentle, reassuring image. But Catherine dismissed it too, as a profanation, as if Pierre de Brezé had tried to conquer her heart and replace the image of Arnaud. . . .

The return of the Dame de la Trémoille drew her from her thoughts. The countess stared at her for a moment and smiled, but there was such cruelty in that smile that it set Catherine on her guard.

"Come," she said. "You will be satisfied."

As on the previous night they left the room one behind the other but there was no concealed door this time. They went down to the courtyard and crossed it, turning aside when they came to the keep towards the prison tower. On the way Catherine recognized Tristan l'Hermite standing with a group of grooms who were playing dice on a large stone. He turned aside as she passed and followed her with his eyes. His gaze was as impenetrable and cool as ever, but from its very persistence Catherine knew he must be wondering what she was doing going to the prisons in such company.

There was a low door at the foot of the tower, made of worm-eaten wood. They had to stoop to enter. Once inside the chill struck Catherine on the shoulders. Light and warmth stopped at the threshold to this world of darkness and pain. At the far end of a low vaulted guard-room, where several men were playing cards in the smoky light of a taper, a dark

200

stairway plunged into the earth. . . . At a dry click of the fingers from the countess one of the soldiers stood up and lit a torch from the lamp, and headed down the stairs in front of them. But Catherine observed none of this because something else had drawn her attention the moment they entered the tower, a sound which froze the blood in her veins: the sound of human groans, which strangely enough grew weaker and yet more distinct as they descended deeper into the ground. By the time the women reached the first landing these groans had become a death rattle. Catherine stared with a stricken heart at the massive door which led off this landing. It was made of solid iron and secured by immense bolts, but a small barred judas window let through a sinister, reddish glow. It was from there that the moans were coming, at the same time as a sort of soft, cracking sound which seemed to coincide with the groans.

Without a word the soldier pushed open the door. Catherine gave a half-stifled cry of horror and fear. . . .

Two torturers dressed in leather, their shaved heads sweating with effort, were alternately whipping a man whose wrists were fastened to the top of a pillar. . . . Catherine did not at once see La Trémoille who sat watching, his triple chins in his hand, on a rough wooden chair. His eyes were riveted to the condemned man who was moaning feebly. His legs no longer supported him and the whole weight of his body dragged on those chained wrists. His head, with its long black hair, hung limp, and his back was nothing but a bloody mess in which the whips struck with an abominable sound. The ground was covered with blood. . . . Sick with horror, Catherine shrank back against the wall but not in time to avoid a splash of blood hitting her on the cheek.

She glanced round at the Dame de la Trémoille with agonized eyes, but the lady was not looking at her. With flaring nostrils and wide-open eyes, she was so clearly enjoying the spectacle that a wave of sickness rose in Catherine's throat. The man had stopped groaning. The executioners ceased their blows, but even before one of them, with a brutal gesture, pushed back the long straight hair hanging over the prisoner's brow, Catherine had recognized Fero . . . and suddenly a terrible vision rose before her eyes. Instead of the gypsy she saw Arnaud, attached to a column as he was, groaning and bleeding under the whiplash, with this atrocious woman standing there, passing her pointed tongue over her dry lips. Arnaud had undergone his torture in the dungeons of Sully before Xaintrailles rescued him. . . . And her vision was so appallingly vivid that Catherine felt a great wave of hatred sweep through her. . . .

Blinded by an uncontrollable rage she felt in her bodice for the dagger. But the first thing her shaking hand encountered was the earthenware bottle, and she paused. The torturer announced flatly:

"The man is dead, monseigneur. . . ."

La Trémoille gave a sigh of annoyance, and finally managed to struggle out of his chair.

"He wasn't as strong as he looked. Throw him into the river. . . ."

"No, don't!" his wife interrupted. "I promised this girl that he would be returned to his people. Return him to them . . . and then send them all packing!" Her crazy eyes turned and sought Catherine, with an expression of malicious glee. Catherine leaned against the wall, ashen pale.

"You see," she said, with dangerous softness, "I have done as you asked."

Catherine's haunted eyes fixed on hers with a look of such passionate hatred and scorn in them that the latter, impressed despite herself, took a step backward. Catherine's hand slowly drew out the little flask. Her fingers squeezed and squeezed, endowed with the strength of her fury, until the little bottle was crushed in her hand. Then with a violent gesture she flung the pieces in her enemy's face:

"And I have given you what I promised you . . ." she said in a voice drained of all emotion.

The countess's pale face was distorted by a dreadful rage. One of the fragments had slightly scratched her lip and the smear of blood gave her a dreadful likeness to a ghoul. She pointed at Catherine with a trembling finger:

"Seize this woman, and chain her up in her companion's place and whip her . . . whip her till she dies too, like the other!"

Catherine realized that in one moment of blind anger she had lost everything, ruined all her plans for vengeance and those of Queen Yolande's too. She realized too that she would never leave this place alive, but strangely enough she had no regrets for what she had done. She would have to content herself, by way of return for Arnaud's sufferings and those she would undergo, with that thin trickle of blood from a cut lip and the countess's fury. But at least the young Comte du Maine would not run the risk of falling, even for a night, into the clutches of this appalling creature.

The two men were already seizing hold of Catherine when La Trémoille, who had been on the point of leaving when the supposed gypsy flung the bottle in his wife's face, and had remained watching the scene that followed with curiosity not unmixed with pleasure, now intervened. He stooped quickly and dipped his finger in the liquid on the floor and sniffed it. Then he said:

"One moment if you please. This woman was given to me. I think I have the right to dispose of her. . . . You will recollect, my dear, that she was only . . . lent to you?"

Now the lady vented all her fury against her husband and marched towards him, with clenched fists.

"She insulted me and struck me, this Egyptian bitch . . . and now you hesitate to punish her?"

"I don't hesitate . . . she shall be punished, when the time comes! For the moment you will have to be content with throwing her into a dungeon. There are certain matters I want to clear up."

"What for instance?"

"What for instance was inside that little bottle whose loss seems to have upset you so much. . . !"

"That is nothing to do with you!"

"All the more intriguing in that case. Go on, you there, put this woman in the cells. And remember that no one is to lay a finger upon her without express instructions. You will answer for her safety with your lives. . . ."

"What precautions!" hissed the countess, raging but defeated. "God forgive me, but one might suppose this girl was infinitely precious to you."

"God cares no more for you, my dear, than you for him. As for this woman, of course she is precious to me. Didn't she seek to harm you? There must be a strong reason for this hatred of hers. I love you too much not to try and discover it . . . by whatever means! Are you coming?"

He held out his hand to her with a smile both mocking and ironical half hidden in his beard. Catherine thought that the Lord Chamberlain seemed somewhat less frightened of his wife than usual. He had just discovered a weapon he could use against her and it looked as though he knew how to make good use of it. They went towards the door together, a curious couple, more tightly bound by their mutual hatred than by the tenderest love. They were like evil spirits out of some nightmare, and she suddenly thought that the worst punishment that could be meted out to them might be to lock them up together in one room, jackal and hyena, and leave them together for all eternity. . . . What damnation in hell could equal that tête-à-tête?

But she did not have time to watch them leave. One of the

203

torturers let drop a heavy hairy hand, clothed in a leather glove, upon her shoulder and drew her towards the other end of the room.

"This way, my beauty!"

Meanwhile his companion was unloosing Fero's inert body, which slid to the ground with a thump. Catherine felt a tear smart in her eyes. This man had loved her once; that tortured flesh had trembled, warm and living, against her own; those bloodless lips had murmured words of love and covered her with passionate kisses . . . and now Fero was no more than a piece of bleeding flesh which they would be carrying back to the camp in a little while. Imagining Tereina's grief, a sob escaped Catherine.

The guard mistook the meaning of this.

"It's hardly the time to start crying now, when you've just signed your own death warrant! Whatever got into you to attack that terrible woman?"

And when Catherine did not reply he shook his great head, which seemed to grow straight out of his massive shoulders, so short was his neck.

"I shall not like torturing you, for there's no pleasure in spoiling a pretty creature like you! But the chances are she will make you pay dearly for what you did to her. . . ."

"She can only kill me," Catherine said scornfully.

"There's killing and killing! I would like just to hang you but she would never be content with that! Eh, well . . . I'll just have to try and be a bit clumsy so it doesn't last too long!"

The man's intentions were kindly, but his words were such as to make one shudder.

"Thank you," Catherine muttered.

When they left the cell, the torturer and his prisoner turned into a narrow tunnel with three iron-barred doors opening off it. One of them was open. The man pushed Catherine in and she found herself in a small damp cell. A mildewed pitcher and pile of dank hay were the room's only furnishings. A pair of iron bracelets hung from the wall. A small shaft of daylight entered through an aperture hardly bigger than a hand high up in one wall. It seemed to be at ground level because a little water came trickling in through it.

"Here you are then," said the man. "Give me your hands."

She held them out docilely enough. The heavy iron bracelets snapped shut over the fragile wrists. The man held them for a moment.

"You have pretty hands . . ." he said, "a lady's hands.

204

. . . Ah, yes, it's a shame! There are days when my job's a sorry one right enough!"

"Why do you do it then?"

The executioner's broad face took on a look of innocent astonishment, while his yellow teeth showed in a sort of smile.

"But . . . well, it's the only one I can do! My father did it afore me and his father afore him. It's a good job you know, and you can go a long way in it if you're handy! Why, one day I may rise to be chief torturer in a big city! Ah, if the King were to return to Paris that would be fine!"

But Catherine, unable to control her horror, could only stare at the blotches of still wet blood on the man's thick torso. He noticed and gave an awkward smile.

"Come, come, I didn't want to frighten you! You must take me for a monster! Try and sleep if you can!"

Afraid that she might have offended him and not wishing to make an enemy for herself, Catherine asked:

"What is your name?"

"It's kind of you to ask me that! It's not often that happens to me, you know? They call me Aycelin the Red . . . yes, Aycelin. My mother used to say it was a nice name. . . ."

"She was right," Catherine said solemnly, "it is a nice name. . . ."

Catherine's eyes rapidly grew accustomed to the darkness of her cell. Small though the skylight was, it would be large enough to enable her to tell night from day and make out the things around her. She sent up fervent thanks to heaven for not having been cast into one of those dreadful *oubliettes* situated so deep beneath the ground that no light ever penetrates there, like the one where she had been imprisoned at Rouen.

She sat on her pile of straw and let the hours slip by. Her chained hands still allowed her a little freedom of movement, despite the weight of the manacles, and she observed that it might even be possible to slip them off. Her hands were so small and slender . . . but perhaps it would be better not to try just yet because it would hurt her so much that she probably would not succeed in getting them on again.

Another cause for satisfaction was that she had not been searched and the dagger was still there, solid and comforting between her breasts. God be praised that she had not drawn it earlier after all! They would have taken it from her and she would never have seen it again. And thanks to it, Catherine was sure to be spared the tortures the countess might devise for her. One swift blow and it would all be over. She would not cry out with pain under her enemy's mocking eyes. . . . All the same she could not fight back the pain which tore at her throat: what was going to happen to her? She could barely hear the sounds of the castle, the walls down here were too thick, and yet from time to time she seemed to make out a sort of distant, lugubrious wailing noise. She realized that it must be the sound of the tribe bewailing its chief's grisly death. She could imagine the women wailing, their long black locks trailing in the dust, tearing at their faces with their hands, the monotonous chants intoned by a mourning tribe, the curses they must be sending up for the woman who unwittingly caused Fero's death!

"My God," she prayed to herself, "please make them understand and forgive me! Especially Tereina! She is going to suffer so much! . . . Have pity on her!"

Would they have time to consign the body to the river with all the ceremony she had witnessed the other night? The countess had given orders for them to be driven off, and La Trémoille had not made any objection. She seemed to hear the orders barked by the King's sergeants, the soldiers' whips cracking as they drove the wandering people away. . . . But now a voice rose up in song, a deep and beautiful voice. And it was a song which Catherine remembered. . . .

Suddenly she realized that the voice was not singing in her imagination but in reality . . . and close at hand! On the other side of the wall to be precise. Then she understood, and the joy in her heart was so great she tried to fling herself against the wall whence the song was coming. But she had forgotten her chains and she fell back heavily against the stone floor, bruising her wrists so badly that her eyes filled with tears. But her bonds could not silence her and she cried out with all the strength in her:

"Sara! Sara! You're there! It is I . . ." she bit her lips. She had been on the point of crying out "It is I, Catherine." She had enough presence of mind to change it to: "It is I, Tchalai." Then she listened with all her heart. The song had ceased in the next door cell. There was a moment's silence. . . . Then to her inexpressible relief she heard:

"The Lord be praised!"

The voice was fainter than the singing and Catherine realized that conversation would be difficult. She would have to shout to make herself heard and it might even be dangerous, but that was too bad. Besides, had Tristan not said that he would keep an eye on Sara? Earlier, when she had accompanied the Dame de la Trémoille to the prison tower, he had

206

followed her with his eyes. He would have been surprised to see the countess leave again without her and must have drawn his own conclusions from that. Feeling a little calmer, Catherine got up and went back to her straw where she lay down. If the countess did not have her put to death in the next few hours she might have a chance of survival. Hope enters most freely in the darkest dungeons, and it was stirring already in Catherine's breast.

She watched the daylight fading in her little window with misgivings, however. When night fell she would be plunged into the most profound darkness. . . . Little by little she was losing sight of her surroundings. The damp sweating walls retreated into the shadows, and the moment came when she could no longer even see her pale hand before her. She felt as though an evil flood was rising which threatened to submerge her entirely. . . .

But then, as if she had guessed Catherine's dismay, Sara's voice spoke out of the depths of the night.

"Sleep now! The nights are short at present. . . ."

That was true. Summer was approaching and the days were infinitely longer than the nights. By straining her eyes Catherine could just dimly discern the little paler square of her skylight. Then somewhat comforted, she lay down and closed her eyes. . . .

Could she have been asleep already when a faint sound reached her ears? But faint as it was it awoke her; she was so used to living with danger that she slept lightly. . . . She lay motionless, not even breathing. She had been awakened by the faint creak of her door being opened. Someone was entering, or had entered already. . . . She noticed the almost imperceptible sound of another living human being in the darkness beside her. There was a faint creak as someone brushed against the stone wall, and Catherine's heart stopped beating. . . . Who could it be?

The idea struck her that it might be rats, and at this her flesh crawled; but she was certain that the noise she had heard was her door being opened. Then a second later she heard that faint breathing again, but nearer . . . much nearer this time! She was bathed in cold sweat. With infinite care she slipped her hand into her bodice, making sure the chains did not rattle, and took out the dagger and gripped it firmly. A terrible fear gnawed at her entrails. She felt as if she had been transported back to that old keep at Malain where, years ago, she had been obliged to fight off the advances of her brutish gaoler every night. It was all starting again. . . .

207

But this time . . . who could it be? . . . Why had they come?

She was so frightened that a scream threatened to burst from her lips and she had to clench her teeth to keep it back. The man was very near now . . . it was a man, she could tell by the smell. . . .

Suddenly a great weight descended on her stomach and she gave a scream which must have echoed through every corner of the castle. The weight on top of her seemed to be crushing her.

She soon realized that the man was bent on strangling her. Two great hairy hands groped for her throat. She felt sharp, odious breathing hot against her face. She twisted and writhed but could not free herself. The man's hands were about to close, they were closing now. . . . A fierce instinct for survival made her lift her arm and plunge the dagger with all her strength into the man's back. The blade sank in up to the hilt. The body crushed upon hers jerked back, and the man gave a brief cry. But then the hands fell limply at her sides. Something warm and sticky flowed over her. The dagger had struck home. The man was dead with a single blow. . . . With a great effort she managed to roll the corpse aside, her teeth chattering with fear. Just then the cell door opened. Two men, one of them carrying a torch, rushed in and stood transfixed by the spectacle of Catherine kneeling, covered in blood, beside a corpse. She gazed at them with the eyes of a sleepwalker, and recognized, without a trace of emotion, Tristan l'Hermite and Aycelin.

"He tried to strangle me. . . ." she said in a toneless voice. "I killed him. . . ."

"Thanks be to God," Tristan, who was ashen pale, muttered to himself. "I almost arrived too late!" Then, turning to his companion who gazed at Catherine with stupefaction, he barked:

"You remember monseigneur's orders? You were to answer for this woman's safety with your life!"

The man's face went muddy gray and he stared at Tristan piteously. "Ye . . . e . . . es, messire! I . . . I remember!"

"Luckily for you I arrived just in time. Take this carrion away, and see that it is discreetly disposed of. Thus, since only you, I . . . and she know about this, no one will be any the wiser. You aren't hurt then, woman?"

Catherine shook her head. Aycelin stooped and took hold of the assassin's massive body. With a colossal effort he raised it on his back.

"I'll throw him in the *oubliette*," he said. "It's close at hand!"

"Hurry up, I'll wait here."

He went out with his burden, throwing a grateful look at the Fleming, and did not even trouble to close the door behind him. As soon as he had gone Tristan leaned towards Catherine.

"Quick, we haven't much time! I was coming to talk to Sara through her grille, as I usually do about this time, when I saw this man—one of the Dame de la Trémoille's valets—slipping into the prison. I had a premonition as to what might be about to happen. I followed him. This livery is a safe-conduct. . . . Then I heard your scream and I came running. . . ."

"Were you coming to get me?"

He shook his head sadly, distressed to see great tears welling up into her eyes.

"Not yet. I cannot. In an hour's time the Lord Chamberlain is coming down here to pay you a visit."

"How do you know?"

"I heard him ordering one of the mutes to put a chicken and a flagon of wine into a basket. Apparently he still has tender feelings towards you. It is important to find out what he wants. I don't imagine that he can have . . . improper designs on you in a hole like this! Besides he is ill . . . much too ill to be capable of the least exploit!"

"I wouldn't let him, anyway! My dagger struck once and it can strike again. . . ."

"Don't go too far! You mustn't let yourself be carried away like you were earlier in the torture chamber. You could destroy us all! I'm going now. Messire de Breze is waiting for me in the orchard. . . ."

He stood up, ready to go. Catherine plucked at his sleeve.

"When shall I see you again?"

"Tomorrow night, perhaps. . . . Before if necessary. Don't be frightened. We shall keep close watch over you now, and I truly believe that De Breze would be prepared to cut La Trémoille's throat at the King's feet for your sake! Courage!"

Aycelin was returning now. Tristan waited by the door for him. Catherine suddenly gave a jump.

"Messire! All this blood . . . how shall I explain it?"

"You will say what happened—and that Aycelin saved you and killed the assassin. That way he will get promotion and you have nothing to lose by the lie!"

The torturer grinned broadly.

"You are kind, messire! If there is anything I can do for you . . ."

"We'll see about that later! Close the door again, and keep better watch this time!"

Tristan left the cell without a glance at Catherine. The cell was pitch dark once more. Catherine's nerves were shattered. She burst into tears. It made her feel better. She wept for a long time, violently, and emerged from it exhausted but calmer. . . . There wasn't a sound from the next-door cell. Sara must have been as frightened as she was, but Tristan must have reassured her. Catherine forced herself to recover her composure. It was essential. She would need all her wits about her to confront La Trémoille shortly . . . very soon now!

Just then a little light glimmered under the door. Heavy footsteps sounded along the passage. Bolts were drawn back, the door opened, only to be blotted out in a moment by the Lord Chamberlain's huge shape. Aycelin stood behind him holding a lantern above his head. La Trémoille's bearded profile flickered up towards the ceiling. But the fat man stopped dead before Catherine's tearful face and bloodstained clothes.

"What's wrong? Are you hurt? What happened? I gave express orders . . ."

Aycelin was beginning to cower away in terror but Catherine came to his rescue.

"They tried to kill me, monseigneur. This man heard me scream. . . . He saved my life!"

"He did well. Here . . . catch! And now leave us!"

He flung a gold piece in the direction of the gaoler, who swooped to pick it up with the agility of a cat, and then retired, bowing and scraping and mumbling words of gratitude. La Trémoille glanced round for somewhere to sit, but there was nothing except Catherine's moldy straw. So he decided to remain standing, wrinkling his nose in disgust. Then he pulled a bag out of his cape and handed it to the prisoner.

"Here! You must be hungry. Eat and drink. Then we will talk. But hurry."

Catherine was dying of hunger. She had not eaten since the day before and she needed no urging. She devoured the bread and chicken in the bag, drank the wine and then flashed a grateful look at the Lord Chamberlain.

"Thank you, milord . . . you are kind."

A wild hope was growing in her. This was the first time she had been alone with him, without danger. Perhaps the time had come to put her plan into effect? La Trémoille smiled, and his face creased into hundreds of little puffy cushions. Then he laid his fat hand on Catherine's head and murmured in a silky voice.

"You see that I don't wish to harm you in any way, little one! You are quite innocent in all this affair. It wasn't of your own free will that you left my apartment, was it?"

"No. A young girl came to fetch me." Catherine said, pretending to be innocent. "A beautiful blonde girl."

"Violaine de Champchevrier. I know her only too well. She is my wife's confidante, but you I think are my own friend . . . aren't you? I've always been good to you, isn't that true?"

"Very good, lord, very merciful."

"Very well, then, now is the moment to show your gratitude. What was in that bottle which you broke earlier this evening, and which you threw the pieces of into my wife's face?"

Catherine hid her face as if she were struggling with herself, and did not reply all at once. La Trémoille grew impatient.

"Come now, speak! You have no reason to keep silent, quite the contrary!"

She looked up and gazed into his face with a look of great frankness. "You are right. You have never done me any harm! This bottle . . . it held a love philter which the lady asked me for. . . ."

The Chamberlain's thick lips set in a cruel line, while his eyes seemed to sink further into his head.

"A love philter, hey? And do you know who it was for?"

This time Catherine did not hesitate. There could be no question of placing the young Comte du Maine in danger. She shook her head vigorously.

"No, Lord, I don't know!"

The Lord Chamberlain's brow darkened. He played nervously with the long gold sash he was wearing, and for a moment, remained silent.

"A love philter?" he repeated again, a moment later. "But what for? My wife doesn't want love, she only wants pleasure. . . ."

Catherine took a deep breath and clasped her hands together, squeezing them together to master the emotion which seemed to be rising in her. The moment had come to stake all on the next throw, to say what she had come to say to this man in order to persuade him to leave his safe retreat. . . .

"It is a very potent drink, monseigneur. It makes the one who drinks it as helpless as a child in the hands of the person

211

who gives him the drink. And the lady wanted it to get a great secret out of a man . . . the secret of a treasure!"

Although she had been warned she was still taken aback by the instant, magical effect of that word! The fat face grew purple, and angry light flashed from the Lord Chamberlain's eyes. He seized Catherine by the shoulders and shook her brutally.

She gave a perfect imitation of abject terror, sinking back on her heels and darting timid, frightened glances at the fat man.

"I am but a poor simple girl, monseigneur, how should I know these secrets? But I listen and I understand things. In my far away country in the East they still speak of the soldier-monks who came to defend the Savior's tomb and left the country with great treasures. When they returned to France the King had them all put to death. . . ."

La Trémoille wiped the sweat off his brow with the back of his sleeve. His eyes were burning.

"The Knights Templar. . . ." he murmured, licking his dry lips. "Go on!"

She flung up her chained hands in a helpless gesture.

"They say that before dying, they were able to hide away the greater part of their treasure, and that the hiding-places are marked by incomprehensible signs and figures. The man who interests the noble lady knows how to decipher these signs. . . ."

The fat man's shining face clouded with disappointment, and he did not hesitate to show it. He mumbled angrily, shrugging his shoulders:

"Yes, but first we have to find out where these signs are to be found. . . ."

An angelic smile spread over Catherine's face, and the look she turned on him was one of candid sweetness.

"Perhaps I shouldn't tell you this, seigneur, but you have been so good to me . . . and the lady so cruel! She promised me to spare Fero's life and she let him die under the lash . . . I think she knows where the signs are. I heard her the other night. She thought I was asleep. She talked of a château where the soldier-monks were imprisoned before going to the scaffold . . . but I can't remember the name!"

This was so artistically played that La Trémoille abandoned the last shreds of mistrust, if he had ever had any. Once more he seized hold of her.

"I order you to remember! You must remember the name! Was it in Paris . . . in the great Templar's Tower? Was it there?"

She shook her head gently.

"No . . . it wasn't at Paris! It was a name like . . . oh, how difficult it is . . . a name like Ninon . . . something like that. . . ."

"Chinon, that's it! It was Chinon, wasn't it?"

"I believe so," Catherine said, "but I'm not certain. Is there a very large tower there?"

"Immense! The keep of Coudray! The Grand Master of the Order, Jacques de Molay, was imprisoned there with other dignitaries during the trial!"

"In that case," said Catherine tranquilly, "the inscription must be in that tower. . . ."

The huge man stood up and paced up and down in a frenzy of excitement. She gazed at him with a fierce joy. She had heard this tale once from Arnaud. One evening, after the sack of Montsalvy, he had sighed and told her how an ancestor of his, a Knight Templar, had been entrusted, along with two other brothers, with the task of concealing the treasure. He had died soon after, his lips sealed upon the secret to which the Grand Master alone knew the key.

"They say that in his prison," Arnaud told her, "in the great tower at Chinon, the Grand Master carved the key to the cipher . . . but alas his marks are indecipherable. I saw them myself when I was there but I didn't pay much attention to them. I was rich, carefree. . . . Now I should like to find that fabulous treasure again to rebuild Montsalvy. . . ."

She had recalled this conversation at Angers when the need arose to think of a lure to attract the Lord Chamberlain to Chinon! But now the bait had been thrown and the fish was hooked. . . . A great relief swept over her. Even if she never left this dungeon alive, she was almost certain that La Trémoille would go to Chinon, and that the trap would close on him there . . . and then she would be avenged!

Almost lightheartedly she watched him circling the cell like a caged bear, and she seemed to see the fever for gold flowing through his veins like a poison. She heard him murmur:

"That man . . . he must be found! I must discover his name! Once I know that I can make him talk. . . ."

"Lord," she interrupted softly, "will you permit me to give you a word of advice?"

He stared at her as if surprised to find her still there. In his newfound passion he had forgotten all about her.

"Yes, speak! You have done me a great service."

"If I were you, milord, I should say nothing which might arouse suspicion. I would go to Chinon with the Court . . .

and even the King, if necessary, and I would watch the noble lady. Once you are there you would be certain to find out which man it is that interests her. . . ."

Now his puffy face brightened. A sly, cruel smile appeared there, smoothing away wrinkles like oil on troubled waters. He picked up his bag, took up the lantern and banged on the door.

"Gaoler! Hey, gaoler!"

He was just about to leave when she cried out:

"Lord, have pity on me! You won't forget me, will you?"

But he scarcely seemed to hear her now. He glanced at her absently.

"Oh, yes . . . don't worry! I'll think of something. But mind you keep quiet about this, or . . ."

She understood. She had suddenly lost all her value in his eyes. With this dazzling vista of gold opening up before him he had even forgotten the violent attraction she had held for him. It mattered little to him now whether she lived or died. The only thing that mattered was the treasure. . . . Tomorrow, tonight perhaps, he would persuade the Court to move to Chinon. Catherine's mission was accomplished. But now she was in greater danger than ever, because she was positive that before leaving for Chinon the Dame de la Trémoille would see to it that she was hurried into the next life. And what if Pierre de Breze and Tristan l'Hermite were not quick enough to save her? She drew the dagger out of her bosom again and pressed the guard to her trembling lips.

"Arnaud," she murmured, "you shall be avenged! I have done what I set out to do. And now may the Lord have mercy upon me!"

But the rest of the night passed silently, without bringing further visitors to the dungeons.

When Aycelin entered Catherine's cell towards midday, bearing a plate filled with a cloudy liquid in which some bits of cabbage floated, a pitcher of water and some dry bread, he seemed dreadfully cast down. His coarse face with its indeterminate features and shaved hair wore a look of deep despair. He placed the bowl and pitcher at Catherine's side.

"Here is your dinner," he said with a deep sigh. "I would have liked to give you something better, because you are going to need all your strength! Eat it though."

Catherine stood up and pushed away the disgusting soup, which she did not need after La Trémoille's fowl.

"I'm not hungry," she said. "But why do you say that I shall need all my strength?"

"Because it's been arranged for tonight . . . they are coming for you after the curfew and I shall . . . I shall have to . . . But you do pardon me, don't you? It isn't my fault, you know. I just do my job."

Catherine's throat tightened. She understood what the executioner was saying. That night, under the Dame de la Trémoille's eyes, she would be tortured to death. Panic swelled in her like a hurricane. Thanks to her dagger she would be spared the torture. But not death. And suddenly she did not want to die! The night before, in her joy at finding La Trémoille prepared to move to Chinon, she had believed that nothing else mattered and that it would be easy to die now because she would be avenged. . . . But now, confronted by this man of blood, who had appointed himself the tragic herald of her last hours on earth, she found herself rejecting her fate with all her strength. She was young, beautiful, she wanted to live! She wanted to get out of his hole and see the sun, and the great blue sky and all the manifold flora and fauna with which God had blessed this earth. She wanted to see her son, little Michel, the mountains of Auvergne, even the sinister place where her love was slowly wasting away . . . Arnaud! She did not want to die so far away from him! To touch his hand again, just once, and then die . . . yes, that she could do. But not before then. . . !

She flung back her head abruptly.

"Listen," she said urgently. "You must find the man who came here last night . . . the one you said you owed such a debt to!"

"Monseigneur's valet?"

"That is the one . . . I don't know his name but you will have no trouble in recognizing him. Go and find him. Tell him what you have just told me. . . ."

"And what if I don't find him? Monseigneur has a lot of valets. . . ."

"You must find him. You must! You say it would upset you so much to hurt me . . . I beg you . . . find him. . . ."

She stood up. With trembling hands she grasped the executioner's huge hairy paws; her great tear-stained eyes gazed at him imploringly. He had shown pity to her. She sensed a sort of fellow feeling towards her in that strange character. It was absolutely essential that he warn Tristan, otherwise the Fleming would almost certainly arrive too late. She would be dead already. Had the executioner not said "after the curfew"? Well it was long after the curfew that Tristan had come the night before.

"For pity's sake, Aycelin . . . if you have a little friendliness towards me, find him!"

The man nodded his big head, whose two large ears gave it a little the air of a cooking-pot. His small eyes blinked under their lashless lids.

"I will do my best . . . but it won't be easy! There is a great to-do in the château today. . . . The King has decided to leave for Chinon tomorrow. They are starting to pack for the journey. Still, I'll see what I can do. . . ."

Catherine collapsed in a heap on the straw. The news Aycelin had just given her was precious, as it was formal proof of her victory. The King was La Trémoille. And he was on his way to Chinon where the Constable de Richemont's men were waiting for him, where the castle was commanded by Raoul de Goncourt, who was party to the conspiracy. The mad boar which had so long and so ruinously trampled the soil of France was going to his last lair. But, if Aycelin did not succeed in warning Tristan, Catherine would not see the dawn of another day. . . .

She stayed there for hours, exhausted, crouched on her mattress with her arms hugging her knees, staring into space and listening to her own heart beats. She was fighting with every ounce of resolution against the onset of despair. Opposite her, the other side of the wall, there was Sara, her old Sara, dear refuge in times of need; but now she had never seemed further away! She had to shout to make herself heard. She was too weak for that! . . . But her agony grew worse as daylight grew into dusk. Outside in the castle yard the sounds of activity were growing more intense every minute. From her dark cell she could hear orders, servants shouting, names called, all the joyous commotion which accompanied a royal departure. It fell cruelly on the ears of one who was about to die. She wondered briefly whether the dead can hear the noise made by the living in the silence of their graves. . . .

The sound of the judas window being opened in the door of her cell made her start. She could see Aycelin's red face through the aperture, lit by the light of a candle. What he said sank like lead into her consciousness.

"I didn't find the man. . . . Forgive me."

"Look for him again!"

"I can't. I haven't time. I have to get ready. . . ."

The judas window shut. Catherine found herself consigned once more to the gathering darkness. A darkness she would only leave to enter one still darker. That was it, then. There was no more to hope for, she should not waste her thoughts

on men. She must turn her thoughts towards God. . . .
Slowly Catherine fell to her knees, burying her face in her
hands.

"My God," she murmured, "since it is Your will that I die
tonight, spare me the torture . . . give me time to kill myself
first. . . ."

She drew the dagger gently from her bodice and held it
against her in a sudden temptation. Why not make an end of
it now? When the torturers entered her cell they would only
find a lifeless corpse. . . . That would be so much simpler. . . .

The sparrow-hawk was warm in the hollow of her palm,
warm as a living bird, and reassuring as a loyal friend. She
knew just where to strike to pierce her heart. . . . Just there
below her left breast. . . . With the point of the blade she
groped for the place and pressed. . . . The sharp point broke
the skin through her dress, and the pain roused Catherine
from the sort of death-like trance she was in. It would be
easy to pierce that fragile skin. She only had to press a little
harder. But some sort of mysterious instinct held her back.
Perhaps after all she should live out the last few minutes
which remained to her. Besides she did not want to die in this
dark hole. She wanted to die in the light, even if it were only
that of a torture chamber. She wanted to die face to face
with the enemy, so that she might enjoy their discomfiture at
seeing her slip through their clutches, and curse them too as
she died. . . . Yes, she must wait till then . . . it would be
better!

Just then the castle heralds blew a blast on their trumpets
in reply to the town bells—the curfew had sounded! It was
like the last trump answering to the funeral knell. Catherine's
blood ran cold. The last few minutes of her time were running out. . . . Soon . . .

There came the sound of mailed feet outside in the passage, and the grating of steel against stone. Catherine shut
her eyes, praying with all her heart for the courage she would
need. They stopped outside her door. The bolts shot
back. . . .

"Farewell," she murmured. "Farewell, my little one. . . .
Farewell, beloved husband! It is I who will await you in Paradise!"

Through the open door Catherine saw that four soldiers
stood waiting. The executioner entered alone, and Catherine
shuddered. Ugly as Aycelin's face was she preferred it to the
way he looked now. The torturer had hidden his coarse features under a red hood which came down to his shoulders

with only two slits for eyes. He was terrifying like this. . . .

Wordlessly he unlocked Catherine's manacles and seized her hands to tie them behind her back. She implored him:

"One small mercy, friend executioner, my last. . . . Tie my hands in front of me!"

She encountered the man's eyes through the holes in his mask. They seemed extraordinarily bright. But he said nothing, merely nodded. Catherine's hands were bound in front of her and she noticed with relief that they were not too tightly secured. She would have no difficulty in seizing the dagger later. . . .

She went towards the door calmly and with a firm gait, and took her place among the soldiers, head held high. She did not turn back as the locks and bolts of her cell were carefully replaced. What did it matter to her now since she would not be returning there? She was not even brave enough to glance into Sara's cell. . . . But she raised her voice and cried:

"Farewell, my good Sara! Pray for me!"

The reply came back, charged with emotion:

"I have prayed. Courage!"

A moment later the door of the dreaded chamber opened before her and she needed all the courage Sara recommended to her not to swoon away . . . it was like entering hell itself. Two powerfully built torturers stood waiting, arms folded, beside glowing braziers where instruments of torture were slowly turning red hot—pincers, blades and hooks; they were both stripped to the waist and wore hoods like Aycelin's. Catherine stared in horror at their arms with their leather bracelets. A rack stood in the center of the room, chains hanging in anticipation of its next victim; and in the red glow cast by the braziers other engines of torture loomed dark and ghastly. . . .

But Catherine soon suppressed the shudder which ran through her body and looked away from the torturers. The Dame de La Trémoille, sumptuously gowned in green and gold brocade, sat in the very chair her husband had occupied the day before, watching her enter the room with a cruel smile playing about her red lips. . . . Violaine de Champchevrier sat coquettishly at her feet on a black velvet cushion, taking long breaths from a gold perfume bottle which she held between both hands. There was something disgusting about the sight of these two women, dressed as for a party, sitting in this torture chamber to watch the sufferings of another. Catherine merely glanced at them disdainfully. The Dame burst out laughing.

218

"How high and mighty we are to be sure! I fancy you will change your tune after Aycelin has practiced some of the refinements of his art upon you. Do you know what he is going to do to you?"

"What do I care! The only thing that matters is that I see no priest here!"

"A priest? For a witch like you? Satan's brood have no need of priests to rejoin their master! What good will a blessing do you on the road to hell. What I'm curious to know is how a witch stands up to torture. Have you any charms, Egyptian girl, to preserve you from pain? Will you stay so composed when the executioner tears off your nails, cuts off your nose and ears, skins you alive and puts out your eyes?"

Catherine did not flinch before the sadistic recital of what was to happen to her. A moment more and she would be nothing but dead flesh. . . .

"I don't know. But if you are a true Christian you will not refuse me the time for a last prayer. Then . . ."

The countess hesitated. Clearly she was tempted to refuse. She looked towards the soldiers standing at the far end of the room. She did not have the right to refuse a dying request, unless she herself wanted to be taxed with impiety. And that was always dangerous.

"Very well," she said grudgingly. "But hurry! Untie her hands."

The executioner stepped forward and untied the cords. Catherine knelt at the foot of one of the pillars turning her back on her foe. She folded her hands on her breast, bent her head and gently drew her dagger. Her heart was pounding. She sensed that the other tormentors were coming towards her. No doubt they wanted to share the spectacle of her last prayer. She grasped the weapon firmly, turned the point towards her heart, and was about to bend forward to drive it home. . . .

A cry of despair broke from her. Aycelin had knocked her over roughly and now he snatched the weapon from her. She thought she was lost. But something strange was going on in the torture chamber. Her cry had been answered by screams from the countess and her maid-of-honor. . . . Catherine saw them, as if in a dream, huddled together, shrieking while the three executioners fought with the soldiers.

She realized, with amazement, that they were gaining ground. Aycelin had driven his dagger through one of the men's throats. His two lieutenants rushed into the fray with swords which had materialized from heaven knows where. The struggle was brief; the executioners wielded their weapons with diabolical skill. Soon there were four corpses on the ground and two swords were held at the women's bare throats by one of the attackers.

"Fiends!" the countess shrieked. "Scum! What do you want?"

"Nothing which need trouble you, noble lady," came the drawling voice of Tristan l'Hermite from beneath Aycelin's red hood. "We merely wish to stop you committing one more crime."

"Who are you?"

"Permit me to say that that is none of your business. . . . Are you ready, you there?"

One of the men raised Catherine, while another returned leading Sara. The two women fell into each other's arms without a word. They were too moved to utter a sound.

Without taking his eyes off the prisoners Tristan ordered:

"Tie these noble ladies up, and stoutly! Then shut them both up in one of the cells."

His commands were executed with praiseworthy rapidity. The Dame de la Trémoille and Violaine, foaming with rage, were dragged toward the cells.

"I would gladly strangle them both," Tristan remarked, "but they still have their part to play. Without his wife La Trémoille would doubtless not go to Chinon!"

As he spoke he removed the hood borrowed from Aycelin, and came towards Catherine with a broad smile.

"You have done well, Dame Catherine. Now it is up to us to get you out of here."

"What have you done to Aycelin?"

"In a short while he should awake from the drugged wine, which he drank in considerable quantities to give him enough courage to torture you."

"And the other torturers? Who are they?"

"I'll show you."

The two men stepped forward and pulled off their hoods. With a blush Catherine recognized Pierre de Breze, but the other man—a dark, stolidly built fellow with an intelligent face—was unknown to her. The young knight knelt before Catherine and kissed her hand, as if it were the most natural place and time for such niceties.

"I should have died myself if I had not been able to save you, Catherine."

With a spontaneous gesture she held out both hands to him and he buried his face in them passionately.

"How grateful I am to you, Pierre. . . . To think that only a few minutes ago I despaired of God and of men!"

"I knew you would kill yourself with the dagger rather than submit to torture," said Tristan, who was busy stripping the dead soldiers of their uniforms. "I was watching you, and I was afraid that you might strike the mortal blow too soon. I needed time to get you away from the real torturers."

Sara had sobbed with joy on finding Catherine again, but now she was growing calmer. She wiped her eyes on her dress and asked:

"We aren't safe yet. What do we do now?"

"You and Catherine, and Tristan, will put on the soldiers' uniforms. I and Jean Armenga, whom I present to you now, and who is squire to Ambroise de Lore, will put on our usual clothes again," De Breze explained. "Then we will go out into the yard. Horses are waiting near the gates. We will take them, and I will place myself at the head of the troop until we have left the castle. I have a pass."

"Who gave it to you? La Trémoille?" Catherine asked, with a smile. "No. Queen Marie, who is on our side . . . and a great deal less dim than you might suppose. I will escort you to the border of Amboise, and then Armenga and I will return to the castle while you carry on with your journey. The lady made sure of being undisturbed during her little entertainment but still we must make haste! There is no knowing what might happen. I must ask you to undress, Catherine, and you too, good lady."

Catherine was already unlacing her dress and she gave Sara, who was grumbling at having to dress as a man again, a push. The three men took De Breze's clothes and the squire's out of the chest where they had been hidden. Catherine and Sara dressed in the shadows. It did not take a minute. They wore the leather doublets but discarded the heavy mail shirts. The tunic with the royal coat-of-arms was enough to give the right impression. Helmets, greaves and enormous mailed shoes were already quite cumbersome enough. . . .

Pierre de Breze could not help laughing when he saw them.

"Lucky it's dark . . . and there are other clothes waiting for you a couple of leagues from here. You would not get far without attracting attention."

"We shall do our best," Sara said. "And it isn't so easy."

Pierre meanwhile came up and took one of Catherine's hands in his. A look of passion flamed in his clear blue eyes.

"To think that I shall have to say good-bye to you in a short while, Catherine. I would so much like to watch over you myself. But I have to stay at the castle. My absence would arouse suspicion. . . ."

"We shall meet again at Chinon, Pierre!"

"You won't meet again anywhere if you don't make haste," Tristan protested. "Now come, let us be off . . . you go first, gentlemen!"

Pierre de Breze and the squire went first. They went cautiously up the slippery stairs which led to the guard-room. In spite of the crushing weight of her clothes Catherine's heart was singing. She had never felt so light-hearted or so happy. After seeing death so near she was to live! Was there any feeling as marvelous and exhilarating as that? Her large shoes slipped on the worn, damp steps. She stumbled and hurt herself but did not even notice. It never crossed her mind that she might have to make use of this long heavy pike which she was dragging along. . . . She felt as though she had nothing to do but follow Pierre de Breze. He led the way, sword in hand. There were two soldiers to be put out of action in the guard-room. . . .

This was done quickly and silently. The soldiers were gagged and bound and laid on the floor.

"Now, outside," Pierre said. "And don't make too much noise this time!"

In the yard there were only a few torches burning, and their light only seemed to make the darkness blacker. Once safely out of the tower, Catherine cast a grateful look heavenwards. The night sky was like dark velvet, striped by the pale glow of the Milky Way. The air had never seemed so soft, or so delicious. . . . Walking with Tristan and Sara beside her, she could just make out Pierre's broad shoulders in front. He had sheathed his sword once more, but she sensed that he was on his guard. . . . Jean Armenga brought up the rear, and walked close behind her, hoping perhaps to conceal this rather undersized soldier from the eyes of the watch. They went close by the keep where two pikemen stood dozing on their cumbersome weapons and Catherine involuntarily looked upwards. There was no light to be seen at Gilles de Rais's windows, but candles blazed from La Trémoille's . . . his lust for gold must be keeping the fat man awake. . . . The hurly-burly of the day had given way to profound calm. The presence of the Queen had put an end to the rowdier distractions of the castle, and the preparations for departure had tired everyone out. The huge courtyard was empty except for the guard-house, where one or two soldiers could be seen going to and fro. Catherine whispered to Tristan.

"Won't those soldiers over there try and stop us?"

"I don't think so. They are the Queen's guards, whom we had specially posted there for this evening. I don't know what it was you told La Trémoille but you excited him so much that everything is quite topsy-turvy here tonight."

"Won't our escape make him change his mind about leaving?"

"Certainly not. He will imagine that it is the work of your gypsy friends. The Dame de la Trémoille did not see our faces if you remember, and the idea that we might have forced her to spend a night in the dungeons is unlikely to cause her loving husband any great annoyance!"

"Silence," Pierre de Breze commanded. For they were drawing near to the gateway and the guard-house. They still had to cross the drawbridge, but Catherine was not afraid. The man walking in front of her must be her guardian angel. She was convinced that no evil could befall her under his protection. . . .

Horses stood waiting near the well, and Catherine thought anxiously that with the great weight of armor she was wearing, she would never succeed in mounting one of them. But De Breze had even thought of that. While he went up to the guards to say a few words, Jean Armenga took Catherine's pike, stood it up against the wall, then grasped her round the waist and hoisted her into the saddle as easily as if she had weighed less than a feather. After which, with Tristan's help, he performed the same service for Sara. Catherine felt like laughing, as she wondered what the guards would have thought if they had seen two knights courteously assisting a common soldier into the saddle. It was very dark where they were. Then she heard Pierre's voice.

"Open the postern gate. There are only five of us. On Queen's business!"

"At your command, monseigneur," said one of them.

The little portcullis was slowly raised and the small bridge lowered. Pierre had presumably wanted to avoid the din made by lowering the main bridge. Now the young man leaped into the saddle.

"Onward," he cried, as he passed through the great archway.

The three false soldiers followed. Catherine and Sara hid their faces as much as possible under their helmets as they clattered past the lighted guard-room, and forced themselves to slouch in the relaxed posture adopted by the men. . . . Instinctively, they expected a cry, or protest . . . or even a joke. But none came. . . . And suddenly there were no more barriers before them, nothing but the great star-spangled sky, and the watered silk ribbon of the Loire, flung round the sleeping township with its faintly gleaming slate roofs. Catherine took deep draughts of the pure night air, filling her lungs with it, savoring its fragrance like that of some heady liqueur. Ah, that soft night breeze with its scent of roses and honeysuckle was delicious after the disgusting stench of the prison, and the countess's sickly perfumes. . . .

Once again she heard De Breze's voice, speaking to the guards on the other side of the bridge.

"Don't draw it up again. I shall be returning in a few minutes. These men are going to keep guard over the southern gate. . . . At the gallop, men!"

They clattered full tilt down the castle mound, skirting round the foot of the rocky spur to reach the fortified gate of the town, which gave on to the wooded countryside nearby. Nothing stirred—Amboise was sound asleep—except for a howl from a lovesick cat and a dog barking faintly in the distance.

De Breze's pass opened the city gates to them as easily as the castle's, and once again he warned the guards that he would be returning. The officer commanding the gate made no objection. At last the open road lay before the fugitives. . . .

They spurred their horses to a gallop. The road wound up to the dark mass of the forest. Until they reached the cover of the trees they made their way in silence. But as soon as the whispering arch of trees closed overhead Pierre de Breze raised his hand and dismounted.

"The time has come for us to go our separate ways," he said. "You will go on alone, for we must return to the château. We must be at the Queen's side when she leaves Amboise. As for you . . ."

"I know," Tristan interrupted. "We carry on to the fort at Mesvres, two leagues hence, where we will be met."

Although it was dark in the forest, a thin ray of light from the sickle moon struck into the glade where the travelers had stopped, and Catherine saw De Breze's teeth flash as he smiled in the darkness.

"I ought to have remembered that you never forget a thing, Sire Tristan! I now entrust Dame Catherine to your care. You know how dear she is to me, and how precious is her safety. The fort at Mesvres belongs to my cousin Louis d'Amboise. There you will be quite safe. You can rest and take refreshment there, as well as finding something more suitable for these ladies to wear."

Not for the life of her could Catherine have explained why she now went up to Pierre and asked him anxiously:

"Where should we go then, Messire Pierre? Where shall we

meet again? May I go to Chinon now? I want to witness the end of La Trémoille."

He bent over her and took off her heavy helmet and flung it into a ditch.

"At least I may see your sweet face again before we part! Yes, of course you may go to Chinon—Queen Yolande will soon be journeying there to join her son-in-law. You will meet her there when everything has been done. You could of course go to meet her at Angers, but you must be weary. You can rest at Chinon. Go to the Inn of the Cross of the Great Saint Mesmes, tell them I sent you there and you will have the innkeeper at your feet. He is a good and loyal subject of the King's, and because he once lodged the Maid there he would be ready to throw himself into the fire alive in her honor. Tell Maître Agnelet that you require discretion and you will not be troubled by a living soul. Your mourning, besides, will guarantee you respect and solitude. . . ."

There was a silence. So profound that Catherine and Pierre could hear their own hearts beating. The others had tactfully moved off a little way. She looked at him with a face radiant with gratitude and held out her hands, which he knelt to kiss as he had done a while before in the torture chamber.

"Thank you, sir knight," Catherine murmured, her heart too full for words. "How can I possibly say what I feel at this moment? It would take too long . . . and my heart is too full."

"My sweet lady, it is my love for you alone which guides me on. If you had died, my life would have stopped. Don't look for words."

He pressed his lips against her hands. Then Catherine stooped and dropped a quick kiss on the young man's short blond hair before gently freeing her hands.

"Farewell, messire! And may God go with you! Help me, sir squire!"

She turned to Armenga who helped her into the saddle. Then she thanked him and he smiled. Sara and Tristan came up. She raised her hand and waved gaily to Pierre, who stood watching and did not take his eyes off her for a moment.

"When we meet again I shall be Catherine once more," she cried. "Forget the gypsy-girl . . . and I shall do the same! And thank you both again."

The track ran straight through the forest, with trees like dark cliffs each side. It seemed to lead on into infinity. Catherine spurred her horse vigorously and sped at full gallop towards the horizon, with Tristan and Sara following hard behind.

CHAPTER ELEVEN

Chinon

The sun was setting in a flaming glory which flung a crimson mantle over the gray walls of Chinon and the slate roofs of the town, solidly girded round by stone ramparts, which seemed to spring straight out of the Vienne. Boatmen guided their craft noiselessly along the shining river towards the dark arches of the old bridge, while swallows darted overhead and river-martins called along the banks. It was a lovely, soft evening, scented with new-mown hay. Catherine, Tristan and Sara passed through the Besse gate into the town and rode along by the walls of the Church of Saint Mesmes. A little further on there was another gate and drawbridge: the gate of Verdun, which led into the heart of the town. High above, the triple castle stretched away in endless perspective: the Fort of St. Georges, built by the Plantagenets; the Château du Mileu; and beyond that, the Coudray, above which towered the massive bulk of its immense keep. Chinon-the-Stronghold undoubtedly deserved its name, and Catherine gazed happily at the majestic stone trap into which her enemies were about to deliver themselves.

But how time did fly! The time at Amboise, with its tragic or merely painful overtones, seemed far away. And yet it was only three days since Tristan and Pierre de Brezé had rescued her from death in those dungeons. After their parting in the forest Catherine, Tristan and Sara, still wearing their soldiers' uniforms, rode on to the little fortress of Mesvres, where Catherine was at last able to cast off her disguise. She bathed, and soaped and scrubbed herself vigorously all over and then rubbed her skin with spirits of wine and softened it with a thick cream made chiefly of lard and herbs. Then she bathed once again and had the satisfaction of finding her skin almost as pale as it had been before. All that remained was a faint golden tan, more probably due to her outdoor existence than to poor Guillaume the Illuminator's dyes. She had also flung away her false black plaits and washed her hair thoroughly. Now that she had stopped blackening the roots a longish band of pale blonde hair could be seen. But alas, to return to her own color she would have to cut it again, and cut it very short! She did not hesitate. She sat on a stool and handed Sara a pair of scissors.

"Now, cut off all the black!"

Sighing like a furnace, Sara obeyed. When she had finished Catherine was left with nothing more than a short, gold thatch which she brushed like a boy's. She looked like a young page with this short crop, but curiously enough it did not make her any less feminine.

"In a few months' time I shall be presentable again," she said, looking at herself in the glass with a happy laugh. "Till then no one will see. Thank heavens the head-dresses people now wear hide one's hair completely. Some ladies even shave their foreheads and temples."

"It looks terrible," Sara cried. "And I don't want to see you like that!"

"Don't worry, nor do I!"

Catherine was dressed in a black silk dress covered with a damask cape in the same color, and on her head she wore a cap of starched black muslin which framed her face. She was once more a noble lady. Sara meanwhile had dressed herself in the costume of a servant of a good house and Tristan wore his usual black leather suit. Passers-by and good wives alike turned to watch as this lovely woman rode by, her fair beauty glowing in contrast to her somber mourning dress.

Once through the Verdun gate the three travelers found themselves in a busy street. People stood about chatting peacefully after the day's work, while children scampered off with jugs and jars in search of wine and mustard. The huge painted shop signs creaked gently in the light breeze. Through open windows there were glimpses of housewives bustling about round their cooking-pots. True, the shops were not as well stocked as they had been formerly. War had struck so cruelly at the kingdom that no supplies were able to reach it from abroad, and foodstuffs were in short supply, but the season of plenty was at hand, and the earth was still fruitful in this part of the countryside which the English had not devastated. Cloth-sellers, furriers and spice-merchants were the worst hit because they no longer had access to the great fairs of former years, but the fruiterers displayed fine vegetables and even some fresh flowers. The river gave its fish and the countryside its fowl and wild birds. . . . A good smell of cabbage and bacon scented the street and made Catherine smile.

"I'm hungry," she said gaily. "What about you?"

"I could eat my own horse," Tristan declared, pulling a terrible face. "I hope this inn is a good one."

All three of them were enjoying the pleasant respite of the journey, after the tragic events of Amboise, and before the violent ones which were soon to follow. It was like a bright interval between two storms, or a light entr'acte between two somber tragedies.

They were approaching a cross-roads where a group of women stood chatting round a well. Not far off some children were riding their hobby-horses, and in the entrance to a house stood a monk, preaching to the passers-by from the top of a big stone. He gesticulated freely in his shabby black robe, claiming that this very stone had once helped the holy Maid to dismount when she had been sent there by God to find the gentle Dauphin . . . and one day, he reminded them, she would return to send antichrist packing. . . . There was a small crowd of men and women standing round, nodding their heads solemnly. The houses round about seemed richer, their gables higher and their turrets more graceful than in the rest of the town. Catherine realized that this must be the Grand Carroi, the heart of Chinon, and Tristan set off to inquire the whereabouts of their inn. It stood a little way off, and its handsome sign could be seen from the cross-roads, liberally daubed with reds and blues and depicting Saint Mesmes in his halo, looking highly dignified but squinting terribly.

They went towards the entrance; Catherine and Sara stayed on horseback while Tristan went in to speak to the innkeeper. It was in truth a very fine, commodious hostelry and it shone with cleanliness. The little leaded panes in the windows glowed like tiny suns, reflecting the fires within, and the finely carved beams which overhung the porch seemed to have been recently dusted. A moment later Tristan returned accompanied by a tall person with an astonishing beard which all but hid his face. From the forest of gray beard, mustaches and eyebrows which covered his face there projected an imposing nose which was shaped somewhat like the foot of a cooking-pot; and a piercing black gaze struck awe into all those who met it. Catherine realized, however, from his spotless white clothing, tall cap and the massive knife at his waist, that this must be Maître Agnelet in person, proprietor of the Cross of Great Saint Mesmes. She suppressed a smile. His name might mean lamb, but he looked more like an old wolf-hound!

Meanwhile the imposing personage bent low before her,

228

and from the white gleam which appeared amid the beard Catherine deduced that he was smiling.

"It is indeed a great honor, noble lady, to receive you in my house. Any friends of Messire de Breze are welcome here. . . . But I fear I shall only be able to give you a small room, albeit newly furnished. News has just come of the King's arrival, and certain of my rooms are booked in advance."

"Don't worry, Maître Agnelet," Catherine replied, taking the hand he gallantly offered her to help her dismount, "as long as you can find lodging for my maid and myself and we can stay here quite quietly, we shall be perfectly content. As for Maître Tristan . . ."

"Don't worry about me, Dame Catherine," the Fleming interrupted, "I shall leave after supper."

Catherine raised her eyebrows.

"You are leaving again? But where for?"

"For Parthenay where I am to join my master the Constable. There is no time to lose. Maître Agnelet, you know what you have to do?"

The host winked and smiled conspiratorially.

"Yes, messire, I know . . . their lordships shall be informed, and the noble lady will be perfectly safe in my inn. Pray enter, you will be served immediately."

The three travelers entered the inn escorted by Maître Agnelet, while three valets led the horses to the stables and another took charge of their baggage.

A lusty housewife, whose red cheeks looked as if they had been polished, and whose full lips were adorned with a faint black down, but who sported a gold crucifix and a dress of handsome, fine material, came forward to curtsy to Catherine. Agnelet introduced her with justifiable pride.

"My wife, Pernelle. She is a Parisian!"

With much simpering the Parisian led the way, and opened a little door at the far end of the room which opened into a fine paved yard, set about with flowers. A wooden stair led up from it to a covered gallery opening into the rooms. She went to the end of the gallery and pushed open a handsome carved-oak door.

"I think madame will be happy here! At least she will be in peace."

"Many thanks, Dame Pernelle," Catherine replied. "As you see I am in mourning and I need peace above all."

"Naturally, naturally," said the innkeeper's wife, "I quite understand. . . . The Church of St. Maurice is not far from here, and you will find the priest full of understanding and compassion. You should hear him preaching . . . and in the confessional! His voice is like velvet on a troubled soul. . . ."

But Maître Agnelet, who knew his wife and her ways, called up now:

"Hulloa, wife! Come down here and let the noble lady rest."

The summons cut a flood of eloquence in the bud. Catherine smiled: "Send my companion to me, Dame Pernelle, and bring us our supper quickly. We are tired and hungry."

"At once, at once. . . ."

With a last curtsy the good woman disappeared, leaving Catherine and Sara alone together. The gypsy was already inspecting their quarters, testing the mattresses to see how soft they were, and inspecting the bolts on the door and windows. These looked out on to the street so that they could watch the comings and goings of people down below. The furniture was simple but of good quality, of oak and wrought iron. As for the hangings which were a cheery, bright red, they made the little room a pleasant place to be in.

"We shall be comfortable here," Sara pronounced. But then she noticed that Catherine was staring out of the window with a dreamy, faraway look and she asked: "What are you thinking about?"

"I was thinking," Catherine sighed, "that I shall be glad when it's all over! However comfortable the inn may be I hope I don't have to stay here long. I . . . I'd like to see my little Michel again! You can't think how I miss him! It's such a long time since I last saw him!"

"Four months!" Sara said, coming closer with a look of astonishment. It was the first time Catherine had ever shown such marked signs of missing her child. She never spoke of him, fearing perhaps that the touching memories of her little boy might soften her courage, but there were tears shining in her eyes tonight. Sara saw that she was gazing out of the window at a woman carrying a blond child who looked about the same age as Michel. This woman was young and fresh faced, and she laughed as she dandled a sweetmeat before the child, who stretched out impatient little hands to snatch it. It was a simple but charming little scene and Sara could understand how Catherine's heart must be smitten by it. She passed an arm round her shoulders and drew her close to her.

"A little more courage, sweetheart! You have been so brave so far! And it won't be long now!"

"I know. But I shall never be like that woman there. She must have a husband to be so happy! She must love him. See

230

how her eyes shine. But when I have done with wandering, all that will be left to me is to shut myself up in a castle and devote my life to Michel at first, and then later, when he has left me, to waiting for death and praying to God. The sort of life my mother-in-law, Madame Isabelle, has led. . . ."

Sara decided that this creeping melancholy which was laying its icy fingers on Catherine's heart must be warded off. She must not be allowed to give in to depression. She pulled her back from the window, made her sit down on a cushioned bench and scolded her soundly:

"Now that's quite enough of that! Just think of what remains to be done and let the future take care of itself! God alone commands our destinies and you have no idea what he holds in store for you. Anyway, it's time to change the subject. Here comes Maître Tristan."

The Fleming knocked and entered, followed by a valet carrying plates covered with white napkins, and another armed with everything necessary for serving and eating a meal. In the twinkling of an eye the meal was prepared, and the three companions sat down to a platter of sausages and haricot beans, and another of saffron flavored mutton. Catherine had calmed down again, and she felt her black thoughts dissipating themselves like smoke as she drank a cup of the good claret of the region, which seemed to have extraordinary restorative powers. When the meal was finished, Tristan, who had scarcely uttered a word, rose to take his leave.

"I must be off now, Dame Catherine. I have to be at Parthenay tomorrow evening to get my instructions. You must stay here. The King will be arriving tomorrow but Messire Prégent de Coetivy and Messire Ambroise de Lore will both be here at the inn by dawn, for it is here that all the conspirators are to assemble. Messire Jean de Beuil is to arrive some time tomorrow too, perhaps during the morning. When everyone has arrived there will be a meeting here. At the far side of the courtyard there are some excellent cellars built into the castle mound itself . . . ideal for storing wine, or concealing conspiracies. All you have to do is wait and keep your eyes open.

"But remember, once the King is here you would do well not to go out. The Dame de la Trémoille has sharp eyes!"

"Don't worry," Catherine said, offering him a last cup of wine. "I may have changed my appearance but I haven't gone quite mad. Here . . . a stirrup cup!"

He swallowed the contents at a gulp, bowed and vanished as silently as a shadow.

The usual bustle of the town grew quite frenzied the following morning, as the King's cortège entered Chinon. When the trumpets sounded in the peaceful afternoon air and all the bells started ringing, Catherine wrapped her head in a veil and leaned her head out of the window, momentarily forgetful of prudence and caution. Above the heads of the crowd below she could see banners and pennants, the colors of the men-at-arms, lances, pikes, the gleaming mail of the knights escorting the King, also in armor, and the litters in which the Queen and the La Trémoille couple were traveling. It was a long time since the Lord Chamberlain had been able to mount a horse. When she caught sight of his colors she automatically drew back her head.

Although she felt safe enough in this inn, she could not help a slight shrinking sensation now that she knew her enemies were near at hand. Until this moment too, she had not really believed in the reality of her triumph, and in imagination she had pictured a whole mass of obstacles. But now at last La Trémoille had come!

The procession went over the cross-roads, amid a crowd chanting "Noel" and "God Be With You," and gradually vanished from sight along the steep road leading to the château. When the last cart and the last footman had disappeared Catherine turned to Sara with shining eyes.

"He has come! I've won!"

"Yes," the gypsy sighed, "you have won! Now it remains to the knights and Queen Yolande to capture the brute. . . ."

"Not without me!" Catherine cried. "I want to be there, and if the plot fails I want to share the fate of the conspirators. I have the right!"

Sara did not reply and started to mend a tear in Catherine's traveling cloak. They had scarcely spent more than twenty-four hours in the inn but Sara was beginning to behave like a caged animal, clutching at any pretext for activity. The forced inactivity was wearisome to Catherine too. She spent the whole time staring out of the window at the life in the street below. The hours passed too slowly for her. She wanted action. She had been so frightened, she had so often despaired of success, that it had been impossible to believe La Trémoille could actually come till she saw him with her own eyes. And now he had arrived she was aching to return to the fray.

When night came and the bell christened Marie Javelle had sounded the curfew from the clock-tower in the castle, Catherine took a chance and put her head out of the window without veiling her face. The night itself should be veil enough, although, according to Sara, it was not dark enough. . . .

It was true. The night was magnificent, with a dark, soft velvety blue sky glittering with stars . . . a night for love rather than intrigue! Not that the view was extensive—only as far as the other side of the road, where firmly barred shutters and total silence spoke of good *bourgeois* families who retired to bed early. On one hand was a helmet-maker's, whose establishment filled the street with noise all day, and on the other an apothecary's, whose shop exuded exotic scents.

Now that the sounds of the day were silenced, the sleeping city assumed an air of mystery. Catherine felt as though she were inside a strong but beautiful sanctuary, an inviolable asylum, and she wondered whether this was not due to the Maid's ghostly presence in the place. In the murmuring river, the rustle of distant trees, the very fragrance of the fertile soil which came to her mingled with scents of fresh water and jasmine, Catherine seemed to hear the clear voice of that tall girl who had come from so far and whose blazing trail had marked her life indelibly . . . Joan the Maid!

How vivid her presence was here in this stronghold where her name would never be forgotten! That name, which was never mentioned above a whisper throughout the kingdom for fear of La Trémoille's spies, was here proclaimed in the public thoroughfares . . . and the very stones of the place were marked with memories. At nightfall her spirit walked and haunted every dwelling.

Almost automatically Catherine gazed up to the milky dome of the night sky as if seeking the gleam of a suit of white armor.

"Joan," she murmured softly. "Help me! In seeking to deliver you from death I found unbelievable happiness! I owed it to you . . . do not let so much suffering be in vain! Give me back my love, and my lost happiness. . . ."

Something soft and scented struck her on the throat, breaking into her thoughts and bringing her sharply back to earth. Without thinking she reached out and caught the bouquet of roses just before they fell, and buried her nose in them. They were fragrant with summer scents. . . . She leaned out and searched the shadows and presently observed a tall dark silhouette standing in one of the doorways opposite.

As she caught sight of it the figure moved. But Catherine knew who it was before he came into sight. Pierre de Breze walked forward slowly into the middle of the street and stood there for a few minutes, gazing up at the window which framed the young woman's charming silhouette. She could not see his face clearly but she heard him utter her name.

"Catherine!"

She did not answer at once. Her heart was beating too fast. She felt herself blushing like a maiden because Pierre had infused more passion into the three syllables of her name than into a love poem. She longed suddenly to hold out her hands and draw him closer, to have him near. . . . Just then the moon peered above a roof, silvering a run of tiles, inundated the street and the young man's motionless figure before pouring through her window and into her room. Catherine shielded her face instinctively from this bright light and stepped back a pace. She just had time to see him blow her a kiss. . . .

It was too bright now, it would be foolish to look out again but the temptation was almost irresistible. She leaned out and sighed . . . the street was empty. Pierre had gone. Catherine shut the window and closed the shutters. Then she took up the roses and inhaled the perfume till her head reeled deliciously. She still seemed to hear that ardent voice which had spoken her name just now from the darkness. . . .

She was trying to recapture its echo, with her face buried in the flowers, when suddenly:

"Extraordinary place this inn!" Sara said mockingly. "I hadn't noticed that there were roses growing on the walls!"

Abruptly shaken from her dream, Catherine flashed her a wrathful glance but then she started to laugh. Sitting up in bed with her graying plaits hanging on her shoulders, Sara had a look of comical dignity, belied by the light of mockery which danced in her eyes.

"They're pretty, aren't they?" she asked.

"Lovely. I'll wager they came straight from the château and were brought here by a certain nobleman in person."

"No need to wager. It's true . . . he threw them to me."

Sara's faint smile vanished. She shook her head sadly. "And you already call him 'he'?"

Catherine flushed and turned away to undress so that Sara should not see her troubled face. She did not answer but it seemed Sara was determined to get a reply.

"Tell me the truth, Catherine. What exactly are your feelings for that handsome blond knight?"

"What do you expect me to say?" Catherine answered irritably. "He is young and handsome as you said, and he saved my life. . . . He loves me, and I find him charming, and that's all there is to it. . . ."

"All," Sara repeated. "That's already a good deal. Listen,

234

Catherine. I know better than anyone how much you have suffered and still suffer from your solitude but . . ."

She paused and looked down, visibly embarrassed by what she was about to say. Catherine slipped out of her dress and picked it up.

"But?" she echoed.

"Take care not to give your heart away. I know that handsome knight has everything it takes to seduce a woman. I'm sure his love is sincere and that it would bring great sweetness into your life. I am sure it would be agreeable for you to be loved, and perhaps to love in return. But I know you well, and I know that you would not be happy for long with another man, because the man whose name you bear has marked you too deeply for you ever to forget."

"Who is talking of forgetting?" Catherine murmured angrily. "How could I ever forget Arnaud when I live only for him?"

"Simply by allowing somebody else to persuade you to live for *him!* I repeat, I know you well, and if you were to let yourself go, sooner or later your old love would reclaim its rights and you would find yourself still more lonely than you are now, and more desperate . . . and burdened with shame and remorse into the bargain."

Standing very straight in her white chemise, Catherine's thoughts seemed to be elsewhere. She murmured, with deep bitterness:

"But wasn't it you who counselled me to surrender to pleasure without regrets, after that night with Fero? Was it because he was a man of your own race that you were more indulgent then?"

Sara went pale. A heavy silence fell between them. Then Sara stood up and came towards her.

"No, it was not because he was a gypsy like myself. It was because I knew he could never capture your heart. Pleasure is good when one is young and healthy, Catherine. It soothes the body and clears the mind and sets your blood flowing warm and swift. Whereas love enslaves and sometimes destroys. . . . If I were sure your heart was safe from that knight I would push you together. A few nights of love would do you good. But you aren't the sort of woman to make love without tenderness. And that would make him . . . your husband, the hermit of Calves, suffer too terribly! He must know you are faithful to him if he is to endure his martyrdom. Everyone believes you are a widow and those black veils seem to deceive you too. It is true that everyone, even the Church, thinks of you as a widow since his name

235

was struck from among the living on entering the leper-house. But he lives, Catherine, he is still alive and it is in your heart that he lives most strongly. If you force him out of there, then he will really be dead!"

Catherine's face was hidden from Sara as she stood behind her. But as she spoke she saw the head with its too short blonde hair start to droop and the frail shoulders to bend. Her words re-echoed through Catherine's heart, re-opening a barely healed wound. She murmured painfully:

"You are cruel, Sara . . . all I did was sniff the roses. . . ."

"No, sweetheart. You have always been honest with yourself and with others. You must be honest now. You have allowed gratitude to lead you along a dangerous path, and one which is not made for you. Your path leads back to the mountains of Auvergne, towards Michel and Montsalvy. . . ."

Very gently she drew Catherine to her and cradled her head on her shoulder and stroked her tear-wet cheek.

"Don't be angry with your old Sara, Catherine. She would give her life and a part of her share in Paradise to see you happy. She loves you like the flesh of her flesh. But," she added, with a catch in her voice, "you must realize that I have given a part of this heart to your husband, to that Arnaud all stiff with pride and passion and suffering whom I saw one night, weeping like a child for his shattered life and condemned love. . . . Don't you remember?"

"Stop," Catherine sobbed, "stop . . . you know very well no man will ever take his place . . . and that I'll never love another as I loved him . . . as I still love him!"

And she meant every word. And yet she could not quite banish the gleam of a smile and sparkle of a pair of blue eyes from her memory. . . . Up there in her tower Marie Javelle struck midnight. Gently but firmly Sara led Catherine to bed. The bunch of roses lay forgotten upon the table.

The following evening there was to be no talk of love, and Catherine did not even give it a thought, for the time for action was at hand.

Towards evening Maître Agnelet went up to Catherine's room and informed her, respectfully but without circumlocutions, that he would be coming to fetch her at midnight.

"Where are we going?" she asked.

"Not far from here, lady. Only to the other side of my courtyard, to be precise. But I must ask you to be as silent as possible. Not all the inhabitants of this inn are as intelligent as they might be. . . ."

"I understand, Maître Agnelet. But could you tell me, please, if the people you were expecting have arrived?"

"Yes, all of them, madame. Messire de Lore and Messire de Coetivy have been playing chess since yesterday morning, and the Seigneur de Beuil has just arrived. But he has gone straight to the château. . . ."

"Why?"

"He is the Lord Chamberlain's nephew, and although he serves Queen Yolande he is still accepted there. Don't forget, noble lady. At midnight!"

The rest of the day passed more quickly for Catherine. It would not be long before they knew the outcome of their schemes. Either the plot would succeed, and it would be a simple matter for young Charles d'Anjou to replace La Trémoille in the King's favor. And that would mean a return to grace, at long last the right to live openly and proudly among those of her own rank. Or the plot might fail . . . in which case nothing would save the conspirators from the anger of La Trémoille. They would all die, irrespective of rank, sex or age. . . .

At curfew time Catherine went over to the window but did not open it. Anyway Pierre de Breze would not be likely to be courting his fair lady at an open window tonight. He had better things to do, and she would not see him again except among all the other knights and nobles. Catherine was too nervous to give much thought to him.

Midnight had just struck when there was a faint scratching at her door. Catherine, fully dressed, stood up from the foot of her bed, where she had been sitting waiting. She had forced Sara to go to bed. She opened the door hastily and perceived a dark figure on the threshold. The house was in darkness, the kitchen fires had been banked up as they were every evening, but the moon cast a milky pool of light into the courtyard, so that the wooden pillars to the gallery and the innkeeper himself stood out in dark relief. Maître Agnelet had changed his spotless white for a dark woolen doublet. There was not a sound to be heard.

Silently Agnelet took Catherine by the hand and led her into the courtyard, slipping along in the shadow of the buildings till they were out of the moonlit zone, and had reached the far side which was bounded by the castle mound itself. Bushes and shrubs stood up here and there, but there were dark openings scattered about.

"They used to be cave dwellings," Agnelet explained as Catherine paused to examine them. "Some of them are still

237

inhabited and others serve as cellars . . . or places of refuge!"

He pushed open a circular door made of rough-hewn planks of wood, which formed the entrance to one of these caves. Then he picked up an oil lamp which was standing by the entrance, opened it and lit it. A huge cave hollowed in the chalk soil met their eyes, stacked all round with barrels of different sizes. There was a strong smell of wine. Some cellarmen's tools stood arranged on a table in one corner, next to a vat full of empty bottles. The whole place had such a cheerful look that Catherine glanced round questioningly at the innkeeper. Could this be the setting for a dangerous conspiracy? By way of reply Agnelet smiled and moved a barrel so that an aperture appeared leading through the wall.

"Go through, noble lady," said Agnelet. "I will replace the barrel after you. This entrance must remain hidden. We are now right beneath the Château du Mileu. The King sleeps just above our heads!"

Catherine stepped straight through into a little passage, lit by a torch, which seemed to lead into a room at the far end. They passed along it in a moment or two, and found themselves in a much larger cave with a rough-looking staircase, hacked out of the living rock itself, leading up out of it. There too there were several barrels but these had all been stood on end and there were four men sitting upon them. They did not say a word. They sat, still as statues, round an oil lamp, and appeared to be waiting. But they all turned as she entered.

Apart from Pierre de Breze, Catherine recognized the red hair and unsmiling face of Ambroise de Lore, the slender and elegant figure of Jean de Beuil, the broad back and masterful features of the Breton Prégent de Coetivy, and as they rose to their feet she dropped them a deep and graceful curtsy. Pierre took her hand to lead her up to the circle of barrels. It was Jean de Beuil who greeted her, after warning Maître Agnelet to keep watch outside.

"We are happy to see you again, madame, and even more so to congratulate you on the success of your undertaking. La Trémoille's presence at Chinon is convincing proof of your success. We are all most grateful to you. . . ."

"Don't thank me too much, Seigneur de Beuil. I worked for you, certainly, and for the good of the kingdom, but I was also working for myself and in order to avenge my beloved husband. Help me to achieve this vengeance and we shall be quits!"

As she spoke she gently withdrew her hand from Pierre's and went forward to speak to the other three men.

"Remember that the lives and honor of the Montsalvys are at stake, messires. So that my name may live, La Trémoille must die!"

"Your wish shall be granted," Coetivy cut in abruptly. "But how the devil did you manage to lead the swine here? I admit that it would be difficult to refuse a lovely woman anything, but, apparently, you are even better armed than we imagined. . . ."

The Breton nobleman's manner was scarcely flattering and full of sly implications. Catherine observed this and her reply was crisp and cool.

"I like to think I am not altogether a fool, messire, but the weapons you allude to are not the ones which I used . . . the bait was a story which my husband, Arnaud de Montsalvy, once told me and which I had remembered."

The missing man's name had its usual effect. Arnaud's personality was too powerful not to bring his image instantly before these men who had fought with him, and it obliged them to show respect towards the woman who bore his name and who had just given them such a commanding example of her courage. Coetivy flushed with shame at his insinuations, and admitted it frankly.

"Forgive me! What I said was unpardonable."

She smiled at him, but did not answer. Then she sat down on the barrel they offered her and recounted her last conversation with La Trémoille to these men. They listened with the wondering, absorbed expressions of children listening to a wonderful story. The word treasure had its usual magical effect. Then there was the mysterious element of the Knights Templar, with their fantastic, disturbing history, rich with the color and mysteries of the Orient. Amusedly Catherine watched their eyes grow dreamy, and glow with excitement. . . .

"Inscriptions!" Ambroise de Lore murmured at last. "If only we knew whether they really existed. . . ."

"My husband saw them, seigneur," Catherine said gently.

A voice spoke up, seeming to boom out of the chalk roof itself:

"I know them too. But the devil if I understood what they meant!"

Two men in armor were coming down the rough-hewn staircase which vanished into the shadows of the ceiling. The man in front, who was bareheaded, was an elderly man but there was nothing feeble or senile about his hardy physique.

Catherine recognized the gray hair, broad face, heavy features and piercing eyes of Raoul de Goncourt, present governor of Chinon, whom she had known when he was governor of Orléans. In all his sixty-odd years Goncourt had never ceased fighting the English and after the siege of Harcourt, which he had defended with great courage, they had kept him ten years in their prisons. He was a slow-moving man from Berrichon, as heavily built as the bullocks from his own country, obstinate and brave, and not devoid of subtlety. He was blindly devoted to the King and quite incapable of deceit. He had mistrusted Joan of Arc at first and had fought against her, but Goncourt was a man of too much honesty not to admit his mistakes. His presence tonight in Agnelet's cellars was proof enough of this.

The man who followed him was considerably younger, but somewhat withered-looking. There was nothing remarkable about his face, save the keen glance of his gray eyes. He was the governor's lieutenant, and his name was Olivier de Fretard. He walked three paces behind his superior officer carrying Goncourt's helmet, and he did not even look at the assembly. But Catherine sensed that this cold-eyed man had not missed so much as a gesture or expression among that company.

Meanwhile Raoul de Goncourt had reached the foot of the stairs. He saluted the conspirators, and then went and stood in front of Catherine. The ghost of a smile flitted over his face.

"It gives me much more pleasure to welcome Madame de Montsalvy to Chinon than it gave me to receive Madame de Brazey at Orléans once upon a time!" he declared without preamble. "The devil take it if I'd guessed that it was love of Montsalvy which brought you into that wasp nest! Especially since that noble lord of yours did his uttermost to get you hanged!"

Catherine could not help flushing. It was true. Had it not been for Joan's intervention on the route to the scaffold, Catherine would have ended her days at the end of a rope, following the command of a tribunal presided over by Goncourt and incited by Arnaud. He was blind with hatred of her in those days and could not wait to get rid of her. . . . But terrible memories though those were . . . they left no bitterness in her. What remained was . . . yes, a shade of regret! She met the old officer's eyes unflinchingly.

"Would you believe me, messire, if I told you I miss those days? The man who became my beloved husband was alive then, in full possession of health and strength, even if he did

240

turn that strength of his against me. Of course I regret those times!"

Something softened in the eyes which were fastened upon her. Abruptly Goncourt seized her hand and took it to his lips and kissed it unceremoniously.

"That makes you a worthy wife to him!" he said gruffly. "And you have done good work! But that's enough flattery! Now, messires, we must plan our campaign. La Trémoille does not like this château and he will not stay long. If you agree, I propose that we should strike tomorrow night!"

"Shouldn't we await the Constable's orders?" asked De Breze.

"Orders? What orders?" Goncourt protested. "We have work to do. And we must do it quickly. By the way what has happened to Agnelet? He must have some wine stored away in his cellar. I'm dying of thirst."

"He is outside," said Jean de Beuil, "keeping watch. . . ."

But, before he could finish, the innkeeper reappeared, carrying his oil lamp and accompanying two men, both covered with dust and clearly exhausted. But the sight of them drew an exclamation of pleasure from Catherine, for the first of them was none other than Tristan l'Hermite. It was Prégent de Coetivy who addressed them first.

"Ah, L'Hermite! Rosnivinen! We were waiting for you. I trust you bring orders from the Constable?"

"Yes, indeed," Tristan replied. "Here is Messire Jean de Rosnivinen who is to—er—execute them! Because of course there was no question of him coming in person. You know how much the King dislikes him. The King must not see this act as one of vengeance but as a decision taken in the national interest!"

As he spoke he went up to Catherine and bowed to her respectfully. "My Lord the Constable has asked me, madame, to kiss the fair hand which opened Chinon on his behalf. He is deeply grateful to you, and trusts that in future you will allow him to include himself among your most devoted servants."

This little speech had a remarkable effect. Catherine felt the atmosphere change at once. Until then, despite their polite speeches, she had been feeling ill at ease among these men. She had the vague sense that the deference they showed her was being paid largely to Arnaud's name and memory rather than to herself as a woman. Her behavior must seem too strange to them, too remote from what they were used to. They no doubt felt that she should have laid the burden of avenging herself upon some champion and waited for the

241

outcome amid prayer and meditation in the seclusion of some convent. But she was determined to see her role through to the very end. What matter what these men might think!

Without a word Raoul de Goncourt came and took her hand, led her into the center of the ring of barrels and sat her down, and then sat down beside her.

"Take your seats, messires, and let's come to a decision once and for all. It's high time we did! Agnelet, bring us something to drink and then disappear!"

The innkeeper hastened to obey, setting goblets and wine pitchers on two large barrels before discreetly retiring. There was silence in the cave while he did this. Then Goncourt glanced round at the company.

"You already know the most important news. La Trémoille is installed in the Coudray Tower guarded by fifteen archers. Which means that without my help you would not have a chance of getting to him. I have the castle's usual garrison of thirty men under my immediate command. Some three hundred men-at-arms arrived here with the King, all under the Lord Chamberlain's orders, of course. The first question is—have you any men?"

"I have fifty men bivouacked in the forest," said Jean de Beuil.

"That will be enough," said Goncourt. "We shall have the advantage of surprise, and of the great scale of the castle, which means that troops have to be spread out over the whole plateau, between the Fort of St. Georges and the Coudray Tower, and of the fact that I, the governor, will be at your head. But on the other hand, the postern gate, which I will open for you at midnight tomorrow if you agree to my plan, and which is the nearest to the keep, stands between the Moulin tower and the polygon tower . . . where La Trémoille's strongest supporter, the Marshall de Rais, is lodged. . . ."

At the mention of Gilles, Catherine shuddered and went pale. She clenched her teeth and bit her lips to stop herself giving way to the fear which the mere sound of his name awoke in her. In her excitement at reaching the end of her mission she had forgotten all about the terrifying blue-bearded nobleman. . . . But Jean de Beuil answered:

"I lodge there too. I will have the men sent into the castle and then I and Ambroise de Lore for instance can go up into the tower and take care of Gilles de Rais between us. He won't be able to leave his apartment."

He spoke so calmly that her fear receded. Gilles de Rais

was not particularly alarming to these knights. The governor made a sign of approval.

"Excellent. You shall have charge of De Rais then. I and my lieutenant here, Olivier Fretard, will see that as many guards as possible are put out of action by having them sent out of the Coudray Tower. De Beuil's fifty men, led by De Breze and Coetivy, together with Tristan l'Hermite and Rosnivinen, shall attack the Lord Chamberlain, who lodges alone in the keep."

"Where is the King?"

"In the Château de Mileu, the lodging which leads out of the great hall. The Queen will ask him to spend the night with her, a thing he never refuses because he loves his wife after a fashion for the calm and gentleness he finds in her. The Queen will do everything in her power to appease him if there should be any alarm given. . . . The hardest part will be the approach to the château. The nights are not dark at present, and the guards on the ramparts may well give the alarm . . . in which case we are lost. You, messieurs, are responsible for seeing that none of these men are wearing any sort of armor or mail, which could make a noise. Nothing but leather and wool. . . ."

"What weapons?" Jean de Beuil asked briefly.

"Sword and dagger for knights, axe and dagger for the soldiers. That is understood then? At midnight we open the postern gate. You come in. Then De Beuil and Lore go towards the Boisy Tower while the rest take care of the keep. Coetivy and Tristan l'Hermite will surround it with ten men, while De Breze and Rosnivinen go up to the first floor and execute La Trémoille."

The conspirators all nodded agreement. Then Catherine's clear voice spoke up.

"What about me?" she asked coldly, for she had been growing steadily more indignant at discovering that no role was assigned to her in the plot, and she could no longer keep silence.

There was a silence. All their eyes turned towards her and she read the same reproving look in all of them, even Pierre's. But it was Goncourt again who expressed the general sentiment.

"Madame," he said politely but firmly, "we asked you here tonight so that you might learn what our plans are. This is customary, and we owed it to you. But what remains to be done is for us, the men, to take care of. Certainly you have earned our gratitude . . ."

"One moment, sir governor," Catherine interrupted, getting

243

to her feet, "I did not come to Chinon simply to receive your congratulations and listen to fine words and speeches and then lie peacefully in my bed while you attacked your quarry. I want to be there!"

"No place for a woman!" Lore cried. "We don't want petticoats mixed up in the fighting."

"Forget that I am a woman. Think of me solely as the representative of Arnaud de Montsalvy!"

"The soldiers will be put off by your presence. . . ."

"I will dress in men's clothes. But I want to be there, milords! It is my right! I claim the right!"

There was silence. Catherine saw them all look questioningly at each other. Even De Breze was hostile to the idea of her being there, she saw that. Only Tristan dared speak up for her.

"You cannot refuse her that," he said gravely. "You accepted the lunatic risks she ran to make this whole attack possible . . . and now you refuse her! It would not be fair to deprive her of the moment of victory!"

Raoul de Goncourt went across to the stairway without replying, and set foot on the first step. Then he turned.

"You are right, Tristan. It would not be fair. Till tomorrow, then, all of you. At midnight!"

There was something unanswerable about the man. No one dared to protest.

"Till midnight," they all cried.

Catherine ignored Pierre de Breze's proffered hand and took Tristan by the arm.

"Come, my friend. It is time you rested," she said affectionately, leading him towards the entrance to the cave. She did not even deign to notice Pierre's unhappy expression. He had not come to her assistance earlier on and she was angry with him for the betrayal.

When she went back to her room Sara was sitting up in bed looking at her.

"Well?" she asked.

"It is planned for tomorrow at midnight. . . ."

"Not a moment too soon. I shall not be sorry to see the end of this wild-goose chase."

Pleased with this conclusion, Sara turned over and was soon fast asleep again.

The June night was clear and warm. In her dark cloth doublet Catherine felt uncomfortably hot as she climbed the hill towards the château with the others. Beside her, shoulder

244

to shoulder, came De Beuil, Lore, Coetivy, De Breze and Rosnivinen. Tristan brought up the rear, with the soldiers.

This troop of more than fifty men moved forward as silently as an army of phantoms. Jean de Beuil's orders were strict and precise: no armor whose steel might rattle or clank. The men wore nothing but thick woolen clothes, but all had a dagger and axe thrust through their belts. It was impossible to read anything on those closed and silent faces. They climbed in disciplined silence, like a well-oiled war machine, towards the walls which drew nearer every moment. The shadow of one of the polygonal towers fell across them and protected them from discovery.

Catherine reflected that this beautiful, blue starlit night was a strange backdrop to murder. She would have preferred it black, opaque and a little misty, but she was filled with a fierce joy all the same. It was she who had set these men moving. The fact that they were there at all, risking their lives in this desperate enterprise, was because she had passionately desired that this should be so. In a few moments she would either be victorious or hopelessly defeated. A little while earlier, on leaving the inn, she had given her last injunctions and requests to Sara.

"If I don't come back you are to return to Montsalvy, and tell my husband that I died for him. And then you must take care of Michel."

"No need," Sara said calmly. "You will come back. . . ."

"How do you know?"

"Your time has not yet come—I can tell."

But as she drew closer to the castle Catherine began to think that Sara might be wrong for once. The troop which had seemed so formidable when they set out seemed to shrink as the immense new curtain walls came into sight, with their slate roofs gleaming. She gave an anxious sigh, and at this Pierre de Breze tried to take her hand. But she snatched hers away instantly. . . . This was not the moment for playing at love, and for the nonce she wanted to be no more to these men than a brother-in-arms.

"Catherine," the young man said reproachfully. "Why do you avoid me?"

She was saved from replying by Coetivy.

"Silence," he ordered. "We are drawing near. . . ."

They were approaching the top of the hill. They could see the guards posted along the wall above them. There were no lights in the castle. The King was doubtless asleep in his immense bed in the Royal Lodgings, with Queen Marie beside him. She no doubt lay there with her eyes open . . . for she had promised to keep watch. Anyway, how could she possibly sleep, knowing what was about to happen?

At an imperious gesture from De Beuil, the whole band flattened themselves and thus became invisible from the battlements while the young captain himself went forward towards the closed postern. Catherine found herself holding her breath. She could see the town and its pointed rooftops spread out at her feet, gathered round the gleaming thread of the river and enclosed snugly by its stone walls. Marie Javelle's deep voice tolled midnight and made her jump. Goncourt and Fretard must be waiting behind that high closed gate. . . .

The door opened, and someone whispered. . . .

Just then a flickering yellow light seeped out through the open door. The man who opened it was carrying a lantern. Catherine caught sight of two tall, armored figures. The governor and his lieutenant, neither of whom were obliged to disguise their presence there and could go in armor. One after the other the conspirators slipped through the gap. Catherine went after De Breze who took her by the arm and tried to pull her after him. She pulled her arm away with annoyance. Then she found herself in the Coudray courtyard, on the far side of the Moulin Tower, which formed the westernmost part of the fortifications. A short way ahead stood the immense round tower where her enemy slept, the keep, behind which one could see the St. Martin Chapel. . . . The end was in sight, at last!

Goncourt examined each man's face as he passed before him, holding up his lantern, and counted them. When the last had passed, the postern gate was closed as silently as it had opened, and the governor took his place at the head of the troop. He pointed towards the silent keep. Catherine could hear the slow, measured pace of the sentries on the roundway above. They did not stop for a moment. The whole operation was carried through in impressive silence. De Beuil and Lore went towards one of the towers, while Tristan and Coetivy, followed by a small group of men, disappeared silently into the shadows round the keep.

As she passed through the Coudray Gate she had to take several deep breaths because her beating heart suffocated her. She felt for the dagger at her belt and gripped it hard with her left hand. By now, silently as a black serpent uncoiling, the conspirators were climbing by flickering torchlight towards the upper floor where the Lord Chamberlain slept.

The guards at the door recognized the governor and did not move. They were overpowered before they could open their mouths. It was not till then that the silence was shattered.

The conspirators flung open the door and rushed into the large room where La Trémoille lay snoring behind velvet hangings. The only light in the room came from a gold oil lamp, and one could just make out an enormous black shape lying on its back.

It was soon over. Four men sprang on top of the monstrous body which they secured and overpowered. La Trémoille, now awake but unable to move, began to shriek. He was momentarily stunned by a blow on the temple with a sword pommel.

"Kill him!" Catherine cried, intoxicated by the prospect of vengeance. She snatched her dagger from its sheath and flung herself forward but a man, whom she recognized as Jean de Rosnivinen, took it from her.

"This is not women's work," the Breton growled as he stepped forward. "Give that to me!"

He plunged the weapon into La Trémoille's belly and the man started screaming. Other blows were struck but without silencing the victim, who screamed like a pig at the slaughter.

People were waking throughout the castle by now. There were disturbing noises. A few moments longer and the guards would come running.

"He is too fat," Goncourt remarked disgustedly. "The daggers cannot reach his heart. Tie him and gag him and take him away. He must be out of the castle in five minutes."

"Take him away?" Catherine cried. "Hang him!"

"We haven't time," the governor said, "or any rope strong enough. Let us take him to Montresor. . . . I left horses outside to be used in such an emergency. A man must go to warn De Beuil. He must gag and bind Gilles de Rais and join us down below."

In the twinkling of an eye La Trémoille was no more than a huge moaning bundle, whose terrified eyes rolled beseechingly above the gag which half-covered his face. Just then Olivier Fretard, who had remained below, came running in:

"The King is awake. He wants to know what the noise is about? He is sending his guards."

"Quick, take him away," Goncourt ordered. "I shall go to see the King."

And in a moment it had been done as he commanded. Catherine, who had been turned to ice by La Trémoille's shrieks, watched in bewilderment. Ten men succeeded in transporting the fat man's huge, bleeding mass down the stairs. They slid rather than walked down the stairs, crossed the courtyard in a twinkling and passed out through the postern gate. Pierre de Breze wanted to take Catherine along with the rest but the smell of blood and the appalling scene of butchery she had just witnessed had been too much for her. She was quietly swooning away beside the great bed. He snatched her up just before she fell to the ground and carried her out.

As they emerged into the courtyard the cool night air brought Catherine round. She opened her eyes, saw De Breze's face close to hers and could not think what had happened for a moment. Then it all came back to her and with a quick, supple movement she slipped from his restraining arms.

"Let me go!" she cried. "Thank you, messire. . . . Where is La Trémoille? What have they done with him?"

Pierre pointed towards the armed company clattering down towards the town, looking like some immense centipede.

"Look, they are taking him away! At Montresor he will be tried and sentenced."

A wave of blood warmed Catherine's cheeks.

"And her?" she stormed. "What about his wife? Are you going to leave her in peace here? She is worse than he is and I hate her even more than I hated him."

"She cannot be seized, Catherine . . . she has her apartments in the château of Mileu, near the King's lodgings. . . . We must go now!"

"Ah, really?" Catherine cried furiously. "Well, go if you like. I stay! I shall not rest till I have disposed of her . . . I have a little account to settle with her!"

As she spoke she felt for her dagger and was surprised to find the sheath empty. Then she remembered that Rosnivinen had taken it from her to plunge into the Lord Chamberlain's belly. The weapon had slid into the fat creature before being snatched out and flung aside. It must still be on the floor somewhere.

"I must go back," she said. "I have lost my dagger."

"What does a dagger matter, Catherine. You must be mad. The guards will arrest you!"

"Well? Supposing they do? I have no intention of hiding anyway; I intend to ask the King to reinstate us publicly and before the whole Court. Queen Yolande promised me that. If I am arrested send word to her. As for the dagger, it was my husband's . . . I value it dearly and I intend to get it back!"

She ran towards the keep once more. A great mass of soldiers swarmed uncertainly round the door, unsure what they should do. She pushed through them, with De Breze behind her, and would certainly have been arrested if Goncourt had not returned at that precise moment from the Royal Lodge. De Breze called him and explained the situation briefly. Goncourt signed the soldiers to move away with a sweep of his sword.

"Leave this . . . this boy!" he said curtly. "I know him. . . . Go back to your quarters."

The men-at-arms went off docilely, dragging their feet as people do when they are still half-asleep. Only De Breze, Catherine and Goncourt remained.

The governor's face, still stained with blood, looked somber and brooding and Pierre concluded that this must mean things had gone badly.

"The King? Does he know now? What did he say?"

Goncourt shrugged and laughed shortly.

"The King has gone straight back to sleep. The Queen assured him that the noise which woke him was in his own interests, and he believed her without further explanations. He merely asked if the Constable was there, and they said no. That gives us until daybreak to find explanations. He behaved exactly as he did when Giac was killed."

"Strange King!" Pierre murmured. "He takes these men, these indispensable favorites of his, to the very pinnacle of power . . . and forgets them in an instant!"

But Catherine was not there to philosophize. She felt she still had work to do. She turned away from the two men and was about to enter the Coudray Tower. Goncourt stopped her.

"One moment. Where are you going?"

"Up there, to find my husband's dagger."

"It is I who should go up there. I still have things to do," the governor cut in dryly.

"Then I will go with you. What is there to fear? La Trémoille is already on the road to Montresor. If they arrest me you can set me free."

"It is true La Trémoille is gone. But his wife is still here. She was woken by the din. Who was not? As I left the King's quarters I caught sight of her running down the corridors, half-naked, like a madwoman. I ran after her but she had a start on me and I saw her running into the keep. She must be up there . . ."

"And you would have me stay here?" Catherine cried. "Ah, no, sir governor, over my dead body!"

She snatched her arm away and rushed up the narrow stone stairs, four steps at a time, with the agility of a cat. Hatred lent her wings. In her joy at the thought of meeting her enemy on equal terms she did not even reflect that she was unarmed. But it was unlikely that the other woman was either. . . . The bells of victory pealed in her ears, and she heard nothing else. . . .

She paused on the threshold, breathless, and astonished by the view which met her eyes. The Dame de la Trémoille, attired in a scanty chemise which revealed most of her bosom and shoulders, was rummaging in a box and taking out jewels which she placed upon a piece of silk close by. Judging by the unbelievable mess she must already have visited the other boxes, chests and coffers. Catherine gave a scornful smile. This woman would never change! One might kill off her husbands and she would always be more anxious about her inheritance than their fate. . . .

So busy was she with her plundering that she did not see Catherine enter. Catherine crept gently in and picked up the dagger which lay on the ground some way off. She grimaced . . . it was still sticky with blood. . . .

Suddenly she started. The countess had become still, panting softly as if she were out of breath, Catherine saw her lift something up to the light, something which sparkled with a thousand somber fires. The black diamond! *Her* black diamond! . . . Never in her life had she seen such a covetous expression on a human face. The woman's eyes were popping out of her head, her lips were dry: it was this above all which she had come to find. She trembled with excitement. . . . Catherine's icy voice made her jump.

"Give me that diamond," she said coldly. "It belongs to me."

The woman turned a bewildered look on her at first. Then her eyes narrowed and once more glittered with cunning and cruelty.

"To you? Who are you?"

Catherine laughed briefly and stepped into the middle of the room where the lamp light fell full upon her, sharply illuminating her slender shape in the masculine garb.

"Look at me. Look well at me! Have you never seen me before?"

The countess stepped forward doubtfully, clutching the black jewel against her bare breast, and examined the face which was framed in a black hood. She shook her head, doubtless disconcerted by the masculine dress.

"They used to call me Tchalai . . ." Catherine began mockingly.

The other woman burst out laughing and turned away angrily.

250

"I dare say. Your face was of so little importance to me! You were lucky to escape me . . . but now clear out, woman, and leave me to my business. As for this diamond . . ."

The smile left Catherine's face. She seized her enemy's wrist and twisted it so that she was forced to look at her:

"Now listen to me, witch! I said that that diamond belonged to me, because you and your swine of a husband stole it from me . . ."

"Get out!" the countess cried furiously. "Since when do women of your sort own diamonds?"

"I am not a gypsy! I only pretended to be one so as to bring about the downfall of you and your husband. Look at me more closely! There is nothing Egyptian about me . . . my hair is light, and so are my eyebrows."

"Who are you then? Tell me and then go to the devil. . . . You are hurting me!"

Catherine slowly pressed her dagger-point against the white bosom.

"If anyone goes to the devil it will be you! And it is I, Catherine de Montsalvy, who will send you to him!"

"Montsalvy!"

The countess stammered the name as a look of abject terror came into her pale eyes. The dagger pressed a little harder. Blood flowed. Catherine's hands gripped the woman's wrist, and she groaned with pain. She clenched her teeth.

"On your knees," she whispered. "On your knees! And ask God to pardon you for the evil you have done, for torturing my husband, betraying Joan of Arc, pillaging the kingdom, sacrificing so many innocent lives. . . ."

"Mercy!" the woman screamed. "Don't kill me! It wasn't me . . ."

"On top of everything, you are a coward," Catherine spat with disgust. "Come now, on your knees. . . ."

Fury gave her fingers unsuspected strength. Little by little the countess's knees gave way. Her teeth were chattering. . . . But unfortunately just then Goncourt's voice, from behind her, broke into her thoughts and distracted her for a moment.

"You cannot kill this woman, Dame Catherine, she belongs to us. . . ."

Her attention only wavered for a second but her enemy was able to profit by it. She twisted like an eel and broke free from Catherine. Then she grabbed her wrist and snatched the dagger. Catherine found herself disarmed and confronted by

251

a veritable fury. The woman's eyes flamed and she ground her teeth.

"This time you will not escape me," she hissed.

Catherine stood with her eyes fixed on her adversary's, then she stepped back a step. Forestalling the two men, who were about to leap upon the countess, she said quickly:

"Stop! I don't care what you say . . . she is my prisoner!"

Behind her Catherine could feel the outline of the pedestal on which the night-light stood. . . . The Dame de la Trémoille's contorted face was coming closer and closer, and she was brandishing the dagger. Catherine reached behind for the lamp and then, with all her strength, flung it at her enemy's face.

There was a scream of agony. The other woman started back, both hands clapped to her face which was spattered with burning oil. A tongue of flame ran through her hair, and another licked at her transparent chemise. She howled with pain. . . . Catherine watched with dilated eyes as Goncourt snatched a coverlet off the bed and rolled the countess up in it. She bent down slowly and picked up the dagger. Her legs shook now that it was all over. Pierre de Breze had to help her to her feet, otherwise she would have fallen on her knees. The screams from beneath the coverlet had turned to moans. The injured woman sounded like a sick cow. Catherine stared at Goncourt blankly.

"I leave her to you now. . . . What are you going to do with her?" she asked.

He bent down, picking up the moaning bundle, and looked Catherine squarely in the face.

"That is for you to decide! You were right—that is your privilege. De Breze told me . . . I was going to send her to join her husband, but I will have her flung into the dungeons if that is your wish. It is no more than she deserves!"

Catherine shook her head, feeling suddenly drained of strength.

"No, let her live. . . . Let them live as they are now, since God has ordained that they shall not die at our hands. Let them live together, one beside the other, with the leprosy in their souls and the horror that they have become! She is disfigured . . . he, impotent with fat, covered with wounds from which he may never recover. . . . Let them make their own hell! And may the world forget them. I am avenged!"

Her overtaxed nerves were beginning to crack. She gripped De Breze's arm, and clung to it for support.

"Take me away, Pierre," she implored, "take me away from here!"

"Do you want to join the others at Montresor?" he asked gently.

She shook her head.

"I don't want to see them again. Complete your task without me, mine is done. . . . I am going back to the inn."

But as she was about to leave the room she suddenly caught sight of Garin's jewel, glittering somberly from a pile of stones. She leaned over and picked it up. The accursed jewel nestled into her palm like a familiar.

"It is mine," she murmured. "I am taking what belongs to me." De Breze passed his arm gently round her shivering shoulders.

"They say that that magnificent gem is accursed and brings bad luck. You have no need of it, Catherine. . . ."

She stared for a moment at the sinister jewel which glowed darkly in her hand.

"That is true," she said gravely. "This jewel brings death and misfortune. But she to whom I am about to offer it has the power to cast out evil and drive death away. . . ."

With De Breze's help Catherine finally left the keep of Coudray. Out in the courtyard she looked up at the sky. The stars had vanished. There was only one left, which glittered with extraordinary brilliance. Over towards the east the sky showed paler. The air was cool. Pierre muffled her tenderly in a cloak.

"Come," he beseeched. "You are going to catch cold."

But she did not move. She held his arm and stood still gazing up at the sky.

"The dawn is coming," she murmured, "a new day! Everything has finished for me . . . the page has turned."

"It can all begin again, Catherine," he whispered ardently. "This could be the first day of a new life, full of sunshine and happiness . . . if you wished. Catherine, tell me . . ."

Gently but firmly she laid a hand over his mouth and smiled sadly at the handsome, anxious face bending over her.

"No, Pierre. Don't say anything more . . . I am weary, weary to death. Just take me back, without saying a word."

Clinging to each other like lovers they slowly and hesitantly made their way down the hill towards the sleeping town.

CHAPTER TWELVE

The Shadow of the Past

When they had passed through the high double gates, reinforced with iron studs and bars, Catherine saw the immense courtyard of Chinon spread out before her. The Scots archers stood in double rows, forming a guard of honor, the heron plumes in their bonnets waving gently in the evening breeze. A dozen heralds stood frozen on the steps leading up to the Great Hall where the King was awaiting her, their trumpets on their hips. . . .

Catherine's heart thumped in her breast. It was now ten days since the daring plot against the Lord Chamberlain had been successfully carried out. La Trémoille languished half-dead in the prisons of Montresor, waiting till the stringent conditions of his ransomed existence should be fulfilled: the payment of a huge ransom, forfeiture of all his offices and honors, perpetual banishment to his château at Sully, the only one which he was allowed to keep. But she was anxious to forget the monstrous tyrant who had treated her and the Montsalvys so cruelly. This was the hour of her triumph. Queen Yolande had sent word to her that this evening, the 15th of June, the King would receive her with all honors.

She had awaited this moment impatiently in the inn although she was no longer obliged to keep hidden. Henceforth she was free to come and go as she wished. No dangers threatened her any more. Had she not seen Gilles de Rais and his followers leaving Chinon at dawn the morning after La Trémoille's downfall? It had been an almost furtive departure! The Marshall's face was arrogant as ever, but it could not conceal the fact that he was returning vanquished and disgraced to his property in the Angevin provinces. She had smiled pensively to herself as he passed: "One day," she murmured, "you too will pay for the wrong you have done me! I shall not forget!"

As she drew near to the ramp the heralds put the long silver trumpets to their lips and the sound made Catherine shiver with emotion. She glanced round involuntarily at Tristan l'Hermite who followed respectfully, at three paces distance. There was some bitterness mingled with her joy tonight . . . she had hoped that Pierre de Breze would be beside her at this important moment. But De Breze had completely vanished since the time he escorted her back to the inn after the attack on La Trémoille. Tristan believed that he had caught sight of Pierre galloping out of Chinon that same day. But no one had seen him since. . . .

The trumpets fell silent, but as Catherine climbed slowly up the steps the high doors of the Great Hall swung open, revealing an astonishing blaze of light within. Hundreds of torches flamed round the walls of the immense chamber. The walls, which were more than six yards high, were all hung about with tapestries. Great drifts of fresh flowers decorated the floor as far as the great fireplace at the far end of the room. There was a brilliant, multi-colored crowd assembled there. As the doors opened they all fell silent. Catherine saw the throne standing close to the fireplace, surmounted by a canopy of blue and gold. The King sat upon it and close at hand stood young Charles d'Anjou, the youth whom she had seen at Amboise, dazzlingly handsome in a suit of cloth of gold. She saw the Queen and her ladies in one of the window embrasures, but her gaze returned to the elderly gentleman who had been standing by the door and now came forward to greet her, leaning on a white stick: this was the Comte de Vendôme. Master of the King's Household and Grand Master of Ceremonies.

He bowed and offered her his hand to lead her up to the throne. But just then a slender feminine figure, wearing sumptuous mourning, stepped rapidly forward between the two ranks of lords and ladies. A great lump rose in Catherine's throat as she recognized Queen Yolande. She spoke graciously to Louis de Vendôme who bent one knee respectfully.

"If it please you, cousin. I myself would like to take Madame de Montsalvy to the King!" she said.

"Protocol is silent where the Queen commands," the Grand Master replied with a smile.

Yolande held out her hand to the deeply curtsying Catherine. "Come, my dear," she said.

Side by side, amid deep silence, the two women made their way up the great hall, the one imposing and handsome beneath her high crown and dark braids, the other radiantly beautiful despite the severity of her dark clothes. Both ladies were in mourning, but Queen Yolande's clothes were of satin and velvet whereas Catherine wore only fine woolen cloth and a crêpe veil on her blonde head. As they approached the throne Catherine's heart skipped a beat and she grew noticeably paler. It was a solemn moment. The King's thin figure in dark blue velvet clothes, seemed to loom taller and taller and Catherine could not help thinking sorrowfully that this helpful hand she was holding should by rights have been Arnaud's. If it had not been for that dreadful illness they would have been walking up that triumphant way together, and they would certainly not have been wearing mourning clothes. Nevertheless it was to him, to her lost love, that she dedicated this moment because it was his by right. She saw him again as she remembered him, struck down like a blasted oak upon the ruins of his gutted castle, razed to the ground by order of that same monarch who now stood waiting to receive her. She almost seemed to hear the despairing sobs which had forced their way out of that proud and valiant man, and she had to close her own eyes for a moment to keep back the tears.

Then she was snatched out of her melancholy thoughts by the sudden realization that Yolande was paying her a supreme honor, for as they went by lords and ladies bowed and curtsied, and the homage paid to the Queen inevitably rebounded upon her young companion. Even the princes of the blood bent one knee as they passed, and as they drew near the throne the King stood up. His lusterless brown eyes fastened upon Catherine's face with some curiosity. Although Charles VII was ill-endowed physically, the majesty which emanated from his slender form and plain face was unmistakable. He was the King despite everything, and it was to him, if one's name was Montsalvy, that one dedicated one's blood, life and fortune. Catherine did not lower her gaze from his but she knelt before him as Yolande spoke up.

"May it please Your Majesty's just and generous heart to receive and honor the Comtesse de Montsalvy, Dame de la Chataigneraie, who has come to kneel at your feet and implore your help in righting the many grievous wrongs and sufferings she has endured at the hands of the former Lord Chamberlain. . . ."

"Sire," Catherine added vehemently, "it is for my husband who died of a broken heart, for Arnaud de Montsalvy who ever served you faithfully and honestly, that I have come to seek justice, not for myself. I am but his wife!"

The King smiled and stepped down towards her, and held out both hands to help her up to her feet.

"Madame," he said, "it is rather the King who should be at your feet asking for mercy. I know all the evil that has befallen the most loyal of my captains, and great is my shame and remorse that this should be so. Now, for the sake of yourself and your son, it is meet that everything should be as it was and that the house of Montsalvy should be restored to wealth and honor. Let the Lord Chancellor step forward."

Once again the brilliant throng parted to make way for Regnault de Chartres, Archbishop of Rheims and Chancellor of France. Catherine watched in some astonishment as the haughty prelate who had been Joan of Arc's mortal foe, and had doubtless abandoned La Trémoille through prudence, made his way forward. She felt an instinctive dislike of him on account of that arrogant expression and calculating fold of the lips. Then she flushed scarlet to the roots of her hair. A little behind the Chancellor there walked a man whose clothes were gray with dust and whose features were drawn with fatigue: it was Pierre de Breze. He smiled at her as soon as he caught sight of her and Catherine found herself returning the smile. But there was no time to start wondering about that because Charles now addressed the Lord Bishop.

"Lord Chancellor, do you have that which Messire de Breze went to seek at Montsalvy?"

By way of answer the Archbishop stretched out his hand and Pierre de Breze placed a parchment scroll, much worn and stained, upon it. Regnault de Chartres unrolled the parchment which was torn at three corners. The blood mounted to Catherine's face. She recognized that tattered, stained and faded piece of parchment. It was the one which had been fixed by three arrows to the still smoking ruins of Montsalvy, the edict which declared Arnaud de Montsalvy a traitor to his King and country and a felon, and condemned him to perpetual banishment. . . . She watched it flutter slightly in the Bishop's hands much as it had fluttered that evening at Montsalvy. And then the spectacle changed. A man dressed in red stepped forward, followed by two varlets carrying a pot full of glowing coals. Catherine recognized the executioner! Her eyes grew wide with alarm and an uncontrollable anguish tore at her throat. This sinister scarlet figure summoned up memories which were all too recent and too horrifying! However, his business now was not with a human being.

Regnault de Chartres stepped forward with the scroll in his hands. His voice rose in the silence.

"We, Charles, seventh of that name, by Grace of Almighty God King of France, decree that the edict outlawing the most high and noble Lord Arnaud, Comte de Montsalvy, seigneur of the Chataigneraie in the country of Auvergne, and likewise all his descendants, shall be annulled for ever more. We command that the said edict be declared false, lying and perfidious and that as such it shall be destroyed this day before our eyes by the hand of the executioner as a mark of our abhorrence of all it contains. . . ."

The Chancellor took a pair of scissors from his pocket, and cut off the faded red ribbon which bore the Great Seal of France, and handed it to the King after kissing it respectfully. Then he gave the scroll to the executioner who took hold of it with a pair of tongs and plunged it into the burning coals. The fine piece of sheep skin writhed like a live thing before going black and shriveling to ashes. Catherine watched fascinated till it was completely consumed. Then she looked up and met the King's smiling face.

"Your place is beside us, Catherine de Montsalvy, till such time as your son is old enough to serve us. You are welcome in this château, and an apartment will be prepared to receive you from this evening. Tomorrow our Lord Chancellor shall draw up the necessary articles restoring to you all your former rights and properties, together with a sum of gold intended to compensate you for the wrongs you have endured. Alas gold cannot make up for everything, and no one regrets that fact more than the King. . . ."

"Sire," she murmured in a voice grown hoarse with emotion, "the Montsalvys will continue to serve you as they have always done. But I humbly thank you for allowing them to do so once again!"

"Now go and greet your Queen. She awaits you."

Catherine turned towards Marie d'Anjou who stood a little way off surrounded by her ladies, smiling at her. Impulsively she went and knelt at the feet of this plain, virtuous lady who did not know the meaning of evil. Marie welcomed Catherine with open arms.

"My dear Catherine," she cried as she kissed her, "I am so happy to see you again! I hope you will take your place among my ladies once more."

"For a while, Madame . . . but I shall have to return to my son one day!"

"There is no hurry. You can have him brought here! Now make a place, ladies, for the Comtesse de Montsalvy who has returned to us once more!"

A flattering welcome met Catherine. She already knew some of the ladies, and it was with great delight that she rediscovered the gentle Anne de Beuil, Dame de Chaumont, whom she had first met at Angers. There was Jeanne du Mesnil too, whom she had known at Bourges, and the Dame de Blosset, but Madame de la Roche Guyon and Princess Jeanne d'Orléans, daughter of the perpetual prisoner of London, were strangers to her. She was astonished not to find Marguerite de Culan, who had been her friend, and was saddened to hear that she had chosen to go into a nunnery. But the happiness she felt at being restored to her rightful station could not be dimmed for long. She was like a stone which a fierce storm had dislodged and which the stonemason has carefully restored to its rightful place, alongside its fellows. It was good to be among her own kind and see those pretty smiling faces and hear their friendly remarks again after so many long days in the saddle, and so many somber times. There were some men now among the crowd of ladies surrounding the heroine of the hour. Almost dizzy with relief and pleasure she saw the handsome Duc d'Alençon come to greet her, then the Bâtard d'Orléans, Jean de Dunois, who had once rescued her from undergoing torture, then the Marechal de La Fayette, and several others. She hardly knew where to look, whom to smile at, yet she sought Pierre among these men, Pierre who had just returned from Auvergne and whom she longed to question about her family. But just then a cheerful voice with a lively Gascon accent spoke up behind her and she turned round.

"I told you we would soon see you at King Charles's Court again! Have you a smile for an old friend?"

She held out both hands to the newcomer, restraining an impulse to fling both arms round his neck.

"Cadet Bernard," she cried affectionately. "How good it is to see you again! So you haven't forgotten us?"

"I never forget my friends," said Bernard d'Armagnac, with sudden gravity, "especially when they bear your name. Come this way. . . ."

He took her arm and led her aside. The courtiers made way for them. Groups were forming round the King and Queen and the normal life of the Court was resumed as they waited for the horn to be sounded for the evening meal. Catherine was part of the community again. As she walked along at his side Catherine examined the Comte de Pardiac's faun-like face. That dark face, with its green eyes and pointed ears, and subtle and witty expression, reminded her of hours both cruel and tender at Montsalvy. Bernard had saved both her and Arnaud from death; he had found them a refuge at Carlat! If he had not, heaven knows what might have become of them!

When they reached a window embrasure Bernard stopped, turned to face Catherine and asked, with sudden seriousness:

"Where is he? What has become of him?"

She went pale and gazed at him in bewilderment. "Arnaud? But . . . didn't you know? He is . . . no more . . ."

"I don't believe it!" he said, with a fierce gesture that seemed to thrust aside the funereal image which had been summoned up for an instant. "Something I don't understand happened at Carlat. Hugh Kennedy, whom I have seen, is as silent as a carp, and everyone here swears that Arnaud is dead. But I am certain that this is not the case. Tell me the truth, Catherine; you owe it to me. . . ."

She nodded sadly, and mechanically pushed aside the black veil which brushed her cheek.

"The truth is hideous, Bernard, and worse than death itself. . . . I owe it to you, as you say, and yet I would rather you had not asked it of me. It is so hard to bear! You must know that to the rest of the world my husband is dead!"

"To the rest of the world, perhaps, but not to me! Look, Catherine, I am like you. It is only a few days since I too was readmitted at Court. Till then I was fighting up in the north with La Hire and Xaintrailles. They also refuse to believe in Montsalvy's inexplicable death."

"How is it that they are not here?" Catherine asked, trying to change the subject. "I had hoped to see them again!"

But the Comte de Pardiac was in no mood to be distracted from his quest. He answered briefly:

"They are fighting Robert Willoughby on the Oise. If I had not been with them I should have returned to Carlat. I am the Lord of that castle, if you remember, and I should have found a way of forcing the truth out of someone there, by torture if necessary."

"Torture? Torture? Is that the only means you know of then?" Catherine asked, shuddering.

"Whatever the means," he answered coolly, "it is the end that matters. Now speak, Catherine, for you know quite well that I am bound to know sooner or later. And I give you my word of honor that your secret will be well kept. You know it is not idle curiosity that prompts me to ask."

She looked at him closely for a moment. Why should she doubt his sincerity after all he had done for them? She made a weary gesture.

"I will tell you then. After all, as you say, you would know one day. . . ."

It did not take her long to acquaint Cadet Bernard with Arnaud's terrible fate. But when she had finished the Gascon prince was ashen. He wiped away the sweat from his brow with the back of a golden cuff. And then, abruptly, he went scarlet, and darted a furious green glance at Catherine.

"And you mean to say you left him to moulder away in that primitive place, surrounded by peasants . . . he, the proudest of us all?"

"What was I to do?" Catherine cried angrily. "I was alone against the garrison, against the village. There was no other way. Besides it was the way he chose himself. You seem to forget that we had nothing else, no other refuge but Carlat, which we owed to you!"

Bernard d'Armagnac turned aside and shrugged, then looked at Catherine uncertainly.

"That is true. Forgive me . . . but Catherine, he cannot stay there! Wouldn't it be possible to install him in some out-of-the-way castle where he could be looked after by a few devoted servants?"

"Who is bold enough to be devoted when leprosy is in question?" Catherine murmured. "And yet . . . I believe, yes, I do think it might be possible. But where? He doesn't want to leave Montsalvy."

"I'll find something, I'll tell you . . . Almighty God, I can't *bear* the idea of him being shut up there!"

Tears rose to Catherine's eyes. Her happiness forgotten, she faltered miserably:

"What about me? Do you suppose I find it easy to endure? And yet this thought has been torturing me for months! If I did not have a son I should have gone off with him, I should never have left him alone. Why should I be afraid to die, even of such an abominable disease, so long as I was with him? But, there is Michel . . . and Arnaud sent me away! I had a task to accomplish. Now, at last, it is done."

Cadet Bernard looked at her curiously, biting his thin lips.

"What do you propose to do now?"

But she had no time to answer him, because just then a tall figure dressed in blue appeared beside them, and a familiar voice inquired dryly:

"Can you be making Madame de Montsalvy weep, Sir Count? There are tears in her eyes."

"You appear to have keen eyesight!" Bernard retorted haughtily, annoyed at being interrupted. "Might I inquire what business it is of yours?"

But if De Breze's interruption had annoyed Bernard d'Armagnac the Count's manner seemed mightily to displease the nobleman from Angevin.

"No friend of Dame Catherine's wishes to see her suffer."

"I am more of a friend of hers than you will ever be, Mes-

261

sire de Breze, and what is more I am likewise a friend of her husband's."

"You *were*," De Breze amended. "Didn't you know that the noble Lord Arnaud de Montsalvy had died a glorious death?"

"Your solicitous attitude towards his—his widow allows one to suppose that the news did not shock you unduly? As for me . . ."

There was real animosity in his voice. Catherine was appalled at this quarrel and hastily intervened.

"Milords! I beg of you! Surely you are not going to mar my return to grace by quarreling? What would the King and the two Queens think?"

Bernard's suddenly aggressive behavior astonished her. But she had long known of the rivalry between the noblemen from the North, and those of Midi. They must hate each other already, and she was nothing more than a pretext.

The two men fell silent, but the look that flashed between them made it clear that there was still bad blood between them. They confronted each other silently like a couple of fighting cocks. Catherine realized that they were burning to air their quarrel and that she would not be able to restrain them for long. She looked about for assistance; her eye fell upon Tristan l'Hermite standing modestly in a corner, and she implored him dumbly. He rushed up, smiling, courteous.

"Queen Yolande was looking for you, Dame Catherine? Would you like me to take you to her?"

Unfortunately Pierre de Breze was quite determined to keep Catherine to himself. He smiled coldly at Tristan.

"I shall take her there myself," he said sharply. Cadet Bernard opened his mouth to protest and Catherine saw with dismay that they were on the point of starting up again. But she was longing to talk to Pierre. He had returned from Montsalvy; he must have so much to tell her! But how was she to find a moment alone with him away from Cadet Bernard's censorious eye now that the gentleman in question seemed to have elected himself the defender of Arnaud's rights? Luckily the question was taken out of her hands, because just then the castle servants announced that dinner was about to be served, and almost simultaneously the Master of the Royal Household came up to Catherine.

"His Majesty desires that you should sup at his table, madame. Allow me to conduct you thither."

Catherine heaved a great sigh of relief. She flashed a grateful smile at the Comte de Vendôme. Then, with a bow to the two enemies and a smile at Tristan, she accepted the old gentleman's arm, and allowed herself to be led away towards the banqueting hall.

The royal supper was both a triumph and a trial for Catherine. A triumph because, sitting at Queen Marie's right hand, she became the focal point of all eyes. In her severe black clothes her beauty stood out among the pale satins, milky complexions and deep-cut necklines, amid flowering bodices and jeweled head-dresses, much as the evil black diamond had gleamed forth among Garin's collection of jewels. The King's eyes kept turning towards her. He ordered delicacies to be served to her from his own plate, and his wine steward served her the same wine as his master's, that same Anjou wine which he preferred to all others. But it was a trial too, because she was able to observe the menacing glances exchanged between Bernard d'Armagnac and Pierre de Breze, who were sitting not far from each other. And Catherine's enjoyment was spoiled by the fear that not even the King's presence would restrain the two men, if their enmity were to flare up once again. She had the unpleasant feeling that she sat perched on top of a barrel of gunpowder. So it was with some satisfaction that she awaited the moment when the supper would end and the company adjourn to the Great Hall for dancing. Since her mourning was an excellent pretext for abstaining she begged Queen Marie and Queen Yolande to excuse her, which permission was graciously accorded, and two torch-bearers were assigned to escort her to her new quarters. She left the hall with head held high, followed by many an admiring glance.

The room she had been assigned was in the Treasure tower, and Sara awaited her there, having been sent for at the same time as her baggage. Catherine's anxious face alarmed her.

"You were the queen tonight. Why this anxious look?"

She told her everything, explaining her natural desire to spend a moment talking to the man who had just returned from Montsalvy, and the fact that Comte d'Armagnac had prevented her.

"I simply wanted to know how my son was!" she cried. "How was I to know that this might provoke a duel?"

"There are times when you don't seem to use your brains!" Sara remarked. "Either that or you must think the Comte de Pardiac a bigger fool than he is!! How could he avoid being surprised by the fact that a great nobleman like De Breze should have galloped all day and night to bring back a faded old piece of parchment when any one of the King's

263

messengers, armed with a royal warrant, could have done the job quite as well? This dash across country is an open declaration of love, as is the knot of black and white ribbons which young De Breze wears everywhere as solemnly as if he were carrying the Host itself!"

"Well?" Catherine remarked acidly. "I don't see what business it is of Messire Bernard d'Armagnac's that Pierre de Breze should choose to be my champion, and even declare his love? The mere fact that he is the King's cousin does not give him the right to interfere in other people's affairs, does it?"

Sara's eyes narrowed as she looked at Catherine.

"It is not the King's cousin who interferes in your affairs, Catherine . . . but your husband's childhood friend! Catherine . . . I have already warned you once against this attraction which you feel for young De Breze! Already it is making you ungrateful! You did not accuse Cadet Bernard of interfering when he saved you from the flames and gave you Carlat to live in! Remember how strong and deep is the love which binds you to Messire Arnaud. That man would never allow you to give yourself to another. He is like a watch-dog who protects his master's property while his master is away. You belong to his friend, and no one should forget the fact."

"As far as I am concerned there is nothing to discuss," Catherine said curtly. She felt uncomfortable and uneasy, not only in herself but in these black clothes of hers which suddenly felt quite suffocating on this hot June night. She tried to take off one of her veils but her fingers were clumsy and feverish; she pricked herself and tore the fine material.

"Help me, will you," she said irritably. "Can't you see that I can't do it myself?"

Sara smiled and started calmly removing the pins, one after another. She made Catherine sit down on a stool and for a moment she did not open her mouth. If a nature as highly strung as Catherine's gave way to bad temper, the best thing was to leave her in silence for a while so that she could calm down. When she had removed her fragile head-dress, she unlaced her dress and took it off. Then, when Catherine had nothing on but a fine lawn chemise she started brushing the short locks which had already begun to curl about the young woman's head, so that she bore a curious but charming likeness to a Greek statue. Then, sensing that Catherine was relaxing little by little, she asked gently:

"Can I ask you one thing?"

"Well . . . yes!"

"How do you suppose Messire de Xaintrailles would have behaved in the same situation . . . or Captain la Hire?"

Catherine did not answer and Sara was well satisfied with this silence, which was better than an answer as far as she was concerned. The irascible La Hire would undoubtedly have provoked a duel, King or no King, with anyone rash enough to parade a love for his friend's wife, for he would certainly have regarded it as indecent. As for Xaintrailles, Catherine had no trouble in picturing the flash of rage in his brown eyes, and the threatening smile which would have curled back his lips like a wolf's. And she was too honest not to admit that there was right on their side, but she could not accept being treated as an irresponsible little fool who had no idea how to behave, and who needed to be watched over. She felt an urgent, imperious need to declare her independence. When her hair was done she asked for a dressing-gown of white, rustling taffetas, which was fastened under the bosom by a high silver belt. Then she touched her lips with a little rouge and turned and fixed Sara with a defiant glance.

"Now go and fetch Messire de Breze," she commanded.

Sara was struck dumb for a moment. Then she flushed scarlet and repeated:

"You want me to . . ."

"Fetch him. Yes I do!" Catherine said smiling. "I want to speak to him straight away. And make sure that Cadet Bernard doesn't follow him like a shadow. Don't worry. You will be present at our meeting!"

Sara hesitated for a moment. She was tempted to refuse. But she knew that Catherine was quite capable of going herself.

"Oh well," she said finally, "it's your life and your business!"

Her exit was made with a dignity which drew another smile from Catherine. Her old Sara was well versed in striking attitudes, and knew how to play tragedy with consummate skill! It was her own way of protesting.

A few moments later the gypsy returned with a Pierre de Breze quite pale with delight. No sooner had he crossed the threshold than he flung himself at Catherine's feet and covered her hands with kisses.

"My sweet lady! I was burning to speak to you. You knew this and you sent for me! I am happy . . ."

He was aflame with passion and ready for any folly; and for a moment Catherine allowed herself to enjoy the pleasure of seeing this young lion, whose strength was only matched by his beauty, prostrate at her feet. What woman would not have been flattered at inspiring love in a man like this? But she was equally aware of Sara standing at the far end of the room, half screened by the bed curtains, hands folded across her stomach, waiting, invisible but immovable, determined to prevent anything she disapproved of happening.

It would be unwise to provoke her.

"Rise, sir," she said gently, "and sit down beside me on this seat. I wanted to see you alone . . . first of all to thank you for having gone to Montsalvy when one of the King's riders could easily have undertaken the task. It was a courteous action and I am grateful to you."

Pierre de Breze shook his blond head and smiled.

"You would not have wanted a stranger involved in matters so close to your heart? Besides, I wanted you to hear news of your family—which you must be thirsting for—from my own lips."

Catherine's lips parted in a happy smile.

"Ah, I long to hear about them," she cried. "Tell me about my son . . . how is he?"

"Magnificent! Handsome, sturdy and happy. . . . He speaks very well now, and everybody there obeys him . . . starting with a sort of red-headed giant called Gauthier, who follows him about everywhere! He is the finest child I ever saw. He looks like you!"

But Catherine shook her head.

"Don't feel you must bring out these lies that parents always seem to expect, my friend! Michel is a Montsalvy from head to foot!"

"He has your charm . . . that is the main thing!"

"To be a true knight he would do better to have inherited his father's," Sara growled from her post behind the curtains. "It's a fine compliment to pay a woman to tell her that her son is her living image!"

Pierre glanced thunderstruck towards the bed. Catherine began to laugh, though a little uncertainly it must be confessed. She felt that the storm was gathering. Sara was not the woman to keep her impressions to herself.

"Now Sara, stop scolding. Messire de Breze was only trying to please me. Come here."

The gypsy-woman came forward ungraciously. She evidently had great difficulty in concealing the dislike which the young man inspired in her.

"Well it wouldn't please me! And it won't please me tomorrow when the gossips start talking because Messire de Breze visited your room."

"I know how to silence gossips," the young man cried. "I

will stuff their lying words down their throats, at sword-point if necessary!"

"You can't throw mud without some of it sticking. If you really love Dame Catherine, don't stay here, messire! This is her first night in this château and she is a widow! You should never have agreed to come!"

"But it was you who came to find me! Besides, what man could refuse a moment of happiness when it is offered to him?" he added, gazing admiringly at Catherine. "Every time I see you, you look more beautiful, Catherine. . . . Why do you refuse to allow me to take care of you for always?"

"Because," Sara cried impatiently, seeing that Pierre showed no signs of moving, "because my mistress is old enough now to look after herself. And anyway I am here to watch over her."

"Sara!" Catherine cried, red with anger. "You go too far! Please leave us alone!"

"I refuse to let you ruin your reputation. If this gentleman cares for it as much as he pretends he will understand."

"You forget that he saved our lives!"

"If it is merely to ruin you, I should have no cause to be thankful!"

Pierre de Breze hesitated for a moment as to what course of action to follow. He was torn between the desire to forcibly silence this tiresome woman, whom he merely saw as some impudent servant, and the fear of displeasing Catherine. He decided to capitulate.

"She is right, Catherine. It would be better for me to leave you. Although I don't quite understand what she reproaches me for. I have done nothing worse than love you with my whole heart and soul."

"That's precisely what I reproach you for," Sara said gravely. "But you couldn't understand. Good evening, seigneur. I will escort you back."

Now it was Catherine who took Pierre's hand.

"Forgive her her excessive devotion, Pierre. She watches over me a little too jealously perhaps. But you still haven't said anything about my mother-in-law. How is she?"

De Breze's forehead puckered. He did not speak for a moment, and Catherine noticed his hesitation and became anxious.

"She isn't ill, is she? What is wrong?"

"Nothing, I swear! She did not seem very strong certainly; her health seemed quite sound nevertheless! But such sorrow! It seems that some hidden grief must be eating away her heart! Oh!" he added hurriedly, seeing Catherine's eyes fill

267

with tears. "I should not have said that. Perhaps I was wrong."

"No," Catherine said sorrowfully, "you were not wrong. This grief you speak of is there . . . and I know it too. . . . Good night, Pierre, and thank you. We shall meet tomorrow."

The young man's lips lingered over her hands, but they stayed cold under the caress. It was as though the Dame de Montsalvy had suddenly entered the room, with that grief-stricken face she had never ceased to wear since the day Arnaud had departed. Sara, who was following Catherine's train of thought on her expressive face, led De Breze away. He went quietly but reluctantly, trying vainly to win a glance from those eyes which no longer saw him. Catherine did not even notice his departure. When Sara returned she realized that he was no longer there and looked up at her old friend with the eyes of a sleepwalker.

"He has gone?" And when Sara made a sign of assent, she asked bitterly, "Now are you contented?"

"Yes, I am . . . and especially that it should only have needed a reference to Dame Isabelle to bring you to your senses. I beg of you, Catherine, for your own sake . . . and for all our sakes, not to let that handsome young blade turn your head. Were you thinking of warming yourself at the fire of his love? You will only burn yourself unless you take care. . . ."

But Catherine was tired of arguments. She shrugged and went over to the window where she leaned her elbows on the sill and stared out into the night. Words suddenly seemed empty and meaningless; they jangled in her head like a peal of bells. She felt she needed air, space. As she contemplated the sleeping town, the soft blue countryside below her, and smelled the subtle odor of river vegetation, she felt a sort of anguished hunger, a sense of emptiness and frustration. . . .

Her triumph that evening seemed to have left a bitter aftertaste. It was true that La Trémoille had been brought down and severely punished, and his wife with him. And it was true that the Montsalvys appeared to be in the ascendant. But what was her victory? She was more lonely than ever, and though the King might have restored rank and fortune to her, she would be unlikely to draw much profit from that. In a little while she would be returning to the wilds of Auvergne, so that she might continue to work towards the glory of the Montsalvys! But always alone!

In this brilliant, joyous Court where everyone seemed bent on making the most of the passing moment, they preached restraint, self-denial and stern duty to her. She was young and beautiful . . . and love was forbidden to her . . . and this at a time when she most needed it, at a time when the thirst for vengeance, which had so long upheld her, had at last been appeased.

Whirling around suddenly she confronted Sara angrily and cried:

"And if I should want to live, what of that? If I wanted to love, to stop being a living corpse whom everyone respects and venerates, and feel my body thrilling, my heart beating and my blood racing? What if I should want to come alive?"

Sara's black eyes met Catherine's without a word, but the look of pity which flashed through them only excited Catherine to further anger. She cried:

"Well, what do you say?"

"Nothing," Sara said dully. "No one would stop you, not even me."

"I see. Very well. Good night. Leave me alone. I want to be alone since that is the only thing left to me."

That night, for the first time in a long while, Sara did not sleep in Catherine's room, but in the dressing-room next door.

In the days which followed Pierre de Breze never left Catherine's side. He carried her missal to chapel, sat beside her at table, accompanied her on walks and spent long hours talking to her in the evening, as they sat together on a window-seat while musicians played for the others to dance. Smiles followed them about, and Queen Marie even raised the subject one day as they were sitting embroidering together:

"Pierre de Breze is a delightful young man, don't you agree, my dear?"

"Delightful, Madame. . . . Your Majesty is quite right."

"He is also a man of valor. He will go far, and I am sure that the woman who chooses him for her husband will have made a wise choice."

Catherine blushed and hid her face over her embroidery, but her embarrassment did not last long. There was a sort of conspiracy surrounding her. Everything and everyone seemed to conspire to throw her and Pierre together and contrive that they should be left alone together. Cadet Bernard was perhaps the only person who might have tried to come between the two young people, but by some sort of miracle the Comte de Pardiac had disappeared. He had gone to Montresor to be with Jean de Beuil. As for Sara she behaved towards Catherine with the reserved manner of a well-trained maidservant, and only spoke to her when it was strictly necessary. No more interminable gossips over Catherine's toilette, no more advice or remonstrances! Sara's face had grown curiously blank. It looked almost stony, but sometimes in the mornings Catherine noticed traces of tears upon it, and for a moment she felt ashamed of herself. But it did not last. Pierre reappeared, with his smile, his love-struck eyes, and Catherine forgot everything which might mar this new-found happiness of hers, and eagerly embraced this source of youthful insouciance which Pierre represented. At night, in the silence of her room, she had to admit that it was becoming more and more difficult to hold out against Pierre's ardent courtship, against his words of love, the touch of his lips on her hand, his eyes which kept asking for more. It was all like a grassy, slightly slippery slope, so starred with flowers that one slid down it almost without realizing it. To Catherine's bruised heart this love was as fresh as a healthful dew, and she felt herself unfurl and expand like a flower.

One evening, as the two of them were strolling through the orchard, the softness of the night, the thick shade of the branches above and the passionate words which Pierre was murmuring in her ear combined to drive Catherine to a state of half abandonment. She let her head drop on to the young man's shoulder and let his arm steal round her waist. . . .

Very gently he drew her against him and they stood there for a moment, hardly daring to move, listening to their hearts beating so close to each other. Catherine gave way to the delicious feeling of having found a refuge, of being protected and defended at long last. He loved her, he was hers. . . . With one word she might chain him to her for life. And this word was the very one he kept asking her to say. . . .

She looked upwards between the leafy branches towards the starry sky, and then a long shudder swept over her. The young man's lips sought hers, gently at first and then fiercely. She felt him tremble against her and reached up to draw his broad silk-clothed shoulders closer to her. But the kiss was still a gentle one, and Catherine sensed that Pierre was fighting against a passionate longing to crush her in his arms and drag her down on to the soft grass. . . . She heard him whisper in her ear.

"Catherine, Catherine, when will you be mine? Can't you see that you are driving me mad?"

"Be patient, my friend . . . I need a little time still."

"Why? You will be mine, I feel it, I know it! Just now when I kissed you I felt you shudder, Catherine. We are both

270

young, both passionate . . . why wait, why spoil the fairest hours which life can offer? I shall have to leave soon. Most of my companions have already returned to the war and I am almost the only one to linger here. The English are still entrenched in the best part of Maine and Normandy. Marry me, Catherine."

She shook her head.

"No, Pierre . . . not yet. It is too soon. . . ."

"Well, then at least give yourself to me, and I shall contain myself until you will at last agree to give me your hand. For you will. You will marry me one fine day, Catherine, and I shall pass my days in adoring you. Catherine, don't let me go without giving yourself to me. . . . The picture I have of you, of the first time I saw you, still fires me every time I close my eyes."

Catherine blushed. She also remembered Pierre's tumultuous entry into her room while she was taking a bath. He had already seen her naked, and strangely enough this seemed to draw them together, as if they had known each other for years. . . . She leaned against him. He fastened upon her lips again and she did not protest. He held her to him with one hand while, with the other, he began gently unlacing the silver ribbons of her bodice, widening the still severe neckline of her dress, seeking the softness of her skin. She did not protest, too deeply stirred herself by this pleasant fever which seemed to be rising in her, soaring up from the mysterious depths of her body.

Abruptly he pulled off her fichu, so that her shoulders were bared. Her dress was open now over the roundness of her bosom, and he began to caress her slowly, intent on arousing equal pleasure in this body he had desired for so long. He stooped and knelt and drew her down to the ground and lay down beside her. . . .

All the scents of summer were in league against Catherine's modesty and she abandoned herself amid the soft grass, eyes closed, her body already stirring in response to the lips which moved from her eyes to her breast. He tried to unfasten the wide belt of her dress but his hands were clumsy with impatience and he could not manage it. She laughed softly and sat up to help him. But her laugh died away and turned into a cry of fright. A man's silhouette stood over them holding an unsheathed sword. She recognized the faun's ears and short beard of Bernard d'Armagnac. . . .

She did not have time to warn Pierre. The Gascon's furious voice roared out:

"On your feet, Pierre de Breze, and give me satisfaction!"

"For what?" said the young man, getting to one knee. "Catherine is not your wife, is she, or your sister?"

"For the slur you have cast on Armaud de Montsalvy's honor! Montsalvy is my brother-in-arms and my lifelong friend. In his absence it is my duty to watch over his property."

"A dead man's property," De Breze said contemptuously. "Catherine is free, she will be my wife. Leave us in peace!"

Catherine guessed the temptation that the Gascon must be feeling to come out with the truth once and for all. She was afraid, and begged him:

"Bernard, for pity's sake!"

The Comte's voice betrayed an almost imperceptible hesitation, then he said, almost wearily:

"You don't know what you are saying. Fight unless you want me to brand you as a coward!"

"Bernard!" Catherine cried in horror, "You haven't the right! . . . I forbid you!"

She clung around Pierre's neck, quite forgetful of her semi-nudity, wild at the thought of the blood which would flow. But he set her aside firmly:

"Leave me, Catherine. This is nothing to do with you now! I have been insulted . . ."

"Not yet! And I forbid you to fight! Bernard has no right to provoke you. I am free to give myself to you if I wish."

"I wish," Bernard growled angrily, "that La Hire or Xaintrailles were here to see you, half-naked like a whore, clinging to your man in case someone kills him for you. They would strangle you on the spot! I preferred you tied to the stake at Montsalvy!"

"I'll kill you for that insult, Pardiac!" Pierre shouted furiously, picking his sword up off the grass. "Defend yourself!"

The clash of their weapons struck sparks. Catherine shrank back trembling and sick with shame under a tree, where she mechanically adjusted the disarray in her dress. She hated herself at that moment, bewildered and embarrassed at the thought of what Bernard must have seen. . . .

The fight was furious and fierce. The two men appeared to be of almost equal strength. Pierre de Breze had the advantage of height and no doubt of greater strength, but Bernard made up for this by an astonishing agility. His heavy sword was like an extension of his slender body. The heavy breathing of the two combatants filled the night air. . . .

Catherine leaned back against the tree-trunk trying to calm the frenzied beating of her heart. If Pierre were killed she would never forgive herself, and it would be as bad if it were Cadet Bernard, because then she would have the feeling that she had struck at Arnaud through him. At all events, if one of them were killed, she would be disgraced and sent away from Court. The whole weight of her shame would fall upon her son . . . Michel would pay for his mother's errors with his future. . . .

She wrung her hands, and choked back her tears.

"Lord have pity on me," she beseeched. "Do something to stop this fight!"

But nothing came from the silent castle, which was almost in darkness at this late hour. And yet it seemed as though the clash of their massive swords must fill the night. To Catherine it sounded like the crashing of cathedral bells. How was it possible that such a din had not brought people running, even if it were only the guards?

And then, suddenly, there came a faint cry, echoed instantly by Catherine. Pierre had been wounded in the shoulder and he sank down on the grass. Cadet Bernard fell back and lowered his weapon. Catherine raced towards the wounded man. He had one hand over the gash, and blood trickled down his hand while his handsome face twisted with pain.

"You have killed him," she faltered despairingly. "He is going to die!"

But Pierre raised himself on one elbow and tried to smile. "No, Catherine, he has not killed me . . . Go back to the château quickly, and don't say a word to anyone . . ."

"I won't leave you . . ."

"Yes you must! I shall be all right. He will help me," he added, nodding towards his foe.

"Why should he help you when he has just been trying to kill you?"

The Gascon's teeth gleamed wolfishly in the darkness. He wiped his blade coolly and placed it back in its sheath.

"You really don't understand the first thing about men, my dear. Are you implying that I could finish him off? You must think me a butcher! Your lover has been taught the lesson he deserved. I hope he will take it at that. Now go back to your room, and keep quiet about this. I will look after him."

He bent forward to help the wounded man to his feet. But Pierre stopped him with a gesture.

"In that case, I refuse! I will never renounce her, Sire Bernard. So you will have to kill me."

"Very well, then, I'll kill you later . . . when you are better," said Bernard calmly. "Now return to your room, Dame

273

Catherine," he added dryly, "and leave this to me. I wish you good night."

Over-ruled by this imperious voice, she went off slowly, leaving the high-walled orchard, and passing through the high gateway which led into the castle courtyard without very clearly knowing what she was doing. She was burning with shame and humiliation. Only instinct guided her, but as she reached her room the first thing she saw was Sara standing at the door. Then her shame turned to anger. She flashed a furious look at her.

"Who sent Cadet Bernard to the orchard? Was it you?"

Sara shrugged.

"Are you out of your mind? I did not even know that he had come back. Decidedly, that De Breze has addled your wits! You must be wandering. . . ."

"Many thanks. Yes, they tried to kill him tonight. Cadet Bernard fought him . . . and wounded him! But you are wasting your time, all of you, because you won't separate us! I love him, do you hear? I love him and I shall belong to him whenever I wish it. And the sooner the better!"

"I couldn't agree more," said Sara coldly. "You are behaving just like a bitch in heat. You need a man and you've found yourself one. As for loving him, I don't believe a word of it! You are just deceiving yourself, Catherine, and you know that very well!"

Sara turned on her heel and went into her little room, shutting the door carefully behind her. Catherine was so stunned by the suddenness of her exit she stood staring at the closed door in a sort of trance. A lump rose in her throat. She felt like running to that silent door and breaking it down with her fists and forcing Sara to come out. She felt a childish need to cry, and shelter for a moment in the safe harbor of those familiar arms. This coldness between them hurt her more than she cared to admit. She had defended herself out of pride and now, all of a sudden, this pride of hers seemed dreadfully fragile! There were so many years of affection and shared experiences between them, so much real tenderness! Little by little Sara had taken the place of a mother to her, and Catherine felt now as if a part of herself had been amputated.

She went towards the door and raised her hand to knock. There was not a sound to be heard. . . . But then, on the screen of her memory, Pierre's face appeared as he had looked when he was wounded, and she heard his voice again murmuring words of love. If she let Sara do as she wished she would end by separating her from the young man, and Catherine was not yet ready to lose this fragile happiness

274

which she had never expected to enjoy again. . . . Slowly her hand fell to her side again. Tomorrow she would go to Pierre's bedside and nurse him herself, and if that was interpreted as a proof of their forthcoming union, that was too bad. After all who could stop her from becoming the Dame de Breze? Pierre would beg her to accept, and she was beginning to long for such an outcome herself, if only to have something solid and unchangeable again in her life. Walled around by her stubbornness, she went towards her bed and sank down upon it.

The last glance she flung towards the closed door was one of defiance.

CHAPTER THIRTEEN

With Open Eyes

It was already late in the afternoon by the time Catherine left her room and directed her steps towards the polygonal tower where Pierre de Breze was lodged. She had pretended to suffer from a migraine so as to have an excuse for not joining Queen Marie and the other ladies in the orchard, where they were purposing to spend a few hours listening to a minstrel's songs and enjoying the soft warmth of the sunshine. . . .

To tell the truth she had not been lying when she claimed to have a headache. Since that morning she felt as if an iron band were pressing in upon her temples. She had slept dreadfully badly and had awakened late that morning, feeling unwell. She called for Sara in vain. There was no reply. And when she finally resolved to open the door which had been so firmly closed the night before she found the little dressing-room quite empty of any human presence. There was no one there, but on a coffer lay a scrap of parchment.

At first she hardly dared touch it. Her heart smote her all of a sudden, and she feared to learn what news it contained. But she knew that already. The few words Sara had written there in her clumsy large handwriting, had scarcely surprised her: "I am returning to Montsalvy. . . . You no longer need me. . . ."

The pain that shot through her then had been so pitiless that she leaned back against the wall, with her eyes closed, waiting for it to lessen a little. But the tears squeezed out from under her closed lids, hot, scalding tears. . . . How lonely she felt suddenly, abandoned . . . almost despised! Yesterday she had had to endure the contemptuous green stare of the Comte de Pardiac. And now this morning Sara had run away from her as if the bond between them had suddenly been severed. . . . Catherine realized now that this bond had been rooted in the tenderest part of her heart. This break with Sara seemed to have amputated a part of herself . . . and the part that she had lost might well be her self-respect!

Her first impulse had been to rush out of her room. She

felt like sending men after Sara, to bring her back by force if necessary. She must have left very early in the morning, as soon as the gates were opened, but she could not have got very far as yet. . . . But then Catherine thought again. How could she send the King's men after the excellent woman, as if she were some common miscreant? She could not do such a thing to her. Sara's native pride would never recover from such a blow, and there would be no chance of reconciliation between them again. The one solution was to go after her herself. She decided that that was what she would do. Why did it have to happen that, just as she finished dressing, a messenger knocked at her door and placed a note in her hands? And this time the message was from Pierre.

"If you love me a little, my beloved, come. Come to see me this afternoon. I will send everyone away, but come. My passion for you burns more fiercely than my wound. I am waiting. Don't refuse."

The words burned her eyes as the young man's breath, the evening before, had set her lips afire. A sudden, violent desire to run to him, to weep in his arms, overpowered her. She fought it back. But the note had had its effect. Catherine no longer felt like racing after Sara, and she found a hundred excuses for this change of heart. . . . After all, she told herself, her old friend was not going away to the ends of the earth. She was simply going to Montsalvy. This whole incident would sort itself out sooner or later. Besides, to chase after Sara like that would be to confer so much importance upon her, that Catherine herself could not but feel diminished thereby. The same feeling which had stopped her knocking on Sara's door the night before now prevented her from ordering her horse to be saddled.

In fact, Catherine took good care not to examine her conscience too closely. In her heart she felt little pride in her behavior, but the more her real nature protested, the more firmly she persisted in her revolt. Pierre's smile had placed a veil over her eyes. He stood for something she had believed forever beyond her grasp—love, pleasure, the sweetness of being adored, and living in a world without pain—everything, in short, which belonged to youth in its prime. She was like the lark fascinated by a sparkling mirror. Her eyes could not, would not see anything else. . . .

At the door of the tower where De Breze was lodged, the same page who had visited her that morning stood waiting to escort her to his master's rooms. He bowed, and then silently carried out his mission. The door opened and Catherine found herself standing, a little dazzled, in a chamber still glowing with the sunset, where Pierre lay stretched out upon a bed.

"At last!" he cried, holding both hands out to her while the page discreetly vanished, and Catherine went across to the bed. "I have been waiting for hours!"

"I was worried about coming here," she murmured, agitated at finding him in bed. He had never looked so handsome or attractive as he did now. His powerful naked torso stood out against pillows and coverlets of red silk. There was a bandage over his left shoulder, but he did not seem to be in much pain. His face was a little pale, perhaps, but his eyes shone. And if the fever was partly responsible for the unusual warmth of the hands holding hers, it was not the only cause.

"You were worried?" he asked gently, trying to draw her to him. "But why?"

She drew away a little, suddenly aware of the impropriety of her presence in this man's room.

"Because I should not be here. Think what people would say if they knew! Especially after last night . . . ."

"Nothing happened last night. I put my shoulder out falling down stairs. I have a slight fever, so I stayed in bed. What could be more normal? You came, charitable as an angel, to see how I was. What could be more natural?"

"And . . . Cadet Bernard?"

"He is out hunting with the King who, as you doubtless know, has been chasing wild boar since this morning. Anyway, do you really think that I would let myself be intimidated by him? Come and sit down. You are too far away. . . . And now take off that veil which hides your delicious face."

She obeyed with a smile, touched by this spoiled-child behavior which was in such contrast to his proudly displayed male vigor.

"There," she said. "But I can't stay more than a moment. The King will soon be back, and Cadet Bernard with him. . . ."

"I don't want to hear that name again," cried the young man, flushed with anger. "Must I repeat—you are free and there is nothing which need stand between us! He treated you abominably. He will have to answer for it to me one of these days. . . . But, sweetheart," he added tenderly, seeing Catherine's face darken, "allow me to watch over you."

"But . . . I'm not stopping you," Catherine said with a sigh. "Watch over me then, my friend . . . I need it so much!"

"And I ask nothing better! You still have no idea how

278

much I love you, Catherine, or you would already have said yes. . . ."

As he spoke he pulled her gently towards him, and very gently touched her eyelids with his lips. His voice grew soothing, almost purringly soft.

"Why wait? Since your return to favor everyone here is waiting for us to announce our engagement. The King himself . . ."

"The King is kind . . . but I don't know, so soon . . ."

"So soon? Lots of women marry as little as a month after their husband's death. You can't remain like this, alone against the world, your beauty wasted. You need a sword, a defender, and a father for your child."

His lips moved down in a series of quick little kisses, till they reached hers and fastened upon them eagerly. She closed her eyes, overcome with the sweet agitation this roused in her, and all her sadness fled.

"Say that you will, my love," he asked tenderly. "Let me make you mine in the eyes of everyone! Say yes, Catherine, my sweet . . ."

This soft word suddenly dispelled the delicious mist into which Catherine seemed to be sliding. My sweet! Arnaud used to call her that . . . and with such passion! She seemed to hear her husband's voice murmuring those words in her ear. "Catherine, my sweet!" No one ever said it like he did. . . . Misty-eyed, she suddenly stammered out:

"No, it's impossible!"

She drew back and pulled herself free of those arms of his which had been holding her so close only a moment before. He cried out a little irritably:

"But why impossible? Why not? No one would be surprised, I've already told you. Not even your own family. Why, the Dame de Montsalvy herself is expecting you to marry me. She understands that you cannot remain single. . . ."

Catherine sprang up. She was white to the lips and she stared at Pierre with incredulous, horrified eyes.

"What did you say? I can't have heard you right."

He began to laugh and held out his hands again.

"What a state you are in! My heart, you are making a mountain out of a mole-hill. . . ."

"Repeat what you said just now," Catherine said harshly. "What has my mother-in-law to do with all this?"

Pierre did not answer at first. The smile vanished from his lips and he frowned slightly.

"I didn't say anything so extraordinary. But what a strange way to speak to me, my love!"

"Never mind the way I speak, but for God's sake answer me! What has the Dame de Montsalvy to do with all this?"

"Nothing much to be sure! I simply said that she expected you to become my wife. During my stay there I confided to her the great love I felt for you, and I told her of my ardent desire to wed you and the hopes I had that you would accept my suit. It was only natural . . . I was so afraid that she might try and force you to live in the past and stay in that old Auvergne of hers. . . . But she perfectly understood. . . ."

"She understood?" Catherine echoed, in anguish. "But what could you have been thinking of to say that to her? Who gave you permission to do such a thing?"

The young woman's agonized face impressed Pierre. He sensed instinctively that he must defend himself against an unexpected danger. He wrapped himself in his coverlets and sprang to the foot of the bed, where Catherine had collapsed on a bench, her eyes heavy with unshed tears and her fingers icy and trembling.

She kept repeating: "Why . . . oh why did you do such a thing? You had no right!"

He knelt beside her and took her icy hands in his.

"Catherine," he whispered, "I cannot understand your despair. I admit I may have been a little hasty, but I had to make sure that there would be no obstacles in the way of our marriage should you ever accept me. And then a little sooner or later, what difference does it make?"

He was genuinely distressed, she could see, and for the moment she was not brave enough to be angry with him. She was brutally awakened from the dream she had been living in for so many weeks now, and the only person she could feel angry with was herself. . . . But she looked at him with sorrowful eyes.

"And what did my mother-in-law reply to all this?"

"That she hoped we would be very happy, that I could give you the rank and style of life to which you were accustomed. . . ."

"She said that?" Catherine cried, in a voice half-choked by emotion.

"Yes indeed. . . . So you see that there is no reason to get into such a state!"

Catherine pushed away the hands which sought to hold her and stood up. She laughed dryly.

"No reason? Now listen, Pierre; you were wrong to tell her

280

that, because I shall never marry you! You have wounded that noble lady for no reason."

He got up with a bound. Now it was he who lost his temper. He seized her by the shoulders.

"Stop behaving like a sleepwalker and look at me! What you are saying is ridiculous. I have not hurt her and you have no right to punish us both like this. It is pride, Catherine! The truth is that you are afraid people will think less of you! But you are wrong, you are free, I keep telling you. Your husband is dead . . ."

"No!" Catherine cried fiercely.

Now it was Pierre's turn to reel back in amazement. His hands fell to his sides, while he stared at the young woman before him.

"Not dead? What do you mean?"

"Exactly what I say. My husband may be dead to the world but he is not dead in the eyes of God."

"I don't understand. . . . Explain what you mean."

And so once again, she recounted the pathetic tale and confessed the hideous truth, but this time as she spoke she had a feeling almost of deliverance. She seemed to be stripping off the intoxication of the past few weeks, the romantic and sensual attraction which had thrown her briefly into the arms of this boy. As she reaffirmed Arnaud's living reality she became conscious once more of her love for him. She had believed she could turn away from him and forget him, but there he was standing before her, unbelievably present, interposing himself between her and the man she had thought to love. When she had told him everything she looked straight at Pierre with her violet eyes.

"So there you are! Now you know everything . . . you know that you did wrong in speaking to that poor mother of marriage . . . but it was a mistake for which I am entirely to blame. I should never have given you the least grounds for hope!"

He turned aside and mechanically tightened the red coverlet round his hips. All of a sudden he seemed ten years older.

"I realize too late, Catherine . . . and I am sorry. It is a dreadful story. But I would like to say that it makes no difference to my decision to marry you sooner or later. My sweet . . . I will wait for you as long as is necessary!"

"My sweet!" she murmured. "He used to call me that . . . and he said it so beautifully!"

He stiffened at this comparison which he sensed as unflattering to himself.

"But I say it with all my heart . . . Catherine," he said in

281

an offended voice. "Wake up now! I know you have suffered abominably, but you are still young, still full of life. You loved your husband as much as anyone ever loved anybody. But there is nothing more you can do for him . . . and now it is me you love!"

And then, once again, and with equal determination, Catherine cried:

"No!" As he fell back a little, with haggard face but a flash of anger lighting his eyes, she repeated: "No, Pierre, I did not really love you. . . . I thought I did for a moment, I admit, and even an hour ago, I still thought so. But, without meaning to, you have opened my eyes. I thought I would be able to love you but I was mistaken . . . I shall never love any man but him!"

"Catherine," he groaned, pitifully.

"You cannot understand, Pierre. I have never loved another, never really lived except through him, for him. I am flesh of his flesh and come what may, no matter what ravages the cursed disease may make in him, he will always remain the unique, irreplaceable . . . the only man for me in the world! My old Sara, who left me this morning because of you, was not deceived. I belong to Arnaud, and to no one else. And as long as I live it will be the same."

There was a silence. Pierre left her and went over to the window. The sun had just set and the golden light was tinged with mauve. Beyond the river, a trumpet sounded, and then another, followed by the howling of a pack of hounds.

"The King," Pierre said mechanically. "He is back. . . ."

There was a cracked note in his voice which made Catherine jump. She turned towards him. He was not looking at her. He stood, motionless, before the window. His head was down and he seemed to be thinking, but suddenly Catherine saw his shoulders shake and she realized he was weeping.

She felt a great pity for him rise up in her. She went slowly across and raised a hand to place it upon his shoulder, but then did not dare.

"Pierre," she murmured, "I wish I could spare you this pain."

"There is nothing you can do," he said harshly. There was a new silence between them, and at last he said, still without turning round:

"What will you do?"

"Go away again," she said promptly. "Go back there, and tell them all that nothing has changed and that I am still *his* wife. . . ."

"And then?" he asked bitterly. "Will you shut yourself up in those mountains till death releases you?"

"No . . . then I will take Arnaud away from that leper-house where I was forced to allow him to go. And I will take him to a quiet, retired spot and stay there with him . . . till . . ."

De Breze gave a start of horror. He whirled round and confronted her with his grief-ravaged face:

"You cannot do that to me! . . . You have a child, you have no right to commit suicide, especially not in that atrocious manner!"

"But it is life without him which is suicide to me. I have finished my task here. The Montsalvys are what they always were. La Trémoille is disposed of. . . . Now I can think of myself . . . and of him!"

Quite silently she went to the door and opened it. The page was waiting outside. She turned back on the threshold. Pierre, still standing by the window, held out his arms as if to embrace her.

"Catherine," he begged, "come back to me!"

But she shook her head and smiled with a sort of tenderness at him.

"No, Pierre. . . . Forget me. It's better that way. . . ."

But then, as if she still feared that she might weaken, and dared not listen to that voice which had stirred her so deeply, she turned on her heels and raced down the stairs. As she ran out into the courtyard the huntsmen were just riding through the gateway, blowing their horns loud enough to burst their lungs. She saw the King in their midst, and the thin figure of Bernard d'Armagnac beside him, laughing. In a second the whole vast enclosure was teeming with warm, colorful life. Some ladies came running up, others leaned out of their windows, exchanging bantering talk with the huntsmen.

There were calls and shouts of laughter. But this time Catherine had no desire to mingle with them. Arnaud had reclaimed her. She felt that a gulf was fixed between these people and herself, a gulf too deep to be crossed. There was only one hand which might have succeeded in restoring her to this world from which she felt herself so separate. And that hand had no longer either the right or the opportunity to do so. Anyway, what did it matter really? She had to return to where her destiny lay, and she was eager now to go back to her family.

The following day Catherine took her leave of the King after having obtained—though not without some difficulty—

permission to depart from Queen Marie, who was perplexed by her haste to leave Court.

"But you have barely arrived, my dear!" she said. "Are you already bored with us?"

"No, Madame, but I am longing to see my son and I am needed at Montsalvy."

"Go, then! But return as soon as you are able, with your child. You are still one of my maids-of-honor and the Dauphin will soon have need of pages."

Charles VII spoke to her in almost the same terms, but he added:

"There are so few really pretty women, and now you are wanting to leave us! What is there so attractive about this Auvergne of yours?"

"It is a fine country, Sire, and you would like it. As for what it is that draws me thither, Your Majesty will pardon me if I say that first there is my son, and secondly, some ruins . . ."

A frown appeared on the King's brow for a moment, only to be replaced almost at once by a smile.

"So you feel the urge to build then? Splendid, Dame Catherine! It pleases me that a woman should unite energy and decision to so much beauty. But . . . where is my friend Pierre de Breze in all this? Were you thinking of taking him with you? I warn you, I have great need of him. . . ."

Catherine stiffened, but then she lowered her eyes to hide her agitation. She was still not quite cured of the dream she had entertained for a while, and the mention of Pierre's name hurt a little.

"I am not taking him, Sire. The Seigneur de Breze has been a loyal friend and true knight to me. But he has his life as I have mine. The war summons him once more, and I must return to rebuild my home."

Charles VII was not lacking in subtlety. The slight quaver in her voice told him that something must have happened, and he did not try to press her further.

"Time solves many things, fair lady. . . . I thought for a moment that we would soon have a betrothal in our midst, but it seems I was mistaken. And now, Dame Catherine, if your King may be allowed to give you a word of advice . . . don't be too hasty! Don't make decisions you might regret. As I have said, time changes men and women. It would be a pity if you were one day to suffer as a result of all this. That would be wrong!"

Touched by this avowal of royal concern on her behalf

Catherine knelt to kiss the hand Charles held out to her. She smiled bravely at him.

"I shall have no regrets. But I am deeply grateful to Your Majesty for your kindness. I shall not forget it."

He smiled back at her, with that touch of shyness which he always showed in the presence of a beautiful woman.

"It is possible that I may pay a visit to Auvergne myself in the not too distant future," he said thoughtfully. "Now you may go, Comtesse de Montsalvy! Return to that duty which you know so well how to shoulder. And know that your King will miss you, that he hopes to see you again soon . . . and that you have his respect!"

And he went, leaving Catherine kneeling in the midst of the Great Hall, where only the motionless guards remained. She heard his footsteps dying away and then she quietly stood up. She felt less sad now, and a sort of pride took hold of her. Charles had spoken to her not as to a woman, but as he might have spoken to one of his captains. As he would have spoken to Arnaud himself no doubt!

All that remained now was to bid farewell to Queen Yolande. She went to her at once, expecting to have to make the same excuses to her all over again. But there was no need. The Queen of the Four Kingdoms simply kissed her:

"You are doing the right thing," she said. "And I expected no less of you. Young De Breze would never do for you . . . simply because he is so young!"

"If you thought that, Madame my Queen, why didn't you say so?"

"Because it was your life which was concerned, my beauty! And no one has the right to interfere with other people's destinies. Not even . . . what am I saying, especially not an old Queen! Return to your own Auvergne. There is work to do because now we have to stitch this poor tattered kingdom together again. We shall need people like the Montsalvys in the provinces. Your family, my dear, are like the mountains where they live: one may use them but one never destroys them. All the same . . . I don't want to lose you entirely!"

With a gesture Yolande summoned Anne de Beuil to her from the corner where she had been sitting embroidering.

"Give me my ivory casket!" the Queen commanded.

When the young woman had brought it to her she placed her long slender fingers inside and withdrew a magnificent emerald ring engraved with her own coat-of-arms, which she slipped on Catherine's finger.

"The Emir Saladin gave this stone to one of my ancestors, who saved him from death without realizing who he was. I had it engraved. Keep it, Catherine, as a memento, to remind you of my friendship and gratitude. Thanks to you, the King and I will rule this land at long last!"

Catherine touched the superb jewel with trembling fingers. Then she knelt once again to kiss her sovereign's hand.

"Madame . . . what can I say? Such a gift! . . ."

"Say nothing! You are like me when you are deeply moved—words do not come easily, and it is better like that. This ring may bring you luck, and it may help you. Everyone who serves me, whether in France, Spain, Sicily, or Cyprus, will help you when they see this jewel. It is rather as a safeguard that I give it to you, because I have a presentiment that you may need one. And I am determined to see you again some day . . . alive and well!"

The audience was ended. Once more Catherine bowed.

"Adieu, Madame . . ."

"No, Catherine," said the Queen, smiling. "Not adieu but farewell! And may God go with you!"

If Catherine supposed that she had done with farewells she was wrong. As she came out into the great courtyard on the way to the Chancelry, where she was to receive her papers of reinstatement, she ran into Bernard d'Armagnac, who was pacing up and down as if waiting for someone. She tried to pass by as though she had not seen him, but he hurried towards her.

"I was waiting for you," he said. "No one here talks of anything but the fact that you are leaving, and when I heard that you were with Queen Yolande I thought you would not take long. You are not the sort of woman to linger over farewells, and nor is she."

"You are quite right. Adieu, sir Count," Catherine said coldly.

A contrite smile wrinkled the Gascon noble's intelligent face.

"Hum! You are still very angry with me, it seems. You are quite right. But I came here to ask your forgiveness, Catherine. The other night I was blinded by anger. I might easily have killed the two of you."

"But you did not. I assure you that I am most grateful."

If she thought that her dignity would bemuse Cadet Bernard she was mistaken, for the Gascon burst out laughing.

"In God's name, Catherine, drop this hoity-toity manner! It doesn't suit you, believe me!"

"Whether it suits me or not it is the only one I find I can use towards you. Surely you did not expect me to fling my arms round your neck?"

"Well, perhaps you should! After all I helped you out of what might have been an embarrassing scrape. If you had succumbed to the advances of that young popinjay, you would regret it now with all your heart."

"What do you know about it?"

"Oh, come now! De Breze was hardly injured by my sword thrust. If you had been really in love with him you would have gone to his room that same night. But you did not!"

"I went the next day. . . ."

"And you came out again with red eyes, and the air of a person who has reached a grave decision. You see how well informed I am!"

"Something tells me that your spies are keeping something back! They haven't told you everything!" Catherine said witheringly. But Cadet Bernard had grown suddenly grave.

"Yes, Catherine, they did. You broke off your relations with De Breze and decided to return to your husband. Otherwise why would you be leaving? Why should De Breze have set off an hour ago at the head of his lancers? He is going to help Lore, whose fortress at St. Ceneri is being attacked by the English."

"Oh!" Catherine exclaimed in a small voice. "So he has gone?"

"Yes, he has gone. Because you rejected him! I was not mistaken in you, Catherine, you are the same woman that the great Montsalvy chose for his wife. I was wrong the other night. And now shall we make peace? I long to be your friend again. . . ."

His apologies were sincere. And Catherine could never harbor a grudge against someone who honestly admitted that they were in the wrong. She smiled and held out her hands.

"I was wrong too. Let's forget all that, Bernard . . . and come to Montsalvy when you return from Lectoure! You will always be welcome there. And later on I shall entrust Michel to you, when he is old enough to become a page. I am sure you will know how to bring him up as Arnaud would have done. And now, bid me farewell!"

"Rely on me! Farewell, lovely Catherine!"

Before she realized what was happening he seized her by both shoulders and planted a smacking kiss on each of her cheeks, then he let her go.

"I shall tell Xaintrailles and La Hire what a good companion you are! I was going to provide you with an escort to accompany you home, but it seems the King has already provided for that."

"Many thanks to him," said Catherine laughing. "And I

must say I prefer something a little quieter than your Gascon devils. It takes a leader to keep those men under control, and I'm no Arnaud de Montsalvy myself!"

Cadet Bernard, who was about to depart, turned for a moment and looked at Catherine. Then he said, very seriously:

"On the contrary . . . I think you are!"

Dawn struck fire from the roof-tops of Chinon, and the calm waters of the Vienne glowed ruddily as Catherine passed under the portcullis of the clock-tower gate the next morning. All the bells of the town were sounding the Angelus, and the carillon soared through the pure air towards the little group of riders who were just leaving the château. The escort the King had provided for Catherine consisted entirely of Bretons, as the soldiers' tabards decorated with ermine tails testified. Tristan l'Hermite commanded them. When he had come the previous evening to tell her that he was to accompany her to Montsalvy before rejoining the Constable of Richemont at Parthenay, she had been delighted. The King could not have chosen a better man to protect her than this taciturn Fleming, whose worth she had come to know. His great qualities were sang-froid, astuteness, quiet courage and a sense of leadership. She told him as much:

"You will go far, friend Tristan. You have all the qualities of a great statesman."

He started to laugh.

"I've already been told that . . . only yesterday! Would you believe it, Dame Catherine, our ten-year-old Dauphin is taking a great interest in my career? He has promised to make my fortune for me when he becomes King. Apparently he was impressed by our exploits against La Trémoille. Not that I am likely to take that sort of promise too seriously. Princes, particularly young ones, have short memories!"

But Catherine shook her head. She remembered the sharp almost unbearably penetrating gaze of the young Louis. A gaze which looked as if it never forgot.

"I think myself that he will remember!" was all she said.

Tristan had merely shaken his head dubiously. Now he rode quietly beside her, slightly slumped in his saddle in the manner of a man accustomed to long, monotonous rides. He was even known to fall asleep on horseback. He rode with his hood pulled well down over his face to keep off the glare of the rising sun, swaying a little in the saddle.

Catherine had resumed the boy's costume she wore on leaving Angers. She liked dressing in men's clothes because they gave her much more freedom of movement, as well as a sort of dash and courage. She stood up in her stirrups and surveyed the town as if seeing it for the very first time. It was there that she had won the victory she had promised herself, not to mention another, more unexpected one over herself. At the moment of leaving Chinon suddenly seemed very dear to her.

The townsfolk's day was just beginning. Shutters were banging open on all sides, shops were opening and the shop-fronts were being got ready for the day's trade. The heavy rain of the previous day had washed all the little cobblestones clean. As they approached the Grand Carroi, Catherine caught sight of a young girl of about fifteen sitting by the wayside arranging bunches of roses. They looked so fresh, those roses . . . and they reminded Catherine of that other bouquet someone had thrown to her one evening through the windows of Maître Agnelet's inn. She stopped her horse.

"Those are lovely roses," she said. "Sell me a bunch."

The child held out the fairest of her scented bunches.

"It costs one sol, kind sir," she said, smiling and curtsying. And then she went quite rosy with gratitude as Catherine handed her a gold piece. "Oh, thank you, kind sir!" she cried happily.

Catherine set off again towards the fortified bridge which crossed the Vienne. She buried her face in the flowers and inhaled their delicious fragrance. Tristan began to laugh:

"I dare say those are the last roses we shall see for a long time. They don't grow at all in your poor Auvergne. But here they are in their rightful element. The Touraine is rose country!"

"That's why I bought these . . . they are a symbol for me of this gentle Loire countryside, and they remind me too of certain memories . . . memories which will have flown away by the time these flowers have faded."

The armed troop crossed the bridge, saluted by the soldiers of the guard, who recognized the Constable's arms. Once across the river, they spurred their horses to a gallop. Catherine and her escort vanished into a cloud of dust.

Part III

THE WAY OF SAINT JAMES

◆◆◆◆◆◆◆◆◆◆◆◆◆◆◆◆◆◆◆

CHAPTER FOURTEEN

The People at Montsalvy

It was after ten o'clock and quite dark by the time Catherine, Tristan l'Hermite and their escort came in sight of Montsalvy, after a gruelling journey. The fine summer weather had dried the mud on the roads but had turned it into dust. Fortunately it had also allowed them to sleep out of doors at night and make long rides without stopping. They had taken sufficient provisions with them and had stopped only occasionally at wayside inns. Most of the latter, moreover, had little to offer.

As the journey progressed Catherine's impatience to be home increased as her mood darkened. She spoke less and less and, driven by an almost feverish haste, would ride silently for hours on end, her eyes fixed on the road before her. When the towers and ramparts of Montsalvy rose above the plateau, like a dark crown against the night sky, she reined in her horse a moment and sat gazing at it with a sudden tightness about her heart. Though it was her home, she had never lived there long enough for the sight to become a familiar one. Tristan rode up beside her anxiously.

"What is it, Dame Catherine?"

"I don't know, friend Tristan . . . but all of sudden I feel afraid."

"Afraid of what?"

"I don't know . . ." she said faintly. "It's a sort of presentiment."

Never before had she been visited by anything quite like this suffocating fear of what awaited her behind those silent walls. She tried to reason it out with herself. Michel was there, Sara and Gauthier too, doubtless. But even the thought of her little son was not enough to chase that lump from her throat. She turned to Tristan with the gaze of a drowning man.

"Let's go," she said at last. "The men are weary!"

"And so are you," the Fleming scolded. "Onwards, the rest of you."

The city gates were closed at this late hour, but Tristan raised the horn hanging at his waist to his lips and blew three long blasts upon it. A moment later a man holding a lantern leaned over the battlements.

"Who goes there?"

"Open up!" cried Tristan. "It is the noble Lady Catherine de Montsalvy returning from the King's Court. Open up in the King's name."

The watchman gave an unintelligible cry. The light vanished, but a moment later the massive gates to the little fortress town swung open slowly, creaking loudly. The man reappeared with his cap in hand, and stepped forward almost under the horses' noses, holding his lantern up in one hand.

"It really is our lady!" he cried joyfully. "May God be praised for sending her back at such a timely moment! They have gone to fetch the bailiff to receive her properly."

Even then a figure came hobbling down the narrow little street as fast as he could go. Catherine's heart lightened as she recognized old Saturnin. He came forward as fast as his old legs would carry him, crying:

"Dame Catherine! Dame Catherine has returned among us! Heaven be praised! Welcome to our mistress!"

He was quite out of breath. Touched, and a little amused, Catherine was about to dismount to greet him, but he literally flung himself against the horse.

"Stay on your horse, milady! Old Saturnin wants to lead you to the abbey as he once led you to his own cottage."

"I am so pleased to see you again, Saturnin . . . and Montsalvy as well!"

"No happier than Montsalvy is to see you, gracious lady! Look!"

Instantly, as by a miracle, all the windows and doors flew open, and cheering heads popped out, together with arms brandishing torches. In a moment the little street was awash with light, while a chorus of happy voices chanted:

"Hail, hail to our good lady who returns to us again!"

"I envy you," Tristan murmured. "A welcome like this must be a comforting thing."

"It's true! I never expected it, friend Tristan, but it makes me happy . . . so happy!"

There were tears in her eyes. Saturnin, stiff with pride, had taken her horse's leading-rein and led it slowly along the street. She rode between two rows of faces, whose cheerful ruddiness could be seen in the torch-light glare. On all sides there were sparkling eyes and mouths shouting their welcome.

"What can you fear now?" Tristan whispered. "Everyone adores you here!"

"Perhaps. But I'm not sure what I was afraid of yet. And this is wonderful . . . it's . . ."

The words froze on her lips. They had come in sight of the abbey gates, which had been opened wide to receive her. The gigantic form of Gauthier stood waiting on the threshold. Catherine expected him to race forward to greet her, as Saturnin had done. But he did not move. Moreover, he folded his arms, as if to bar the way to her. His face was dour as granite. There was not a trace of a smile upon it. And when she met the icy glare of his gray eyes Catherine could not help shivering.

With Saturnin's help she dismounted and went towards the Norman. He watched her come towards him without moving a muscle. She tried to smile.

"Gauthier," she cried. "How happy I am to see you!"

But there were no words of welcome to be heard from that tight-lipped mouth. Only a curt:

"Are you alone?"

"What do you mean?" she asked, dumbfounded.

"I asked if you were alone," the Norman repeated stonily. "Is that handsome blond gallant you are to marry now with you? I dare say he stayed a little way behind so that you could make an entry on your own!"

Catherine flushed, as much with humiliation as with rage. Gauthier's insolence staggered her. Did he dare to attack her like this in front of everyone, and put her through her paces? If she did not want to lose face hopelessly before all these peasants she must fight back. Setting her little chin haughtily, she stepped up boldly towards the gates.

"Give way," she said curtly. "What right have you to cross-question me?"

Gauthier did not stir. He remained in the doorway, his giant bulk effectively blocking her path. Tristan frowned and his hand went to his sword. But Catherine stayed him with a gesture.

"It is all right, friend Tristan. This is my affair. Come

now," she commanded coldly, "let me pass. Is this any way to receive the mistress of a place on her return home?"

"This is not your home, but the abbot's! As for being mistress here, Dame Catherine, are you still worthy of the title?"

"What outrageous rudeness!" Catherine cried, beside herself with rage. "Am I supposed to account to *you* for my actions? I have come to see my mother-in-law!"

Reluctantly, as it seemed, Gauthier stepped aside. Catherine stepped by, head held high, and entered the courtyard of the abbey. Then he called after her, coldly:

"I should hurry up then. She will not live much longer!"

Catherine stopped dead as if she had been struck by a whip. For a moment she stood rigid with shock, then she slowly turned and stared at the Norman with horrified eyes.

"What," she stammered, "what did you say?"

"That she is dying! But I don't suppose that worries you too much! Another tiresome bond gone!"

"I don't know who you may be, friend," Tristan shouted angrily, "but you are strangely uncouth! Why treat your mistress so brutally?"

"Who are you?" Gauthier asked disdainfully.

"Tristan l'Hermite, Squire to Monseigneur the Constable, commanded by the King to escort the Comtesse de Montsalvy to her home and watch over her to see that no harm befall her. Are you satisfied?"

Gauthier nodded affirmatively. Then he snatched a torch from its iron holder beside the gateway and silently led the way across the courtyard to the abbey guest-house. After the hubbub in the village, the silence in here was striking. The monks were already in their cells for the night, and the abbot was not to be seen. Only a few candles remained burning behind the guest-house windows. There was no one waiting to receive them on the threshold, and Catherine suddenly stopped Gauthier by taking his arm:

"What about Sara? Isn't she here?"

He looked at her in astonishment.

"Why should she be here? She never left your side. . . ."

"Nonetheless she left," Catherine said somberly. "She told me she was returning to Montsalvy. That is all I know; except that I saw no sign of her along the way."

Gauthier did not reply at once. His gray eyes met Catherine's searchingly. Then he shrugged his broad shoulders, and muttered with bitter sarcasm:

"She too! Dame Catherine, how could you have done all this harm to us?"

She almost shouted in her exasperation:

"Harm, what harm? What have I done to earn all these reproaches? What do you accuse me of?"

"Of sending that man here!" Gauthier said harshly. "You might have become his mistress, it seems to me, without sending him here to strut around and vaunt his great love for you. What do you think is killing the Dame de Montsalvy . . . the *real* one? Your lover's confidences!"

"He is not my lover!" Catherine protested angrily.

"Your future husband then, it's all the same!"

Catherine snatched up the Norman's huge fist in both hands. She felt an urgent need to justify herself. She could not endure this weight of accusation much longer.

"Listen to me, Gauthier. Will you believe me when I say that not only will he never be my husband, but that, in all likelihood, I shall never set eyes on him again?"

The giant did not answer at once. He seemed to be looking for an answer in Catherine's eyes. Gradually something softened in his face. All of a sudden he imprisoned her hands in his.

"Yes," he said, with a new warmth, "I believe you! And I'm glad to! And now come quickly and tell her that it isn't true and that you never dreamed of replacing Messire Arnaud! She has suffered so much!"

Tristan l'Hermite watched all this round-eyed. Clearly he was quite mystified by this scene. That a great lady like Catherine should stoop to explain herself to this rustic oaf was more than he could comprehend! Catherine noticed his bewilderment. She turned and smiled faintly at him, and then said briefly:

"You could not possibly understand, friend Tristan. I shall explain everything to you later."

He bowed silently and then, guessing no doubt that his presence would be *de trop* in the events which were about to follow, he asked if someone would be so good as to show him where he and his men might spend the night. Gauthier pointed to a fat sleepy monk who was yawning gigantically a few steps behind.

"That is Brother Eusebius, the porter, who will take charge of you. The animals will go to the stable, the men will find hay in the barn, and you will be given a cell."

Once again Tristan bowed to Catherine and then turned and followed the porter, with his men behind him. The young woman stepped, not without qualms, across the threshold of this guest-house which she had left so many months before with Arnaud and Cadet Bernard. They had been on their way to Carlat, where she had hoped to find happiness. But then she pushed aside these depressing images. She needed all her courage to go through with what awaited her here.

She looked at Gauthier as they stood in the little low-ceilinged hall.

"My son?"

"Asleep at this hour."

"Let me see him! It's been so long. . . ."

Gauthier smiled briefly and took Catherine by the hand.

"Come. It will cheer you up."

He took her into a dark little room with a door opening into another, rather dimly lit chamber, where Catherine noticed Donatienne, Saturnin's wife, fast asleep on a settle. The candlelight showed up the marks of fatigue on the old woman's face. Gauthier pointed to her and said:

"She has been watching over our mistress for three nights now. Usually she sleeps with the little lord. But she must have dropped off. . . ."

As he spoke he took a candle from the coffer and quietly carried it outside and lit it from the torch which burned outside the door. Then he came and stood by the head of little Michel's bed, holding the flame aloft so that Catherine could see his face. Catherine fell to her knees, ecstatically, joining her hands as though she were praying before the tabernacle.

"Heavens!" she faltered. "How handsome he is! And . . . how like he is to his father already," she added, in a strangled voice.

It was true. Below the thick forest of untidy golden curls little Michel already had his father's clear-cut profile. His cheeks were still round and rosy and shadowed by long sweeping lashes, but there was a proud tilt to the little nose, and a stubborn set to his mouth.

Catherine's heart overflowed with tenderness, but she did not dare lean over the child. He looked like a sleeping cherub and she feared that the slightest movement might awaken him.

Gauthier, who had been looking down on the child with a sort of pride, noticed her hesitation.

"You can kiss him if you like," he said. "Once he is asleep the skies could fall in and he would not waken."

Then she bent over adoringly and placed her lips on the little damp brow. Michel did not wake but his closed lips softened in a half smile.

"My little one," Catherine whispered, almost choked by love, "my little baby!"

She could easily have stayed there all night long, kneeling beside her son, but then a rasping, choking sound came from

295

the next room. Donatienne woke with a start and disappeared through the doorway.

"Dame Isabelle must have awoken," Gauthier whispered.

"I'll go in there now," Catherine said.

Now the pitiful sound of labored breathing reached her, interspersed with dry coughs and faint groans. She ran into the room, hardly larger than a monk's cell, and scarcely more elaborately furnished. Isabelle de Montsalvy lay stretched out upon the narrow bed standing in one corner. She was dreadfully thin. Donatienne bent over her, trying to persuade her to drink a little herbal potion from a bowl which she had taken off a small oil flame. But the old lady was choking, unable to drink even a drop.

Catherine bent over the sick woman and gazed with a stricken heart at the convulsed, tortured face. How greatly the old lady had aged since her departure, how frail and small she had become! Her body seemed to have shrunk to nothing and the only noticeable features in her face were the dry lips gasping for air, and eyes grown suddenly too large,

Donatienne turned, with a sigh of discouragement, to set the bowl down, and found herself face to face with Catherine. Her tired eyes shone with joy and tears of relief all at once.

"Dame Catherine!" she stammered. "Lord be praised! You have arrived just in time!"

Catherine put a finger hastily to her lips to motion the old woman to keep silent, but she shook her head sadly.

"Oh, we can speak! She cannot hear! The fever is so high that when she speaks she is merely delirious!"

Even as she spoke a few words issued from the sick woman's parchment-colored lips. Disconnected and confused as they were, Catherine managed to make out her name and Arnaud's. The fit of coughing which had shaken the poor, exhausted body so roughly seemed to have calmed down a little. Isabelle's face slowly returned to a more normal color, but her breathing stayed hoarse and gasping. There was an imploring expression in her eyes. Isabelle seemed to be suffering torment in her delirium, and Catherine could not help feeling that she was the cause of this suffering.

She gently took the burning hand, which clawed feverishly at the coverlet, and raised it to her lips. Then she laid it against her cheek, as she had so often done formerly.

"Mother," she said softly, "mother, listen to me! Look at me! Here I am . . . beside you! It is I, your daughter. It is Catherine . . . Catherine!"

Something seemed to come to life in that cloudy, tormented gaze. The mouth closed, then opened again and whispered:

"Catherine!"

"Yes!" the young woman insisted. "It is I . . . I am here!"

The eyes rolled, and seemed to grow fixed as they stared at the young woman who bent forward, clasping the withered hands in hers.

"It's no use, Dame Catherine," Donatienne whispered, "her mind is wandering again."

"No it isn't. She knows me, I think. Mother, look at me! Don't you recognize me?"

Her will was strained and concentrated in the effort to get through to the cloudy mind of the sick woman. She longed to be able to pour her own strength into the wasted body, and her longing was so strong that she actually felt as if the warmth were flowing from her hands into the other's. Once again, she implored her:

"Look at me! This is Catherine, your daughter! Arnaud's wife!"

A shudder raced across Isabelle's parched skin at the mention of that name. Her eyes, quite lucid now, rested on the young woman's anxious face.

"Catherine!" she breathed. "You have come back?"

"Yes, mother . . . I have come back! And I will never leave you . . . never again!"

The sick woman's shadowed eyes gazed at her with a look of slightly doubtful anxiety.

"You are going to stay? . . . But that young man . . . De Breze?"

"He mistook his dreams for a reality! I shall never see him again. I am Catherine de Montsalvy, and so I shall remain, mother. I am *his* wife . . . and only *his*!"

A look of intense joy and relief spread over the sick woman's drawn face, and her hand, which had been clutching at Catherine's, grew supple and limp and a faint smile parted her lips.

"God be praised," she murmured. "Now I can die in peace."

She closed her eyes for a moment, opened them again and looked tenderly at Catherine. She beckoned to her to come closer and whispered mysteriously:

"I have seen him again, you know. . . ."

"Who, mother?"

"Him, my son! . . . He came to me. . . . He is still as handsome as ever! Ah yes! So beautiful!"

A violent burst of coughing cut her brutally short. Her

297

face grew purple and her eyes wandered again. The poor woman fell back fighting for breath. The moment of respite was over. Donatienne came up with her cup.

"The herbalist says that when she coughs she should be made to drink this brew of poppy seed, dried violets and mallow, but it is not easy. . . ."

With Catherine's help, however, she managed to make the sick woman swallow a few drops at a time. Her coughing grew less harsh and hollow. Slowly the tense body relaxed, but her eyes did not open.

"She may sleep a little now," Donatienne whispered. "Go and get some rest, Dame Catherine. That long journey must have tired you. I will keep watch till day-break."

"You are exhausted, Donatienne."

"Bah, I'm stoutly made!" the old peasant woman said with a brave smile. "And besides it gives me new heart to know that you are here."

Catherine nodded towards the sick woman who seemed to be falling asleep.

"Has she been ill for long?"

"More than a week, gracious lady. She insisted on going there, to Calves, with Fortunat! It seems she could not endure being parted any longer from her son. . . . On the way back she ran into torrential rain which poured down unceasingly for three days. But she refused to stop or take shelter. She got back soaked through, chilled to the marrow, teeth chattering wildly. The following night she had a severe fever. Since then the sickness has not left her. . . ."

Catherine listened to Donatienne, frowning, but did not interrupt. She was eaten up with remorse. She understood Isabelle's reaction so well. Her mother's heart had sought to make up for the hurt Catherine had done Arnaud, even though he himself was as yet unaware of it. Besides how could he have learned about it in that living tomb which leprosy represents? Did not all the rumors stop on the threshold of the living-dead, who were only tolerated on condition that they kept apart from the rest of the world and allowed themselves to be forgotten?

Catherine asked mechanically:

"By the way, where is Fortunat?"

This time it was Gauthier, still in his position near Michel's bed, who answered:

"It is Friday today, Dame Catherine. Fortunat left yesterday for Calves, as he does every week. He has never missed a single visit . . . and he always goes on foot, as a token of humility."

"Have you so many provisions to send there then?"

"No. Sometimes Fortunat takes only a small loaf of bread or a cheese, and sometimes, even, nothing at all. But he sits down on a tree-stump near the leper-house and stays there for hours on end just gazing at the place. . . . He is a strange boy, but I swear to you, Dame Catherine, that I have never met a more loyal soul."

Catherine turned her face away to hide the flush which had risen to the roots of her hair. The little Gascon squire had certainly given her an object lesson in fidelity. Nothing would part him from this master of his whom he could never forget. When she compared her behavior with the Gascon's, Catherine told herself that Fortunat undoubtedly carried off the honors.

"Nor I," she murmured. "Who would have thought the boy would have attached himself so passionately? Come to think of it, when will he return . . . from there?"

"Tomorrow, some time during the day."

But there was no sign of Fortunat the next day. She spent the whole day at Isabelle's bedside and the old lady seemed a little stronger. She also had a long talk with the abbot. It was time, she said, to rebuild their castle, and she had the means to do so. The King's Treasurer had granted her a handsome sum in gold ecus, and there were always her jewels, minus the few which she and Isabelle had been forced to sell latterly to live on.

Bernard de Calmont d'Olt, the young abbot of Montsalvy, was a forceful and intelligent man. She made him a present of a superb ruby brooch to fasten his ceremonial cope and then set about discussing her plans for reconstruction. One of the monks, Brother Sebastian, was charged with drawing up the plans while another was sent to find a quarry from which the stones for building it could be brought. Like all large abbeys, Montsalvy offered a complete range of crafts and talents.

"In any event," the abbot told her, "you can remain here as long as you like. The guest-house is sufficiently far from the monastery buildings for the presence, however prolonged, of a young woman not to become a matter for malicious gossip."

Reassured on this point, Catherine then turned her attention to Tristan l'Hermite and his men, who were due to leave for Parthenay the following morning. The soldiers had received a generous reimbursement. As for Tristan, she presented him with a heavy gold chain set with turquoises which had once belonged to Garin de Brazey.

"It will serve to remind you of us," she said, slipping it round his neck. "Wear it often in memory of Catherine."

He gave his three-cornered smile and murmured, in a voice somewhat more emotional than he would perhaps have wished:

"Do you really think I need a sumptuous jewel to be reminded of you, Dame Catherine? I might live a hundred years without forgetting a single thing about you. But I shall wear this chain with pleasure on festive occasions. And with pride too, since it comes from you."

The supper they were taking together was to be the last before their parting. Catherine felt a real regret at having to part from this good companion of hers, a somewhat taciturn one at times, but a man whose loyalty could be trusted and whose courage never failed. She had, therefore, given orders that, despite her mother-in-law's condition, their meal together should exhibit a certain elegance. With the help of Donatienne and the good-will of the monastery poultry-run, she had succeeded in producing a supper which was respectable if not luxurious. Wearing one of her few elegant dresses she and her guest took their places on the seignorial dais where they were served, with more enthusiasm than elegance, by Gauthier. However, this detail in no way impaired the two friends' appetites for cabbage soup and the abbot's roast capons.

When they left the table Catherine saw that night was falling and she asked for word of Fortunat. She had been waiting all day for his return, absurdly hoping for good news. But how could there be good news where a leper was concerned? Yet it was disappointing to find that he had not yet returned. And on top of this she felt anxious because she could not help noticing that Gauthier himself was uneasy.

"He must have stopped on the way," she said, after returning from the gate-house for the hundredth time, "I expect he will return tomorrow."

But the Norman shook his head.

"Fortunat? He is as punctual as a clock. He always leaves at the same time and returns at the same time, just before supper. It isn't normal for him to be late!"

His eyes met Catherine's. They both shared the same thought. Something must have happened to Fortunat, but what? He might have fallen among thieves, though the district was fairly safe now that the Armagnac had increased the garrison at Carlat and the abbey was presided over by the vigorous Bernard de Calmont. The English, moreover, were abandoning the strongholds of Auvergne one by one.

"Let us wait," Catherine said.

"At day-break tomorrow I will go in search of news. . . ."

Catherine felt like saying, "And I will go with you. . . ." but she stopped herself. She could not leave Isabelle just now. The old lady always sent for her in her rare intervals of lucidity, and she took such an obvious delight in her presence that Catherine would not have dreamed of depriving her of it. So she sighed:

"Very well. Do as you think best."

Before going to bed she made a tour of the house, anxious to fulfill all her duties as a hostess. Now that the abbot had given her free use of the guest-house she was determined that it should run as smoothly as possible. She even went as far as the stables, where the soldiers' horses had been installed, but her motive here was more sentimental than housewifely. Faithful to his promise, Hugh Kennedy had sent Morgane, the white mare, here before he left Carlat, and thus given Catherine the unexpected pleasure of finding her again. For to Catherine, Morgane was a special personage, almost a friend. They understood each other perfectly and their reunion had been a joyful moment.

"Now here we are destined to lead a quiet life together," said Catherine, a little wistfully, stroking Morgane's snowy coat. "You will be the good little palfrey of a good little country lady!"

Morgane's huge, intelligent eyes gazed at her with an expression which struck Catherine as quite devilish, and the challenging neigh with which she accompanied the look gave her clearly to understand that the little mare, for her part, did not believe a word of it. . . . Catherine could not help laughing. She offered Morgane a lump of sugar she had brought specially for her, and then slapped her rump gently.

"We want a little excitement it seems? Ah, well, my pretty, we shall have to find a pretext!"

On leaving the stables Catherine would have liked to linger for a moment in the fresh air because the night was exceptionally clear and fine, but Donatienne came to tell her that a bed had been made up for her in the room next to Isabelle's.

"But I wanted to be in the same room!" Catherine protested. "You have stayed up long enough, Donatienne. You need rest."

"Bah, I sleep just as well on a bench!" the old peasant woman asserted stoutly. "Besides I have the feeling that she will sleep soundly tonight. The apothecary has given me a soothing-draught for her. You would do well to take a little yourself. You seem so nervous!"

"I think I shall sleep quite well without that!"

She went to kiss Michel who was lisping a prayer under Gauthier's impassive eye. The comradeship between the little boy and the giant Norman had both amused and surprised her. They understood each other perfectly, and though Gauthier might treat the little lord with a certain deference, that did not mean that he put up with all his whims. As for Michel, he clearly doted on Gauthier and admired his immense strength.

He welcomed his mother as though she had left only the day before. He had come running to her on his still slightly unsteady little legs and thrown his little arms round her neck. Then he nestled his blond head in her shoulder and let out a happy sigh.

"Mamma!" was all he said, but it made Catherine cry with happiness.

That night she put him to bed herself, and kissed him, and then left him to hear the story which Gauthier was starting on. Every night the Norman told his little friend a story, or part of a story if the recital took too long, and they were always the strange Norse legends, full of djinns and fantastic gods and virgin warriors. The little boy listened, open-mouthed, and finally began to nod off. . . .

Catherine tiptoed out as Gauthier began:

"Then the son of Eric the Red took ship with his companions and set sail across the sea . . ."

There was something lulling about Gauthier's voice. The child was too young to understand this legend of an earlier age but he listened with wide, wondering eyes, none the less, attracted by the cadence of the foreign names and the charm of that solemn voice. Catherine meanwhile dozed off in her little narrow bed, lulled by the sound. Her last thought was for Sara. She had traveled so fast, she and the Bretons, that they might have passed her on the road without realizing it. But she could not be long in coming now. . . . The idea that something might have happened to her did not even cross her mind. Sara was indestructible; she knew the secrets of nature and nature was her friend. Yes, she would soon be there . . . yes, soon. . . . The son of Eric the Red had barely reached the open seas when Catherine was fast asleep. . . .

She had a strange vision towards midnight. Was she asleep or half-awake then? Had it all been a dream? It seemed to her that she opened her eyes to the still unfamiliar surroundings of her room. The silence was undisturbed, but Isabelle's night-light still lit up the room. From her bed Catherine could see Donatienne sleeping, curled up with her bonnet all

302

awry on a cushion-strewn bench. Then suddenly a dark shape slipped across to the sick woman's bedside . . . the shape of a man dressed in black and wearing a mask. . . . Panic rose in Catherine's throat. She tried to cry out but no sound came. She tried to move, but her limbs and body were so heavy suddenly that she felt as if she had been tied to the bed. In a nightmare fog she saw the man stoop, and stoop still further, over Isabelle's bed, make a gesture, and then stand up again. Convinced that the stranger was trying to murder the sick woman Catherine opened her mouth again, but still no sound would come. . . .

Now the man stepped back and turned round, his mask in his hand . . . and Catherine's fear turned to immense joy, because she recognized the haughty profile, dark eyes and firm mouth of her own husband. Arnaud! It was Arnaud! A wave of marvelous happiness, such as is only found in dreams, washed over Catherine. He was there, he had come back . . . God must have worked a miracle, for that handsome face, which she remembered so clearly, was intact. There was not a trace of the dreadful malady upon it. But why then was he so pale, so deathly sad? . . .

Buoyed up by her love, which she had believed weakened but which came back to her now with a new strength, she tried to call him, to stretch out her arms to him . . . but she found herself as helpless as before. This fog around her seemed to be suffocating her. . . . She saw Arnaud disappearing into it, in the direction of Michel's room. And then there was nothing left but a terrible feeling of solitude and abandonment. . . .

"He has gone," Catherine reflected despairingly. "And I shall never see him again . . . never again!"

She woke at day-break. Outside Tristan's horn was summoning the Bretons to their saddles. The hour of departure was at hand and Catherine got up to assist at it. But not without a struggle. She felt dreadfully weak this morning, her head was heavy and her legs trembled. But already a ray of sunlight was struggling through the window of her cell and next door she could hear Michel chuckling and murmuring to himself in his little bed. She splashed her face with cold water and hurried into her clothes, fighting as best she could against a rising feeling of dismay.

She could not forget that dream of hers. The more she thought about it the more she felt like weeping, for she remembered dreadful tales of people appearing, at the hour of their deaths, to the people who loved them, as if to warn them of their departure. Might not that extraordinarily life-like dream of the previous night have been one of those tragic premonitions? And was Arnaud then . . . No, she could not even imagine the word! All the same, this prolonged absence of Fortunat's? What if he had just heard the dreadful news over there? The sickness might perhaps have made rapid progress. . . .

"It's enough to drive one mad!" Catherine murmured aloud. "I must know. Gauthier must leave at once . . . or, no . . . I shall go too. Donatienne can keep watch over my mother-in-law today, and Morgane can take me there and back before nightfall!"

She ran to embrace her son, made sure that Isabelle was still asleep, and raced out into the yard. The Bretons were already mounted, but Tristan and Gauthier were talking near the stable door. They separated on seeing Catherine. She forced herself to smile to her departing friend despite her heavy heart, and held out her hand:

"Bon voyage, friend Tristan! Tell Monseigneur the Constable for me how grateful I am to him for sending you with me."

"He will certainly want to know when we may have the pleasure of seeing you again, Dame Catherine."

"Not for a long time, I fear, unless fate brings you back perhaps. I have so much to do here! Everything must be restored to its former state."

"Bah! The Auvergne is not so far! I know the King thinks of coming here, and when he is finally reconciled with Richemont it is possible we may all be reunited!"

"I hope God is listening. Good-bye, my friend."

He kissed her hand and leaped into the saddle. The abbey gates swung wide open for him, revealing the village square where the housewives were already milling about at their duties. Tristan l'Hermite rode at the head of his men, but, just as they crossed the threshold of the holy place, he turned and waved his hat in the air.

"Till our next meeting, Dame Catherine!"

"Till then, friend Tristan, and may it be soon!"

A few seconds later the heavy gates swung shut and the courtyard was empty. Catherine went over to Gauthier who stood by the open stable door.

"I had a strange dream last night, Gauthier. . . . I am plagued by sad thoughts. So I have decided to go with you to seek news of Fortunat. Even if it means going as far as Calves we should be able to return within the day. Find a horse and saddle up Morgane!"

304

"I would be glad to," the Norman said calmly, "but unfortunately it is quite impossible."

"Why is that?"

"Because Morgane is not there!"

"What!"

"I'm telling you the truth: Morgane has vanished. Go and see for yourself. . . ."

Catherine followed Gauthier into the dark stables. There were still many horses there, but it was obvious that the white mare had gone. Catherine stood stock-still on the threshold, and looked at Gauthier.

"Where is she?"

"How should I know? No one has seen or heard a thing. . . . I might add that there is another horse missing, Roland, one of those the abbot placed at our disposal . . ."

"But this is ridiculous! How could those two animals have walked out of here without anyone seeing?"

"Doubtless because the one who took them had means of entering without attracting attention. He must have known the abbey well."

"Well then?" Catherine asked, subsiding on a heap of straw. "What conclusion have you reached?"

Gauthier did not answer at once. He was thinking. A moment later he glanced uncertainly at Catherine:

"The fact is that Roland, the horse which has been stolen with Morgane, was the one Fortunat used to use when he went to Aurillac or elsewhere. . . ."

"But not when he went to Calves?"

"No. As you know he refused to go there except on foot . . . because of Messire Arnaud!"

Now it was Catherine's turn to fall silent. She had plucked a wisp of straw and was chewing it abstractedly. A mass of ideas crowded into her brain. . . . At length she looked up.

"I wonder if I was really dreaming?" she said. "If it wasn't one of those premonitions?"

"What do you mean?"

"Nothing. I'll tell you later. Saddle two horses and let the people know that we shall be out all day. I am going to put on my boy's clothes."

"Where are we going?"

"To Calves, of course. And with all speed!"

CHAPTER FIFTEEN

The Empty Valley

The riders paused at the cross-roads to decide which road to follow. The wretched village of Calves was not far now, and Catherine could see the basalt cliff of Carlat, bristling with towers and turrets, on the horizon. The sight was strangely moving. She had spent the most agonizing hours of her life there and fled from the place under the threat of imprisonment, but nevertheless, at the sight of this imposing edifice which had grown so familiar to her, she felt her courage weaken.

A peasant returning from work with his hoe over one shoulder was approaching the cross-roads. Gauthier called out to him from his mount.

"Do you know where the leper-house is, my good man?"

The man crossed himself hurriedly and pointed down one of the roads.

"Go down as far as the river . . . and you will see a big closed building. But don't come to the village afterwards!"

He hurried on towards the hamlet. Catherine turned her horse's head in the direction in which he had pointed.

"Let's go," she said.

The road led downhill to the Embene, a small river which farther along flowed round the rock of Carlat. A line of willows marked its course. Catherine rode on ahead in silence, swaying to the rhythm of the horse's steps. She felt herself becoming deeply agitated as they approached the place she had so often dreamed about and never dared to visit. In a few seconds she would be close to Arnaud, only a few paces from the spot where he lived. Perhaps she might even succeed in seeing him. . . . The mere thought made her heart beat faster, but despite this she had difficulty shaking off a vague sense of foreboding which had clung to her since that morning. . . .

The road now turned aside to cross a small thicket of overgrown trees. The soil here, furrowed with ancient cracks and muddy pits which had never dried up, had the air of being but rarely trodden upon. The evening sky—Catherine and

Gauthier had taken far longer over the journey than they expected—vanished behind the thick foliage. This wood was like a natural barrier which had grown up to protect men from the unclean accursed dwellers of Calves. . . . And then, suddenly, at the foot of the slope, the two riders turned a corner and found themselves on the river bank and clear of the wood.

This narrow valley, where the only sound was the melancholy rushing of the stream, was a dreadfully gloomy place. Catherine stopped her horse in the shadow of the trees. Gauthier joined her and the two of them remained there, not moving, shocked into silence. A few yards ahead stood the outer walls of a sort of large farm . . . but only the outer walls, for there was nothing left in the center but a few blackened slabs and a standing arch, which must have been the entrance to the chapel. The great door swung from one hinge and revealed the interior of the leper-house, full of charred remains. . . . The only sound troubling the silence was the sinister cawing of ravens circling overhead.

Catherine went as pale as death, closed her eyes and swayed in her saddle, on the verge of fainting.

"Arnaud is dead," she cried. "It must have been his ghost I saw last night!"

Gauthier sprang to the ground and snatched Catherine from her saddle. Then he laid her down, ashen white, by the wayside and began rubbing her frozen hands vigorously.

"Dame Catherine, please! . . . Take hold of yourself! Courage! I beg you," he implored.

But she seemed to be losing consciousness more rapidly every minute, and she felt as if her life were draining out of her body, ebbing from her like water. Then he struck her twice across the face, carefully controlling himself from hitting her too hard. Her pale cheeks turned bright red and Catherine opened her eyes and stared at him with a sort of bewilderment. Then he smiled contritely:

"Forgive me, I had no choice! Wait, I am going to fetch a little water."

He ran past the burned buildings, filled his goblet which hung at his belt with spring water and came back and made Catherine drink it, fussing over her like a mother. The reaction was swift and violent. The young woman burst into hysterical sobs.

He stood beside her and let her cry, trusting to the calming power of tears. He neither said nor did anything to stop the terrible sobs which seemed to be tearing her apart. Little by little, Catherine grew calmer. . . . A long while later she raised a tear-stained face and red eyes towards him.

"We must find out what happened," she said, in a voice growing gradually stronger.

Gauthier held out a hand to help her to her feet. She did not let go, needing this strength and warmth of his for the trials to come. With his assistance she went up to the doorway of the building above which the arms of the Abbey of St. Geraud d'Aurillac could still be seen. Her heart missed a beat at the thought that Arnaud had once stepped across that threshold . . . for ever more!

She paid no heed to the tears which trickled silently, ceaselessly, down her cheeks. Inside, the building was completely gutted. Nothing remained but charred, twisted fragments, which reminded Catherine of the ruins of Montsalvy. The fire had destroyed everything except for a few walls of particularly stout stone which had survived. Not a roof remained; nothing but a few stones scattered about. Gauthier examined them.

"The fire is recent," he said. "The stones are still warm."

"My God!" Catherine moaned faintly. "I can't believe that he is lying under all that . . . my darling . . . my beloved husband!"

She fell on to her knees on the stones and tried to move some of them away. But her hands were trembling and clumsy and she cut herself. Gauthier picked her up bodily.

"Don't stay here, Dame Catherine, come with me."

But she fought and struggled violently.

"Leave me . . . I want to stay here. He is there, I tell you."

"I just don't believe it, and nor do you! . . . Anyway, even if he were, what good would it do to hurt yourself on those scorching hot stones?"

"But I tell you he's dead!" Catherine cried angrily. "I tell you I saw his ghost last night. . . . He appeared, masked, in my mother-in-law's room. He bent over her and then he vanished!"

"And he didn't go into your room? Was Dame Isabelle awake or asleep?"

"She was asleep. She did not see a thing. At first I thought I was dreaming. But now I know it wasn't a dream, that I saw Arnaud's ghost. . . ."

She began to weep again. Gauthier took her by the shoulders and shook her hard, and shouted:

"And I'm telling you that you did not see a ghost! And you were not dreaming either! . . . A ghost would have come to *you!* Obviously Messire Arnaud did not know of your return since he made no effort to see you."

"What do you mean?"

Calmer all of a sudden, Catherine stood open-mouthed looking at Gauthier as if he had suddenly taken leave of his senses.

"I am trying to say that a ghost would know everything about the living. He would have come to you. Besides, why the mask?"

"You aren't trying to tell me that that was Arnaud I saw . . . Arnaud in person?"

"I don't know. But some strange things have happened. Let us suppose that Fortunat went to Messire Arnaud and told him that his mother was dying. Leprosy need no longer be feared on the threshold of death. . . . He might have wanted to take his leave of her for the last time. Whereas he did not come to you because he had no idea that you had returned. Fortunat did not know about it, for instance."

"Where can he be now then? And what has happened here? Why these ruins, this silence and desolation?"

"I don't know," Gauthier replied thoughtfully, "but I am going to try to find out. As for his whereabouts, I have an idea Fortunat might be able to help us there . . . just as he might be able to tell us of the whereabouts of Roland and Morgane!"

Very gently he started to lead her out of the ruins. Catherine clung to him like a frightened child, and gazed at him with wondering eyes.

"Do you really think that?"

"Do I ever say things I don't mean? Specially to you."

She gave a shaky smile, so near the verge of tears still that the Norman's heart melted with pity. He loved her enough to forget his own love of her and only wished to see her happy. Alas! Destiny seemed to prey on her, and how many tears were still to be shed for a moment's weakness she had already repented of?

"Don't raise my hopes too much," she implored. "Don't you see I might die of disappointment. . . ."

"Stay as strong as you have always been. And let us try to find out. Let us leave this place; we are bound to find someone who knows what happened here. . . ."

They got back on their horses again and left the deserted valley, climbing uphill towards the village, towards the open sky. . . . This time Gauthier went ahead, seeking a sign of life in this deserted spot. Catherine followed, head lowered, trying to put her thoughts in order. She was torn between despair and hope. All of a sudden everything she had cared about seemed irrelevant. Only one thing mattered now: and that was to find out if Arnaud was alive or dead! She would never know a moment's peace till she knew.

As they rode out of the dark wood Gauthier stood up in his stirrups and pointed southwards.

"Look! I see a cottage chimney smoking. . . . They must be able to see the roof-tops of the leper-house from there . . . or at least they must have been able to. . . ."

It was a small house, modestly tucked away under a thick thatch. Gauthier and Catherine left their horses tethered to a tree, so as not to frighten the inhabitants, and climbed the path leading to the door on foot. The sound of footsteps brought an elderly peasant woman in a yellow bonnet to the door. In one hand she carried a rush basket. She must have been very old indeed for she was quite bent, and leaning heavily on a blackthorn stick, but the eyes with which she fixed the new arrivals were young and keen, like two forget-me-nots in a tanned, immensely wrinkled face.

"Do not fear, good mother," Gauthier said, making his voice as gentle as he could, "we do not mean any harm to you. But we would like some information. . . ."

"Come in, my pretty gentlemen. My home is yours. . . ."

"We don't wish to disturb you," Catherine said now, "and we have not got much time. . . ."

As she spoke she turned and stared out over the countryside unrolling at her feet. The ruins of the leper-house were just visible in the distance beyond a line of trees.

"Do you know what happened there?"

The old woman's face became the picture of terror. She crossed herself several times and murmured something unintelligible, then:

" 'Tis an accursed place . . . it is bad to speak of it, it brings bad luck!"

"That depends," Catherine said, pulling out a gold piece and letting it flash in the sunlight before slipping it into the old woman's palm. "Speak, good woman, and you shall have another. . . ."

The old woman gazed unbelievingly at her, then tested the coin by biting on it, to see if it were genuine.

"Gold," she exclaimed, "real gold! Ah, 'tis a long time since I saw any of that. What is it you wish to know, my young sprig?"

"When did the leper-house burn down?"

Despite the gold, the old woman looked away, obviously

loth to speak. Then she hesitated, closed her hand round the gold piece and finally made up her mind.

"On Thursday night! The lepers went mad! Or rather the monk who cared for them, and watched over them . . . a real saint . . . he died the day before, bitten by a viper. Such a noise they made! All evening long one could hear them crying and howling . . . like demons! The mountains shook with the din. It was as if hell had suddenly opened. . . . The people of the village were afraid. They thought the lepers would come out and attack them. They went to Carlat to ask for help. Then some soldiers came. . . ."

She stopped, looking towards the ruins with eyes which spoke of the horrors they had seen. Then she crossed herself again.

"Then?" Catherine prompted.

"They arrived at night," the old woman went on, more faintly. "The lepers were still bemoaning their fate. It was dreadful. But what happened next was still worse!"

Catherine felt quite weak. She sank down on a stone bench by the door, and wiped the sweat off her brow with her sleeve.

"Finish . . . for pity's sake!"

"The soldiers were mercenaries, real barbarians," the old woman cried with sudden violence. "They barricaded the door of the leper-house and then set fire to it!"

A double cry of horror greeted this news. Catherine slumped back against the wall, cut to the heart.

"Arnaud!" she moaned. "My God!"

Now that she had got into her stride the old woman went on in a sort of fury.

"The soldiers were drunk, because the villagers had made them drink to give them enough courage to go to the leper-house. They shouted that these godforsaken wretches should all be destroyed . . . that the valley should be cleansed! It burned all night long. But before midnight there was nothing to be heard . . . nothing but the crackling of the flames!"

She fell silent at last, and not a moment too soon for Catherine was swooning away.

Gauthier leaned over her hastily and took her by the arm.

"Come," he said softly, "we must be on our way. . . ."

But she was almost unconscious and she fell back limply. The old woman gazed at her with curiosity.

"The young lord seems to grieve! Did he know any of those unfortunates?"

"The young lord is a woman," Gauthier replied curtly. "And she did . . . know one of them!"

311

Catherine heard no more. Her body felt as if it were made of stone, and only one thought sounded in her head, thundering there monotonously like a clanging bell. . . .

"He is dead! They killed him. . . ."

She had quite forgotten what Gauthier had said earlier. Her eyes saw nothing but flames leaping high into the night sky. And her heart ached as though steel claws were dragging it out of her breast.

The old woman had entered her house without a word. Now she came out again carrying a bowl.

"Here, poor lady," she said, "drink this! It is wine in which herbs have steeped, and it will do you good!"

Catherine drank, felt better and would have got to her feet, but the old woman interrupted.

"No, stay here! Night is closing in and the roads are dangerous. If no one waits for you, why not stay till morning? I have not much to offer you, but what there is is yours."

Gauthier studied the young woman's pale face. She was scarcely able to stand. She would never be able to reach Montsalvy that night.

"We will stay then," he said. "Many thanks."

Gauthier spent the whole night sitting up beside the straw mattress where Catherine was vainly trying to snatch a little sleep. And all that night he labored to infuse a little of his own courage and confidence into her suffering heart. He repeated the same words over and over again. It was not a ghost Catherine had seen. She had seen Arnaud himself. He had no doubt escaped from the fire with Fortunat's help . . . and the two men must have fled on the stolen horses. But she no longer believed him. Arnaud had no cause to flee from Montsalvy. He could have taken refuge with Saturnin, who would have accommodated him despite his fear of the disease. . . . No, Gauthier replied, the master would never have risked infecting his own people. The fact that he had gone to see his mother only proved that he knew her to be dying . . . and Fortunat, perhaps, had taken him to another leper-house. They said that there was one near Conques.

"Don't despair, Dame Catherine. We shall return to Montsalvy, and in a few days you will see Fortunat returning. Believe me!"

"I wish I could," Catherine sighed. "But I dare not! I have been disappointed so often!"

"I know. But with a little courage and perseverance one can come out the other side! One day, Dame Catherine, you too . . ."

"No, don't say any more. I will try to be sensible, and believe you. . . ."

But she could not. The dawn found her still desperate and broken-hearted. She thanked the old peasant woman graciously for her hospitality, and then, in a great blaze of sunshine which afflicted her tired eyes and sad heart, she set off for Montsalvy.

Catherine saw nothing of the magnificent countryside of the Truyère valley with its green wooded slopes. She rode along slumped in her saddle, eyes half-shut, dragging her heart like a cannon-ball. Her vision the other night had so persuaded her of Arnaud's death that the world seemed a gray place to her now. She did not see the exuberant greenness of the trees, the flowering meadows and hedgerows, or the golden glory of the sunlight. Something seemed to have died in her. Her desolate spirit could not even find a prayer to beseech heaven with.

Catherine came within a hair's breadth of blasphemy as she reproached God bitterly for his injustice and cruelty. . . . How heavily he made her pay for the few favors he grudgingly accorded her!

She discovered, too, that she had never really believed that Arnaud was lost to her till this minute. He might no longer be with the living, but he had been somewhere beneath this heaven above, a living, breathing being, whom she had always felt she might one day rejoin when her duties were completed. But now what was left for her? Nothing but a great emptiness and the taste of ashes bitter on her lips. . . . From time to time Gauthier rode his horse alongside hers and spoke to her, trying to rouse her from this shattering sorrow. She replied in monosyllables and then spurred her horse, and went ahead a short way. At the moment she could not bear to be anything but alone. . . .

And yet when Catherine got back to Montsalvy, she felt something revive within her, a feeling strangely akin to joy. For standing on the threshold of the guest-house, with little Michel in her arms, was Sara! She stood quite still with the baby clutched against her heart, like some peasant madonna, but as the riders came nearer the gypsy's sharp eyes noticed Catherine's ravaged face and sleepwalker's eyes. Sara's features, which had been stern to begin with, softened. The almost maternal affection she had for Catherine allowed her to guess her misery merely from the way she sat her horse. Without taking her eyes off her she handed the child to Donatienne and went to greet the new arrivals.

Not a word was spoken. As Sara drew near, Catherine slid

313

to the ground and collapsed sobbing into her arms. How dear that familiar refuge seemed to her now in this moment of despair! The young woman's face was so pitiful that Sara began to weep too. They clung together, weeping, for a moment and then went slowly into the house.

Once inside Catherine gradually regained a little self-control and looked up at her old friend with eyes drowned in tears.

"Sara! My good Sara! . . . I can't be altogether accursed if you have come back to me!"

"Accursed? You? Poor little one. . . . What could have put such an idea into your head?"

"She is convinced that Messire Arnaud perished in the fire which destroyed the leper-house at Calves," Gauthier's grave voice explained from just behind them. "She won't listen to what you tell her, she is quite determined to believe it!"

"Ouf!" Sara cried, all her old combativeness returned at the mere sight of her old enemy. "Tell me all about it!"

She left Catherine to hug and kiss her child with a warmth which came straight from her overflowing heart and took the Norman aside to question him. Gauthier told her everything briefly: Catherine's return, the strange nocturnal visitor, how the two horses had vanished, and, at last, about the drama at Calves. Sara listened attentively, frowning, concentrating on every detail of the story. When he finished she stood there silently for a moment, with arms folded and her chin resting on her hand, staring into the black hole of the fireplace.

At length she came back to Catherine who was sitting on a stool, as she rocked Michel to and fro on her lap, watching her covertly.

"What do you think?" Gauthier asked her.

"I think you are right, my lad! The master is not dead! It is not possible!"

"How could he have escaped?" Catherine asked.

"I've no idea. But it wasn't a ghost you saw. Ghosts don't wear masks. I know them."

"I wish I could believe you," Catherine sighed. "But then, if you're right, tell me what I should do now!"

"Wait a few days, as Gauthier suggested, to give Fortunat time to return. Otherwise . . ."

"Otherwise?"

"We could go back to Calves and take Saturnin and several other strong men with us and search the ruins till we are sure one way or another. But, for my part, I am already certain: there is no body at Calves . . . at least not the body you are concerned about. . . ."

This time Catherine did feel a little more hopeful. The bonds which united her to Sara were so powerful that she had come to think of her as not quite an oracle perhaps, but a person who was usually right, and sometimes had strange moments of insight. She said nothing, but took her friend's hand and laid it humbly against her cheek, like a child seeking forgiveness.

Sara's eyes grew tender as they rested on the blonde head beside her. The monastery bell rang for compline.

"The monks are going into chapel," Sara said. "You should go and pray too. . . ."

Catherine nodded hopelessly.

"I don't feel the wish to pray any more, Sara! What is the good of it? God only remembers me to strike me down."

"That is not fair. He has given you the bitter fruit of vengeance, and the sweeter one of victory! You have given Montsalvy back its right to exist!"

"But at what a price!"

"A price you cannot estimate as yet . . . unless perhaps you are still sighing over the one you left behind at Chinon?" Sara remarked slyly. She wanted to see how Catherine would react to this mention of the man who had been the cause of their separation. But she was instantly reassured on that point. Catherine shrugged impatiently.

"What is there to regret except that I don't know where Arnaud is?"

There was nothing to add to that!

The fever which consumed Isabelle de Montsalvy seemed to be abating. The old lady was no longer delirious and she coughed less, but she grew gradually weaker and weaker like a lamp which is burning down.

"We cannot save her," Sara said, as she and Catherine took over at the bedside so that Donatienne could rest and look after her husband. He had been sorely neglected by her since the beginning of her mistress's illness.

"It seems as though she has lost the will to live," Catherine replied.

All the herbal remedies which the monastery could offer, all the science of the physician of Aurillac, who had returned to visit her that day, seemed powerless to halt the ebb of the vital spirit from that exhausted body. Isabelle was gently being snuffed out. She lay for hours now, stretched out upon her bed, hands folded on her rosary or prayer-book, which she no longer read, silent and motionless. Only the faint movement of her lips showed that she was praying.

One evening, three days after Catherine's and Gauthier's

visit to Calves, the old lady opened her eyes and glanced up at Catherine who was standing beside the bed.

"I am praying for you, my child," she said softly, "and Michel and for my son too. Don't abandon him in his wretchedness, Catherine. When I am gone keep watch over him from afar! He suffers so much!"

Catherine clasped her hands and wrung them, then she cleared her throat so that her voice should not tremble. Isabelle knew nothing of the drama at Calves which had been scrupulously hidden from her, but it was becoming so difficult to play her part and feign the requisite, soothing calm, when her soul was ravaged with uncertainty. Every minute of the three days which had just elapsed had been a moment of torture for Catherine. Trusting to Sara's judgment she had been waiting for Fortunat to return, and Fortunat had not yet returned. . . . But she managed to smile tenderly at the careworn face.

"Do not fear, mother! I shall never leave him. I want to build him a home, not far from here but apart from the other dwellings, where he could live more comfortably, and more in the style to which he is accustomed . . . in a manner suited to his tastes and rank. I have so longed to get him out of that awful leper-house!"

The sick woman's eyes became radiant with joy. She stretched out her emaciated hand to squeeze Catherine's.

"Oh, yes! . . . Do that! . . . Save him from poverty and misery! Now that we are rich. . . ."

"Very rich, mother," Catherine smiled, fighting back her tears. "Montsalvy will rise again, stronger and more handsome than ever. Brother Sebastian, the monastery architect, has already begun plans for the new château and Saturnin, helped by Brother Placide, has started working a quarry near La Truyère. The whole village will have work once the harvest is over. Soon you will find a dwelling worthy of you!"

Isabelle shook her head with a sad smile. Her eyes lingered on Catherine's hand, where Queen Yolande's emerald flashed like a green eye. Since the day it had been given to her Catherine had never once removed the ring. But now, seeing that the old lady was looking at it, she slipped it off and placed it on the still beautiful, though emaciated, hand which lay upon the coverlet; a hand modeled with the same precise, almost masculine strength as Arnaud's.

"This is the gage of friendship towards our family which I received from Queen Yolande. Look, here are her arms engraved upon the stone. Wear it, mother; it suits you so well."

Isabelle contemplated the jewel with a dazzled smile, an almost childish joy, then she looked affectionately at Catherine.

"I accept it only as a loan. Soon . . . my child, I shall be able to return it to you. No . . . no, don't protest! I know this and it does not frighten me. Death has no terrors for me, rather the contrary . . . for it will give me back the loved ones whom I have mourned my whole life long . . . my dear husband, my little Michel whom you tried to save! And that will be well."

She remained silent for a moment, admiring the emerald which cast a deep, sea light upon her skin. Then she asked:

"And what happened to the fabulous black diamond?"

Catherine's face darkened slightly.

"I lost it and then I found it again. But it had already done a great deal of harm. I swear it will do no more!"

"How so?"

"In a few days' time I will go and offer the accursed jewel to the only one who has nothing to fear from its devilish powers."

"Is it really so evil?"

Catherine stood up, and her gaze went out beyond the walls of the little cell. Again, as on the previous occasion, she saw as in a vision the flaming walls of the leper-house at Calves. . . . Then she clenched her teeth so as not to cry out with pain, and murmured with a look of inexpressible hatred and horror:

"More than you realize. It has never stopped doing evil! It still does it, almost every single day, but I have a plan which will cancel its power. I shall chain the devil once more at the feet of the one who once stepped upon the serpent barefoot. On the cape of the Black Madonna at Puy the black diamond will be harmless."

There were tears now in Isabelle's eyes, but also a sort of quiet happiness.

"You were rightly destined for our family, Catherine. Almost by instinct you seem to have stumbled on the old tradition by which the châtelaines of Montsalvy would go to Puy, in times of war and danger, to implore divine help and offer their most beautiful jewels to the Madonna. Go, my daughter, you think as a true Montsalvy would!"

Catherine did not reply. There was no longer any need of words between Isabelle and herself. Silence was enough. For they understood each other now. At that very moment Abbot Bernard came into the sick woman's room to pay her his regular nightly visit. After kissing his pastoral ring Catherine withdrew, leaving them alone together. She was on her way to join Sara who was feeding Michel in the kitchen. But as she passed through the great hall the porter monk came running up.

"Dame Catherine," he cried. "Old Saturnin would like you to visit him at his home at once. He says it is a matter of importance."

In his capacity as bailiff of Montsalvy, Saturnin was in charge of recruiting workers for the reconstruction of the castle. Catherine assumed that some problem connected with this had arisen, and did not bother to warn Sara of her absence.

"Very well, I will go at once," she said. "Thank you, brother."

Casting a quick glance into the little mirror in her room to make certain that her blue fustian dress was tidy and her high white starched cap perfectly clean, Catherine went out of the gates and hurried towards the house in the near-by Grand Rue, where Saturnin lived. The peasants were returning from the fields now, for evening was drawing in, and it was the middle of the harvest season. For the first time in years nothing had stopped the wheat and oats from growing. They were all hastening to load the harvest on to carts and store it for winter. . . .

Catherine encountered happy groups of peasants in the streets, tanned faces smiling out from under their straw hats, blouses opened wide across their sweating chests. The women had kilted up their skirts and went barelegged, with winnowing flail or gleaner over one shoulder. They all greeted Catherine with a smile and a wave of their caps, or a bobbed curtsy and a merry "Good even to you, m'lady!" which warmed her heart. These good folk had taken her to their hearts for the sake of the suffering they shared, their common loss in Arnaud. . . . She was really at home now in Montsalvy!

The house belonging to Saturnin and Donatienne stood close to the southern gate of Montsalvy, and the square tower which guarded it. With its high gables it was one of the most imposing buildings in the town, almost rivaling a town merchant's house, and Donatienne kept it as clean as any Flemish housewife could have done. When Catherine arrived she found old Saturnin standing waiting on the threshold, both sleeves rolled up, cap in hand. His face was wrinkled with worry. So much so that his chin, which was somewhat prominent, nearly met his long nose. He greeted Catherine respectfully and gave her his arm to lead her into the house.

"There is a shepherd in there, Dame Catherine . . . he has just come here from Vieillevie, a village four leagues distant, in the Lot valley, and he has strange tales to tell. That is why I preferred not to take him as far as the abbey and sent for you, begging pardon for being so bold, to come here."

"You did well, Saturnin," Catherine replied, her breath coming a little faster as he mentioned the Lot valley. "What are his strange tales?"

"You are about to hear them. But first go in."

In the kitchen, where the pewter dishes gleamed on the dresser like silver, and the stone floor was so white it looked like velvet, a young lad, wearing a sheepskin coat over his rough clothes, was seated on a bench near the black chest-nut-wood table. He was eating bread and cheese, which Saturnin had doubtless given him, but he stood up politely when Catherine entered, bowed clumsily and then remained standing, waiting to be spoken to.

"This lad," Saturnin explained, "is one of the Lord of Vieillevie's shepherds. As for you, my friend, you find yourself before the Lady of Montsalvy. Tell her what you saw on Sunday morning."

The shepherd blushed a little, no doubt embarrassed by the presence of this great lady, and his voice was scarcely audible to begin with; but no sooner had he begun his tale than Catherine found herself enthralled.

"Sunday morning, I was watching my sheep on the plateau, a little way above the Garrigue . . ."

"Speak louder," Saturnin ordered; "it is hard to hear you."

The boy coughed and raised his voice.

"I saw two riders who seemed to come from Montsalvy. The first, who was tall and well-built, was dressed entirely in black: he even wore a black mask, but he rode a beautiful white mare. . . ."

"Morgane," Catherine murmured, "Morgane and . . ."

"The other was a thin, sallow little man, with fiery black eyes and a pointed beard. They stopped close by me, but it was the little man who spoke to me. The other . . . the rider with the mask, did not even open his mouth. He kept a little to one side, stroking his horse's neck, while it pawed the ground impatiently."

"What did the little man say?" Saturnin asked.

"He asked me if I knew the bailiff of Montsalvy, and I said that I had seen him two or three times, and that I was shepherd to the Lord of Vieillevie. Then the little sallow man asked if I would agree to take something to Master Saturnin, and if I could be trusted. I said yes, but that it would be necessary for me to come here first. As it happened I had some cheeses to sell. I said that I would come by some time during

319

the week. Then he asked me a question. He asked me if I could read. I said no . . ."

"Then?" Catherine asked, tormented by impatience. "What did he say?"

"Not much," the boy replied. "He took a roll of parchment from his pocket, folded it and sealed it and told me to take it to Master Saturnin as fast as possible. And he gave me a gold écu for my trouble!"

"Where is the letter?" Catherine asked.

"Here," said Saturnin, holding out the sealed missive which she took with a shaking hand.

"Haven't you opened it?"

"It wasn't my place to," said the bailiff, shaking his head. "Look at it. . . ."

And the few lines traced on the roll bore these words "For Dame Catherine de Montsalvy, on her return."

All at once Catherine felt as though the whitewashed walls were spinning about her. Those words—it was Arnaud himself, and no one else, who had written them! Instinctively she clutched the note to her heart, fighting against a rising tide of emotion. Saturnin noticed this and would have sent the shepherd away.

"You have done your task well, boy. Now go and rest."

But Catherine stopped him.

"Wait, I want to thank you, shepherd. . . ."

She searched in her purse, but the boy refused with a gesture.

"No, noble lady. I have already received my wage. Buy my cheeses if you will, but I shall accept nothing else."

"I will buy all your cheeses, child. And God bless you!" And with that she tipped the contents of her purse into the astonished boy's hands. He went out muttering blessings which she did not even hear. She was dying to be alone, to read the precious message. When the shepherd had gone she looked up at Saturnin.

"No one," she said, "must know the shepherd's tale, no one in Montsalvy. And especially not Dame Isabelle!"

"It must have been Messire Arnaud?"

"Yes, Saturnin, it was he! The leper-house at Calves burned down the other night. He must have escaped, by some miracle, but it would be better that she should not know about it. Only Donatienne, Sara and Gauthier may know."

"Have no fear. No one will know a thing. As far as everyone here is concerned, including the abbot, Messire Arnaud died at Calves. They will continue to believe this. Now I will leave you for a moment."

"Thank you, Saturnin . . . you are kind!"

He tiptoed out and carefully shut the door behind him. Catherine sat down on the immaculate hearth-stone and slowly unfolded the parchment. Her hands trembled with excitement and joy, but her eyes were so blurred with tears that at first she could scarcely decipher her husband's bold hand. She passed her hand over her eyes as if to tear off the veil which seemed to cover them.

"My God," she said, laughing nervously, "I shall never read it if I go on like this."

She took two or three deep breaths and wiped her eyes. This time the text was quite clear.

"Catherine" [said the parchment], "I have never been agile with my pen, but before disappearing forever, I wanted to bid you a last farewell, and wish you the happiness you deserve. You have found it now, so they tell me, and my good wishes are superfluous. For what am I but a living corpse, who still breathes and thinks, alas! But I still have the power to tell you that henceforward you are free, and that this is my wish and command!

Catherine's heart missed a beat. Her fingers clutched the parchment, but she forced herself bravely to read on. What came next was worse.

"The man you have chosen will give you everything I could not. He is brave, worthy of you. You will be rich, fêted, honored! But I, Catherine, I, dead thing that I am, have never succeeded in killing the love my heart holds for you, and I can no longer remain in this country once you have left it. What was tolerable while you were near is no longer so once you have gone. I don't want to perish like a rat in a hole, rotting in a cave somewhere. I want to die in the open . . . and alone. Fortunat, who has never stopped communicating with me, at the risk of his life and despite all my remonstrances, has helped me to escape. He will be my last friend on earth. . . .

"Do you remember that pilgrim we met together once? His name was Barnaby. I believe, and I can still hear him saying: 'Remember me, during the evil times which have yet to visit you, remember the old pilgrim of St. James of Compostela!' Do you remember, Catherine, how he recovered his sight at the apostle's tomb? . . . If God wills I shall be cured of my sickness too in Galicia. Afterwards I shall go to fight the infidel using a borrowed name. And if God's grace is not vouchsafed to the sinner that I am, I shall still find a way to meet death like a man.

"It is here that our ways must part. Forever. You journey on towards happiness and I go to meet my fate. Farewell, Catherine, my sweet. . . ."

The letter fell from Catherine's icy hands. In her heart there was a searing pain, mingled with rage, wild, torrential, murderous rage against De Breze. What damage his clattering tongue and protestations of passion had done! It had caused Isabelle's death, Arnaud's flight and Catherine's unendurable remorse! Arnaud had gone away, far, far away . . . believing her inconstant! He said that he still loved her and that that was why he was going . . . but how long could this love last now that it felt itself betrayed? She felt rage against herself too! How could she have forgotten the old pilgrim and the advice he had given them? Why hadn't she abandoned everything, including that far-fetched plan of vengeance of hers, in order to guide the man she loved towards a possible cure? Why had she not set off with him, months ago, to attempt the impossible? In her fury she forgot that Arnaud would never have allowed her to become involved in any such adventure. After all he had refused even to touch her for fear of contagion.

And then her anger melted away, and left nothing but pain. Catherine collapsed on the hearth and sobbed bitterly, desperately, calling his name between sobs. . . . The thought that Arnaud believed himself betrayed, forgotten, was unbearable. It seared her soul like a branding iron. . . . Horrified she saw herself swooning into Pierre de Breze's arms in the orchard at Chinon, and cursed herself furiously. But how dearly was she to have to pay for that moment of dire folly?

She lifted her head, found herself alone in this little room, trapped like a fly in a spider's web. Her eyes went desperately from door to window. She must flee too, she must set off at once in pursuit of Arnaud! She needed a horse, a swift horse. . . . She must fly over walls, over mountains and plains. . . . She must find him again! That was what she must do, at whatever cost; find him, throw herself at his feet, beg his forgiveness and never leave him again . . . never, never!

She ran to the door like a madwoman, opened it and cried:

"Saturnin! Saturnin! . . . Horses!"

"Dame, what is the matter?"

The old man came running up and at the sight of this red-eyed, disheveled woman, he instantly became alarmed:

"Lady, what is wrong?"

322

"I need a horse, Saturnin . . . straight away! I must leave at once. I must go after him!"

"Dame Catherine, night is falling, the gates are closing. . . . Where must you go?"

"I must find him—my Lord . . . Arnaud!"

She cried out the beloved name in despair. Saturnin shook his head and came towards her. He had never seen her so pale and shaken.

"You are trembling! . . . Come with me. I am going to take you back to the monastery. I don't know what has happened, but at all events it is too late to do anything about it tonight. You must rest. . . ."

He picked up the parchment, placed it gently in her hands as if she were a child, and led her outside. She allowed him to take charge, still protesting, however, like someone lost in a nightmare.

"You don't understand, Saturnin. I must catch up with him. . . . He has set off on such a long journey . . . and he means never to return!"

"He had already departed never to return, Dame Catherine. And he had departed on a journey from which there is no turning back. Come with me. At the monastery you will find Dame Isabelle, Gauthier, Sara. . . . They love you, and they will help you when they see you so deeply distressed. Come, Dame Catherine. . . ."

The cool evening air made Catherine feel better, and she calmed down a little. As she walked along, leaning against Saturnin, she managed to stop her mind revolving the same desperate thoughts, and she began to think more coherently. Was it not wise to reason it all out as coolly as possible and plan her next move? Saturnin was right when he said that Gauthier and Sara would help her. . . . But first she must calm her nerves, and not allow herself to think that Arnaud had parted from her forever, and severed the frail thread that bound them. . . .

She held up her head, trying to put a brave face on things for the benefit of those she met in the street. But when they reached the monastery they found the abbot himself standing on the threshold of the porter's lodge. . . .

"I was just going to send someone to fetch you, Dame Catherine. Your mother has had a relapse and lost consciousness. . . ."

"But she was so well a little while ago!"

"I know. We were chatting peacefully together when she suddenly fell back against the pillows, choking. . . . Sara and the apothecary are both with her."

Catherine was obliged to forget her own troubles and rush to the old lady's bedside. She valiantly put the fatal letter away in her purse and went to Isabelle. The sick woman was still unconscious. Sara bent over her trying to revive her with smelling salts, while the apothecary rubbed her temples with Hungary Water. Catherine leaned over her:

"Is she very bad?"

"She is coming round," Sara whispered, frowning. "But I really thought this was the end."

"In any case she won't last much longer," said the monk; "she is barely holding her own."

Isabelle was gradually returning to consciousness. With a sigh of relief Sara stood up and smiled at Catherine, but her smile as instantly vanished.

"Why, you are paler than she is! What has happened?"

"I know where Arnaud is," Catherine replied faintly. "You were right, Sara, when you warned me that if I listened to Pierre de Breze I would regret it all my life. Regret has not been slow in coming."

"Tell me what has happened."

"Not now. Later. Saturnin is waiting in the great hall. Tell him to stay. Go and find Gauthier too and ask the Reverend Father if he would kindly join us. I have serious things to discuss."

An hour later the council Catherine had convoked met, not in the guest-house, but in the monastery itself where the abbot had summoned them. Brother Eusebius guided the four of them, Catherine, Gauthier, Sara and Saturnin, across the church, which was still and silent at this late hour; only a faint light burned before the statue of Our Lady, to whom the foundation was dedicated. Then they entered the great hall. It was lit by four torches fixed to pillars which supported the vaulted ceiling. The abbot, a frail wraith of a man in his long black robe, was alone beside the abbot's throne. He walked slowly to and fro with his hands swallowed up in his voluminous sleeves, and head bowed beneath a shaved tonsure of fair hair. The torch light gave his yellow ascetic face the color of old ivory. He was both a man of action, who ruled his monastery with a firm hand, and a man of prayer. His love of God was immense, his life was without a stain, and, though his youth might force him to adopt a severe, even austere manner to enforce his authority, he concealed a warm heart and great compassion for mankind beneath that glacial front.

When he saw the others entering, he stopped pacing,

placed one foot on the step which led up to the throne and pointed to a stool for Catherine.

"Sit, daughter! You find me ready to hear your tale and give you my advice, as you requested."

"Many thanks, father, for I am sorely distressed. An unforeseen event has shattered my life. And I wanted to ask your help. These people here are my faithful servitors, from whom nothing is hidden."

"Speak. I am listening."

"First, I feel I must tell you the truth as to the supposed death of my husband, Arnaud de Montsalvy. It is time you knew . . ."

The abbot's pale hand gestured to Catherine to stop.

"Spare yourself the trouble, child! Dame Isabelle has already confided the painful secret to me, in the confessional. And now that you wish to speak of it, it is no longer a secret. . . ."

"Very well. Then, father, would you be so kind as to read this letter . . . and read it aloud. Gauthier here cannot read and Sara can barely do so."

Bernard de Calmont agreed, took the letter and began to read it. Catherine folded her hands and closed her eyes. The abbot's deep, slow voice lent the farewell words a heartbreaking charm and pathos, and she had to fight to control herself. Behind her she heard her companions' smothered exclamations. She did not open her eyes again till the abbot stopped reading.

Then she saw that all eyes were fixed upon her, and that the abbot's held an expression of profound compassion. Sara laid a reassuring hand on her shoulder.

"What advice is it you seek, daughter," the abbot asked, "and what help?"

"I am going after him, father. Despite the sorrow I shall feel at parting from my child, who is all I have left in the world, I must go in search of his father! A dreadful misunderstanding has come between us. I cannot bear it. Messire de Breze believed in good faith, because I was friendly towards him, that I would agree to become his wife. But he did not know the truth and could not know that nothing on earth could ever induce me to bear another name but Montsalvy. He acted rashly, but he was in love . . . and he has brought about this appalling disaster. I want to ask you to take care of my son and watch over him like a father, to take my place as Lord of Montsalvy, and supervise the rebuilding of the castle. My servants will remain here . . . but I must leave!"

"Where will you go? In pursuit of him?"

"Of course. I don't want to lose him forever. . . ."

"He already is lost forever!" the abbot said severely. "He turns towards God. Why seek to bring him down to earth again? Leprosy shows no mercy towards its victims."

"Unless God wills! Must I remind you, father, that miracles can happen? How do you know that he will not be cured at the tomb of St. James, in Galicia?"

"Let him go there then. But alone!"

"And if he were cured. Must I let him set out to fight the infidel and meet his death in some faraway land?"

"What else did wives do during the Crusades?"

"Some wives went with their husbands. For my part I want to find the man I love," Catherine cried, with a note of such passion in her voice that the abbot turned away, wrinkling his brows slightly.

"And . . . if he were not cured?" the abbot said at last. "It is a rare sign of grace, and one not easily won."

There was silence. Till then Catherine and the abbot had given question and answer in rapid, staccato succession, like the clashing steel of two duelists. But the abbot's last words summoned up the great terror which all felt for the accursed sickness. A shiver ran down their spines. Catherine got up and went towards the great crucifix which hung on the wall.

"If he is not cured I shall stay with him and live as long as he lives, and die of his sickness, but I shall stay with him!" she said firmly, eyes fixed upon the cross as if to summon it as a witness to her words.

"God forbids suicide! To live with a leper is to court death knowingly," the abbot objected dryly.

"I would rather die with him than live without him . . . and I do not even fear damnation, if it is offensive to God merely to love someone more than oneself."

The abbot's voice rang out while his thin hand was raised towards heaven.

"Silence! Human passion causes you to offend God even more surely! Repent, if you would be saved, and remember that the cries of carnal passion offend God's purity!"

"Forgive me, but I cannot lie when something which affects my whole life is concerned, and I cannot speak otherwise! Tell me one thing, father. Do you agree to replace me at Montsalvy, protect my people, and act as both lord and abbot till my return?"

"No!"

The word rang out, precise and final.

Again there was silence. Behind Catherine the three silent

witnesses to this scene held their breath. The young woman looked at the thin, severe face disbelievingly.

"No? . . . But why . . . father?"

It was a cry of real pain. Slowly, she sank to her knees, holding out both hands in an instinctive gesture of supplication.

"Why?" she asked brokenly. "Let me go! If I lose my love forever my heart will stop beating of its own accord. I could not live!"

The rigid features softened into an expression of profound compassion and understanding. Bernard de Calmont came towards the young woman, stooped and gently raised ner to her feet.

"Because you cannot leave just yet, daughter. You think only of your human passion, and your legitimate . . . and possibly merited . . . regret and remorse. Did you not encourage that young man to hope that you might love him? No, don't answer me. But tell me this—does this love of yours make you cruel, is there no room in that heart of yours for pity for anyone else?"

"What do you mean?"

"Just this: I will not mention your son, who should detain you here by rights, but would you leave that old woman to die alone, without your comfort and love? Would you abandon that mother whose suffering, doubtless, is still greater than yours, since somewhere in your heart you still nurse a secret hope of seeing him again? Whereas she knows that she never will. . . . Would you be capable of such cruelty?"

Catherine hung her head. In her despair she had forgotten Isabelle slowly passing away in the narrow monastic cell. Her heart had only trembled for Michel. It had been he who caused her painful indecision; he alone could have held her back. She had not thought of the old lady. She was ashamed of herself now. But behind the reproaches of her conscience she still heard the voice of her love speak loud and clear. No one else meant anything to her when it came to Arnaud. However, she acknowledged defeat gracefully.

"No, you are right," she said. She turned to seek the comfort of Sara's arms which clasped her protectively. She added, with a sigh, "I will remain."

Then Gauthier's rough voice spoke up.

"You must stay, Dame Catherine, for the sake of the child and the dying woman. But I am free, if you give me your permission to leave! I can go in pursuit of Messire Arnaud! Who could stop me?" He turned towards the abbot, towering above him by a head. "Give me a horse and an axe, man of

God. I am not afraid of the highways, nor of long days in the saddle!"

Catherine, revived by this explosive interruption, turned gratefully towards the tall Norman.

"It's true . . . there is you! You could find him and tell him that I never betrayed him . . . but even so he would never agree to come back to me, I know that. No one has ever succeeded in making him change his mind."

"I could do my best. At least you would find your duty less bitter then. If Messire Arnaud is cured, I shall bring him back, by force if necessary! If not . . . I shall return alone! Do you permit me to go?"

"How could I refuse? You are my only hope. . . ."

"Very well, then, let us be off!" cried Gauthier, who despised words like all men of action. "We have already wasted enough time. Have them open the town gates for me, and find me a horse. By Odin, I'll find him all right . . . even if I have to chase him as far as Mahomet!"

"This is the house of God," the abbot cried indignantly. "False idols have no place here! Come with me, Catherine my child . . . we will go to ask Our Lady's protection for this great barbarian who does not even recognize her existence! And then we shall send him off together. . . . I will help you!"

An hour later Catherine stood between Sara and Saturnin by the gate to Montsalvy, listening to Gauthier's hoof-beats receding into the distance. Provided with some provisions, stout clothes, a full purse and a large and powerful horse, the Norman was launched in full pursuit of Arnaud and Fortunat.

When the sound had died away in the starry night, Catherine drew her dark cloak more tightly about herself and searched for the pale trail of the Milky Way above her head. In those times it was known as the Way of St. James. Then she sighed.

"Will he ever find him? Those southern lands will be as strange to him as the country of the Great Khan."

"Monseigneur the abbot told him to follow the way which was marked with cockleshells," said Saturnin. "And he taught him the names of the first stopping-places, since he could not write them for him," Saturnin continued. "You must have courage, Dame Catherine! Even though he does not believe in them I am confident that Madame the Virgin and Monseigneur St. James will watch over Gauthier! They never abandon those whose greatheartedness sends them wandering the pilgrim ways."

"He is right," Sara scolded her. "Gauthier is strong, intelligent and cunning. And he has enough faith in himself to move mountains! Now come, let us return! Dame Isabelle needs us both. And you will find the courage to persevere in your duty when you embrace your child!"

Catherine did not answer. She silenced the sigh of regret which rose in her and went silently towards the abbey. But she knew very well that she had merely bowed before superior reason and that her desire to be off in pursuit of Arnaud would not be stifled so easily! She sat for long hours that night rocking Michel in her arms, and trying to warm her sore heart with her love for the child.

CHAPTER SIXTEEN

The Minstrel

Isabelle de Montsalvy died the day after the feast of St. Michel, without pain or agony, almost peacefully. She had known one last joy, on the eve of her death: that of seeing her grandson receive the homage of his vassals for the first time. . . .

Saturnin, in his capacity as bailiff, and in agreement with the notables of Montsalvy, had decided that the child should be officially recognized as lord of the little city on the occasion of his name day. Now that the King had returned their titles and possessions to the Montsalvy family, the date of the 29th September had struck the good man as ideally suited for the occasion, especially since it coincided with the shepherds' feast-day, when all the shepherds of the region gathered on the plateau of Montsalvy.

That day a dais was set up in the town square, outside the church door, dressed and decorated in the Montsalvy family colors. After a solemn mass, at which Abbot Bernard officiated, Michel and his mother took their places there to receive the homage of their vassals, all dressed in their finest clothes for the occasion. Saturnin, dressed in brown wool, with a silver chain about his neck, presented them an offering of wheat and grapes upon a cushion. He made a fine, slightly muddled speech, which the inhabitants of Montsalvy judged eloquent to a degree, and then all the people of the town came forward, one by one, to kiss Michel's little hand. The child laughed with pleasure, delighted with the fine white velvet suit in which Sara had dressed him, but even more pleased with the chain of gold and topazes which his mother had fastened about his neck. The ceremony went on a little too long perhaps for a little lord who was not quite two years old. But the shepherds' dances and wrestling bouts which followed delighted him beyond measure. He stood up in his chair, despite all his mother's efforts to hold him still, and jumped about like a little devil. From nearby his grandmother, who had been carried out on a stretcher covered with rugs, so that she might witness the ceremony, watched him adoringly. . . .

The day ended with a great celebration bonfire, lit on the plateau by Michel himself, with Catherine guiding his hand. And then, while boys and girls sang and danced upon the green grass, to the sound of pipes, the new Lord of Montsalvy was borne off to bed exhausted by the day's excitement. He fell asleep in a moment, his blond head nestled in Sara's warm shoulder.

All night long Catherine listened to her vassals dancing and singing, delighted with their mirth which even her own somber mourning could not dim. She had hidden her own deep sadness all that day so that they should not know how cruel this occasion seemed to her. Michel's accession seemed to push his father into the past, this father of whom no one had heard a word for the past month and a half. . . .

The following morning the good people of Montsalvy, who had gone to their beds happy and full of contentment, but very late, were awakened by the lugubrious tolling of the funeral bell and thus learned that their old châtelaine had passed away. . . .

Sara had gone in that morning to take her a bowl of milk and found her dead in her bed. Isabèlle lay quite straight and still, with her eyes shut and her hands fastened upon her rosary; a ray of sunlight sparkled on Queen Yolande's emerald which she still wore on her pale hands. Sara stood for an instant on the threshold, struck dumb by the dead woman's extraordinary beauty. The ravages of illness had vanished, and her face was relaxed and smooth, looking infinitely younger than it had the day before. Her white hair framed it, hanging in two thick white plaits, and the resemblance to her son was quite striking.

Sara crossed herself. Then she set down her bowl of milk and went into Catherine, who, towards dawn, had at last fallen asleep. She shook her gently. The young woman sat up abruptly and stared at her with wide startled eyes as she explained gently:

"Dame Isabelle's sufferings are over, Catherine . . . you must get up. I shall go and tell the abbot. Meanwhile take Michel from the room next door and hand him over to Donatienne. Death is not a sight for small children!"

Catherine obeyed her like a sleepwalker. She had been awaiting this moment ever since she returned. She knew the old lady longed for death as a deliverance, and reason whispered that there was no cause for sorrow, that Isabelle had found peace at last. But reason was powerless against the sudden grief which tore at her. . . . She was discovering that Isabelle's presence was more precious to her than she had ever realized. As long as Arnaud's mother was living, there was someone with whom Catherine could talk about him, someone who knew him even better than she did, and whose memories of him were inexhaustible. And now the soft voice was silent, and her own solitude seemed the more dreadful. . . . Arnaud had vanished, Gauthier had been swallowed up by the unknown for more than a month, and now it was Isabelle's turn. . . .

When she and Sara had laid the dead woman out, they both stood for a moment at the foot of the bed where she lay, dressed in the religious habit of the Sisters of Clare in which she had expressed a wish to be buried. The austerity of the flowing black robes gave her a look of extraordinary majesty and her eyes, beneath the violet lids, seemed just about to open. . . .

As they dressed her in the habit, Catherine had very gently slipped off the chiseled emerald, whose profane splendor seemed ill at ease with the nun's habit. Then, together with Sara, she contemplated the dead woman for a long while before kneeling for the first prayers, just as the abbot arrived, preceded by two acolytes carrying censer and holy water.

The three days which followed unrolled like a mournful dream for Catherine. The corpse lay in state in the church choir, with four monks keeping vigil. But Catherine, Sara and Donatienne took turns kneeling on the cushion at the foot of the catafalque. For Catherine these long hours of vigil in the silent church had something strangely unreal about them. The monks standing about the body, with their hoods pulled down over the top half of their faces and their hands hidden in their flowing sleeves, looked like phantoms, and the wavering light from the huge yellow wax candles gave their immobility a sinister touch. Catherine forced herself to pray so as to keep off this sense of unease, but the words did not come easily . . . she had forgotten how to speak to God. She found it easier to speak quite simply to the dead woman.

"Mother," she whispered softly, "everything must be so much simpler and easier where you are now! Help me! . . . Make him come back or at least let him know that I have never stopped loving him! I am so unhappy!"

But the wax face remained quite still and the half-smile on her lips did not yield up its mystery. Catherine's heart grew heavier as the time passed.

On the eve of the third day, the body of Isabelle de Ventadour, Lady of Montsalvy, was placed in the family tomb in

332

the presence of the whole village. Behind the wooden grille of their cloisters, the abbey monks chanted the Miserere. And Catherine, whose habitual mourning took on a double meaning tonight, watched the slender form of the woman, who thirty-five years before had given birth to her own adored husband, disappear forever beneath the stone floor of the church. . . .

As she left the sanctuary the young woman's eyes met those of the abbot who had sung the Requiem mass. She read a look there which was both question and prayer, but she turned her head away as if to avoid replying. What was the good? Isabelle's death had not freed her. Michel's little hands clutched her more strongly than ever. And she had no reason to leave him now, since Gauthier had gone to find Arnaud. Until she had news of him, she must stay here and wait . . . wait!

Autumn set the mountain blazing with crimson and gold. The countryside round Montsalvy flamed with color, while the clouds sank lower in the sky and swift black flights of swallows sped by towards the south. Catherine followed them with her eyes from the monastery towers, until they disappeared. With each flight that passed overhead she felt a little more sad and dispirited. She found herself envying those carefree birds with all her heart, flying southwards in search of sun to the lands whither she longed to follow!

The days had never dragged by so leadenly or monotonously. Every afternoon, if the weather were fine enough, Catherine went with Sara and Michel to the south gate where monks and peasants had begun to dig out the foundations for the new château. On the abbot's advice she had decided not to reconstruct the castle where it had stood formerly, on the flanks of the Puy de l'Arbre, but right beside the gates of Montsalvy. The ravages inflicted by the brigand Vallette were still all too present in everyone's minds.

The two women always stood for a while on the site of the castle and then went a bit further on to watch the woodcutters at work. Now that the threat of the English had gone, everyone was at work reclaiming the land which had gone wild during the times of great distress. The shrub, which had so often provided them with a hiding-place, had overgrown everything. It had to be cut down before the lands could return to crops of wheat and pasturage. But Catherine's eyes always wandered afar off, to the deep blue distances beyond the dark line of trees, where Arnaud had disappeared. Then, holding

Michel's little hand tightly in her own, she walked slowly back home.

Then one night the wind came down like a wolf and the trees were stripped of their leaves. And the following night the land was covered with snow. The clouds were so low they seemed to touch the earth, and the icy mists which clung to the countryside every morning took a long time to clear. It was winter and Montsalvy went to sleep; work on the castle stopped and everyone in the town huddled in the warmth of their own homes. Catherine and Sara did likewise. The monastery life, regulated by the tolling bell, became a desperate monotony which succeeded nevertheless in softening and soothing Catherine's grief. Day followed day, each the same as the one before. They spent the time spinning at the corner of the hearth, watching Michel playing on a coverlet on the floor. The countryside remained spotlessly white and Catherine began to doubt whether it would ever change. Would spring return one day?

Each day she forced herself to go out for a walk. She put snowshoes on her feet, wrapped herself in a thick cape with a hood and left the monastery to take a walk, always the same one. She went a little way beyond the southern gate. Then she sat down on an old wall where, impervious to the gusts of wind and eddies of snow, she remained for a long time, staring at the road which traveled up from the Lot, watching an undying hope of seeing a familiar shape traveling along it. It was so long now since Gauthier had gone! . . . It would be three months by the time Christmas came! And no one had brought so much as a word from him in all that time. He might have dissolved into that great white expanse out there. . . . When night began to close in Catherine slowly returned home, a little heavier in spirit, a little less hopeful.

Christmas came and went without bringing relief. She thought incessantly about the ones who were not there. Arnaud first of all! He must have reached Compostela in Galicia by now. But had he obtained the miraculous cure he had hoped for? And Gauthier? Had he managed to catch up with the fugitives? Were they all together somewhere now, just as they were in her mind? She brooded on these and similar questions and it was torture not to have an answer.

"When spring comes," she promised herself, "and there is still no news of them . . . I shall go myself . . . I shall go to find them. . . ."

"If they come back it will not be before spring," Sara told her one day when Catherine absentmindedly spoke her thoughts aloud. "No one would try to cross the mountains

334

while the roads are deep in snow. Winter sets up obstacles which even the hardiest will and most obstinate love could not hope to cross. You must wait!"

"Wait! Wait! I'm always waiting! I can't stand this endless waiting!" Catherine cried. "Must I see the rest of my life slip away in waiting for something which never happens?"

Sara preferred not to answer questions like those. It was better to let the conversation drop, or talk about something else, because trying to reason with Catherine only seemed to increase her misery. The gypsy did not believe that Arnaud could be cured. No one had ever heard of leprosy relinquishing its victims. It was astonishing enough that St. Meen de Jaleyrac, the patron saint of this particular dreadful malady, should still have clients. St. James of Compostela was renowned for miracle working, but Sara's Christianity was still too strongly colored by paganism for her to place much confidence in miracles. On the other hand she was convinced that unless some fatal accident befell him, they would sooner or later hear from Gauthier. But still, when she saw Catherine's small, black silhouette setting off across the snow to see if he were not coming along the valley road, she could not help sighing.

One evening in February as Catherine reached her observation post after a painful time of being shut up at home by the weather, she suddenly seemed to distinguish a dark speck against the white road, a speck which seemed to be growing slowly larger as it passed along between the black pine trees. She leaped to her feet, her heart thumping painfully, catching her breath. . . . It really was a man and he was climbing up from the valley. He was coming on foot, and making painfully slow progress, his back bent against the icy wind. . . . She ran forward a little way, but when she reached the fringe of trees she stopped disappointedly. It was not Gauthier . . . and still less Arnaud. The man, whom she could see quite clearly now, was short, thin and very dark. For a moment she thought it might be Fortunat, but then this hope too vanished. The traveler was a total stranger to her!

He wore a green hat, whose brim was turned down in front and up behind over a plume which was little more than a quill and a few wisps of feather, but the brown face below it had bright, lively eyes, and the wide sinuous mouth smiled cheerfully on seeing that it was a woman who stood by the wayside. Catherine saw that his back was distorted by a square object which he was carrying under his cloak.

"A peddler," Catherine thought, "or a minstrel. . . ."

She decided upon the latter when he drew nearer. He wore

a green and red costume under his cloak, a bright and cheerful, though somewhat shabby outfit. The man swept off his faded hat in a bow.

"Woman," he said in a thick foreign accent, "what is the name of this place if you please?"

"Montsalvy. Is that where you wish to go, sir minstrel?"

"It's where I plan to go tonight. But, by Our Lady, if all the peasant lasses are as fair as you, this Montsalvy must be a veritable Paradise!"

"Alas, it is no Paradise," Catherine replied, amused by the young man's accent. "And if you were hoping to be welcomed to a château, you will be disappointed, sir minstrel. The château of Montsalvy no longer exists. You will only find an ancient abbey where they sing few songs of love."

"I know," said the minstrel. "But though there may be no castle there is a châtelaine. Do you know the Lady of Montsalvy? She is the fairest lady in the world, so they tell me . . . though I reckon she might find it hard to surpass you!"

"You will be disappointed then," Catherine said. "I am the Lady of Montsalvy."

The smile vanished from the traveler's merry face. Once more he swept off his faded cap and knelt in the snow.

"Most noble and very gracious lady, forgive my ignorant familiarity."

"You could not have known. Not many châtelaines venture upon the roads in this weather, especially alone!"

Just then, as if to underline her words, a rough gust of wind blew the minstrel's cap off and forced Catherine to shelter against a tree.

"Don't stay here," she said, "the weather is terrible and the night is closing in. The castle is in ruins but the monastery guest-house where I live will provide you with food and shelter for the night. How is it you know my name?"

The minstrel stood up and dusted off his thin knees. He was frowning worriedly and his gay smile had vanished.

"A man I met in the high mountains of the south spoke to me of you, noble lady. . . . He was very tall and mightily strong! A real giant! He told me his name was Gauthier Strongitharm. . . ."

Catherine gave an exclamation of relief and joy and seized the minstrel unceremoniously by the arm to make him walk faster.

"Gauthier sent you? Oh, then you are truly blessed, whoever you may be. How is he? Where was he when you met him?"

She hurried towards the village, pulling the minstrel—who seemed more uneasy every moment—along with her. They went through the gates and as Saturnin appeared at the window of his house she cried out to him:

"This man has seen Gauthier. He brings news!"

The old bailiff came out to greet them with a cry of joy. The minstrel looked at them both with a sort of terror.

"By heaven, noble lady," he groaned, "you have not even given me time to tell you my name and . . ."

"Tell me what it is then," Catherine cried gaily. "For me you will always be Gauthier. . . ."

The man shook his head miserably.

"They call me Guido Cigala. . . . I come from Florence, the beautiful city, but I wanted to pray at the tomb of the apostle in Galicia in penance for my many sins. . . . Lady," he begged, "do not welcome me so warmly or show so much joy! The news I bring is not good."

Catherine and Saturnin stopped dead in the middle of the road. The happy color which had risen in Catherine's cheeks gave way to a tragic pallor.

"Oh," was all she said. Her eyes went from the minstrel to Saturnin, anxiously, almost imploringly. Then she took hold of herself and flung back her head proudly.

"Good or bad, you still need rest and food. Your welcome is still the same, sir minstrel. But tell me this: how is Gauthier?"

Guido Cigala hung his head, like a guilty man.

"Lady," he murmured, "I fear that he is dead!"

"Dead!"

The cry broke simultaneously from Catherine and Saturnin. It was the old man who voiced the thought uppermost in their minds.

"It isn't possible! Gauthier cannot be dead!"

"I did not say I was certain of the fact," Cigala said contritely, "I said I feared it was true."

"You must tell us all about it," Catherine interrupted. "Now let us go in."

Back at the guest-house Sara took charge of the traveler, washed his sore feet, served him hot soup, bread and cheese and a cup of wine, before sending him in to the great hall where Catherine was waiting, with Saturnin and Donatienne. The laws of hospitality had to take precedence over her natural impatience. She smiled sadly on seeing that the minstrel carried his harp in one hand.

"It is a long time since a song was heard here," she said softly. "And I have not the heart for music now."

"Music comforts the soul, especially when it is downcast," Guido said, placing his instrument on a bench. "But first I will answer your questions."

"When, and where, did you see Gauthier?"

"It was on the mountain range of Ibañeta, some way before the guest-house at Roncevaux. I slipped into a ravine and Gauthier came to my assistance. We spent the night together in a mountain shelter. I told him I was returning to my own country, but that I would be stopping at all the castles I met along the way. He asked me then if I could come as far as this to bring you news. Naturally, I agreed. After the service he had rendered me, I could refuse him nothing. And besides, for those like me, a little more traveling makes little difference! . . . Then he gave me a message."

"What was it?" Catherine asked, bending forward eagerly.

"He said, 'Tell Dame Catherine that the white horse is only a little way ahead. I hope to catch up with it tomorrow. . . .'"

"Was that all?"

"That was all. Or rather that was all he told me, but then something happened. We separated the next morning. He was to continue along the road whence I had come, and I went on towards Roncevaux, but my road wound uphill and I was able to see your friend for a long time, noble lady. He rode quietly along. And then just as he was about to vanish from sight the drama happened. . . . I must tell you that the inhabitants of that region are fierce, uncouth people, and the place swarms with brigands. They did not attack me because no doubt they decided I was not worth their attentions. But the tall traveler was well-dressed, well mounted. . . . I watched as, hidden by rocks, they gathered about him; then they swarmed like a cloud of wasps. He defended himself magnificently, but there were too many of them. I saw him fall beneath their blows, and then, while one seized the horse, and another the baggage, three men stripped the body and flung it into one of those bottomless ravines whose sight alone is enough to terrify you. . . . He must have already been dead, or the fall must have killed him. But I cannot *swear* that he was dead!"

"And you did not go back?" Saturnin asked indignantly. "You did not even try to find out whether the man who had helped you was still alive, or really dead as you imagined?"

The minstrel shook his head, shrugged and made a hopeless gesture.

"The bandits' lair must have been quite near because they stayed where they were, no doubt awaiting more travelers.

What could I have done, alone and weak, against those savages? And the precipice was alarming enough. How could I have got down it? Lady," he said, turning towards Catherine with a beseeching look, "I beg you to believe that if there had been anything I could have done for your servitor, or your friend, I would have done it even at the risk of my life. Guido Cigala is no coward . . . please believe me."

"I believe you, sir minstrel, I believe you," Catherine said wearily. "There was nothing you could do, I quite see that . . . but you will forgive me if I give way to my grief before you. Gauthier was my servitor, you see, but his life was far more precious to me than that of my most intimate friend and the thought that he is no more . . ."

Emotion cut short her speech. Her eyes were dimmed by tears and her throat was too tight to speak another word. She rushed from the hall to her room and then threw herself down on her bed and burst into desperate sobs. This time it was all over, finished! She had lost everything. With Gauthier's death her last hope of seeing Arnaud again was gone. Whether he were cured or not her husband would never know that she had remained faithful to him, and that her love for him was greater than it had ever been. . . .

He had vanished as finally from her life now as if the tomb had closed over his head. It was the final blow for Catherine. . . .

She wept for long hours unaware that Sara was with her, standing by the bed, silent and powerless for once to ease her terrible grief. At last Sara ventured:

"Maybe the minstrel did not see as clearly as he thinks. . . . Maybe Gauthier is not dead."

"How could he have escaped with his life?" Catherine said with a nervous catch in her voice. "And if he wasn't dead already he cannot have lived long. . . ."

Silence fell again. Far off, in the great hall, they heard the soft lilting strains of the viol, which was being played for some of the servants, for Donatienne and Saturnin, and also for some of the notables of Montsalvy who had asked for permission to come and hear the wandering minstrel, a pleasure they had not enjoyed for a long time past. The Florentine's supple, well-rounded voice reached the cell where the two women stood facing each other, without finding anything to say. Guido was singing an old roundelay of the loves of Tristan and Queen Yseut:

"Yseut, my lady, Yseut, my fair,
In thee my life, in thee my death . . ."

Catherine stifled a sob. Beyond the minstrel's plaintive song, she seemed to hear Arnaud's warm passionate voice whispering in her ear, "Catherine . . . Catherine, my sweet . . ." and the sorrow which pierced her was so sharp that she had to clench her teeth to keep back a cry of pain. If she were never to see her love again on this earth it would be better to quit this world at once than drag out a lifetime of suffering. . . . She closed her eyes for a moment, twisted her hands together, and then opened her eyes and looked at Sara with an air of quiet determination.

"Sara," she said, in such a calm voice that the gypsy-woman jumped, "I am going to leave. Now that Gauthier is dead, I will have to go in search of my husband myself."

"In search? But where?"

"Where I know he certainly has gone: to Compostela in Galicia. And along the way I shall try to find the corpse of that unfortunate Gauthier so that it can at least receive decent burial. I cannot bear the thought that he should be left to the vultures."

"But the road is long and dangerous. How could you succeed, my pretty one? How could you hope to succeed where Gauthier failed?"

"The Holy Day of Easter is not far off. There is a tradition that on that day a group of pilgrims leaves Puy en Velay to journey to the tomb of St. James. I shall go with them. That way there will be less danger and I shall not be alone!"

"And me?" Sara cried defiantly. "Am I not to go then?"

Catherine shook her head negatively. She stood up, laid both hands on her dear friend's shoulders and looked at her fondly.

"No, Sara. . . . This time I shall go alone. For the first time, really the first time—because our quarrel at Chinon does not count—I shall set off without you! But that is only because I need you to look after the most precious thing I have in the world . . . my little Michel! If you were to come who would look after him? Donatienne is too old and Saturnin is not young. They will help you a great deal, but it is to you that I confide my son. You are so much a part of me, Sara, that I know he will be happy with you, as happy and well looked after as if I were there too. You will be my mind, my hands and my lips to him. You will talk to him of me and of his father. And if God wills it that I should not return . . ."

"Hush!" Sara cried. "I forbid you to talk like that . . . it hurts me too much. . . ."

She had tears in her eyes. Catherine embraced her warmly.

340

"Being forearmed against everything does not kill anyone, Sara. If I should not return you must send messengers to Xaintrailles and to Bernard d'Armagnac, and ask them to take over the education of the last of the Montsalvys and bring him up. But," she went on with a brave smile, "I am certain I shall return."

Sara wiped her eyes angrily, and then went a little way away from Catherine.

"Very well then," she grumbled. "We agree that I should stay and you should go. But how will you leave Montsalvy? Do you believe the abbot will allow you to go now any more easily than he did in September?"

"He will not know I have gone. I decided long ago that I must go to Puy to offer Our Lady the accursed diamond which I still have in my possession. I must get rid of it. . . . It is absolutely essential, and the sooner I can the better! See how the misfortunes are piling up! Gauthier, my messenger, my only hope, Gauthier the indestructible, has been felled by the wayside. My cause will be ill-starred as long as I have that diamond. The abbot knows that I am anxious to complete my vow. He will let me go. The Easter holidays are a good time to pay my respects to Our Lady. He will think my desire quite natural."

"You have an answer for everything," Sara cried, a little bitterly. "I find it hard to believe you thought this plan up all in a moment, after that accursed minstrel arrived. . . ."

"No, I have been thinking of it for a long time," Catherine admitted. "But will you do what I ask of you?"

Sara shrugged and started to turn back the coverlets for the warming-pan.

"What a question! It would be the very first time I had ever refused you anything. And I suppose there really is no alternative. . . . But God knows what it costs me none the less. . . ."

As Sara opened the door to take her basin into the kitchen Guido Cigala's voice filled the little room. Now he was singing an old song by the troubadour Arnaud Daniel, and the words of the old lay made such an impression on both women that they stood there not moving for a moment, looking at each other.

"Gold will cost no more than iron
The day Arnaud forswears his ladylove. . . ."

Catherine suddenly had the air of someone who had been struck by lightning. She was ashen to the lips, but there were

341

stars kindling in her dark eyes, the shining stars of hope. The minstrel's voice seemed to have answered the questions she no longer dared to ask. Sara clutched her utensil against her crossly.

"I'd like to know who sent that damned singer here? The Devil? Or God? In any case his voice is singularly like that of Fate herself. . . ."

Catherine had guessed aright in supposing that the abbot of Montsalvy would not prevent her from going to Puy en Velay for the Easter week feasts. He merely offered her the monastery porter, Brother Eusebius, as an escort, for it was unseemly that a noble lady should travel the roads alone. The company of a monk would protect her from dangers both terrestrial and spiritual.

"Brother Eusebius is a gentle and peaceful fellow," said the abbot, "but he will be a good protection for you none the less."

It must be said that Catherine was not enchanted with the company of the worthy porter. His round pink face looked too honest, and she had learned to mistrust everyone and everything. She asked herself if Abbot Bernard, in making him her bodyguard, were not also posting a sort of spy beside her, who might turn into a new problem. How, once she reached Puy, was she to get rid of the good man?

But the difficulties of her past life had taught the young woman that each day is sufficient unto itself, and that nothing is gained by tormenting oneself in advance. Once she was there she would find a way of tricking her guardian angel. Now she thought of nothing but this great journey of hers, undertaken more in love than hope.

The Lent weather finally cracked the white crust over the countryside with explosive force. Snow and ice melted into a network of tiny rivulets which darted this way and that, streaking the hillsides and mountain ravines like a net of silver thread. The earth appeared again, first in dark patches, then in great stretches which slowly, timidly grew green again. A touch of blue relieved the eternal gray cloud expanse of the sky, and Catherine decided that the time had come to set out.

The Wednesday after Passion Sunday, Catherine and Brother Eusebius left Montsalvy, both riding mules the abbot had lent them. The weather was mild, slightly drizzling, and the clouds ran swiftly, driven by a southerly wind, the wind which, according to Saturnin, "puts flesh on the sheep." . . .

Sara and Catherine had said farewell rapidly. Both, in tacit

342

agreement, avoided the sort of tenderness which saps courage and softens resolutions. And besides too agonized leave-takings would only have served to arouse the suspicions of Abbot Bernard. One does not weep for a separation of two weeks. . . .

The hardest thing was parting with little Michel. Catherine's eyes were heavy with unshed tears as she kissed and hugged her little boy. She had the impression that her arms would never be able to relinquish him. Sara had to take him and carry him off to Donatienne. The child was infected by his mother's agitation and began to cry, without realizing why.

"When will I see him again?" Catherine murmured, suddenly feeling intensely miserable. Her misery was so great that it would not have taken much to make her give up the whole expedition.

"When you wish!" Sara said calmly. "No one will stop you returning if you don't succeed in carrying out your plan. And I beg you, Catherine, don't tempt fate! Don't overtax yourself. There are occasions when it is wiser to accept one's destiny, cruel as it may be. Remember that even though I may be here, no one can replace a mother! If the obstacles are too great come back, I beg you! For the love of God. . . ."

"For the love of God," Catherine cut in, smiling through her tears, "don't say another word! Otherwise in five minutes' time I shall have completely lost heart."

But when the abbey gates opened for the mules to pass through, Catherine had an extraordinary, almost intoxicating feeling of freedom. She was not afraid of what was to come. Her will must triumph over every obstacle. She felt stronger, younger and braver than ever. . . .

She carried the diamond in a little skin purse slung round her neck on a ribbon. It had lost almost all its value in her eyes. But it had this virtue: by offering it to the Virgin of Puy she could open up the long road which might eventually lead her to her husband.

When the walls of Montsalvy were out of sight she pulled the folds of her heavy cape closer about her shoulders, with the traditional gesture of a peddler shifting a heavy pack. Then she flung back her head, ignoring the bells which seemed to be accompanying her on her journey, and set her mule trotting over the short-cropped grass of the wayside, staring before her dry-eyed and resolute.

343

CHAPTER SEVENTEEN

The Final Link

The Puy en Velay! A town which flowed like a gigantic, multi-colored stream from the porch of the immense Roman church, with its crown of towers and cupolas. When Catherine and Brother Eusebius arrived, they paused for a moment to contemplate the amazing spectacle which presented itself to their eyes. Catherine's marveling gaze went from the holy hill, the ancient Mont Anis, which stood out against the blue distances of the surrounding countryside, to the huge rock which kept it company, and to the volcanic peak of St. Michel d'Aiguilhe a little way off, which pointed proudly towards heaven like a finger, crowned by its little chapel. Everything in this strange city seemed created to serve God. Everything came from him and returned to him. . . . But as they passed through the gates and made their way towards the center of the town, they were struck by the vivid decoration of the streets and the hurly-burly which reigned there. On all sides banners and pennants fluttered from roof-tops, great lengths of colored silk and tapestries hung from windows overlooking the street. . . . Everywhere the French royal coat-of-arms was in evidence. With a feeling of bewilderment Catherine watched a noisy group of Scots bowmen push past, dragging their arms behind them.

"The town is celebrating something!" said Brother Eusebius, who had not spoken all that day. "But what?"

Catherine had cultivated silence in his company. She decided there was no point in answering him, but she hailed a small boy who was running past with a pitcher, on his way to the nearby spring.

"Why all these banners and silk hangings, and all these people?"

The child looked at Catherine with a saucy freckled face in which a pair of brown eyes danced gaily, but he doffed the green fringed bonnet he wore with great politeness.

"Our Lord the King rode into the town the day before yesterday, with Madame the Queen and the whole Court, to pray to Our Lady and pass Easter here, before going on to

Vienne where the States-General are to meet. You will find it hard to get lodgings. All the inns are full because Monseigneur the Constable is due to arrive today. . . ."

"The King and the Constable?" Catherine queried in astonishment. "But they have quarreled!"

"Exactly! Our King has chosen the cathedral as the place to receive him once more into his grace. They will be performing the Easter vigils tonight together. . . ."

"Are the pilgrims gathering here now for the journey to Compostela?"

"Yes, gracious lady! The guest-house by the cathedral is full of them. You will have to hurry if you wish to join their party. . . ."

The boy pointed out the road to the guest-house to Catherine. It was simple to get there: she only had to follow that long, long road which climbed upwards from the Tour Panessac, which stood nearby, as far as Notre-Dame, where it became a long flight of steps. These steps went up within the entrance itself. Before leaving the boy added:

"All the pilgrims equip themselves at Maître Croizat's shop, near the guest-house. His clothes are the strongest and best made . . ."

"Thank you," Catherine cut in, noticing that Brother Eusebius's normally expressionless eyes were fastening curiously upon her. "We must go and find lodgings."

"And may God guide you to them! But you will not find anything. The Bishop's palace itself is packed full. The King keeps his Court there."

The boy went running off. Catherine reflected for a moment. There was no time to lose. Tomorrow, after High Mass, the pilgrims would be setting out. And she wanted to leave with them. She slid down from her mule and turned towards Brother Eusebius who was placidly waiting for her to make up her mind.

"Take the mules, brother, and go to the guest-house where you must ask them if they can supply us with accommodation. Here is gold to pay for it. As for me, I intend to go straight to the cathedral to offer the Virgin my gift, and it would not be seemly for me to approach a holy place on horseback. Go on without me. I will meet you again later."

The worthy brother porter of Montsalvy nodded briefly to signify that he had understood and then, gathering up the bridles of the two mules, set off tranquilly along the road.

Catherine climbed slowly up the cobbled street which was hung with innumerable shop signs; there were souvenir shops, inns, chop-houses, stalls of all kinds, and women sat on the stone steps in front of each one, bent over little pillows covered with fine threads, making dozens of little shuttles flash to and fro with their nimble fingers. The traveler stopped for a moment by one of these lace-makers who was young and pretty and smiled sweetly at her. She would not have been a true woman if the fragile marvels spun by those fairy-like fingers had not enchanted her. But now a procession of penitents was coming downhill from the cathedral, chanting the canticles for the dead at the tops of their voices, and Catherine was suddenly reminded of her vow. She went on up the hill and as she climbed she forgot everything around her. . . .

On the steps of the huge staircase which vanished into the shadows under the immense Roman arches, crowds of people were slowly and painfully ascending on their knees, up stones hollowed out by centuries of religious fervor. The hum of prayer and invocation pressed on Catherine's ears from all sides like the buzz of myriad bees, but she ignored it. She stared up at the high polychromatic façade, whose strange Arabic designs evoked far-away countries and mysterious craftsmen from the depths of time. She did not want to kneel, not just yet! She must walk upright to the celebrated altar, just as she would walk upright to the apostle's tomb. She vanished into the shadows of the porch. Beggars clustered there, exhibiting their real or false afflictions and whining on a monotonous unbroken note for alms. Others surrounded the ancient fever stone where the sick congregated every Friday, claiming that only last Good Friday a paralytic had recovered the use of his legs. Catherine paid no attention to them.

Her eyes were fixed upon a step which stood at about the level of the great gilded doors to the sanctuary. There were some Latin words inscribed upon it: "If you are not afraid to sin, fear to touch this lintel, for the Queen of Heaven demands that her servitors be spotless." Could she really be said to approach her without sin, since she was purchasing her freedom with a lie? She stayed there for a moment fighting the dismay in her heart. But the resolve which had carried her that far was too strong to be shaken so easily. She passed through the doors and continued climbing in the murky darkness of the church. The steps climbed up through a sort of tunnel, at the far end of which, in the very heart of the sanctuary itself, wax candles stood massed in a fiery forest. Up there the blackness of the ascent broke into a luminous, dazzling aureole. A solemn, melancholy, monotonous chanting filled the stone chamber. . . .

When she finally emerged from the darkness Catherine felt

as if she had entered another world, so strange were her surroundings. The Black Madonna stood on a stone altar between two blood-colored columns of porphyry, surrounded by hundreds of wax tapers and red glass lamps, gazing at her with enameled eyes. . . .

The choir was empty, but on the walls the ferocious, hieratic characters of Byzantine frescoes seemed to come to flickering life in the trembling candle-light. Catherine was seized by superstitious terror, the ancient dread of heaven and hell forever latent in the hearts of men and women throughout that century of war. She slowly sank to her knees on the steps of the altar, fascinated by the strange statue.

Small and stiffly upright in the gold, jeweled cone of her cape, the Black Madonna had the frightening, hieratic air of a heathen idol. It was said that the crusaders had brought her back from the Holy Land in olden times, and that she was ancient as the earth itself. . . . Her heavy black face with its fixed expression gleamed beneath the gold crown surmounted by a dove. But the disconcertingly white enameled eyes seemed strangely alive, and Catherine began to tremble beneath their gaze, shaken by the barbaric majesty of the statue.

The lugubrious chanting had stopped. Now the church was enveloped in silence, in which it was possible to hear the faint flapping of innumerable candle-flames. Slowly, Catherine took the diamond from its purse and held it up to the Virgin on both outstretched palms. This traditional gesture made the evil jewel flash with all its incredible, bloody fires. It had never sparkled as it did now in this sanctuary devoted to the majesty of God. It lay like a black sun of death on Catherine's hands as they reached towards the sacred statue.

"All-powerful Virgin," Catherine whispered, "accept this jewel of blood and pain. Hold it so that the devil may at long last be exorcised from within it, so that misfortune may leave us at last . . . and happiness return to Montsalvy! And above all, so that I may find my husband again!"

Very gently she placed the jewel at the feet of the statue and then prostrated herself, her terror forgotten in the new emotion which flooded through her.

"Give him back to me," she implored, "give him back to me, merciful Virgin! Even if it means more suffering, even if it means I must sorrow through days and nights without end . . . please let me find him at last! Let me at least see him again . . . just once, only once . . . so that I can tell him that I love him, that I have never belonged to anyone else, and that no one . . . ever . . . can ever take his place! Have mercy upon me! Oh, have mercy upon me! Let me find him again! After that do with me what you will!"

She buried her face in her hands which were soon wet with tears. She stayed there for a long time, praying for her child and for Sara, weeping softly, and unconsciously waiting for an answer to her impassioned prayer. Then suddenly she heard this:

"Woman . . . be of courage! If your faith is great, your prayer will be answered."

She raised her head. A monk stood before her in a long white robe, his gray head bent towards her with a look of ineffable sweetness. Such serenity emanated from his white form that Catherine remained kneeling before him, hands folded, as if he were an apparition. The monk pointed with a pale hand towards the jewel which sparkled near the Virgin's golden cape, but he did not touch it.

"From where does this fabulous jewel come?"

"It belonged to my late husband, the Lord Treasurer of Burgundy."

"You are a widow?"

"I married again. But my husband was struck down by leprosy, and he has journeyed to the tomb of the apostle to pray for a cure, and I too wish to journey thither, to find him."

"Have you taken your place among the pilgrims? You will need a note from your confessor and you will have to be accepted by the chief pilgrim. They leave tomorrow."

"I know. . . . But I have only just arrived. Do you think I shall be too late, father?" Catherine asked, in a sudden terror.

A kindly smile lit up the white monk's face.

"You are very anxious to go, are you not?"

"I want it more than anything in the world!"

"Then come with me. I will hear your confession and then I shall give you a note for the Prior of the guest-house."

"Have you the power to admit me at this late hour?"

"No time is too late to approach God! And I am Guillaume de Chalençon, Bishop of this city. Come, my child."

With a new surge of hope swelling inside her, Catherine followed the white-robed prelate.

Catherine left the cathedral on wings. She had the feeling now that everything was going to be all right, that her hopes were no longer impossible, that she could achieve anything. She only needed courage and she had enough courage now and to spare.

She found Brother Eusebius waiting for her at the entrance to the guest-house, whose high arched doorway, guarded by stone lions, opened off the steps of the cathedral itself. He was sitting on a step, placidly telling his beads. When he saw her coming he looked at her unhappily.

"Dame Catherine, there is no longer any place in the dormitories. The pilgrims are sleeping in the courtyard and I was unable to find you even a mattress. I can always seek admittance to a monastery. But what about you?"

"Me? It doesn't matter. I shall sleep in the courtyard with the rest. Besides, Brother Eusebius, the time has come to tell you the truth. I am not going back with you to Montsalvy. Tomorrow I shall be leaving for Compostela with the other pilgrims. . . . Nothing can stop me now. But I want to ask your pardon for any trouble I may have caused you. The lord abbot . . ."

A great smile lit up the little monk's round face. He drew a scroll from under his robe and handed it to Catherine.

"Our most reverend father," he interrupted, "asked me to give you this, Dame Catherine. But I was not to give it to you till you had accomplished your vow. You have done so now, have you not?"

"Yes, I have."

"Then here you are!"

Catherine took the roll with a hesitant hand, broke the seal and unrolled it. It contained but few words, yet reading them brought a joyful color to her cheeks:

"Go in peace," Bernard de Calmont had written, "and may God go with you. I shall watch over the child and Montsalvy. . . ."

She rewarded the little porter with a look which was radiant with joy. In her emotion she kissed the signature before replacing the letter in her purse. Then she held out a hand to the monk.

"Our ways part here. Return to Montsalvy, Brother Eusebius and tell the most reverend father that I am ashamed of myself for not having trusted him, and that I thank him. Return the mules to him, I shall not need them. I shall go on foot like the rest."

Then she turned and ran, light as a freed bird, across the street to a shop with a handsome sign depicting a pilgrim in his wide hat, staff in hand. On the sign Maître Croizat begged to inform all those who traveled the Pilgrim Way that his shop supplied everything necessary for the pious journey.

There were some fifty people among the pilgrims, men and women come from as far as Germany, from Franche-Comté and the Auvergne. They tended to form groups according to their nationalities and tastes, but some few kept apart, preferring their solitude and their own company.

Catherine heard High Mass on Easter Sunday amid her new companions. She saw King Charles VII pass, only a few steps away, right in front of her on his way towards the high chair placed in the choir for him. Next to him she recognized the powerful figure of Arthur de Richemont, Chief Constable of France. On this Easter day the Lord Constable resumed his rightful rank and duties. She saw the great blue and gold sword of state gleaming in his powerful hands. She saw Queen Marie too, and among Richemont's followers she recognized Tristan l'Hermite's tall form . . . Tristan, her best friend and ally! She was sorely tempted to break the silence and rush towards him. . . . It would be good to hear an exclamation of pleasure and go over memories of past experiences together again. . . .

But she resisted the impulse. No! She no longer belonged to that bright, colorful, luxurious world. Between her and them stood her vows of the day before. The invisible barrier which separated her from that Court to which she still rightfully belonged was one Catherine did not want to overthrow. The future lay elsewhere and, far from revealing her presence there, she only shrank into as small a space as possible, between a gigantic fellow with a graying beard, who sang lustily and noisily, and a pale, withered little woman whose fanatical glance was fastened on the glittering altar. Catherine was torn between pity and revulsion when she looked at her. She doubted, however, that the woman, who was clearly ill and kept coughing hollowly, would survive the rigors of the pilgrimage.

As for her, who would be likely to recognize the Comtesse de Montsalvy, the beautiful widow of Chinon, whom Pierre de Breze worshiped on his knees, in this woman dressed exactly like her companions: a thick frieze cloth dress over a linen chemise, stout shoes, a thick cloak which would keep off all weathers, and on top of the fine lawn cap, which closely framed her face, a black felt hat whose broad brim was fastened back by a tin cockleshell in front. There was gold in the purse hanging at her waist, and also Arnaud's dagger, her faithful companion in hard times and dangerous places. Finally, in her right hand, she held the pilgrim's emblem, the famous staff: a long stick with a round gourd attached to one end. No, no one would have known her in that garb, and Catherine was relieved by this. She was merely a pilgrim among others. . . .

The mass was coming to an end. The bishop's solemn

voice had delivered his parting good wishes to the pilgrims. Now he blessed their staffs as they raised them in unison. The priests who were to lead the procession as far as the city gates, with the great cross held aloft, were already moving off. Catherine threw a last glance towards the choir, taking in both the King, the Queen and the Constable and his escort of men-at-arms. They already seemed like shadowy figures receding into the mists of past history. Higher up, above them all, she could still see Garin's evil jewel blazing darkly against the gold circlet which crowned the stiff-backed little Madonna in the gold mantle. The great doors swung open to the pale blue sky, where clouds raced swiftly. . . .

On the threshold Catherine took a deep breath. She felt as though the doors were opening on to infinity, on to a new hope as vast as the world itself. . . .

Behind the priests and monks the pilgrims ran down the steep hills, crying aloud for joy. On both sides of the street the townspeople thronged to see them pass. Some shouted good wishes, others cried a last farewell to a friend or parent.

Once past the stone ramparts where the royal banners flapped in the wind, the priestly escort parted from the pilgrims. In front of them a steep hill rose into the air, looking as though it were climbing into heaven itself. In the front of the column the chief pilgrim, a solid fellow with lively eyes, struck up the old marching song which had upheld so many flagging spirits over long and exhausting marches. It was a strange song, couched in an ancient tongue which fitted well to the rhythm of walking feet:

> "E ul treia!
> E sus eia!
> Deus aia nos!"

The simple, rhythmic chant swept along the column of pilgrims like fire along a trail of gunpowder. Catherine began to sing with the rest. Her heart felt light, her mind was at peace and she had never felt so vigorous. Behind her, in the town which was already receding into the distance, the bells were ringing a triumphant carillon. That victorious note seemed to efface the lugubrious funeral bell of Carlat whose mournful tolling had echoed for so long in her mind and heart. Catherine, uplifted by a new faith as ardent as that which once sent the crusaders to conquer the Holy Land, was convinced that one day, at the end of the long road ahead, she would find Arnaud again! Even if endless miles stretched before her,

351

even if it were but to die at his side, she would go to the ends of the earth. . . .

At the top of the steep climb the pilgrims were met by a sharp gust of cold wind, and a fine cold rain which lashed their faces. Catherine bent her head to protect herself against it, and marched stoutly against the wind, leaning on her staff. She was determined not to let the elements have the last word in this first skirmish, and she sang louder than ever. This wind came from the south. Before reaching her it must have crossed unknown lands, lands she would be crossing herself ere long in search of her lost love. . . . The south wind was her friend!